## A GRAVE UNDERTAKING

Earl Cradle has put together the perfect bank heist. He's got a safecracker, a gunman, some extra muscle—and a crooked undertaker. All the details are set. They'll access the bank from the funeral home next door and hit the bank when it opens, then escape as part of a funeral procession. All they need is a body. When Earl discovers that a bowery bum has just died and is laying in the morgue, he has his girlfriend claim the body as her father. There's only one problem. Newspaperman Jake Epstein has been researching this death, and discovers that the bum is a disgraced professor, with a real daughter. And she wants to know what the hell has happened to her father's body!

## OBSESSION

Conrad Madden is out of work and irritated at his wife and kids when he takes the babysitter home that night. Which is no excuse for getting drunk and spending the night with her. But how could he know that he would wake up to a corpse in the living room the next morning? The babysitter, Allie, claims the man was going to kill him while he slept. It was self-defense. She *had* to kill him. If Madden wasn't falling for the young woman, becoming obsessed with her, he could call the cops. He probably should call the cops. But there's the suitcase full of cash to consider. Now he is on the run, trying to keep one step ahead of the cops—and the hoods whose suitcase Allie has stolen.

## LIONEL WHITE BIBLIOGRAPHY (1905-1985)

**Fiction**

Seven Hungry Men (1952; revised as *Run, Killer, Run!,* 1959)

The Snatchers (1953)

To Find a Killer (1954; reprinted as *Before I Die*, 1964)

Clean Break (1955; reprinted as *The Killing*, 1956)

Flight Into Terror (1955)

Love Trap (1955; reprinted in UK as *Right for Murder*, 1957)

The Big Caper (1955)

Operation—Murder (1956)

The House Next Door (1956; first published in *Cosmopolitan*, Aug 1956)

Hostage for a Hood (1957)

Death Takes the Bus (1957)

Invitation to Violence (1958)

Too Young to Die (1958)

Coffin for a Hood (1958)

Rafferty (1959)

Run, Killer, Run! (1959; re-write of *Seven Hungry Men*, 1952)

The Merriweather File (1959)

Lament for a Virgin (1960)

Marilyn K. (1960)

Steal Big (1960)

The Time of Terror (1960)

A Death at Sea (1961)

A Grave Undertaking (1961)

Obsession (1962) [screenplay published as *Pierrot le Fou: A Film*, 1969]

The Money Trap (1963)

The Ransomed Madonna (1964)

The House on K Street (1965)

A Party to Murder (1966)

The Mind Poisoners (1966; as Nick Carter, written with Valerie Moolman)

The Crimshaw Memorandum (1967)

The Night of the Rape (1967; reprinted as *Death of a City*, 1970)

Hijack (1969)

A Rich and Dangerous Game (1974)

Mexico Run (1974)

Jailbreak (1976; reprinted as *The Walled Yard*, 1978)

As L. W. Blanco

Spykill (1966)

**Short Stories**

Purely Personal (*Bluebook*, May 1953)

Night Riders of the Florida Swamps (*Bluebook*, Jan 1954)

"Sorry—Your Party Doesn't Answer" (*Bluebook*, July 1954)

The Picture Window Murder (*Cosmopolitan*, Aug 1956; condensed version of *The House Next Door*)

To Kill a Wife (*Murder*, Sept 1956)

Invitation to Violence (*Alfred Hitchcock's Mystery Magazine*, May 1957; condensed version of novel)

Death of a City (*Argosy*, Jan 1971; condensed version of novel)

# A GRAVE UNDERTAKING

# OBSESSION

## Lionel White

### Introduction by
### Brian Greene

**Stark House Press • Eureka California**

A GRAVE UNDERTAKING / OBSESSION

Published by Stark House Press
1315 H Street
Eureka, CA 95501, USA
griffinskye3@sbcglobal.net
www.starkhousepress.com



ISBN: 979-8-88601-087-9

Book design by Mark Shepard, shepgraphics.com
Proofreading by Bill Kelly
Cover art by James Heimer, jamesheimer.com.



First Stark House Press Edition: June 2024

# Lionel White: The "Lazy" Crime Novelist

by Brian Greene

I interviewed Lionel White's son January White while working on an introduction to a previous Stark House edition of Lionel's crime novels. Over that thread of emails, January passed along a funny comment he remembered his dad making to someone who asked him why he became a novelist:

> "It's one way to make a living if you're too lazy to work or too incompetent to hold a job."

It's a great crack from a man whom January says had a sharp sense of humor. But the truth is, when you look at White's history as a writer, he hardly comes off as either a couch potato or an inept guy. White (1905-1985), who dropped out of school in seventh grade according to his son, eventually found work hustling as a beat reporter for newspapers before becoming a long-time editor of lurid true crime magazines. Then he turned to authoring novels.

Like Raymond Chandler, White started relatively late in life, being in his latter 40s when his novels began circulating. But unlike Chandler, White pumped out his titles at a furious rate, producing close to 40 works of edgy crime fiction over a span of a little more than two decades, finally ceasing in the mid-1970s. So, the guy put in his years in the working man's grind before settling into the existence of an author, and as the latter he was plenty productive. Lazy? Doesn't look like it. And, judging by the quality of his work between the covers of those novels, he was far from incompetent.

White seems to have put the knowledge he gained through his pre-author jobs into the text of *A Grave Undertaking* (1961), one of the two titles in this edition. One key character in the tale is an eager, nervous cub reporter who needs to pull off a big scoop for his paper if he hopes to keep his newfound position. One wonders if White may have worked under similar pressure during his early years as a journalist on a crime beat. And the multi-layered criminal plot that's at the heart of the story could have been drawn from information White amassed while editing publications that detailed actual illegal ploys.

*A Grave Undertaking* is, like so many other White novels, a heist story. Set in New York City (White was born in Buffalo), the tale involves a complicated plan to rob a bank. Many people become involved in the scam, either as part of the robbery team or unintentionally. One in the latter group happens to be a corpse, thus the wordplay in the title.

I'll let readers new to the book learn the details of the heist themselves. But what I will say is that, while not as well-known as White classics like *The Big Caper* and *A Clean Break* (both 1955), *A Grave Undertaking* is a highly effective heist thriller penned by a master of the subgenre. There's a whole panorama of character types, including well-intentioned individuals, ill-intentioned ones and innocents who get pulled into the drama by chance. And there are those who didn't expect to find themselves on the wrong side of the moral compass, but that get led that way when life beats them down. There are crooks, cops, doctors, college professors, a grief-stricken daughter, an overprotective mother, the aforementioned cub reporter, a mortician, and, as referenced above, an as yet unburied dead man whom the police originally thought was just a typical Bowery bum but who turns out to have had an intriguing life story himself. In telling the tale, White expertly takes us inside the lives, minds, and hearts of many of these characters. We see the planning of the crime, the execution of it, and then the aftermath. It's all compelling. Typical of White, the writing here is economical. The tale moves briskly and the tension builds gradually yet remains taut throughout. It's vintage Lionel White and pure noir.

Lionel White was married multiple times. Tracking the history of his marriages is a brain-teasing exercise. When I asked January White (he was born out of Lionel's second marriage to Helaine Levy and was Lionel's only child as far anyone knows) a question about his dad's marital history, January made it clear that he didn't care to discuss the matter.

A marital overlap comes into play in *Obsession* (1962), the second of the two White novels included here. The lead male character marries the female lead, which might be okay if not for the fact that he's already married to someone else. But then, he uses a false name on the certificate that legally validates the wedding that occurs in the story, so did he actually commit polygamy? Hmm, kind of a head-scratcher, just like White's real-life marriage history.

The man in question is Conrad Madden. Things haven't been going Con's way. A 38-year-old denizen of Stamford, Connecticut, Con is a currently unemployed fella who sometimes writes TV teleplays. He can't find work of any kind at the moment. And meanwhile he drinks too much, his beautiful wife is icy towards him, his two kids don't think much of him, and he feels disillusioned by and alienated from the other adults in his and his spouse's social circle. So, what does he do? After having a miserable time at a party, he winds up sleeping with the teenage girl who babysat his kids that night. And when he wakes up in her place the next morning, he learns that his wife came looking for him there in the wee hours and saw him in the young girl's bed. And, oh, there's also a dead guy in the apartment.

As Con and the young girl go on the lam and travel across various states together, it's natural to think of Vladimir Nabokov's 1955 novel *Lolita*, and the same-titled film Stanley Kubrick made from it in '62. But Allison O'Connor, the girl Con Madden takes up with in the White story, is a much different kind of character than Nabokov's titular one. Allie is 17 to Lolita's 12. And Allie is an already-hardened, worldly-wise girl who lives alone in that apartment when Con beds down with her. Besides Con, everyone in her social sphere is a criminal of some kind. She's an attractive young girl who knows what men want from her and knows how to play them to suit her needs. And if they cross her, well, she's handy with knives. She's usually several steps ahead of the hapless Con in all of their doings, and he can't do shit about it because he's given up his previous life for her and is fully under her spell. She's a teenage femme fatale leading a lost soul of a man into danger.

There is a significant connection between White's literary output and the cinema. Kubrick turned *A Clean Break* into his 1956 film noir gem *The Killing*. And *Obsession* was adapted for film by another acclaimed auteur: Frenchman Jean-Luc Godard used it as the (loose) basis of his 1965 avant-garde title *Pierrot Le Fou*, starring big screen luminaries Jean-Paul Belmondo and Anna Karina. In his shape-shifting movie, Godard took the story to all kinds of places not seen in the book. But the foundation of the tale is the same in both versions. Godard, like Kubrick, was a cutting-edge filmmaker who was inspired by the content of White's novels. That's an impressive testament to the strength of White's writing and an important facet of his legacy.

So, was White's own complicated romantic history on his mind when he penned this tale of a guy pushing 40 leaving his wife for a teenager? Who knows? Whatever gave him inspiration for the novel, it's another well-written, suspenseful, memorable White work of literary noir. Some might find the premise of a love/lust/infatuation-fueled relationship between a 38-year-old man and a girl 21 years his junior a bit unsettling. But White's evocative writing makes one see how the dire circumstances of Con Madden's existence led him down the path of getting tangled up with Allie O'Connor, and how she has the wise-beyond-her-years cunning to be able to keep him chasing her no matter how perilous their adventures together become.

*Obsession* isn't a heist novel per se. Unlike *A Grave Undertaking* and other White titles, its plot isn't totally dominated by a crime ploy. But the author, who must've learned much about the plans and methods of actual cons while writing and editing true crime articles, managed to work a heist into the story of *Obsession* along the way. Heists were his thing. But what makes this one White novel a keeper is that it is the story of a formerly upstanding man's descent into desperation-driven acts that grow increasingly more hazardous the longer he remains in this mode of existence. What's more noir than that?

Lionel White spent most of his middle-aged years living around the Eastern Shore of Maryland (January says he loved being on the water, and fishing). Then, after some amount of time residing in L.A., he lived out his final years near Asheville, North Carolina. The executor of his last wife's estate says that he and she enjoyed a healthy and happy relationship, and that White was devoted to the woman. It looks like he ended his time on Earth living well, after all those "lazy" years of being a working novelist.

—March 2024

..............................................................................................................

Brian Greene writes short stories, personal essays, and journalism features on the arts. His articles and essays on crime fiction and film noir have been published online by Crime Reads, Criminal Element, Mulholland Books, The Strand, Cinema Retro, Crime Time, Crimeculture, and others, and in print by PM Press, *Film International*, and *Paperback Parade*. Brian lives in Durham, North Carolina.

# A GRAVE UNDERTAKING

Lionel White

# Chapter 1

Shortly after eight o'clock on the morning of May fifth, a Monday, the body of an elderly derelict was discovered propped in the doorway of a tenement house, just south of the Bowery on Stanton Street, on the East Side of New York City.

The uniformed sergeant of the prowl car who made the discovery conducted a cursory examination. The man had been dead for several hours. The fact that no one had reported the death failed to surprise him. The man's head had fallen so that his face was concealed and he could have been merely another drunk who had passed out from the cheap sherry he had been drinking. An empty pint flask was clenched in the corpse's gaunt hand where it lay on the cement step at his side.

The sergeant beckoned his partner who still sat behind the wheel of the patrol car and when the second policeman stepped to his side, instructed him to put in a call for an ambulance.

"Tell them he is dead," he said, his voice without emotion.

The intern who arrived with the ambulance realized at once there was no need to use his stethoscope, but he made the check in any case.

"Heart, I should imagine," he said, standing up and signaling the ambulance driver to bring the stretcher.

"Booze," the sergeant answered laconically. "It's always the booze."

He was right, of course.

The body was removed without causing any undue commotion and as soon as it arrived at the morgue in Bellevue, a check of the dead man's possessions was made. His pockets yielded an empty wallet, some twenty-eight cents in odd change, two soiled handkerchiefs, a crumpled cigarette package containing two cigarettes, a safety pin, and a worn newspaper clipping.

The clipping was so old and tattered that it was almost impossible to tell from what paper it might have come or how long ago it had been printed. But analysis under a glass established that it concerned a scientific discovery made at a Midwestern university laboratory some three years previously. This might have been a clue to the dead man's identity had the article carried any names, but it did not. On the reverse side of the clipping was an ad for a patent medicine and this too might have been considered the reason that the dead man had the fragment of newspaper in his pocket.

There was an old-fashioned, plain gold ring on the third finger of the left hand. It was obviously a wedding band, but upon its removal, it proved to be so worn that whatever engraving might at one time have been on the inside had completely disappeared. Examination of the teeth showed that the dead man wore a complete upper plate and a partial lower. He had two platinum fillings in the pivot teeth in his jaw and the dental work had been expensive.

There were no scars on either the head, limbs, or torso and no unusual physical characteristics. The autopsy surgeon estimated the man's age in the late sixties, he was five feet eight inches tall, weighed a hundred and twenty-eight pounds, was probably Caucasian and had obviously been suffering from extreme malnutrition. Cause of death was acute alcoholism.

There was nothing at all unusual about either the corpse or the method by which the dead man had become a corpse. In short, merely a case of another Bowery bum—a wino, a sneaky Pete drinker—ending up dead in the inevitable gutter.

It happens every day.

A routine report was made to the Bureau of Missing Persons; the patrolman on the beat where the body had been discovered was supplied with a morgue photograph and instructed to check out as to whether the man had a room or apartment in the neighborhood. Certain flophouses and cheap hotels also would be checked in case the dead man had resided in any of them, but the fact that he carried no key in his pocket or any sort of identification discouraged any optimism that the results would be anything but negative.

Actually, no one really expected to discover his name or much of anything else about him. No one really cared. The death, in a sense, was "natural" and if he cleared with missing persons, then very obviously it was just a routine case of another down-and-outer reaching the end of the road. The end would come when the city buried him in Potter's Field, after the passing of a certain legal interval of time.

By midafternoon the Police Department had instigated its routine procedures, photographs and fingerprints had been taken and sent to the proper sources for possible identification, the autopsy had been completed.

The cadaver was reassembled with the aid of a few surgical clamps and some silk medical thread and consigned to a slot in the cold storage vault.

For purposes of identification, the number Z-12-77 was typed on a card and pushed into a cellophane holder which was tied to the large toe of the right foot.

To all intents and purposes the case was closed.


## 2.


Shortly after eight o'clock on May fifth, a Monday, a Midtown New York City undertaker who was facing bankruptcy, compromised with his conscience and made a decision. The decision resulted in a telephone call and this telephone call was the initial step in the series of carefully laid plans which resulted some seven days later in the quarter of a million-dollar robbery of the Upper West Side branch of the Citizen's National Bank.

The undertaker's name was Mario Gallucci. He was forty years old, tall, thin and with a sunken face. He had lost most of his hair, his eyes were very dark and deep-set, his ears were too large and he had a bony, slightly twisted nose. His demeanor was one of perpetual melancholy.

Mario Gallucci decided on that Monday morning to meet his destiny halfway. In fact, a little more than halfway. He telephoned his cousin, Joey Gallucci, at a delicatessen down in Chelsea, where Joey had an arrangement with the management to receive his personal phone messages. Joey did a little side business as a bookmaker and found the delicatessen phone booth both a convenient and reasonably safe spot from which to operate.

Joey, a short, fat, good-natured man with the doughy face of a comedian and the physical contours of a Kewpie doll, was ten years younger than his cousin. He was partial to silk shirts and large plaids, suede shoes and hand-painted neckties. He moved in a constant miasma of expensive perfume. His tiny hands were beautifully manicured and in the right one was invariably a cigar, in the left a scratch sheet.

He was eating a salami sandwich on rye when the owner of the delicatessen leaned out of the phone booth and called to him. "Your cousin, Joey," he said.

Joey dropped the sandwich and picked up the cigar and his wide mouth split open in a grin. His small black eyes were like twin raisins in an ocean of dough.

He had to edge into the booth sideways and it was still a tight fit. But he was careful to close the door before picking up the dangling receiver and speaking into the mouthpiece.

"Joey," he said. "This you, Mario?"

"Yeah."

There was a decent interval and Joey waited until he realized that Mario apparently was through talking.

"Well," he said, "what gives?"

"I've decided," Mario Gallucci said. He spoke in the voice of doom.

"So?"

"So all right, I'll go along."

Joey breathed a long sigh of relief. He didn't realize it, but he had started sweating the second he'd entered the phone booth. He carefully took the receiver away from his ear, and dropping the cigar which he held in his other hand, reached for his breast pocket handkerchief.

He wiped his forehead.

"Tell Earl," Mario said.

"Don't worry—don't worry kid." Joey sighed again and then smacked his lips. "We'll be along," he said. "About an hour. You sit tight."

"Sure," Mario said. "Why not—I got nowhere to go."

They hung up simultaneously.

Joey stepped out of the phone booth and again wiped his brow. He walked over to the counter and reached into an opened box and took out a handful of cigars.

"Gotta go out," he said. "Guess I won't be back until late, maybe not at all today."

"Whatcha want me to say should anyone—" Bobby, the cashier, began, but Joey cut him short.

"Tell 'em I gone to Miami, tell 'em to go to hell, tell 'em anything," Joey said. "I'm retiring for a while."

Bobby stared at him as Joey turned and started for the door, hesitating only for a second to bite off the end of the cigar and spit it out.

He stepped into the cab sitting at the curb and gave the driver the address of a rundown theatrical hotel in the West Forties.

## 3.

Billy Dale yawned voluptuously, stretching her bare arms over her head and kicking the sheet so that she uncovered herself from the waist up. She blinked quickly several times and her cornflower eyes opened wide, staring sightlessly for a moment at the dirty gray ceiling.

Earl Cradle was sitting on the edge of the bed in his T-shirt and a pair of slacks, barefooted, rolling a brown paper cigarette in his left hand, when the telephone rang. He flipped the completed cigarette into his mouth and took time to light it before reaching to the night table and picked up the receiver.

He listened for a minute and then said, "Come up."

He dropped the paper to the floor and turned to Billy, who sat cross-legged on the only chair in the room. She was a tall, handsomely built blonde, in her mid-twenties. She sat staring at the floor, her startling blue eyes half closed and a pensive expression around her lush, rather large mouth. She had not looked up when the phone rang and she seemed completely lost in some private dream of her own.

"Joey is coming up now," Cradle said. "You better blow, kid. Call me later."

Slowly she lifted her head, staring at him blankly. Her mouth twisted and she smiled, simultaneously uncrossing her legs and standing up.

"Earl," she said, "what did he say?"

"He didn't say anything, kid," Cradle said. "But it must be set or he wouldn't be here. Anyway, you better …"

"But Earl," she said, pouting again. "Why can't I stay? After all, I am going to be in …"

"I know, I know," he said quickly. "But I think it's best I see him alone. Let me find out what it's all about. You run along now and I'll call you later."

She stepped toward him and leaning forward, brushed his cheek with a kiss.

"How later?"

"As soon as I know what's on his mind. Now …"

"All right Earl," she said. "But call me. I'll be in my room."

"I'll call."

She moved quickly then, picking up her bag where she had dropped it on the bed and pulling her jacket together. She paused for a second as she passed the dresser mirror and her finger touched her mouth and then her hair.

Two minutes after she had closed the door there was a soft knock and Earl Cradle called out, "Come in."

Joey didn't waste any words.

"It's set," he said. "We got it made. Mario called me downtown. He'll go along."

He crossed in front of Earl and fell into the chair which was still warm from the heat of the girl's body. His face broke into a pleased smile as his eyes remained on the face of the other man.

For a moment or two, Earl Cradle stood completely still, his eyes half closed and his thin-lipped mouth opened enough to expose the edges of his even white teeth. And then his lean, angular head nodded slowly. He smiled and suddenly he looked ten years younger, looked like a man in his early thirties. He released a deep breath and not speaking, went to the dresser and pulled open the top drawer. He took out a half-empty bottle of Canadian Club and filled two water glasses half way and handed one to Joey. Lifting his own glass, he spoke in a low, husky voice.

"To the Citizen's National Bank," he said. "To your cousin Mario. To us. To money."

"To the neatest caper that will ever be pulled in this town or any other town," Joey said.

They drank.

**4.**

Shortly before eight o'clock the morning of May fifth, a Monday, Jake Epstein, latest addition to the general assignment staff of the *New York Blade*, was given a lesson in basic journalism by a past master at the craft. The teacher was Carlton Dewey, day city editor of the *Blade*, a hard-bitten, old-school newspaperman. Dewey was a bitter, sardonic, completely efficient martinet who had no use for the new type of journalists being graduated by the universities. He didn't mince his words.

"How old are you, son?" he asked.

Jake Epstein blushed. He was standing at the side of the city desk, in the center of the editorial room and there were at least thirty people within earshot. He had worked for the Blade for only three months and it was his first newspaper job.

"Don't you know?" Dewey asked, not really giving Jake time to fumble for his answer.

"I'm twenty-one, sir."

"Don't call me 'sir,' damn it!" Dewey said. "Pull up a chair. Sit down. Do you think I want to yell?"

It was exactly what Jake did think, but he didn't say so. He pulled up a chair.

"All right you're twenty-one. You been here about a year and …"

"Three months," Jake said in a sort of desperate whisper.

"Shut up," Dewey said. "I'm doing the talking. Anyway, you've been here three months. You've covered a few luncheons, you've filled in on a couple of beats, you've gone to a fire or so. You've—but the hell with it. The point is this. You can't write and God knows maybe you will never be able to write. But it doesn't matter. In this town a newspaperman doesn't have to know how to write. I don't expect anyone to know. And even if you did know how to write it wouldn't matter. Until you learn how to be a newspaperman, nothing else is important. Now, what is a newspaperman?"

He stopped, staring at Jake with a bitter eye.

"Why I suppose …"

"Shut up. I said I'm doing the talking. A newspaperman is just what the word says. It's a man who knows how to get news. Now I have a staff here …" he hesitated, lifting his head and looking around at the room which suddenly became a beehive of industry. "I have a staff of meatheads, of experts, of geniuses, of God only knows what. But I don't have any newspapermen. They don't make newspapermen anymore. They make journalists or columnists or critics or.... Anyway, the point is this. You come in here this morning and you ask for an assignment. You ask for an *interesting* assignment."

His voice rose to a near bellow on the last few words. Again he swung his eye around the room, but again there was a studied effort to avoid that poisonous gaze.

"An *interesting* assignment," he repeated. "There is no such thing. And if there was, I'll be double damned if I would give it to some young cub who is still wet behind the ears. But I am going to give you something else."

Jake felt the blood leave his face. This was going to be it. The louse, he thought, can't he just fire me? Do I have to get the lecture thrown in for free?

"I'm going to give you a piece of forgotten information and then I am going to give you a week to act on it. And if at the end of the week you don't come back with an *interesting* story from an *interesting* assignment, you don't have to come back at all."

The sudden reprieve came with such a shock that Jake heard his own voice, the words coming quite free from any conscious desire to speak.

"Thank you," he said.

Dewey looked at him sharply and then half nodded.

"The information is this," he said. "A real newspaperman doesn't have to wait for news—he finds news. And that son, is exactly the difference between these journalism school graduates who have merely learned how to parse a sentence and accept a free handout from some press agent, and the legitimate article. A newspaperman who is worth his salt goes out and *finds* the news. He *makes* the news. He *digs!* Damn it he ..."

Carlton Dewey stopped talking and shrugged his shoulders and sat back in his seat.

"Okay." he said, his voice suddenly tired. "You are going to have your chance. You got a week. Go where you want, do what you want. You can even have a few bucks a day expense money. You can try City Hall, you can try a police station, you can go down to the morgue, you can go up to the Waldorf and find Adolph Hitler hiding out as a waiter. I don't care. You got a week. A complete seven days. At the end of that time, I expect a story. A real story. An *interesting* story, as you say. And if you haven't found one by then, why you'll never make a newspaperman anyway. So now get the hell out of my sight."

Jake stood up.

"Can I get the expenses in advance?" he asked.

Dewey squinted his eyes and then for the first time his face broke into what might have passed for a smile.

"Maybe you'll make a newspaperman after all," he said.

Ten minutes later and Jake Epstein, the *Blade's* newest cub reporter, was on a bus heading downtown. He had a cousin who was interning down at Bellevue who might be able to help him in some way or other.

## 5.

Shortly before eight o'clock on the morning of May fifth, a Monday, Dr. Martin Jordan told the prettiest girl in Sandusky, Ohio, that she had an Oedipus complex.

The girl was by no stretch of the imagination neurotic and Dr. Jordan was not a psychiatrist. Dr. Jordan was merely a man who had suddenly lost his temper and the girl was Jane Mercer, his fiancée.

The scene took place at the back right-hand booth of the Rexall Drugstore while the two of them were having a hurried breakfast. It had to be hurried of necessity as Dr. Jordan was due back at the hospital within fifteen minutes and the hospital was very strict about its interns. Even though the intern might be a particularly brilliant young man who had only another three weeks to go before he was scheduled to accept an exceptionally fine opportunity as a resident physician at a famous Edinburgh hospital.

It also had to be hurried because Jane Mercer, who was indeed the prettiest girl in Sandusky, and very possibly in Ohio and most of the Midwest as well—because Jane Mercer was due to report to work at eight-thirty. She was the private secretary of the president of one of the biggest banks in town. One of the reasons that she was able to hold this important position at the tender age of twenty was because of her trustworthiness and respect for punctuality. There was no question about it, that is what he said.

He said she was suffering under an Oedipus complex and, to compound the insult, added that it was about time she grew up and faced reality. It is quite sure that Dr. Jordan would never have made these remarks if he hadn't been suffering under extreme tension and a complete loss of temper. However, the moment the words left his mouth, Dr. Jordan realized he had gone too far.

Jane Mercer's small body suddenly went taut and the blood drained from her lovely, childlike face. She shook the dark, curly hair from her eyes.

"So!" she said. "So!"

The word had a certain frightening significance and Dr. Jordan opened his mouth to say something, to try and undo the damage before it was too late. But she didn't give him the opportunity.

"So, Martin Jordan," Jane said. "Because I love my father, because I want to keep the very last promise I ever made to him, I have an Oedipus complex. I …"

"Now darling …"

"Don't you 'darling' me. Just because I refuse to suddenly up and marry you and go off to God knows where …"

"God knows where Scotland is," Dr. Jordan said.

Her mouth opened slightly and she stared at him and then quickly her body relaxed and her face broke and she closed her eyes tightly. A small sob escaped from her throat and Dr. Jordan quickly reached across the table and took her by the forearms.

"Oh, honey," he said. "Please try to understand. I'll be leaving in three weeks. I want you to come with me, can't you understand? We'll be married in another few months and I can't see why …"

Her eyes snapped open and she shook off his hands.

"I've told you why, Martin," she said.

Her voice was cold and concise and he shrugged and looked a little desperate.

"I have explained to you. I promised Daddy. The very last thing he said, that night he came into my room before he left. The last thing. He said, 'And baby, I *will* be back. You must wait here and by the time you are a big girl, by the time you are twenty-one, I'll be back.'"

Dr. Jordan sighed.

"But Jane," he said, "we've been over it so many times. That was five years ago. Five long years during which you have never heard from him. And you yourself have told me a hundred times that he was sick. That he had had a breakdown. That he probably had no idea of what he was doing or saying. You have to be sensible and face the truth. Five years. You know as well as I do that there is almost no chance he is still alive. Think of the money your mother spent looking for him before she died. The police, the people at the university, everyone. And you have never had one word. Not one single word. Now honestly, darling …"

Jane shook her head and wiped at her eyes and interrupted him.

"I know, Martin," she said. "I know. But don't you see, dear, it doesn't matter. It isn't a case of whether they ever find Daddy or not. It is a case of my promising. I told him I would be here waiting and he told me that he would be back by the time I was twenty-one. And so I am going to stay right here and wait. Stay at the old house and wait."

She leaned forward and this time she took one of his big square hands in both of hers.

"Try to understand," she pleaded. "I have to. If I didn't—well, I would just never feel right again. And you know, darling, that I will come. The day I am twenty-one, I'll put the old house on the market and I'll take the first jet plane. To Scotland or to the ends of the earth for you."

They left the drugstore some five minutes later and Jane let Dr. Jordan know that she had forgiven him for his outburst of temper in the most pleasant way possible.

She stood on her toes and lifted her face to be kissed. He blushed at the lack of privacy, but it didn't keep him from accepting the offering.

"You'll pick me up at the bank for lunch?" she asked as she turned to go.

"Not today, honey," he said. "I have to be sitting in on an autopsy— but I'll see you tonight, as soon as I can get away."

# Chapter 2

Mario Gallucci's grandfather, one Salvatore Gallucci, had been an undertaker and stonemason in the old country. A decent, sober, hardworking man, he had been fairly successful in spite of the poverty of the particular section of the country in which he lived and worked. He had had a connection with the church, since his brother was the local priest, and this had helped a great deal. When anyone died in his village, he buried him, and if the family had any extra money at all, he sold them a carefully chiseled stone to mark the grave.

Mario's father, Giuseppi Gallucci, had followed the family calling, coming to the United States shortly after the advent of Prohibition to establish a small mortuary on the lower East Side in New York City. Giuseppi, who was anything but a hard-working and sober man, had a connection with the Maffia and this had been a big help in his business. In spite of a passion for strong liquor and gambling, the senior Gallucci had attained a certain prosperity. He was a jolly, happy man, large both in body and in spirit, and he had a following.

In the early nineteen fifties, he had moved to a new location in the West Eighties, just off of Amsterdam Avenue. He had purchased the building outright. It was an old brownstone, the second house from the corner on the west side of the street. The business continued to thrive and by the time Giuseppi Gallucci finally died—the result of a combination of gastric ulcers, high blood pressure, and cirrhosis of the liver—his son Mario had been taken in as a partner and was already sufficiently experienced in the profession to be able not only to inherit the establishment but to take care of the final needs of his deceased parent.

Mario was typical of the second generation of immigrant. He was Americanized, but retained certain very definite characteristics of his father. He spoke Italian as well as he did English, had attended grammar school, high school, and four years of college, and had studied his profession not only as a journeyman in the family business, but in academic institutions designed to turn out modern-day, streamlined morticians. He knew how to dress properly, how to handle the family, how to cope with the body from the moment of its arrival in his establishment. But he also had learned a great deal about advanced business methods and efficiency.

He was up to date.

He was also, in many ways, a throwback to his staid and respectable grandfather. He had disapproved of his own parent, believing that his profession called for a serious, dedicated outlook on life. He neither drank nor gambled and long ago had been forced to give up cigars as his doctor had told him that they probably contributed to his chronic indigestion.

Mario Gallucci had ambitions and an almost maniacal desire to become a tremendous success. He was confident, once his happy-go-lucky father was dead and out of the way, that he, Mario, could make Gallucci's Funeral Home one of the biggest operations of its type in the city.

Mario's first move, once his parent was safely laid away, was to run down to the main office of the Citizen's National Bank, which was the trustee of his father's estate. He talked with a second vice-president and outlined his plans. Mario Gallucci was going to expand. He wanted to purchase the building next door, the structure which was on the corner and adjoined his own, and completely rebuild it after tearing out the insides. He would install a small private chapel with a cathedral ceiling; stained glass windows, and an electric organ. There would be several reception rooms and smaller parlors for his less prosperous clients.

The two elderly hearses and the ancient flower car would be junked and he would purchase new and modern vehicles which would be in keeping with the luxury of his refurbished establishment. He would purchase half a dozen long black limousines.

The funeral home would be completely refitted and brought up to date.

Mario had his facts and his figures. He knew to the penny exactly how much money he would need and he had already made overtures to the owners of the property that he wished to acquire.

The bank had a rather complete dossier on both Mario and the business which he had inherited and they were more than willing to go along. Not only did they consider the sixty thousand dollars which they were prepared to lend an excellent investment, but they had the additional security of a first mortgage on both the new property and the old as well.

Mario progressed rapidly with his plans. He bought shrewdly and personally oversaw all construction and work as it was being accomplished. He was equally meticulous in seeing that there was no waste.

Upon completion of the expanded facilities, he used what was left in his depleted bank account on an advertising campaign.

According to all of the laws of finance and business, as well as the laws of basic justice, he should have been eminently successful. But he wasn't. He was a complete failure.

The tragedy lay in one simple fact, a fact which in itself was an utter contradiction of nature, so to speak.

Mario Gallucci looked like exactly what he was—an undertaker.

His father had looked more like a racetrack tout or a vaudeville actor than a mortician, and the people had loved him. They even liked the simplicity of his establishment, its lack of pretense and show. They were old-fashioned people for the most part, first-generation Americans, and they distrusted anything new and modern. They liked the elder Gallucci because, with his sunny disposition, he was able to cheer them up in their time of trouble. They liked a happy undertaker the same way that the Irishman likes a bottle of strong spirits at his wake. And they simply could not stand young Mario, with his long sad face, his funereal manner, and his doomsday approach.

The live ones stayed away in droves and they took their dead with them—to other funeral homes.

At the end of four years, Mario was in dire trouble. The Citizen's

National Bank very likely would have foreclosed on him at this time but for one factor. The board of directors had recently decided to open a new West Side branch and they felt that a location in the neighborhood of the West Eighties and Amsterdam Avenue would be extremely suitable.

The building which Mario had purchased and turned into a small chapel, being on the corner, made a perfect spot for the new branch. It was a simple matter to readjust Mario's delinquent loan by taking title to the structure and then also taking possession.

Within no time at all, the cathedral ceiling was torn out, the electric organ was sold to a second-hand dealer, and the builders were busy installing the iron cages, the long counters, and the ersatz marble floor which would lend tone to the newest branch of the Citizen's National Bank.

The same vice-president who had arranged the original loan for Mario, also suggested that he might do well by selling off the recently purchased hearses, limousines and flower car, but Mario sadly informed him that there was a certain lag in the market for this type of transportation and he hung onto them.

Later, after the branch bank opened, Mario would stare over at it from his own place of business, unable to keep a certain bitterness out of his heart and mind.

He grew more melancholy than ever.

Had it not been for the physical fact that the branch was standing there, next door to him where he must look at it a hundred times a day, it is doubtful if Mario Gallucci would ever have consented to the plan which his cousin Joey had presented to him. That he would have agreed to cooperate with Earl Cradle in what would be the very first criminal act of his entire life.

He was thinking this very thought as the doorbell rang.


**2.**

Earl Cradle sat on the side of the stainless-steel drain table in the center of the white tiled room and stared hard at Mario Gallucci.

"And you are sure," he said. "Absolutely sure. The second Monday of each month?"

Mario looked at the small pile of ashes which Earl had carelessly dumped on the cement floor and frowned.

"Mario knows what he's talking about," Joey said.

"Right," Mario said. "Always the second Monday. I've been over there in the vaults a dozen times. Been there when it happens. Every second Monday. About three o'clock the armored car drives up and the dough is moved. Taken down to the main vaults in Midtown, I suppose. As near as I can guess, the branch just chooses that day once each month to move the surplus dough. Maybe they get big deposits during the first few days of each month—I don't know. But I do know that there is between a half and a million moved each month. On that particular day. The manager himself once mentioned it to me."

Cradle nodded.

"Okay. So it gives us exactly one week. A week from today. Not a lot of time. Now about the passage. Go over that again."

"It's like I said," Mario said. "At one time this building and the one next door were a single structure. The two buildings shared one basement. There was a wall put up when the buildings were separated and later, when I had both buildings, before the bank took over, I had the passageway cut through. It made it easier to move the bodies ..."

"Sure—sure," Cradle said quickly. "I understand. But how come, when the bank took the building over for a branch, they didn't ..."

"I'm trying to explain," Mario said, irritated. "They did. They blocked up the passage. But that was just the one we used for the bodies. There is a second passage, back of the furnace rooms. That was because I had two heating plants, but wanted to get the ashes all out through one entrance—or exit, I guess you would say. Anyway, right after I turned the place over to the bank, I just went ahead and blocked off the furnace passageway with board. I guess their builders didn't pay any attention to it or maybe they just overlooked it. From their side, it goes into the old coal bin, which is no longer used. They changed over to oil heat. All I can tell you is, they didn't do anything about it and the boards are still there. Never been touched. Take out a few nails and you can cross right into their basement."

Joey looked at his cousin and smiled.

"Somebody goofed," he said.

Mario frowned at him.

"All right," Earl Cradle said. "That takes care of that. The dough will be there and we can get in. That's half of it, but only half. The easy half. It's the getaway that is the trick. Now here's exactly how I got it lined up."

Joey and his cousin leaned forward and listened intently as Cradle continued to speak. He went on for more than an hour, not hesitating, not stopping when one of the other started to question him. He spoke in a low, tense voice and several times he got off the drainboard to pace as he talked, using his hands and arms to demonstrate one point or another. By the time he was through, the pile of ashes at his feet had grown to a small mound.

At last he hesitated, drew a long breath and stretched.

"And that," he said, "is about it. Any questions?"

"Plenty," Joey said. "For instance ..."

"Be quiet," Mario interrupted. "A couple of things I want to know. Just how many you expect to bring in on this? How many is it going to take?"

Earl looked at the ceiling speculatively.

"Well," he said, "I'd say about eight altogether, counting us. Seven live ones and a dead one."

"A dead one?" Mario said in surprise.

"Sure," Earl said. "A dead one. We have to have someone in that hearse, don't we? Suppose the cops stop it at a roadblock? Suppose ..."

"Where the hell do I get the dead one?" Mario asked.

"Hell, you're an undertaker," Earl said. "Don't ask me. That's your department."

Joey got off his chair and turned to his cousin.

"You must have 'em laying around all the time, Mario," he said.

"Don't be a fool," Mario said. "If I had dead ones laying around, I wouldn't be going in on this deal. I get maybe one or two a month, business is that lousy."

"Well, you work it out," Earl said. "I'm going to be having plenty to take care of on my end of it. I gotta round up the boys, get the tools together, get the signs painted, take care of the equipment for cracking the vault. A million things. And only a week. You start thinking about the dead one and leave the rest of it to Joey and me."

"Mario can manage," Joey said. "Mario is smart. Anyway, let's call it quits now and get started on something besides talk. Suppose we have a drink to seal it."

He turned to his cousin.

"You got something to drink down here, Mario?" he asked.

"Yeah," Mario said. "Formaldehyde. What the hell you think this is, a saloon?"

Earl Cradle looked around the sterile white walls of the room and a shiver went through his body.

"Let's get out of here," he said. "This place gives me the creeps." He turned to Mario. "We'll be back tomorrow—same time. Go over the rest of the details. In the meantime, get me the dope I want. The routine of the cops on the beat, street maps, a layout floor plan, and the rest of it."

He started for the door and Joey walked over and slapped his cousin on the shoulder before turning to follow him.

"It's in the bag, kid," he said. "Your troubles are over. Earl Cradle never misses. He knows exactly what he's doing."

Mario looked at him sourly.

"If he knows so much," he said, "maybe he knows where I'm going to get a body between now and next Monday morning."

3.

Dr. Enoch Frogg, the assistant to the assistant medical examiner, was a short, stout man in his mid-fifties who suffered from acne and a bad stomach. The first gave him an inferiority complex and the second gave him a feeling of extreme antagonism toward his fellow man. He hated his work and he hated himself even more for having neither the courage to give it up nor the competency to do anything else if he should.

He sat back in his oak swivel chair and his small, faded blue eyes took in the figure of Jake Epstein. What he saw failed utterly to make his day any better.

"So," he said, drawing the word out to permit it to carry the full depth of his disgust, "you come here in hopes of getting a story." He grunted and leaned over to spit in the wastebasket.

"My cousin," Jake began, but the man facing him quickly looked up and interrupted.

"Cousin, indeed," he said. "What right has some snot-nosed young intern got sending you down here to bother a man who is involved in serious ..." He hesitated, seeking the proper word and then apparently deciding there was no proper word, grunted again and stood up.

Jake also stood up.

"And you are from the *Blade,* you say?"

"That's right, sir. And I thought that perhaps I might, well you know, sort of pick up something colorful …"

He was interrupted by a snort.

"Colorful! There is nothing colorful in a morgue, young man. Of that I can assure you. However, I am a public servant, receiving my salary from the taxpayers. And I suppose I shall have to pamper the press. All right. Follow me. We will step downstairs and you can look around. We can start with the cold-storage vault first. Maybe *that* will give you some color."

Ten minutes later, Jake Epstein stood shivering at the side of the long drawer Dr. Frogg had pulled from the wall vault. He forced himself to look down on the thing which lay on the slab and for a moment the thought crossed his mind that he probably never would make a real newspaperman. It also occurred to him to wonder, for the first time, if he really cared.

"This one came in early this morning," Dr. Frogg was explaining. "As you can see, we have already done an autopsy."

He took the pipe from between his thick lips and reversing it so as to use the stem for a pointer, leaned down and delicately lifted a flap of flesh from the dead man's skull.

"I can see," Jake said in a whisper, at the same time quickly turning so that he could avoid seeing.

"Yes," Dr. Frogg said. "He's all wrapped up and waiting."

"Waiting?" Jake asked. He felt that if he could only keep talking he might just possibly last it out until he could leave the vault without fainting.

"For identification," Dr. Frogg said, again poking the dead man with his pipe stem. "But there won't be any identification. There never is. He's just another drunken bum who finally let the juice catch up with him. They come in all the time and no one ever bothers to identify them. No one cares."

He reached down and lifted up the tag which was tied to the dead man's big toe.

"Z-12-77," he said. "That's who he is, Z-12-77. One more for Potter's Field."

Five minutes later and Jake was seated in a straight-backed chair in an anteroom to the morgue proper, drinking water from a paper cup, his face completely white and his body still shaking from the combination of the low temperature in the cold-storage room and his recent traumatic reaction to seeing his first dead man.

Dr. Frogg leaned against a desk and glared at him and was talking in an angry voice. He had the habit that is characteristic of so many men who are essentially antisocial; he was unable to resist capturing an audience and then haranguing it incessantly.

It was as though he really enjoyed wallowing in the acid of his own vitriol.

"Drunks and deadbeats—no-goods! All of them," he said. "Worthless scum. Better off dead than alive. Just a shame we have to bury them."

"But don't the police make an effort to find the families?" Jake asked.

"The police!" Dr. Frogg's voice found a new level of disgust. "The police can't find their own tails. And why should they care? It's pretty obvious that the families themselves don't care or we wouldn't be getting these creeps. Oh, of course there are the routine checks, but if Missing Persons doesn't have a wanted on them, and their fingerprints fail to show who they are, then they go to Potter's Field."

Jake shook his head sadly.

"But a man like that one in there," he said. "Why he could have been anyone. He might have been a great man in his day. A famous singer or writer or something. Maybe he suffered from amnesia …"

"He suffered from booze."

"But," Jake persisted, "I should think that there would be a real, vital, human-interest story in finding out just how a man suddenly …"

"Look son," Dr. Frogg said, "I got no time for finding out real interesting, human drama stories or whatever it is you are talking about. I got work to do. You want to find one of those real, human-interest stories, I suggest …"

"You suggest?" Jake said, suddenly alert.

"Oh for God's sake," Dr. Frogg said. "The guy was nothing but a drunken bum. The autopsy showed acute concentration of alcohol." He shrugged and stood away from the desk.

"Look," he said. "If you got time to kill, why go right ahead, but I got work to do. You wanted to see a stiff and I showed you one. Now what else …"

"Well, could I find out where he was picked up and who found him and …"

"Come upstairs and I'll give you what we've got. But make it snappy. As I say, I've got work to do."

## 4.

Sergeant Emile Jannsey was down in the locker room, in the basement of the precinct house, changing out of his uniform just prior to signing out for the day. He was in a hurry. He wanted to stop at the tavern a couple of blocks down the street and check up on the first couple of races. He had a daily double going and, for a change, he was feeling optimistic about it.

It was an omen. The last time he had felt optimistic, his nags had come in and he had been paid thirty-six dollars on the winning combination. That had been six months ago and he was damned if every time since then, the minute he had laid a bet on the daily double, he'd at once had a hunch it was going to go down. And sure enough it always did.

But this time might be different and if he just hurried, he might be able to get to the tavern before Benny left and …

Jake Epstein took his hat off and said, "Sergeant. Sergeant Jannsey?"

Sergeant Jannsey twisted his neck, looking up from the stooped position which he had assumed as he retied his shoelaces.

"Yeah?"

"I'm Epstein—from the *Blade*," Jake said. "I understand that this morning you encountered—" he hesitated and looked down at the slip of paper he held in his hand "—you encountered Z-12-77 on a stoop."

The sergeant slowly stood up and stared at Jake. His trousers began to slip and he quickly grabbed them, but he didn't move his eyes.

"I found *who?*"

Jack checked the slip of paper again.

"Why, Z-12-77. You know, down on Stanton Street."

For a moment the sergeant hesitated and then he slowly shook his head.

"Look, son," he said, "you got the wrong department. You just go up to the desk and the lieutenant—well, you tell him your troubles." He half turned putting his arm out to pick up the loop of his suspenders.

"You are Sergeant Jannsey?" Jake asked weakly.

The sergeant turned back to him, his mouth suddenly grim. "I am and I ..."

"Well," Jake quickly interrupted. "They told me at the morgue that you found—that you found this elderly dead man early this morning down on Stanton Street and I am doing a story and ..."

"What's this bit about Z something?"

"Oh that," Jake said. "That's the number they tagged the body. You see, I am anxious to learn ..."

Ten minutes later Jake followed the sergeant, now in street clothes, into the ABC Tavern and crowded into a booth.

"Now you just wait here, son, while I make a check on a little business matter and then I'll be right back and I'll be very glad to talk with you. We can have a beer."

"I don't drink," Jake said.

The sergeant stopped as he was about to turn away. He stared at Jake for a moment and then slowly shook his head.

"New on the job," he said, not unkindly. "Well, you wait right here and I'll be back and tell you anything I can."

<br>

## 5.

It wasn't until he was just about ready to give up that Jake Epstein ran into Mrs. Markowitz and even then the whole affair would have evaporated into another of those things which merely might have been had it not been for the fact that Jake's dead father had insisted he learn rudimentary Hebrew.

Jake had, following Sergeant Jannsey's kind but pessimistic advice, canvassed the entire neighborhood in the area in which the dead man had been discovered. He had rung doorbells and where there were no doorbells, he had knocked. Often he had been rebuffed, almost never had he been invited in and even more discouraging, mostly he had been ignored. Jake had the picture and he had the description and he was further armed with a knowledge of exactly what had happened that morning.

But of those he talked with who had the vaguest idea of what he was getting at, none admitted as much as knowing that there was a dead man or that he had been found in the neighborhood. That is, until he encountered Mrs. Markowitz.

Mrs. Markowitz was a tiny, gray-haired little woman in her seventies and she lived in the second-floor front of a tenement a half a block away from the place where the body had been picked up. She answered the door when Jake knocked and listened as he identified himself as a reporter. Jake went into his well-rehearsed routine quickly, before she would have a chance to close the door in his face. He flashed the photograph of the dead man and asked if she knew who he was or where he lived.

Mrs. Markowitz started to close the door. And then she hesitated, looking up at Jake with near-sighted eyes.

"You look like my Benny," she said.

"Thank you," Jake said. "Now I wonder if you …"

"You a Jewish boy?" Mrs. Markowitz asked, ignoring his question. Jake nodded.

"Yes, Ma'am."

"Speak Hebrew?"

Jake spoke Hebrew. Not having any conversational Hebrew, he merely began on the Kiddush, and suddenly Mrs. Markowitz's face lit up.

Five minutes later and Jake had what he wanted. He had the key to the room across the hall, which Mrs. Markowitz had rented to the dead man. He had learned that the man had lived there for two weeks, had paid his four dollars a week rent in advance and that Mrs. Markowitz knew absolutely nothing else about him, not even his name.

Jake's use of Hebrew had so impressed the little gray-haired landlady that she didn't even bother to accompany him when he entered the dead man's room.

It was a small room, not more than ten by twelve feet overall. In the center of the room, against one wall, was an ancient iron bed on which was a lumpy mattress and two tattered gray blankets. There was an old-fashioned washstand against one wall which held a round porcelain basin half filled with clear water. On the opposite wall was a three-drawer bureau, with one missing drawer. In front of it was a straight-back chair.

A faded oriental rug covered a few square feet near the bed. Aside from dozens of empty sherry bottles, tossed in the corners of the room, there was nothing else at all in the place.

Jake looked around for a second door, seeking a closet, and found none. He crossed to the bureau and after a moment's hesitation, pulled open one drawer. It contained a half-filled bottle of a cheap domestic wine, a dirty pair of socks, and a shoelace. He opened the second drawer.

In one corner was a curved pipe with a broken stem. In the other was a rolled-up pair of trousers. Jake lifted out the trousers and spread them on the bed. Reluctantly he put his hands in the pockets. They were empty. He looked for a label and found none and was about to turn away when he hesitated.

Reaching down again he sought for the watch pocket. It yielded a tightly folded envelope and Jake carefully spread it out and then lifted the sealed flap. Inside were several folded newspaper clippings.

The first clipping was very old and it took him a long time to decipher it. It was a wire service story with a Washington date line and it had to do with an impending investigation by the Senatorial Committee Investigating Un-American Activities. The story said that the chairman of the committee had announced that an inquiry was to be started into the background of a well-known Midwestern scientist and college professor. The chairman refused to name the man, but said he could be identified as one of the leading …

And there the clip ended, the piece containing the rest of the story having been torn off.

The second clip appeared to have come from a more recent edition of a newspaper. It was a two-column reproduction of the photograph of a very pretty girl and contained a short caption. There was no date line. The caption read:

"Miss Jane Mercer, graduate of the Bigger's Business School, who has recently joined the staff of the Erie Trust and Loan Company."

The picture had been badly smudged but Jake could see that she was a very pretty girl.

A third clipping was so badly worn that Jake was unable to make anything of it and the fourth was almost as bad. By piecing together a word here and there, he was able to see that it had something to do with the appointment of a new professor at some unreadable university.

Carefully he replaced the clips in the envelope and then put the envelope in his pocket. He spent the next fifteen minutes diligently searching the room and found absolutely nothing else that would indicate any human being had ever lived and breathed and slept in it.

On his way out he stopped again at Mrs. Markowitz's door and knocked.

When she answered she looked at him as though she'd never seen him before. He started to thank her for all she had done, but she quickly mumbled something about not knowing what he was talking about. She closed the door as he was trying to find something to say.

Mrs. Markowitz's action didn't actually surprise Jake, any more than had the peculiar reticence of those whom he had previously questioned. If there was one thing Jake understood, it was the uncommunicativeness of the poor. Poor people minded their own business. They didn't want trouble. If they knew nothing, saw nothing, it was easier to stay out of trouble. Especially when it might have to do with the police.

Leaving the neighborhood, Jake felt a definite sense of elation. He still didn't know the real name of Z-12-77, but at least he had found out a lot more than the police had been able to discover.

For a moment he wondered if the proper thing to do was not to contact the authorities immediately and tell them what he had learned. But then he hesitated.

After all, this was not a case involving crime. There was no murder or other bit of wrongdoing at stake. Merely a nameless dead man who was going to be buried in Potter's Field unless someone showed up to claim the body. And that hardly seemed likely from the evidence he had at hand.

His next instinct was to call his paper and tell them what he had learned. And again he hesitated.

What, in fact, had he really learned? Nothing actually. It was merely that he was on the trail of a slender clue that might just possibly turn into something. He had a couple of clips and a girl's picture. And a name. That was all.

He had a week's grace. A week in which to turn up that story which, if it were good enough, would ensure him his place in the sun.

He made his decision at once.

He would go to an inexpensive restaurant and get something to eat. And then he would go to the public library.

He wanted to find out the location of something called the Erie Bank and Loan Company. He wanted to look up old newspaper stories on the activities of the Senate Committee for the Investigation of Un-American Activities. He wanted to discover the location of an institution which called itself the Bigger's Business School.

Jake Epstein was twenty-one years old and for the first time he was beginning to feel like a real honest-to-God newspaperman.

# Chapter 3

Earl Cradle was standing in front of the hotel when Joey Gallucci wheeled the long black limousine to the curb on Thursday morning just before ten o'clock.

Joey, wearing a black whipcord uniform, touched the peak of his chauffeur's cap and smiled sardonically as he reached over to open the front door.

Earl climbed in, sitting next to him, and he spoke as soon as Joey put the car into motion.

"Well, what's the trouble?"

"My cousin's a dope," he said. "He's beginning to panic."

"Great," Earl said. "What's his problem?"

"That body. Mario don't know how to get a body. He had one call, but the family insisted the burial be Saturday at the latest. Anyway, it would be one of those big family things and a couple of hundred relatives would be there. No good."

"Right," Earl said. "Is there anything else bothering Mario?"

"No. But he just don't know …"

"It figures," Earl said. "A guy who can go broke as an undertaker can't have much imagination. Anyway, don't let it worry you. I have the angles figured."

Joey took his eyes off the street ahead and looked quickly at his companion, a trace of alarm on his face.

"Now, Earl," he said quickly, "we don't wanta start this thing with a …"

Cradle shook his head and interrupted.

"Don't be a jerk," he said. "There are plenty of dead people around without helping to decrease the population."

He pulled a newspaper out of his pocket and opened it. A small, single paragraph story was encircled with pencil and he read it aloud.

"The body of an unknown man was found slumped on the front steps of a tenement house on Stanton Street early this morning and removed to the morgue at Bellevue Hospital, to await possible identification. The man was in his late sixties and poorly dressed. It is believed he died of alcoholism. Police are investigating."

Joey shrugged.

"So what? You suppose they'll just turn him over to us because we need him?"

"I said, don't be a jerk, Joey," Cradle said. "I had a feeling Mario would goof off and so I kept my eyes open and I saw this. Last night I went down to the morgue and I told them that my older brother had disappeared and I showed them the clipping and said I thought this might have been him. They took me in and let me have a look at the stiff. He was still there and so far no one else had even bothered to check on him. Anyway, I got a good look at him."

"And where does that get us?"

"It gets us the stiff," Earl said. "Bright and early tomorrow, I am having Billy go down and identify him as her father. I have told her exactly what he looks like so she can make a convincing story. After she identifies him, she'll arrange to have the body released. There will be a little red tape, but not much. The authorities are always happy to be saved the trouble of planting the drifters they pick up. And by Friday night I want the hearse from Mario's to pick him up. Billy will call and give the time and other details. Then, once he's safely tucked away uptown, we just hold him until Monday morning."

Joey shook his head and made a tsk-tsk sound of admiration. "You're great, Earl," he said. "Great."

"Sure—sure," Cradle said. "I'm great. But just you be sure to see that Mario takes care of the coffin. You think he can handle that without any trouble? Without panicking?"

"Oh he can handle it all right. He's a good carpenter."

"Well just tell him this stiff is about five feet seven or eight and as thin as a rail."

"Thin is good," Joey said. "The height don't count."

"And don't let him forget," Earl continued. "It must be one of those jobs where you just lift the upper half of the lid—you know, to see the kisser, not the whole body."

"He knows," Joey said. "Anyway, that's that. Now how about Herman. Is he expecting us?"

"He's expecting me. When we get out to Queens, you just stay in the car and wait. I'll go in alone. You know the place don't you?"

"I know the place, Earl."

**2.**

Bertha Wonder held out the pills in one fat hand and the glass of water in the other. Standing in front of her husband, she looked down at him and shook her large head to get a wisp of straggling gray hair out of her eye. There was a note of concern in her voice when she spoke.

"Take the pills, Herman," she said. "They'll settle the nerves. You should take it easy, get your rest. You know you shouldn't be getting all stirred up before work. Here you are, not sleeping good and already worrying and the job less than a week off."

Herman Wonder raised bloodshot eyes and stared at her. He reached for the pills and the water and swallowed first one and then the other. He was a frail man, in his late sixties and his bony head was completely bald. His hands were thin and deeply veined and shook a little as he returned the glass.

"He'll be here any minute, Mama," he said. "You go on in and put the tea on."

"Maybe a little schnapps, Herman …"

"Tea, Mama. This is business," Herman said. He leaned forward and pulled the curtain aside and looked out of the window which faced the street.

"Just drove up," he said. "You better go to the door."

Earl Cradle hesitated a moment in the hallway before entering the living room. Looking down at Mrs. Wonder, he asked, "How is he, Mama? Is he feeling okay?" He spoke in an undertone.

Bertha Wonder looked up at him and her large, matronly face smiled in friendliness.

"It's good to see you, Earl," she said. She nodded toward the living room. "He's fine. Like a racehorse. Always gets all tensed up before a job. But you don't have to worry about him, Earl. The kidneys are giving him a little trouble, but he's all right. Worried and jittery, but that's the way he always is. Like a racehorse. That's Herman."

Earl patted her on the shoulder and crowded past her short, rotund body.

"I'll see him."

The old man looked up without expression as Earl entered the room.

"Well, Herman …"

"My kidneys," Herman said. "Bad."

"Mama told me."

"Sit down, Earl," the old man said. "Sit down, boy. I have been thinking. You know—well, you know I'm beginning not to like it."

"What's the trouble, Herman?" Earl asked, his voice conciliatory. "Now you know …"

"I'm not used to working with a lot of people around. Not my kind of thing at all, Earl. I like quiet. I get nervous when I don't have quiet. I don't see why we can't do it Sunday night. Just go in after dark and do it at night."

Earl Cradle sighed.

"Now, Herman," he said, "I've explained all that to you. It is just too risky. We have to wait until eight-thirty on Monday morning. Don't you understand? This isn't like some small-town bank out in Iowa or Oklahoma. They have Holmes' protection. The place is bugged and wired and God knows what. We wouldn't get as far as the main office before someone would trip over an alarm."

"So why should eight-thirty be any safer?"

"Because when eight-thirty comes around the staff show up. The branch manager comes in first and cuts off the main night alarm system. And then at exactly eight-forty the time lock on the safe cuts out. We have to wait for that, Herman."

The old man nodded, his lips pouting.

"Well, I guess you're right, Earl," he said. "I don't like time locks. Did you bring the dope on the vault?"

Earl reached into his pocket and took out a folded piece of paper.

"As much as Gallucci was able to get. It's a new job with the latest combination electronic alarm device, installed last year. Diebold. Circular door. There's a stainless-steel gate barring off the room itself, but that presents no problem. Night alarm ties in with the gate, but it will be off when we crack through."

He extended the paper.

"Gallucci has written down everything he knows, but it won't be much help. You still think you can handle it all right, Herman?"

"I can handle anything—just so I got peace and quiet, Earl," the old man said. "All I want is you have someone to carry my tools for me. I'm getting too old to lift much anymore."

"We'll take care of that, Herman. And you won't have to worry about peace and quiet. There won't be any trouble. You'll have enough time—and plenty of protection."

"Just be sure I do," Wonder said. "Just be sure I do. And I don't want any trouble when we blow. I'm getting old and I got this game leg. I want to do my work in peace and leave in peace."

"There'll be no trouble, Herman. You'll have forty minutes—fifty if you need it. And you leave like a gentleman. In the back seat of a chauffeur-driven limousine."

The old man looked across at Earl Cradle and for the first time a thin smile split his seamed face.

"Not like the old days, eh boy?" he said. "Not like the old days. No back roads and no screaming tires and nobody leaning out of a car door and blasting away with a Tommy gun trying to get the radiator of a squad car."

"No, Herman, not like the old days."

Herman Wonder shook his head and his rheumy eyes took on a sad, nostalgic expression.

"Tell Mama to hurry up with the tea, Earl," he said. "Tea is good for the kidneys."

3.

Crossing the Whitestone Bridge into the Bronx, Joey said, "You know, Earl, you're asking me to have a lot of faith in you. Here you expect me to be a part of a million-dollar heist and I don't even get to meet the guys who are in on the caper."

"That's right, Joey," Cradle said. "You don't meet them and they don't meet you. That is, until the right time comes. The less you know about them, the better it will be—should anything happen."

"Why, Earl? Don't you trust me?"

"I trust you or I wouldn't be in this thing. I'm just trying to protect everybody. Don't forget, if you don't know anything about them, they don't know you. Anyway, this thing is no damned kaffeeklatsch. There's no need for sociality. You have to remember one thing. These are my people. I know them. I've worked with them for years."

"This guy you are going to see now," Joey said. "This guy what works for the gas company. You told me you didn't know him."

"That's right. I don't know him personally. But his brother was my cellmate for three years up in Sing Sing. And you don't live in a place like that with a guy for three years without knowing a hell of a lot about him. I know him and he knows his own twin brother and it's the twin brother I'm seeing."

"But if this twin brother you're seeing is such a square he's working for a utility company, what the hell makes you think he'll go along …"

"I don't think, I know. He's already been talked to and he knows the score. He needs dough and he needs it bad. He needs money for a mouthpiece so that his brother can make an appeal and maybe get sprung. Understand, if the brother doesn't get sprung, he does the whole bit. Life. So this twin brother I'm going to see is ready to do anything and everything to get the right kind of dough. He knows he'll never get it as a foreman of a construction gang for the gas company. Not with a wife and three kids to support."

"But for a guy like that to agree …"

"You have to understand how twins feel about each other, Joey," Earl said. "Anyway, stop worrying about it. Leave the masterminding to me. It's safe because I say it's safe. You have to remember one thing. This guy is not in on the overall plan. He knows something is going to happen, but he doesn't know the details. All he has to do is be there early Monday morning with the truck and the air hammers and the saw horses to shut off the street, the signs and the rest of the stuff. He knows how to handle it once he's on the job."

"But if he uses a company truck …"

"My God, Joey, I said leave it to me," Cradle said. "He isn't taking a company truck. He merely tipped me off as to where one can be stolen for the time we need it. I'm arranging to handle that part of it. The truck and the tools and stuff. He just shows up and grabs an air hammer and starts making the hole in the sidewalk in front of the door. That is exactly the kind of work he's been doing for the last eight years and he knows how to go about it to make it look professional."

Joey shrugged his shoulders.

"Okay, Earl, if you say so," he said. "I guess you know what you're doing all right. Anyway, should a cop stop by and question him, he'd probably sound convincing."

"The cop won't question him," Cradle said. "The cop will be out in the intersection, diverting traffic. I've already seen to that."

Joey looked over at his companion and then whistled softly in quiet admiration.

"You see to everything don't you, Earl," he said.

"To everything," Earl Cradle answered.

### 4.

Mary Lou Shannahan waited until the man left and then went into the kitchen where Mike sat over a cup of coffee, staring at the floor.

"Mike," she said, "you should get to bed. You have to go to work at five o'clock and already it is past noon. You need your sleep."

Mike Shannahan looked up at the slender, girlish figure of his wife and the same thought struck him which had so often struck him before. She didn't look like the mother of three husky young kids. She looked like a high school girl. A pretty, black-eyed high school girl—in spite of the droop to her thin shoulders and in spite of the paleness of her pretty heart-shaped face. She looked young and sweet and innocent—and very tired.

"I'm fine, baby," he said. "It's you should be getting some rest."

"Who was that man, Mike?"

His eyes crinkled and he ran a hard, muscular hand through his short red hair.

"Sit down, baby," he said. "We got to talk." He reached out and pulled her to him, sitting her on his lap.

"Baby," he said. "You aren't going to believe this. That man was a bookie. He was Santa Claus. He was an angel in disguise. Look at this."

He reached into his pocket and a moment later laid the sheaf of bills on the table.

"Four thousand bucks," he said.

It took him several minutes to calm her down. To get her over the shock. To wait until she stopped crying.

"For you," he said, kissing her wet cheeks. "So you can do what Doc said and go on out to Arizona and spend a year. Take the kids and get that sunshine you need. Get those lungs of yours back in shape."

She shook her head, staring into his blue eyes.

"But Mike," she said, "I just can't believe it. You say you won a bet? I can't believe ..."

"That's right, a bet, baby."

She moved suddenly, pushing his arms away and quickly stood up. Putting her hands on her hips, she spread her legs and looked him in the eyes.

"Mike," she said, "you're a good man and I love you. But Mike, don't try and lie to me. I guess the reason I know you are lying is because you have never done so before. Except the time you tried to keep what the doctor said from me. But you don't make horse bets. I want to know about this money. How did you get it? Why did the man give it to you?"

"Now honey …"

"Don't 'honey' me. And don't try and get around me with any of your sugar talk. I want to know the truth. Is this some deal that your brother Charlie …"

Mike stared at his wife for several seconds, his face rapidly becoming scarlet. At last he sighed deeply and stood up, pacing the floor of the tiny room.

"Okay, honey," he said. "Okay. I don't lie to you and I won't now. You're right. It's a deal Charlie cooked up. A job I'm doing."

"And it's crooked?"

Mike shrugged.

"Maybe—maybe not. I'm not going to tell you the details. In fact, I don't even know the details myself. As far as I'm concerned I'm getting this four grand to play a sort of practical joke. I am going to dig a hole in a sidewalk."

Mary Lou shook her head and sucked at her small white teeth. "Now Mike …"

"I'm telling the truth, baby," Mike said. "As much as I know of it. What I got to do is spend a couple of hours digging a hole in a sidewalk. Then I just walk away."

For several moments his wife stared at him and then slowly sat down.

"And for that you get four thousand dollars? You said your brother Charlie …"

"Charlie arranged it."

"Then it's crooked and you know it is. And if Charlie arranged it, I can guess why. He wants you to take this money and hire a lawyer and …"

"This money is sending you to Arizona," Mike said, his lean, lantern-jawed face suddenly stubborn.

"All right, Mike," Mary Lou said. "All right. I'm not going to argue with you or fight with you. I know when your mind is made up about something. But I am your wife and I love you. I want you to tell me everything there is to tell me about it. I want to know."

"Make some coffee," Mike said. "I'll tell you."

He talked while they drank one cup of coffee and continued to talk while they had the second. At last he pushed the cup away and stood up.

"And that's it, honey," he said. "The whole thing. In a way I guess I'm double-crossing Charlie. But then again, I'm the one who has to take the chance, take the risk. I'm earning the dough. I guess I love Charlie as much as it's possible for one brother to love another. But I love you a lot more. Getting Charlie a lawyer would be, in any case, a hopeless gesture. Even if the lawyer finally got him out, he'd be back again within six months.

"But getting you out to Arizona, giving you a real chance to get well like the doctor said, that's something else. I don't care what I have to do to do it."

Mary Lou looked at her husband and slowly shook her head.

"Are you going to tell the priest about it, Mike?" she asked. "You know in your heart it's wrong—will you tell the priest?"

The stubborn expression returned and Mike's jaw tightened.

"The priest hasn't told me how to get my wife out to Arizona where she might have a chance to live and get well," he said. "The priest hasn't told me how I can protect the life of the mother of my children and the girl I love. No Mary Lou, I'm not going to tell the priest. I'm just going to do the job I have to do—and keep my own counsel."

**5.**

Dr. Martin Jordan carefully removed the black horn-rimmed glasses and folded the bows before slipping them into the breast pocket of his tweed jacket. His dark, shaggy eyebrows lifted and one corner of his wide mouth twisted as he cocked his head.

"But what I don't understand," he said, looking across the table into the excited eyes of Jane Mercer, "what I don't understand is how this man knew where to find you. How did he ever …"

"Martin, you really don't listen to me," Jane said in exasperation. "I've already explained to you. He said that he called the Bigger's Business School and that they gave him my telephone number."

Dr. Jordan looked more perplexed than ever.

"And how did he know about the Bigger's Business School?" he asked.

"For goodness sake, how should I know that?" Jane answered. "All I can tell you is what he said to me. He said he called them and that they gave him my address and phone number and so then he called me."

"All the way from New York City?"

"All the way from New York City. Of course, you ninny. What's so unusual about that? The Bell Telephone Company does advertise long distance you know. Anyway …"

"Now just take it easy, honey," Dr. Jordan said, reaching out and patting Jane on the arm. "Just take it easy and give it to me slow. And we'll have another …"

"We'll have nothing," Jane said. "I've already had three cups. And I can't help but have a feeling inside of me …"

"Never mind the feeling, honey, just tell it to me again. Now you say this man called you and …"

"Epstein. He said his name was Jake Epstein and that he was a newspaperman. I think he said the *New York Blade*. Or maybe it was the *Times*. I'm not sure, I was so excited. Anyway, he wanted to know about my father. What his name was and everything about him."

"Well, I think that if you really believe this fellow is on to something, you should at once contact the police department and …"

"But Martin, I've explained to you. He made me promise. He made me give him my solemn promise that I wouldn't say a word to a single soul until he calls back tomorrow."

"I'm a single soul," Dr. Jordan said.

"Oh you idiot," Jane said. "You don't count. After all, we're going to be married, aren't we?"

"That's why I should count," Dr. Jordan said. "Anyway, go ahead and give it to me again. Now exactly what was it he said?"

"He wanted to know all about Daddy. So I explained that Daddy was Dr. Creighton Fairwell Mercer and that he had been a professor at Ohio State and that he had disappeared five years ago. This man, this Mr. Epstein, seemed quite excited and he said that he thought that he might have a clue as to what had happened to him. I tried to question him, but he couldn't seem to hear me very well. Maybe it was a bad connection. In any case, he asked me a lot of questions and then before he hung up he made me promise not to say anything to anyone. That he would call me back the first thing tomorrow morning and that if he was right, I should be prepared to get a plane and come to New York at once."

Dr. Jordan shook his head.

"You'll do nothing of the sort," he said. "I'm not going to have you traipsing off to New York on some wild-goose chase just because some stranger telephones you."

"Now see here, Martin," Jane said. "Don't you dare tell me what to do and what not to do. If this man knows something about Daddy, then I ..."

"Then you should go to the police this very minute."

"Martin, I promised."

Dr. Jordan threw up his hands.

"Darling, listen. You don't even know who this Epstein creature is. You know nothing at all about him. Sure, he said he'd call back. But you don't really know if he will or will not."

"If he doesn't call back he won't be keeping his word and in that case, I'll feel free to break mine," Jane said. "In that case I'll go to the police. But, in the meantime, I'm going to wait and see what happens. I'm going to do just what he said for me to do and say not a word to anyone about it. And if he does call, and if I have to go to New York ..."

"Listen, darling," Dr. Jordan said, reaching for the check and starting to get up from the seat in the booth. "Listen, if he calls, you get in touch with me at once at the hospital. I have to get back—I'm late already. And one thing, honey—please don't set your hopes too high. I don't want to have you disappointed all over again."

"Both our hopes," Jane said, looking up at him with sudden tenderness in her eyes. "Both our hopes. You remember what I promised, darling? As soon as I really know what happened to Daddy, why then ..."

Dr. Jordan leaned down and kissed her.

"I love you," he said. "I love you very much."

He turned quickly then and was gone.

# Chapter 4

"I'm superstitious, Earl," Billy Dale said. "Do I have to do it today—on Friday?"

Earl Cradle reached for the shot glass and downed its contents in a gulp.

"Listen, Billy," he said, "just because you are a blonde, don't be dumb. Of course you have to do it tonight. And never mind this superstition stuff. Tell me now, just how did it go? Was there any hitch at all?"

Billy shook the blonde hair out of her face and took a quick puff of the cigarette before putting it in the ash tray on the dresser.

"Well," she said, "it was spooky. You know I can't stand looking at dead people and they made me look at him. Of course I told them exactly what he looked like but I had to go down there and see him anyway. They didn't ask very many questions. I gave them the story we rehearsed. Said he had disappeared a couple of years ago. That he was a drunk. Told them he used to be a vaudeville actor and had taken to the bottle when it was no longer possible for him to get work.

"They made me identify myself and they took down my name and address. There wasn't a great deal else. I guess you were right; they're glad to have them claimed. Anyway, I had to sign about a million papers and they wanted me to try and get someone else down to verify the identification, but I explained about not knowing very many people in town and told them after all I was his daughter and I should know.

"So after I signed the papers and all, I went out and said I'd make arrangements. I went to a gin mill and had a couple of slugs and sat around for a while. I needed a drink and a breath of fresh air. Then I went back and I told them that I had contacted a funeral home and that he would be picked up."

"And that was all there was to it?"

"They said I should come back when the undertaker came to get the body. I had to sign something called an out slip. So, like you said, I told them that the hearse would arrive this evening between seven and eight o'clock."

"You did great, kid," Earl said. He stood up and put his arms around her and she lifted her face and he kissed her.

"Great."

"I kinda hated to use my own name and all ..."

"You had to, kid. But don't worry. There won't be any trace. Who will ever know? Just another bum who is, after all, getting a break. He won't land up in Potter's Field at least. Now you go on back to your room and take it easy. And tonight, when you go down there with Gallucci, I want you to wear something conservative. Black, if you have anything like that. You're supposed to be in mourning."

"If I have to take one more look at that stiff," Billy said, "I probably will be."

He gave her a pat on the fanny.

"Pour us each one," he said, "before you go. And then take it easy this afternoon. Go to a movie or something. I don't want you showing up with a half a load on."

"You know I won't get stoned," Billy said. "But I can use a drink. This sort of thing makes me jittery. I don't have your nerves."

Cradle took her by her arms and pulled her close.

"You aren't going to crack up now, baby?"

"Of course I'm not," Billy said. "It's only …"

"A drink isn't what you want honey," Earl said. His hands moved up on her arms and around her shoulders and he pulled her close. After a long minute, Billy pulled back and looking up at him, said, "Earl, hon. You have to see Karl and Georgie, remember?"

"They can wait."

"But Earl …"

**2.**

They were playing eight-ball, over on the table in the northwest corner of the almost deserted poolroom, which was on the second floor over the Chinese restaurant. Neither of them looked up as he sauntered over and sat on the high stool next to the cue rack.

The tall thin boy in the sweat shirt was very good. He had a nice way of handling his cue stick and a very easy, sure manner.

He ran the solid colors and then called the eight ball in the side pocket and put it in with deadly precision.

The husky kid with the crew cut shrugged and racked his stick. He flipped a half dollar across the table and the tall thin boy pocketed it.

The husky youth began to rack the balls and Earl drifted over to the window, followed by the thin boy.

"You talk to him, Karl?" he asked.

"Yeah."

"Everything all right?"

"Yeah. He'll go along. It's all set, just the way we lined it up. He'll pick up the truck on Sunday night, late. I showed him the maps."

"Fine," Earl said. "And about after?"

"Well, Georgie squawked a little about the cut, but we straightened that out. I told him five percent up to fifty grand and that made sense to him. Another thing made him a little nervous was about afterward. He wanted to leave with the rest of us, but I explained that that was out."

"Go over and break," Earl said. "Send him over here for a second."

Karl went to the table and whispered something and the husky youth came across and stood next to Earl.

"Everything okay, Georgie?" Earl asked.

"I guess so."

"Don't guess."

"Everything is okay."

"Just do it the way your buddy Karl tells it and things will go fine. But don't miss up on the timing. Set your watch Sunday night. This is a split-second deal and if the timing misses the caper falls apart."

"I'm not an amateur," Georgie said, sullenly.

"The amateurs are all in prison," Earl said. He moved over to the table and when Karl missed his next shot, Earl chalked his cue and drew a sight on the seven ball.

Georgie lost the game and paid up and then left and Earl and Karl went downstairs to the Chinese restaurant and found a secluded booth. Earl ordered the special Chinese dinner for two, asking for a double order of egg rolls.

"I'll want you at the funeral parlor Sunday," he said.

"Why Sunday?"

"Several reasons. I want to keep my eyes on the rest of them. You gotta remember, you and I and Herman are the only real pros in this thing. Joey Gallucci is nothing but a second-rate heister and con artist. He's okay or I wouldn't be doing business with him, but he's never had experience in the big time. Old Herman, of course, can handle his end of it, but he's good for nothing else. We have to babysit him just a little bit. The two outside guys are good enough for what they have to do. But Mario Gallucci, the undertaker, is something else again."

"What do you mean Earl, something else? You don't think …"

"Oh, I'm not worried after it's all over and done with. He'll have his cut and he'll be safe enough then. But he's a square and he's never been mixed up in anything like this. I don't want him to panic. If some little thing should go wrong …"

"I thought you said nothing could go wrong with this one, Earl?"

"Don't be a damned fool," Cradle said. "You know as well as I do that something can always go wrong. Why the hell do you think Lloyd's don't give insurance on this sort of thing?"

"Are there any others I should know about?"

"Two more," Earl said. "A stiff who will be waiting in a coffin for a fast ride and a girl who is supposed to be his daughter."

Karl looked up, interested.

"A girl?"

"My girl," Earl said shortly. "Don't get any ideas."

Karl shrugged and reached for the egg rolls.


### 3.


Mario Gallucci softly whistled an aria from *Bohème* as he carefully tacked down the purple satin on the false bottom of the plyboard slab he had meticulously cut to fit exactly on the cleats he had nailed to the sides of the coffin. He had taken his time with the jig saw and done a really nice piece of work. One of his few pleasures was working with the tools in his small shop in the basement of the funeral home and although he realized that it wasn't really necessary to do a first-class job, he had nevertheless taken pains.

Friday had been a hard day. And he still had things to do. When he finished with the coffin, he would just have time to go upstairs and make himself a cup of black coffee and a salami sandwich. And then he would have to get the hearse out and go down to Bellevue.

Yes, it had been a busy day. First there was the business with the four Caddie limousines. It had really hurt him to part with them. The dealer had robbed him. He'd taken a real loss there. But any kind of money was better than none.

And the business with the instruments had been a crime. A couple of thousand dollars in lances and clamps and medical tools and the swine down at the pawnshop had given him less than two hundred bucks.

The place up in the Catskills hadn't been quite so bad. After all, he had known for a long time that he was going to have to let it go. Swartz, his neighbor who owned the summer hotel, had been after it for a long time. Old Swartz had really been surprised when he had called and told them he'd decided to sell.

It was a lucky thing Mario had been smart about it, and had gotten a price agreed upon before he'd mentioned that he needed the money at once. That the only way the deal could go through was if he could have the cash that weekend.

Swartz had been a little skeptical when Mario explained he had to meet a note and he hadn't liked it when Mario said he wanted to retain possession until the end of the month. But he had finally come through.

Sixteen grand wasn't a bad price at all, actually. It was seven thousand more than Mario's father had paid for the farm when he'd purchased it ten years ago. And, after all, no one had ever really used the place. No wonder either, with that lousy three-mile dirt road and the loneliness and all.

Well, that was gone and the limousines were gone and there was nothing really much left except this building itself and the furnishings. And they were mortgaged to the hilt.

Mario laid the completed false bottom in the coffin and it fitted perfectly, as he had expected it would. He carefully closed the mahogany top of the casket, giving it an affectionate pat. He stood up and switched from Puccini to Verdi.

Earl Cradle. Mario had to laugh. Of course he didn't actually laugh, as he never laughed. But Earl must think that he, Mario Gallucci was a real damned fool. Trying to make him believe they could fool the cops. That the police wouldn't find out sooner or later.

Cradle must take him for an idiot. Of course Earl was right about one thing. It would take the cops a little time to put everything together. But Mario understood about the police and he was quite sure that sooner or later they would have all the answers. Just as he was equally sure that Earl Cradle knew they would.

Oh it was easy enough for Cradle, a professional crook, to talk. Sure the job would be done and they'd have the money and cut it up and Cradle and that fancy blonde of his would disappear. Mexico or the Riviera or South America and they would be safe enough. And Mario was supposed to linger on and hold the bag.

But Mario was far too smart for that. Let Cradle and the others think what they wanted.

He had his phony passport and everything was ready. Once it was over and done with, his plans were made.

First across the border into Canada. Then the flight to Italy. Mario had his connections and once he was on the plane, to all intents and purposes, Mario Gallucci would have disappeared from the face of the earth.

Yes, Mario Gallucci would be dead, but some day, not too far in the distance, there would be a new funeral home opening up in that little town where his grandfather had first started in the undertaking business. A funeral home which wouldn't have to depend on a volume business but could be run as it should be run. After all, the owner would have a couple of hundred grand in back of him and that kind of money goes a long way in Italy.

For the second time within an hour Mario actually smiled, breaking what was almost a lifetime record.

He only wished that it was Monday night instead of Friday.


## 4.


Jake Epstein felt just a little bit like God.

His eyes went to his wristwatch and he saw that it was five-fifty. In exactly ten minutes the rates would change and he would put in the telephone call.

He sat back in the leather chair in front of the desk and his eyes traveled around the walls of the room. It was the back bedroom in which he had lived almost as long as he could remember. For a while he had shared the room with his older brother Herbert but then Herbert had gone away to law school and he had had the room to himself. It wasn't a big room, but it was comfortable.

There was the desk at which he sat, the twin bed which had been left after he had taken out Herb's bed to give himself more room. The banners and trophies on the wall (Herb's for the most part) the long bookshelves with all the books (his), the small portable television set. The stereo outfit his father had given him on his last birthday.

It was a boy's room, warm and comfortable and cluttered with the things of boyhood.

But Jake felt like a man. In fact, he felt something like a God.

He pushed the portable typewriter back and looked down on the sheaf of clippings and his series of notes. Three days of hard research. Three days of real work.

Maybe they would take him seriously now. Maybe …

His mother's voice dissipated his fantasies as she called through the closed door.

"Jake, if you don't come out and get your dinner I'll come in there and box your ears."

"Later, Ma," he said.

The door opened.

"Later, schmater," Mrs. Epstein said. "What's this later business with you anyway? I been hollering for ten minutes. What are you doing in here all by yourself anyway?"

"Ma," Jake said, "you don't understand. I've done it. I have really done it. Who could eat now?"

"You could," Mrs. Epstein said. "And just what is it you have done? Staying at home, not working, sitting on your tokus and ..."

"Ma, I have really made it. I've actually dug up a dead man and brought him back to life."

Mrs. Epstein stepped into the room and carefully closed the door.

"Keep your voice down," she said. "Gertie and Morris might hear you. Have you lost your mind? What do you mean you have dug up a dead man?"

Jake turned and threw out his arms in exuberation.

"Oh I don't mean literally," he said. "I just mean there was this dead man and I have found out who he was and all about him."

"So what business is it of yours, Jake? Isn't it enough the poor man is dead without bothering to put your nose in? How do you suppose the poor man's family will feel, young Jake Epstein digging up ..."

"They'll love me," Jake said. "They'll ..."

"Good God!" Mrs. Epstein cried, throwing up her hands. "What kind of business is this newspaper business anyway? Digging up dead men! People should love you for it. You sit here in your room all day and don't go to the office. You make telephone calls. A hundred, two hundred dollars maybe in telephone calls to all over the good Lord should only know where. You don't eat and you don't sleep. And you call that a business."

"Now, Ma ..."

"Don't 'Ma' me, Jacob. I don't know what is with you. Here your brother Herbie is already a lawyer. Your father is a decent honorable dress manufacturer. Your sister is studying medicine and even little Gertie is getting honors in school. But you: What's with you? A bum who sits in his room all day and makes phone calls and when I tell him to come eat a decent meal he tells me he's digging up dead men."

Jake stood up and put his hands on his mother's shoulders but she quickly shrugged him off.

"It's a story, Ma," he said. "A great story. And I have done it all by myself. The police couldn't do it, nobody could. But me, your son Jake, I've done it."

Mrs. Epstein took a step back and sighed deeply.

"So you've done it, Jakie?" she said. "All right, fine. Now come downstairs and get your dinner, yes?"

"One more phone call, Ma," Jake said. "Just one more. Then I'll be right down."

Mrs. Epstein opened the door and again sighed.

"One more phone call," she said, "and then dinner. After dinner you can come with Papa and me to the Margolieses and ..."

"After dinner," Jake said, "I have to go down to the morgue."

"A son I have raised," Mrs. Epstein said. "A monster I have raised."

She closed the door and spoke over her shoulder as she started for the staircase.

"So come down and eat the dinner, monster. Make the phone call and come downstairs."

Jake laughed and again sat down at the desk. For several moments he studied a sheet of paper in front of him and then he picked up the telephone and dialed long distance.

"I want to make a person to person call to Sandusky, Ohio," he said. "To Miss Jane Mercer at ..."

5.

Acting Captain James Xavier Cooney sat beside the uniformed driver of the patrol car as he made his first rounds of the precinct which he had taken over temporarily, until the Commissioner made up his mind about his promotion to the status of Deputy Inspector. The Captain knew that this assignment was a test. He had been down in headquarters, working on a desk job, for the last four years and in a good many ways had actually lost track of the type of police work a man out in the field was expected to do.

One thing he was thankful for at least. It wasn't a really tough precinct. Not like one of those up in Harlem or over in the Red Hook district in Brooklyn. It would have been murder there. Here everything was fairly safe and sure. Brownstone residences, most of which had been turned into rooming houses. A large number of middle- and upper-class apartment buildings. The usual run-of-the-mill taverns and restaurants. A few commercial establishments and a fair share of small businesses and retail stores. Routine.

He could expect the usual amount of trouble—the Amsterdam and Columbus Avenue saloons were always sore spots. There would be a few robberies, a few muggings, possibly a murder or so. But nothing really big. Nothing spectacular. Nothing that would make the front page.

What he had to do was run a tight precinct, keep traffic moving, watch the trouble spots. Keep the men on their toes, and be damned sure nothing happened that he wasn't right on the top of. He didn't want to blow this temporary post. If he did, then he'd miss that promotion he had waited for all these years.

The promotion meant not only more money and more pension, but also that he would be assigned back to the safe and loft squad and would be working out of headquarters, and that is exactly where he wanted to be. He didn't like precinct work and he didn't want to go back to the old desk job.

The driver, a detective first grade, pulled over toward the curb and slowed down. He nodded at a tavern on the corner.

"Hot," he said. "Guy got stabbed there the other night. They average one fight a week."

The Captain growled something under his breath about places that had pull and couldn't be closed. The driver stepped on the gas again. He swung into Amsterdam Avenue and as he passed south into the eighties, he said, "A quiet stretch. A mugging now and then but nothing else much."

The Captain nodded.

He looked out the window and saw the hearse as it came to a stop at the corner.

"You got a funeral parlor around here?" he asked.

The driver nodded.

"Yeah. Gallucci's," he said. "But he doesn't do a big business. No traffic problem there, usually."

The Captain grunted again.

"I see there's a bank on the corner," he said.

"Right. But we've never had to worry about it. Has private protection nights and weekends and the way it's located, no stickup man in his right mind would try to knock it over in the daytime."

"Stickup men are never in their right minds," the Captain said.

The patrol car rolled on down the avenue and was soon lost to sight.

Back at the corner the hearse crossed with the green light and pulled down the street several yards and then turned into the private driveway leading to the basement of Gallucci's Funeral Home.

Mario Gallucci pressed the button on the electric eye device and overhead doors swung up and he drove inside. The blonde girl at his side couldn't resist a slight shudder.

"I'm sure glad to get here," she said. "And I'll be just as glad to leave. I didn't think we'd ever arrive."

Mario looked at the clock on the dashboard.

"It's only eight-thirty," he said. "We made good time."

## 6.

The night attendant looked up from his reception desk and frowned. Tossing his still lighted cigarette into the waste basket between his feet, he said, "Say, boy you been hanging around here since nine o'clock. You waiting for someone in particular?"

Jake Epstein stopped pacing and looked at his wrist watch. It showed ten fifteen.

"I don't suppose Dr. Frogg ..."

"Dr. Frogg doesn't come on until nine tomorrow morning," the attendant said. "Now if you intend to ..."

"My name is Epstein and I'm from the *Blade*," Jake said. "I am waiting here for a young lady."

"Well this is a hell of a place to meet a girl."

"She's coming here to identify a body," Jake said. "You see ..."

"Not tonight she ain't," the attendant said. "Only way you can get in the vault tonight is with a special pass. Either the police or one of the Assistant Medical Examiners ..."

"But it's the girl's father," Jake said quickly. "Z-12-77."

"Did you say Z-12-77?"

"That's right. This girl is coming in from Ohio and I ..."

The attendant began to laugh.

"What's so funny?" Jake asked.

"You say you was a newspaperman?"

"That's right."

"Well, son, you better start getting on your toes. You've missed your young lady. She's come and gone."

"Come and gone?" Jake again checked his watch. "What do you mean come and gone? I've been here since before nine and ..."

"I'm just saying she has been here and gone." The attendant checked a paper on his desk. "Was here between seven and eight," he said.

Jake looked at him unbelievingly.

"But that's impossible," he said. "Why I talked to her in Sandusky late this afternoon ..."

"Not this dame you didn't talk to. This dame was here at seven o'clock." He checked the paper again. "Seven-fifteen and she signed the release and by seven-thirty her old man was in the hearse and on his way. Z-12-77 you said, didn't you?"

"That's right, Z-12-77," Jake said. "But you must be wrong. Miss Mercer could never have gotten here from Sandusky ..."

"Who's talking about a Miss Mercer. I said the young woman who claimed Z-12-77—her old man—was here and got the body and left with it."

Jake stopped pacing and stared at the man, the blood slowly draining from his face.

"Listen," he said, "there has been some terrible mistake. You have done some awful thing. Z-12-77 is a man named Creighton Fairwell Mercer, a famous scientist and scholar, and his daughter is on her way from Sandusky, Ohio, to claim his remains. Mr. Mercer ..."

"I don't know nothing about any Mr. Mercer and I don't know nothing about any girl from Sandusky, Ohio," the attendant said, looking belligerent. "All I know about is Z-12-77." Again he checked the paper on his desk.

"Z-12-77," he repeated, "a derelict picked up last Monday morning down off the Bowery. Name, James Dale. Daughter's name, Billy Dale. Z-12-77. Died drunk. Now on his way to a funeral parlor from which he will be buried. Now son, if that's all you got on your mind, you had better be on your way. This is no place to be hanging around waiting to keep a date."

"See here," Jake said. "I tell you ..."

"And I tell you to get out of here and be on your way. The man was positively identified—by his own daughter. She obtained the proper papers from the Medical Examiner's Office and from the Police Department. The body was released to her and she has had it picked up. I guess a girl knows her own father, don't she?"

For several seconds Jake just stood there, his mouth open.

Suddenly the whole and complete reality of what had happened came to him and he felt his limbs beginning to shake. Good Lord! What had he done? Any moment now some young woman from the Midwest was going to burst in wanting to see the body of a man that he had led her to believe was her missing parent. Any moment now …

Jake staggered toward the door. He might be able to face his mother and his family, he might even be able to face his city editor, but he knew that right now he would never be able to face a girl named Jane Mercer, from Sandusky, Ohio.

On the way through the door Jake passed the man who was coming to relieve the attendant while he took his coffee break.

Outside on Twenty-third Street, a cab was pulling to the curb. Jake walked like a man who was drunk as he lurched toward it. He never even noticed the pretty young girl in the trim, tailored suit who was standing at the side of the cab paying off the driver.


## 7.


At eleven o'clock the man who filled in on the reception desk looked up and spoke, his voice sympathetic.

"Listen, Miss," he said, "honest, you should do what I say. We got no Mr. Epstein here. I never even heard of a Mr. Epstein. This place is closed to the public nights. Even if there was a Mr. Epstein, he couldn't help you. Go somewhere and get some sleep and come back in the morning. Please."

Jane Mercer stared at him and she wanted to cry.

"But," she said, "but he said he would be here. It's about a man—a man …" her voice broke but she quickly gathered herself together and took a slip of paper from her bag "… somebody you have here. A number Z-12-77. He's my father."

The temporary attendant got up from behind the desk.

"I'm going to see you to a cab," he said. "I can't tell you anything. Nobody can. Not until tomorrow morning. You come back in the morning and ask for a Dr. Frogg. He'll be able to help you, I'm sure."

An hour later, in the room at the Midtown hotel she had taken, Jane remembered her promise to Dr. Martin Jordan. She was to call him as soon as she got in.

Instinctively her hand reached for the phone, and then she hesitated.

She was confused. First that business at that terrible place downtown and then trying to get the man Epstein at his newspaper without any luck. Everything seemed to be conspiring against her.

A few hours wouldn't matter. She'd wait until morning and call Martin then. At least she might have some news—good news, please God—to tell him then.

# Chapter 5

"If you don't open that door, Jake," Mrs. Epstein said, "I'm going to call your father at the office and tell him …"

Jake lifted his head from the pillow.

"Go away, Mama," he said. "I'm sick."

"Sick you are. That's just fine. So you lock yourself in your room and won't even see your own flesh and blood. What is this with you, Jake? All night long some strange woman telephones the house and you won't even pick up the receiver. This morning that newspaper office of yours calls and again you won't answer. What is it Jake?"

"The newspaper just wants to fire me," Jake said in a muffled voice.

"So good—let them fire you. Then maybe you will begin to live like a human being again. Let them fire you, I say. You can go back and study to become a …"

"I don't want to become anything. I just want to be alone."

"You and Miss Garbo, Jake," his mother said. "I tell you, son, you better snap out of it. The newspaper should fire you, so much the better. But in the meantime, what am I supposed to tell these people who keep calling? Huh? What should I tell them?"

"Tell them to go to hell," Jake said thickly.

"Ah-hah! So now he swears at his own mother. That does it, Jacob. That does it. Right now I am going down and telephone your father."

Jake buried his head again in the pillow as the sound of his mother's receding footsteps reached him through the locked door of his bedroom.

## 2.

Dr. Frogg looked at the slender, nervous girl who sat across from his desk. His dyspepsia was giving him trouble and he felt more grumpy than usual, but there was some quality about this youngster that seemed to act as a catalyst and his voice was almost pleasant when he spoke.

"Yes, yes, I remember a young newspaper fellow named Epstein. Haven't seen him around for several days."

"And he assured me that the man was my missing father," Jane said. "Mr. Epstein assured me …"

"But I don't quite understand how Epstein could have assured you of anything," Dr. Frogg said. "I have already explained. The man you were told about has been positively identified. By his daughter. He …"

"But when he died he was carrying a picture of me. From an old newspaper. It had my name and everything and …"

Dr. Frogg shook his head.

"I'm sorry, Miss," he said, "but I am afraid you have it wrong. There were a couple of newspaper clippings. I saw them. But there was no clipping with any picture, of you or anyone else."

"Mr. Epstein told me …"

"A newspaperman? Never believe anything a newspaperman tells you, my dear."

"But Mr. Epstein seemed so absolutely positive."

"Well, Mr. Epstein was wrong. I'm sorry that the cadaver has already been removed. Otherwise I would be glad to take you down and let you see for yourself."

Jane Mercer blanched a little at the word "cadaver."

"You must have a picture," she said, tentatively.

Dr. Frogg nodded.

"We do," he said. "If it will serve to set your mind at rest, I'll see if I can get a copy." He pushed a button on his desk.

Five minutes later Jane laid the large glossy photo down and faced Dr. Frogg. Her eyes were serious and her small jaw was very firm.

"I told you that I hadn't seen my father for five years. I can tell you now, however, that although he has changed a great deal, this is a photograph of him. I am absolutely sure."

Dr. Frogg shook his head.

"Now my dear," he said, "you are upset and disappointed. Also photos of elderly men often look very similar. Especially if they have met their deaths in a way ..." He hesitated, and then coughed. "There is only one thing I can advise you to do. The body of this man has been picked up and taken to an undertaking establishment in Manhattan, as I recall. I suggest that you go up there and tell them your story. I am sure that you will find them very reasonable. If you insist they will let you look at the remains."

"And if I still insist it is my father?"

"Then you must contact the police, or come back here and I'll get in touch with them. A further investigation will be made."

"But why should anyone want to take my father's ..."

Dr. Frogg stood up and rounded the desk and laid a pudgy hand on Jane's shoulder.

"I don't think anyone claimed your father's body," he said. "After all, the other young lady was quite sure it was her father. She recognized him at once. Immediately. I am quite sure she isn't anxious to assume the expense of burying a complete stranger."

"Well," Jane said, "she was wrong."

"In that case, you do as I have suggested. If you'll wait just a moment, I'll give you the name and the address of the funeral home and I will also write a short note which you may give them. I am sure they will cooperate."

"And if they refuse to let me ..."

"As I say, if you see the body and still feel that you are right, contact the police at once."

3.

Dr. Martin Jordan pushed his horn-rimmed glasses up on his forehead and spoke in a controlled, tight voice.

"I tell you, sir," he said, "she has been gone since six o'clock last evening. It is now Saturday noon and I have not heard a word. I know that she arrived in New York—I checked the airport. From there she has completely disappeared. She promised to call last night as soon as she had checked into a hotel."

The superintendent of the hospital looked up sympathetically.

"I understand, Doctor," he said. "I understand and I know you are worried. But I don't exactly see what you can do about it unless you want to report it to the police."

"I want a pass for the weekend," Dr. Jordan said. "I want to get a plane to New York and find this newspaperman she was supposed to meet."

The superintendent smiled.

"Well, they always told me that newspapermen are pretty gay, attractive, careless types. Perhaps …"

He suddenly noticed the expression on Dr. Jordan's face and the smile faded from his own.

"Frankly, Doctor," he said, "I think you are worrying prematurely. And you know how shorthanded we are here. Suppose we do this. It is now noon on Saturday. If you have heard nothing within the next twenty-four hours, then I will give you a leave of absence. For three days."

Dr. Jordan thanked him curtly and turned on his heel to return to his ward. He was praying that he wouldn't need that pass. That he would have some word of Jane long before then.

**4.**

Herman Wonder stood in front of the dresser, looking into the mirror. His wife, Bertha, reached over and flicked a piece of lint from the sleeve of his black suit and straightened the white handkerchief in his breast pocket. She watched him admiringly.

Cocking her head, she said, "You're still a fine figure of a man, Herman. A regular racehorse."

"No, Mama," Herman said. "No, I'm an old man. I've got arthritis, I'm half blind, and I wheeze when I talk."

He took off his rimless bifocals and handed them to her. "Wipe them for me, Mama," he said. "I'm an old man—but I can still work."

Mrs. Wonder took the glasses and wiped them on her apron.

"They should be here any minute now," she said. "Seems a shame you have to leave already—only Saturday—and you won't be needed until Monday morning. Have you got everything packed?"

"All packed," Herman said. "Leaving now is a good idea. Earl wants plenty of time to get things organized. Earl knows what he's doing. He's a good boy."

"Well, I just hope they take care of you. I worry."

Herman turned to his wife and frowned.

"You worry, Mama? That isn't like you."

"Oh, not about the job," Mrs. Wonder said. "I worry about your health. Nasty weather for you to be sitting around in some cold vault."

"I won't be in a vault until Monday," Herman said. "I'll be in a nice warm funeral chapel. Might as well get used to it; they'll have me pretty soon anyway."

"Don't talk like that, Herman."

Mrs. Wonder lifted her head and listened.

"The doorbell," she said. "That will be them. Hurry now—I'll let them in."

Joey was wearing the chauffeur's uniform again and this time he followed Earl Cradle into the living room of the house. Earl kissed Mrs. Wonder on the cheek and looked down at the three suitcases on the floor.

"This all of it?" he asked.

Bessie Wonder nodded.

"Take them to the car," Earl said to Joey.

Joey reached down and picked up two of the bags, swinging them carelessly as he started for the door.

"I'll toss them in the back," he said.

Herman Wonder, stepping into the living room, spoke in a soft voice.

"Sure son, toss 'em," he said. "There are four vials of raw nitro in one of them—enough to put you in orbit."

Joey hesitated, suddenly paling, and then moved cautiously toward the door.

Mrs. Wonder handed her husband an overnight bag and said, "You remembered the aspirin, Herman?"

"Yes, Mama, I remembered. You put the brandy in didn't you?"

"Three pints, Herman," Bessie said. "One for each day."

She kissed him goodbye and a couple of minutes later Earl helped the old man into the back of the limousine and then climbed in after him and closed the door.

"We'll pick up Karl at his place on East Fourth, Joey," he said. "Drive carefully."

"You don't have to tell me," Joey said. "You don't have to tell me."

Herman turned to Earl.

"Karl Hansom?" He asked.

"Yeah, Hansom. A good boy."

"Used to be trigger-happy and woman-crazy," Herman said.

"He's quieted down," Earl said. "Since he's switched from the choppers to the sawed-offs, he's quieted down. You don't have to worry about him."

"Got no use for gunmen," Herman muttered, "but I guess he's as reliable as any of 'em."

He reached into his pocket and took out a pipe and began to fill it from a leather pouch. "You get the mattresses, Earl?"

"Four of them—doubles."

"It's a shame, Earl, we have to do it this way. Be a lot easier if we could just wait until that safe was opened up by the manager."

"I know, Herman, I know," Earl said. "But the timing is all wrong. Mario Gallucci has cased it and he knows. If we waited until the manager opened the box, the place would be filled with customers and it would make the whole thing far too risky. But the way we got it planned, the outside door will be locked and there won't be any problems. No, this one is planned right—there's only one foolproof way to handle it. I'm sure about the timing. It would be different if we were only interested in the small safe. He opens that one immediately. But the one we are interested in can't be touched until nine-fifteen when the time lock is released. He doesn't bother with it until around nine-thirty, usually."

Herman nodded. "I know you're doing it the right way, Earl," he said. "If I didn't have confidence in you, I wouldn't be playing along."

"Thanks, Herman," Earl said. "A great deal will depend on you, Herman. A great deal."

"I know my business," Herman said, his voice a little touchy. "You've seen to everything else, haven't you?"

"Had a little trouble with the diamond bits," Earl said, "but I managed finally."

Herman Wonder grunted and put the pipe into the corner of his mouth, but didn't light it. By the time they had reached the Midtown Tunnel he had closed his eyes and was softly snoring.

Karl was waiting on the curb in front of the apartment house. He had a trombone case and a small airline bag. He nodded briefly at Earl and climbed in beside Joey.

It was just twelve noon on Saturday when the limousine pulled into the driveway at the funeral home. They had to wake Herman when the car came to a stop.

Ten minutes later the five of them were seated around a table in the main chapel, Mario and Joey Gallucci, Earl Cradle, Herman Wonder, and Karl Hansom. Cradle was doing the talking, drilling each one of them in his role.

He stopped talking suddenly as the sound of a doorbell reached his ears. He looked over at Mario.

Mario shrugged.

"Customer maybe," he said. "I'll get it."

He was gone for several minutes and when he returned, his long, horselike face was white and his eyes were popping.

Earl Cradle sprang to his feet.

Mario carefully closed the door and for a moment he struggled to get his breath.

"What …" Earl began.

"A girl," Mario said.

Earl sat back in his chair.

"So take it easy pal," he said. "Get rid of her, or did you?"

Mario shook his head.

"She's come for her father," he said in a ghastly whisper. "She's from Ohio and she says she's come for her father."

"What the hell are you talking about?" Earl asked. "Have you blown your stack, Mario? Who's come for whose father?"

Mario took a handkerchief from his pocket and wiped the sweat from his face.

"This girl," he said weakly. "She's come for the stiff. You know …" he nodded toward the basement. "The one we got from Bellevue. She says that he belongs to her and she's here to get him."

Joey let out a soft whistle.

"This cuts it," he said.

Cradle slowly got to his feet.

"Damn it," he said, "take it easy. Just take it easy. You, Mario, get a hold of yourself. Where is this girl?"

"In the reception room."

"All right. I'll see her. The rest of you stay here. Mario, can you control yourself long enough to take me in and introduce me? Just say Mr. Jones, your funeral director, and then get out. I'll handle this. Don't worry. I'll handle it."

**5.**

Jane Mercer stepped into the cab and gave the driver the address of Gallucci's Funeral Home.

She sat back on the leather seat and drew a long, tired sigh. Her emotions were mixed.

From the very moment when she had first talked to the man named Epstein, she had unconsciously realized that her father was dead. The long five years of waiting, of not knowing, had muted her grief.

When Epstein had made the appointment to meet her at the morgue in Bellevue, there had of course no longer been any doubt. And then there had been these last terrible hours when she had thought that the whole thing was a mistake and it was about to start over again.

But now she knew. Finally and ultimately and completely, she knew. There had been no mistaking that photograph.

She experienced a sudden sense of complete relief; almost of freedom. It was over and done with.

The thought crept into her mind that somehow this marked the end and the beginning of things for her. Yes, in truth, it would be the beginning. It would no longer be necessary to hold Martin Jordan off. There was no reason in the world why, once things had been properly taken care of, they couldn't be married. She would be able to go to Scotland with him. To …

She leaned forward suddenly, conscious-stricken. Lord, she still hadn't telephoned! Of course she had tried to early that morning when she had first gotten up, but had been unable to get a through circuit. She should have called again from the morgue, but it had completely escaped her mind in the excitement of talking with that strange little man with the odd name.

She tapped on the driver's shoulder and he instinctively slowed down and turned his head.

"Would you stop some place where I can get to a telephone?" she asked.

He nodded and a couple of minutes later pulled to a parking spot in front of the Madison Hotel.

"In the lobby, Miss," he said. "Next to the cigar stand."

She dropped the dime in the slot and asked for Long Distance. There was a wait of a minute or so and the girl's voice reached her. "The circuits are busy. If you will let me call you back …"

"But I'm in a phone booth and I really must …"

"I'm sorry. All circuits are busy. If you will …"

She hung up. There was a click and she reached into the return coin box but there was no dime.

"New York!" she said, in disgust, and returned to the cab.

It took the driver almost an hour to get through Midtown traffic and he stopped at a drugstore on Columbus Avenue, a couple of blocks from his destination. Jane again went to the telephone. And again the circuits were busy.

"If you will wait," the operator said, "I will ring as soon as I have an open circuit."

For a moment Jane was tempted to stay in the booth. But then she quickly decided that there was no point in letting the cab stand there running up its meter. She would put the call in again from the funeral parlor and if there had to be a wait, at least it wouldn't be costing her money.

The driver asked if she wanted him to stand by when she alighted in front of Gallucci's, but she told him not to bother. She had already spent too much money on cabs. In any case, she really didn't know how long she might be detained.

Three minutes later and she had explained herself to the gaunt-looking man who called himself Mr. Gallucci.

The man was very odd.

At first he hadn't seemed to know exactly what she was talking about. But at last she had gotten through to him and when he did understand, instead of saying anything, he had merely looked startled and bewildered and gotten up and excused himself.

Well, she supposed that it would be a little upsetting. Thinking he had one customer and then discovering that there had been this awful mistake. He was gone a long time and now he was back, accompanied by a slender, athletic-looking man with a lean, handsome face and very sharp, black eyes.

"Mr. Jones, our funeral director," Mario Gallucci said. "He will …"

His voice died out and Earl Cradle stepped forward, holding out his hand.

"How do you do," he said. "I understand there has been some sort of …"

He hesitated and Mario quietly faded through the doorway, closing the door softly after himself.

"As I have explained," Jane said, "my name is Jane Mercer. I am from Sandusky, Ohio. Several days ago a newspaper man from New York telephoned me and said that he believed he had identified a body in the morgue as that of my father, Creighton Mercer, who has been missing for five years."

"I am sorry," Earl said, his voice soft with sympathy.

"I came to New York last night," Jane continued, "and I went to the morgue. The body, I discovered, had been removed and brought here. Some woman made a mistake and thought it was a relative of hers."

Earl nodded encouragement.

"Well, I just couldn't believe it and I returned to the morgue again this morning. They showed me a picture of the deceased. It was my father."

"I see," Earl said. "Now Miss...."

"Mercer—Jane Mercer."

"Miss Mercer, aside from the photograph, have you any other means of identifying the dead man?"

"I know my own father."

"How long since you last saw your father?"

"Five years. But I ..."

"Miss Mercer, a man may change a lot in five years. Did anyone come with you from Sandusky who might have known your father? Who might be able to help in the identification?"

"No one else is needed," Jane said, a little sharply. "No, I came alone. But I would certainly ..."

"Miss Mercer, a woman already has positively identified the dead man as her parent. She has obtained all the official papers and ..."

"I want to see him," Jane said. "If I see him I will know for sure."

Earl hesitated a moment.

"My dear," he said, "why don't we do this before you subject yourself to such an ordeal? Why don't I have the lady who has already identified him come here. It will only take a very few minutes. In all fairness ..."

"I have no objections," Jane said. "But I still want to ..."

"And you may, you may," Earl said. "Now if you will just excuse me for a moment, I will contact Miss Dale, the young lady I mentioned."

"When you're through calling her," Jane said, "I would like to make a telephone call. I'll reverse the charges."

Earl looked at her sharply for a moment and then nodded. "Certainly," he said.

He left the room and hurried back to the chapel.

"Get Billy Dale, at the hotel, and tell her to get up here as fast as she can move her fanny," he barked at Joey. "Give her the pitch. This dame thinks the stiff is her old man and he probably is. I'm going to try and talk her out of it."

He turned to Gallucci. "And Mario, the second Joey gets through calling Billy, I want you to take that receiver off the hook and leave it off. She wants to make a call to someone and we've got to see that that call doesn't go through."


**6.**


Jane looked into the blue eyes of the tall, blonde woman and thought, "She looks frightened. I wonder why?"

"Why don't we do this," Earl Cradle said. "You have seen the deceased, Miss Mercer, and you are still convinced that the dead man is your father. You have no proof, of course, but you are convinced. On the other hand, so is Miss Dale. Why don't we just let things rest for a couple of days, say until Monday afternoon, and then sort of review the entire thing and make our decision?"

Jane looked at him with wide eyes.

"Until Monday. Why ..."

"He'll ..." Cradle quickly throttled his words. He had been about to say "He'll keep," but it struck him as a little indelicate.

"What I mean, Miss Mercer," he said, "is that it will give you time to return home and find some substantiation. You know, early photographs, that sort of thing. Perhaps friends who knew your father and would be willing to come here and aid in a positive identification."

Jane stood up and her face was red with anger.

"Now see here, Mr. Jones," she said. "I have told you that he is my father. I *know*. Now if you are not prepared to let me have possession— Well, Dr. Frogg at the morgue told me that if I was sure I had any trouble, I should go to the police and that is exactly what I shall do!"

"Good God!" Billy Dale said.

"I beg your pardon," Jane said.

"Now ladies, please," Earl said. "Sit down, Miss Mercer. It will not be necessary for you to go to the police. We'll settle this here and now to your complete satisfaction." He turned toward Billy and spoke in a soft, quick voice.

"Miss Dale," he said, "I am afraid Miss Mercer has a point. She has made a positive identification. Now as you remember, you weren't really sure when you first saw the dead man. I honestly believe you have made a mistake. Won't you reconsider …"

Billy looked at him baffled and then quickly recovered. She fumbled for a moment for words, and then spoke.

"Of course I don't want to have any trouble. If Miss Mercer honestly thinks …"

"I do," Jane said.

"All right," Earl Cradle said. "That settles it. Now here is what I suggest. Let me handle the details. I will at once straighten out the technicalities with the morgue. Miss Mercer, you may rest assured that everything will be taken care of. Because of technicalities," he looked at his wristwatch, "and the fact that it is now Saturday afternoon, it will probably be late Monday before I have everything taken care of. And then if you wish, we will be very happy to do anything you desire. If you care to have your father's body shipped to Ohio …"

There was something wrong. There was something terribly wrong here. Jane knew it. Five minutes ago this girl was absolutely positive, as positive as I am, that the man was her father. She was hanging onto him for dear life. And now …

And this Mr. Jones? He has certainly made a very fast turn back.

"I shall have him cremated in New York," Jane said. "And I don't really think we will have to wait until Monday. Dr. Frogg, down at the morgue, told me he would be in all afternoon and he was very cooperative. I am quite sure that he will help me and that I can have my father removed …"

"But, Miss Mercer," Earl said, "because of our mistake, I feel that the least we can do is to take care of things for you. In your time of grief …"

"Your mistake?"

"Well, that is to say, Miss Dale's mistake."

Jane stood up again.

"You are acting very oddly, Mr. Jones," she said. "I believe that I will telephone Dr. Frogg. I think that …"

"I'm sorry, Miss Mercer, but the telephone is temporarily out of order. They started work on the lines this morning and we have been without ..."

Jane's eyes suddenly opened wide.

"Did you say this morning?"

"Why yes ..."

"You told me less than an hour ago that you had telephoned Miss Dale. To tell her to come here. Apparently the telephone was working then. And that was long after noon."

She started toward the door as she finished speaking.

"Miss Mercer, if you will just ..."

"I am going out and telephone Dr. Frogg," Jane said.

Her hand was on the door when Earl Cradle moved. He moved like a cat, with silent, lightning speed. She felt his fingers dig into her shoulder and started to turn, her eyes furious. And then she saw his face and her mouth fell open and she gave a small cry.

"All right, sister," Earl said. "That will be all. You are not going anywhere. Not for the next forty-eight hours."

"Why what—what ..."

"Take care of her, Billy," Earl said. "If she starts to yell, slap her, slap her hard. Now get her in the back."

Three minutes later Earl entered the small reception room which clients passed through before entering the funeral parlor.

He tore a sheet from the calendar pad on the desk and printed the words in large letters:

WILL BE CLOSED
FOR TWO WEEKS

He signed Mario Gallucci's name at the bottom and found a thumbtack and tacked the message on the door leading from the reception room to the office of the establishment. He left the door to the street unlocked, but carefully locked the other door behind him before returning to the others.

**7.**

Billy Dale looked at her wrist watch and yawned.

"A great way to spend a quiet Sunday night," she said. "I can't see why it would matter if I went out for a while and hit a movie."

Earl Cradle looked up from his cards and frowned.

"You can't because I told you I want you to stay in there with that girl," he said.

"But, Earl," Billy protested, "I was just in with her. She's fine. And Herman said he would rather stay in there than sit around here watching you guys playing pinochle. He *wants* to stay in there with her. Anyway, she finally fell asleep. I guess the pills took effect. Herman is reading and he said it wasn't necessary for me to hang around."

"Let her go out," Mario said, laying down a ten-spot. "What the hell, she can bring back a few containers of fresh coffee and some sandwiches."

Karl looked up and grunted.

"Good idea."

Earl thought for a moment and then nodded.

"All right, kid," he said, a bit reluctantly. "But don't be gone too long. Be back before midnight. I want Herman to get some sleep before morning. Someone has got to stay there with her."

Mario tossed his hand on the table.

"What the hell is this?" he asked. "A card game or a debating society? And that brings up another question. Just what do you plan to do about her—tomorrow? You still haven't said, Earl."

"I haven't said because I haven't yet decided," Cradle said shortly. "How the hell do I know—at this time? We have to wait and see just exactly what …"

"Well, I don't want any …"

Cradle slammed down his cards and stood up.

"Listen," he said, his voice tight with anger. "Lay off, will you? I didn't ask her in on this party. I didn't tell her to come here. And I don't know what I'm going to do yet. All I can tell you is one thing. We're going to pull this job and pull it the way we planned it. I don't like killing any more than you do. But nothing is going to interfere with this caper. Nothing, understand?"

"She's …" Billy began, but Cradle cut her short.

"Keep out of this," he said. "Go on out now if you want to get away for a while. And the rest of us—let's just take it easy and get back to the card game."

He sat down and Joey reached for the deck to shuffle for a new deal.

Mario shrugged.

Karl pushed his chair back.

"Cut me out for a while," he said. "I'll just watch."

Billy left the room as Joey offered the cards for a cut.

They played silently for several minutes and Karl wandered around the table, looking over shoulders. Finally he yawned deeply and spoke.

"Think I'll go on in the other room," he said. "Get some shuteye."

No one bothered to look up as he slouched out of the room.

Herman turned as the door of the small antechamber, where he sat guarding the girl, quietly opened. He looked up and frowned when he saw it was Karl. For a moment Karl leaned against the door jam, a toothpick hanging out of the corner of his mouth and his small, dark eyes watching the girl as she lay breathing deeply on the couch at the side of the room.

Jane Mercer lay on her back, her elbows bent and her bound hands locked together on her breast. Her hair was tumbled over the pillow under her head and her face was very pale but relaxed, as she slept. They had removed her shoes and the jacket of her suit. Her skirt was hitched up exposing one thigh a little above the knee. She wore a light silk blouse.

Karl's eyes went from the girl to Herman.

"Out like a light, eh?"

Herman nodded.

"What do you want?"

"Earl sent me," Karl said. "He sent Billy out to get some coffee and sandwiches. Said for me to relieve you for a while and that you should go in and get some sleep."

Herman shook his head.

"I'll sleep when I get tired," he said shortly.

"Makes no difference to me, Pop," Karl said unconcernedly. "I'm just telling you what Earl said. Billy will be back in a couple of minutes and stay here and he wants you to get some sleep."

The old man stared at him for a moment or so, and then slowly got up, dropping his newspaper to the floor.

"I'll wait …" he began, but Karl quickly interrupted.

"She don't look like she'll be any trouble," he said, looking over at the bed on which Jane lay, "but I'll just stay outside, near the door, until Billy gets back."

The old man crossed the room and Karl stepped aside as he passed through the door. He followed him out and closed the door behind himself. Herman moved down the hallway without speaking.

Karl waited for a full five minutes and then carefully reopened the door.

Jane Mercer hadn't moved.

His gaunt body moved silently. He crossed the room until he was standing over the bed looking down at her. His eyes went from her tumbled hair down across her face to her half-opened lips and then moved on to the thin blue vein barely discernable as it pulsed at the side of her neck. He leaned forward, his hands instinctively twitching. He saw the soft curves of her body and one hand went out, but he didn't touch her.

Jane moved in her sleep and bent one knee and the skirt hitched up higher.

Moving soundlessly, Karl reached down with one hand and took the edge of it between his fingers.

He sensed, even as he started to drop to the side of the bed, that she had suddenly awakened.

His hand tightened at the same moment his eyes went to her face. She was staring wide-eyed at him, not really seeing him. Her mouth began to open in a scream.

"Don't yell," he said in a hoarse whisper. "Don't let out one damned sound or I'll smash your teeth down your throat."

She began to struggle, moved her bound hands, her long nails raking the side of his neck.

At the same moment she screamed.

The pain was so sudden and unexpected that instead of reaching to throttle the scream, he himself let out a sharp yell of pain and his hand doubled into a fist and he struck her a glancing blow on the side of the face.

She screamed again.

He was reaching back to swing a second time when the door burst open.

He barely had time to half turn when Earl Cradle's fist smashed between his eyes.

He was on his feet like a cat, half crouched and ready to spring. "Go ahead," Cradle said, "go right ahead! I'll break every bone in your body if you make one move."

Karl held the pose for a second and then slowly straightened up, rubbing his face.

"What the hell's the matter with you?" he said. "Can't a guy ..." Cradle ignored him and moved quickly to Jane's side as she struggled into a sitting position.

"Just lay back and take it easy, lady," he said. "It's all over. I don't want to have to put that gag back in your face."

She stared at him with wide, frightened eyes for a moment and then slowly slumped back on the bed, softly sobbing.

Earl turned to Herman who stood in the doorway.

"Stay with her," he said. "You—come on."

Karl followed him out of the room, his eyes mean and his mouth sulky. His nose was dripping blood.

"What the hell," he said, "twenty minutes ago you didn't know if you were going to rub her out or not and now you squawk if a guy wants to have a little fun. You got one dame of your own, so why be a pig about somebody else ..."

Earl turned like lightning and grabbed him by the throat.

"You stupid fool," he said, "get something through your head. I don't care what happens to that girl or what happens to anyone. The only thing I care about is seeing that this thing goes off without a hitch. You want her screaming and bringing every cop in town down on us?"

"All right, so I gag her," Karl said.

"You leave her alone—understand? Leave her alone. We got work to do. The games can come later."


# Chapter 6

At eight o'clock on Monday morning, May twelfth, Acting Captain James Xavier Cooney replaced the receiver of his desk telephone and reached for the half-smoked cigar butt he had placed on the edge of his ash tray. He turned to the uniformed sergeant sitting at the desk opposite him.

"Never a dull moment," he said. "You know where the Citizen's National Bank is over on Amsterdam?"

"Yep."

"Well, that was the trouble department at Consolidated Gas," the Captain said. "They got a leak in a gas main and they're digging up the sidewalk in front of the bank. Got the street partly closed off. You better get a man over there right away to redirect traffic."

"How bad is it, Captain?"

"How the hell do I know? The guy just said they have to dig up the sidewalk. But if it's gas, it could be dangerous. Keep the main line of traffic open if you can, but reroute pedestrian traffic to the other side of the street. Don't let anyone park, not even for a moment. Keep things moving. If one man can't handle it, send a couple. Send four. I don't want no jam-ups this time of the morning. Hell, we tie up an intersection around there and they'll feel it all the way down to Forty-second street."

"Right," the sergeant said. "I'll get on it immediately. You have no idea how long …"

"I have no idea."

## 2.

Patrolman Hardy stepped out of the squad car and half saluted the driver. He turned and noticed at once the saw horses blocking the sidewalk in front of the bank. He saw the two men working on the sidewalk with the air drills, digging a hole directly in front of the four wide granite steps leading into the bank. The sound of the drills as they hit the cement was deafening.

He shrugged and walked toward the center of the intersection. His eye traveled down the side street and he spotted the blue convertible parked at the curb with the hood raised. He started toward it.

Billy Dale looked up just in time to see the patrolman start for her car. Quickly she ducked the walkie-talkie out of sight.

"Trouble, lady?"

"The motor won't start," Billy said.

"Well, I'm sorry, but you can't leave it here," Patrolman Hardy said. "We got orders …"

"But it won't start. I've already called a garage and they're sending a tow car."

Patrolman Hardy nodded.

"Okay, lady. You did the right thing. How long ago did you call?"

"Five—ten minutes."

"Well it may take them a little time," the patrolman said. "Traffic is tough this time of morning. Just take it easy." He turned and started back for the intersection.

So far things weren't too bad. All he had to do was keep the cars moving. He just hoped the guys from the gas company would finish what they were doing and find the leak as soon as possible. It made him just a little nervous, the idea of a gas leak. He sniffed the air. Yeah, he thought he could smell it all right.

**3.**

Mrs. Epstein looked up at the man in the horn-rimmed glasses and blushed.

"He's up in his room," she said, "and he won't come down. He says he doesn't want to see anybody."

Dr. Martin Jordan stared down at her and gritted his teeth.

"You tell your son, Mrs. Epstein, that if he isn't down here in just one minute flat, I'll go up and get him. I'll ..."

"Now, now, Mister—what did you say your name was?"

"Jordan. Dr. Martin Jordan. And if ..."

"Look, Doctor, I think that's what Jake needs. A doctor. Maybe if you come up and talk to him—of course, he won't open the door, but ..."

Dr. Jordan moved toward the stairs.

"If he doesn't open the door he's going to need a doctor," he said grimly.

A moment later and he rapped on Jake Epstein's locked bedroom door.

"Go away," Jake said.

Martin Jordan pounded his fist on the door.

"You open that door, fellow," he bellowed, "or I'll smash it in."

"Who are you and what do you want?"

"I am Miss Jane Mercer's fiancé and I want to talk to you. Right now!"

Jake said, "Oh, my God."

A moment later the key turned in the lock and Dr. Jordan quickly shoved his way into the room. He stopped, staring at the pathetic figure of Jake Epstein, who had fallen back on the bed.

"So you're Epstein!" Dr. Jordan said, his voice venomous.

"I'm Epstein."

"What have you done with my girl?"

Mrs. Epstein squeaked in the doorway and pushed into the room.

"Jakie," she said. "Jakie, you didn't ..."

"Go away, Ma," Jake said. He turned and looked up at Dr. Jordan. He spoke in a thin voice.

"I'm sorry. Honest to God, I'm really sorry."

Dr. Jordan's face went white.

"Why you ... I asked you what you have done with my girl. Where is she? Where is Jane Mercer?"

Jake shook his head.

"I ran out," he said. "I didn't wait. I just couldn't. I couldn't bear to face her."

The doctor reached down and grabbed Jake by his pajama lapels. "Listen," he said, "you start talking! And talk straight. Jane came to New York Friday night to meet you. Now I want to know exactly what happened."

A half hour later and Dr. Martin Jordan, accompanied by Jake Epstein, were in a subway, on their way down to the morgue. It was nine-thirty, Monday morning, May twelfth.

**4.**

The redheaded, wide-shouldered man in workman's clothes was standing on the corner, right where Georgie was told he would be. Georgie pulled the truck over to the bus stop and pushed in the clutch. He wound down the glass in the door and leaned out.

"Mike?"

Mike Shannahan nodded, not speaking. He opened the door and climbed into the truck and Georgie put the engine back in gear.

After a moment Mike spoke.

"Any trouble?"

"None. Right where they told me it would be." He looked over at Mike curiously. "They told me that you told them this pile wouldn't be missed. How come?" he asked.

"That's right," Mike said. "I should know. This is the one I drive myself."

"Oh. You mean you actually work for the gas company?"

"That's right, chum," Mike said.

"And ..."

"Well, I pulled it in for repairs yesterday after work. Told the mechanic the motor was acting up. It's routine. They tag it and it takes two or three days for them to get around to checking it over."

"And it won't be reported stolen?"

"No. There are a bunch of them waiting for repairs. It will only be missed when its turn comes up and they check the sheet against the trucks."

"I see," Georgie said. He was silent for several minutes as he continued on uptown. And then he spoke again.

"You say you actually work for the gas company?"

"That's right," Mike said.

"Boy, you *are* taking a chance," George said. "You'll really have to blow after this is over."

Mike shook his head. "Don't tell me about it," he said. "I made a deal to dig a sidewalk—for two hours. That's all. When I get through, I just walk off and that is it."

George turned and looked at him again.

"You mean to tell me that you don't know …"

"Look," Mike said. "I don't know nothing and I don't want to know nothing. I'm getting paid for a job and I'm doing that job. Understand?"

George shook his head unbelievingly.

"I don't get it," he said. "I guess you know …"

"I know there's some kind of caper, sure," Mike said. "But that's all. I don't want any details."

"Brother! I suppose you realize that you might get questioned afterward? What happens if they ask you about me?"

"You're safe," Mike said. "I'm not stupid. I told you I got the general picture. If by any chance I should be questioned, you can be sure I'll know how to handle it. I guess Earl told you that I can be trusted."

"Yeah, he told me. But I still don't get it, you working for the gas company and all. If someone should spot you there working on the pavement, and remember you …"

"I've had a lot of experience," Mike said. "I told you this was the truck I handle, didn't I? Listen, one thing you got to understand. A guy digging a hole in the pavement is the most anonymous man in the world. Five, maybe ten thousand people can pass him. Can even stand around and watch him work. And ten minutes later you ask them, and they won't have the faintest idea what he looks like. That's New York for you."

George shook his head.

"Yep, I guess it is at that," he said. He turned a corner and began to slow down. "Here she is," he said, "and everything seems nice and quiet. They told me to park directly in front of the bank. What then?"

"We get the saw horses out and set them up. Hang the DANGER signs on 'em. Block off the sidewalk completely. You just follow me and do what I do." He looked down at his watch. "Only thing, we got to leave a passage so the people who work there can get inside. Once they're in, then we close it all up. By that time we'll have the hole pretty well started."

George shut off the ignition.

"And you really mean to say no one will stop us?"

"Who's to stop us?" Mike asked. "Somebody is always digging up the streets in New York."


**5.**


Clarence Chance arrived at the bank at exactly eight thirty-eight. Chance was a stout man in his middle sixties who had more than thirty-five years before, been a member of the New York Police Force. He had acquired a double hernia and been forced to resign after three years as a patrolman and since that time had been working for the Citizen's National Bank. He still had the double hernia, but it hadn't bothered him too much in recent years.

Chance carried a thirty-two automatic in a shoulder holster under his coat, but he hadn't fired the gun since the day he had purchased it. He had fired no weapon of any sort in more than a quarter of a century. He was a quiet, dignified man who looked more like a bank president than a bank guard.

His oldest boy had graduated from college on a scholarship, his next oldest was a druggist. His daughter Grace was a trained nurse and little Betty, who was eighteen, was finishing business school. He was a widower. His salary was eighty-two dollars a week; he owned his own home in Brooklyn and he had a lot paid for on the west coast of Florida. In three years, at the age of seventy, he would retire on a pension of around two hundred and eighty dollars a month. He had twelve thousand five hundred dollars in government bonds. He didn't trust banks.

Mr. Chance had observed the men digging the hole in the sidewalk in front of the institution when he arrived. He had had to step carefully around them. He had not stopped to question what was going on. Mr. Tilford, the branch manager, would do so if he thought it necessary.

Gerald Tilford arrived one minute after Clarence Chance and he did hesitate a moment as he observed the large hole rapidly expanding in front of the steps leading to the double doors of the bank. But Mr. Tilford didn't question the workmen either. After all, what the Consolidated Gas Company did was hardly any of his business.

He climbed the four steps, nodded to the bank guard and took a key from his pocket.

They entered the building together and Mr. Tilford reached for the switch cutting off the night alarm. Chance went at once to the basement. Neither had spoken.

Chance had one foot in his trousers and one foot raised in the other leg, when he heard the slight noise. He lifted his eyes and suddenly his hands dropped the trousers he was holding and slowly raised over his head.

"Don't shoot," he said. "Please—for God's sake—don't shoot." Karl stepped into the washroom, holding the sawed-off shotgun under his right arm. Earl Cradle was behind him.

"One yell and you are dead," Cradle said in a soft whisper. He moved around Karl and deftly removed the gun from Chance's shoulder holster. Putting it into the side pocket of his jacket, he crossed to the locker and took out the belt that held Chance's cartridges and thirty-eight. He pulled the gun out and flipped open the cylinder and dumped the shells into his hand.

"All right," he said, "finish dressing. Do it fast but not so fast that you don't hear every word I say."

Chance nodded dumbly, fumbling for his uniform trousers.

"You want to keep on living," Earl said, "then you will do exactly what you're told. Finish getting dressed. Strap on your gun belt. Then you go upstairs. You stand by the door as you always do and you let the others in. Behind you, every minute of the way, will be a man with a gun. The gun has a silencer. The man doesn't care whether he uses the gun or not. If you make one single false move, you are dead. Understand?"

Chance tried to find his voice, but ended up nodding.

"If you have any doubts about it," Earl said, "say so now. Dead heroes don't get medals."

"—I want to live," Chance said.

"Then follow instructions," Earl said. He turned and spoke over his shoulder. "He's coming out, Joey."

He turned on his heel and left the washroom, Karl followed him as Joey moved in to stand next to the bank guard.

Mr. Tilford was arranging the ash tray on his desk—the cleaning woman never would remember to put it back on the right side—when he became aware of the fact that someone had entered the office. He looked up, expecting to see Chance.

There was an expression of annoyance on his face. Chance should be at the doors leading into the bank.

The stranger stood less than three feet from him and the thing that Tilford saw was the gun which he held in his hand. A gun with an odd contraption on the end which Tilford at once recognized as a silencer, although he had never actually seen one before. Even as Mr. Tilford raised his eyes to the man's face, his mouth opened and the scream started.

Earl Cradle moved fast and the barrel descended with a sickening thud on Tilford's skull.

The door of the bank opened and Warren Fidman, the bookkeeper, entered. He said good morning to Mr. Chance, automatically noting that Chance seemed very pale. Mr. Fidman was a little surprised to observe the short fat man standing at Chance's side.

He would have to speak to Mr. Tilford about that. Chance had strict orders not to let anyone in the bank until the doors officially opened at nine o'clock.

"Mr. Tilford wants to see you at once in his office," Chance said, stuttering a little over the words.

Fidman nodded curtly, tucked his umbrella under his arm and purposefully strode to the end of the room. Joey took his eyes off Chance long enough to see him enter the manager's private office.

Miss Grace Clark and Miss Alice Langley entered together. Again Chance gave them his message.

"Mr. Tilford," he said. "In his office. Right away."

"Why Clarence," Miss Langley began, but Chance spoke up quickly to interrupt her.

"Please hurry," he said.

They both turned and looked at him over their shoulders as they moved away. A moment later Joey heard a small scream from the back of the room.

"All right, lock the doors," he ordered.

After Chance had locked the doors, Joey handed him the sign. "Hang it so that it can be seen through the window from outside," he instructed.

Chance did as he was bid and Joey moved back out of sight, some ten feet from the guard.

"Okay, buddy," he said. "Now just relax. You been fine so far. Just keep it up. We have a little wait. Stay where you can be seen from outside, but don't make a move. If anyone comes and tries the door, just shake your head and point to the sign."

Five minutes after the doors had been locked, Karl and Earl had handcuffed the two women, Tilford, and Fidman. They had taken all four to the women's rest room, on the main floor, and pushed them inside. They had taped their mouths and tied their ankles.

Herman Wonder and Mario Gallucci were waiting by the passageway when they returned. Mario helped Herman through and then handed in the heavy suitcases.

"I'll take this stuff upstairs," Earl said. "Karl, you start bringing up the mattresses." He turned to Herman. "How's it coming Herman?" he asked. "You feeling okay?"

"I'm fine boy, fine," Herman said. "Let's get on with it. And be careful with those bags."

As soon as they were upstairs, Earl took Herman to the room which held the vault. He handed him a collection of keys.

"One of them probably opens the steel gate," he said. "I took them from the manager. I'll be right back."

Leaving Herman, who was removing his black coat and carefully folding it, he quickly went into the main office. He stepped to the small telephone switchboard beside one of the cages and saw that there were three trunk lines. Reaching down he picked up a telephone and dialed the weather station, WE 6-1212. As soon as he heard the tape-recorded weather being repeated, he laid the receiver on its side and stepped to a second phone and repeated the maneuver. He did it a third time and then relaxed a little. He knew that anyone calling the bank would get a busy signal.

When he returned to the vault room, Herman already had the gate open and was checking an old-fashioned watch he had taken from his vest pocket.

"We'll give it a couple of minutes more, Earl," he said. "Want to be sure about that time lock."

He turned and studied the door of the large safe for several minutes and then said: "It's going to be a tough one, Earl."

"Listen Herman," Earl said, "maybe it would be best if we just get that combination from the teller. Maybe …"

"I've told you boys that it's too risky. They've figured out a perfect protection against that. He'd give you a combination, all right, but the minute I'd start to dial it, it would set off an alarm over at the nearest station house. They give a phony series of numbers and that does the trick. It's the latest wrinkle. I am not sure that this box is rigged that way, but we can't take any chances. I may be an old fogy, but I know what's going on these days."

"All right, Herman, just as you say. There's no point in taking the gamble. But I should think blowing the box would be just as likely to set off that alarm."

"It could and it couldn't," Herman said. "A fifty-fifty chance. But even if it does, it'll take them about four minutes to get here. By that time we should be in and out and back next door. On the other hand, you start fooling with a combination and you never know if that teller is going to trip you up. Give you the wrong one first and then by the time you beat the right one out of him, the law will be down our necks. You just let me handle it my way."

Earl nodded.

Herman began rolling up his sleeves.

"Open that black suitcase," he said. "I want the high-speed drill." Karl came in lugging a mattress as the old man started to work.

<h2 style="text-align:center">6.</h2>

Dr. Frogg's oyster eyes went from Dr. Jordan to Jake Epstein and then back to Dr. Jordan.

"I've told you everything I know," he said in a querulous voice. "Yes, the girl was here. I talked to her myself on Saturday morning. I believe that she was downstairs making inquiries sometime late Friday night. In any case, I saw her Saturday.

"She did ask about the body and I showed her the photograph. As I've already said, she insisted that it was her father. Well, I told her what had happened and she left."

"But …"

Dr. Frogg shrugged his thick shoulders and rubbed his bald head.

"I told you. I gave her the address of the funeral parlor where the body had been taken. She left and said she was going right up there. And that was last Saturday."

He looked at the round clock on the wall and stood up.

"Ten already," he said. "I got an autopsy and I can't be wasting any more time."

Dr. Jordan and Jake stood up as the doctor walked to the door, dismissing them. He stepped through and turned. He glared at Jake.

"You," he said. "You, Epstein. Stay away from me. Stay away from here altogether. You're a troublemaker. I don't want any more of your foolishness."

His eyes went to Dr. Jordan. "Would you like to see how we handle an autopsy in this town, Doctor?" he asked.

Dr. Jordan shook his head.

When they were in the cab and on the way uptown, the doctor turned to Jake.

"God only knows what could have happened to her," he said.

"Well, this man Gallucci will know what happened to her father, anyway," Jake said. "By the way, Doctor, how did you ever manage to find me?"

Dr. Jordan stared at him bitterly and then sighed. He was finding it increasingly difficult to maintain his dislike for the youth at his side.

"Jane had mentioned that a Jake Epstein called her from New York. She said he was a newspaperman. When I got into town Sunday night I started calling the papers. I finally located you on the *Blade*."

"And they gave you my address?"

Dr. Jordan shook his head.

"Not until this morning early. I talked to a man named Dewey."

"That's my city editor," Jake said proudly. "And he gave you my address?"

"Not right away. Not until he asked what I wanted to see you about and I told him I thought I probably would murder you."

"Oh."

"Which reminds me, Epstein," Dr. Jordan said, "just how did you find out that this dead man of yours was Jane's father?"

"It wasn't too difficult," Jake said, with a certain false modesty. "I traced him down to where he had taken a room and I found a clipping with Miss Mercer's name, the bank where she worked and the business school from which she graduated. There was also a clipping about the work of a Senate Committee investigating Un-American

Activities.

"Well it wasn't too hard to find the business school. They gave me Miss Mercer's phone number. When she told me her father had been missing for some time, I checked the old files on the Un-American Activities Committee. The name of a Dr. Mercer was mentioned as one of those to be investigated. It seems he had, years previously, donated money to the Spanish Loyalists and had lent his name to several liberal causes.

"We had figured the dead man might have been a scientist. I just put two and two together. Persecution by the committee was enough to cause a breakdown. He disappeared and became a Bowery derelict. The whole thing all added up."

Dr. Jordan looked at Jake with a certain admiration.

"Well Jake," he said, "you better start using that brilliant, deductive mind of yours and figure out what has happened to Miss Mercer."

# Chapter 7

The uniformed sergeant put the receiver back in the cradle and looked over at acting Captain Cooney. He shook his head, looking sad.

"The things the people expect from the police," he sighed.

"What was that all about?" Cooney asked.

"Some guy down at the Citizen's National Bank," he said. "They've been trying to get in touch with the Amsterdam Avenue Branch and the lines have been busy."

"So what the hell are we supposed to do?" Cooney asked. "Tell people not to make phone calls? Why don't they call the telephone company?"

"The man said they did, but all they could learn was that the lines were all tied up. The branch has several trunk lines coming in and the people downtown seem to think it strange that they can't get through. Thought maybe we might know if the service is out of order in the neighborhood."

"There's nothing wrong with the service here," the captain said sourly. "Every idiot and his brother finds no trouble in calling us and …" he hesitated, a thoughtful looking frown crossing his face.

"You know," he said, "they might have something at that. Those phone lines are all underground, aren't they?"

"They are. I haven't seen a telephone pole in …"

"All right, all right," the captain said. "You don't have to draw a diagram. Anyway, someone called from the gas company this morning and said there was a leak and they would have to dig up the sidewalk and street in front of the bank. Probably one of the workmen hit a wire and screwed up the works. Could happen. On the other hand, the phones are probably just in use. People like to talk these days—it's only the police who don't have time for …" His voice faded out and he turned back to the papers on his desk.

"The people down at the main branch seemed a lot concerned," the sergeant said. "Sort of half suggested we might have a man stop by and check."

Captain Cooney looked up, annoyed.

"My God," he said, "we have a man stationed in front of the place keeping traffic moving. If anything was wrong …" Again he hesitated, thinking for several seconds.

"Couldn't really be anything to it," he said speaking more to himself than to the sergeant.

A minute later he looked up and spoke again.

"Sergeant," he said, "Maybe we just better send a patrol car over to make a check. Probably silly, but I'm damned if I like to take any chances on anything happening."

**2.**

Herman Wonder stood back from the safe and began to peel off his white gloves.

"She's all set, Earl," he said. "Get everyone out of the room."

Earl and Karl followed the old man outside and the three stood still and tense. In a moment there was a hollow boom and they quickly reentered the vault room.

The mattresses, which had been placed around the front of the strong box had been blown back and the door hung open. Earl moved forward and Karl helped him with the crowbar. It took only a few seconds to pry the round steel door open and then Earl turned and Herman handed him a key from the ring they had taken from the bank manager.

"This is it, Herman," he said, a second later. "You go on now and get back in the other building. Karl and I will start collecting."

Karl was dumping the contents from the suitcases which had held the tools as the old man turned and left the room.

Earl spoke into the walkie-talkie as he worked.

"Signal the boys they got exactly four minutes," he said.

"Did she blow?" Billy asked.

"Yeah."

Two minutes later and Earl had what he wanted. He didn't bother with change or securities; he was interested in only the fives and tens and twenties, fifties and hundreds. The money was already neatly bundled, waiting for the afternoon pickup when the armored car was scheduled to arrive.

Karl grabbed the suitcases and had already started for the basement and Earl was halfway to the front of the bank to warn Joey to get ready to leave, when Joey turned and signaled him. At the same moment Billy's voice again came over the walkie-talkie.

"John Law," she said in a quick whisper. "One in a car. Just stopped in front."

Earl made a gesture, pointing at Chance, the guard, who still stood in front of the glass doors where he could be seen from the street.

Joey had turned back and he was directly behind Chance now. His gun was prodded in the guard's back. Through the doors Joey could see the cop outside as he opened the door of the patrol car.

"When he looks up, you wave," Joey hissed. "Hold up your hand and give a signal. Now!"

Chance lifted one hand in a semi-salute.

"He's going over to talk to the cop at the intersection," Billy said over the intercom.

"You get going, kid," Earl said.

He slid quickly behind Joey.

"Hold him a minute or two more until the cop leaves. Then bring him downstairs and put him away in the washroom. Handcuffs and gag. After that, get inside as fast as you can."

He turned and ran for the rear of the bank.

When Earl reached the basement of the undertaking establishment, Mario was already packing the money he had taken from the bags into the false bottom of the coffin. He was mumbling figures as he worked.

"Good God, don't take time to try and count it now," Earl said. As he spoke he began stripping off the overalls he was wearing, revealing the dark suit underneath. He took a black four-in-hand tie out of his pocket and knotted it around his neck.

"Everything set?" he asked. "The cars …"

"Hearse is in the driveway under the canopy," Mario said. "The limousine is just behind it."

"Well we'll do it just as planned," Earl said. "You drive the hearse and I'll be beside you. Joey drives the limousine. Karl gets in back with Herman and we put the girl in between them."

"Why don't we just leave her?" Mario asked. "Suppose she starts to yell or something?"

"Yell? How can she yell? Her mouth is taped and we'll have the heavy veil down over her face. Her arms are strapped to her sides and they are covered by the black cloak."

"I still think …" Mario began, but Earl cut him short.

"Don't be a damned fool," Earl said. "Suppose the cops decide to come in here the first thing and look around? They find her and the whole thing goes out the window. We take her with us. Karl will make damned sure she don't yell."

"All right," Mario said, "but I wish they'd hurry. Here, give me a hand with the stiff; he's hard to handle alone."

"Not yet," Earl said. "I want to get all the guns in with the money first."

"Why not leave them. We won't be needing …"

"We won't be needing them until we get past the roadblocks—if there are any roadblocks," Earl said. "But later on, who knows? We may not have more than an hour of safety at the outside. We keep them under the body until we are out of town and hit the first stop off."

Earl looked down at what was the last remains of Dr. Creighton Fairwell Mercer and felt a sense of repugnance.

"My God!" Earl said, "you could at least have put on a pair of pants and some shoes and underwear couldn't you?"

"Waste of money," Mario said. "Nothing shows except from the waist up."

Joey burst into the room.

"You get the boards back over the opening?" Earl asked.

"I'm wasting no time on anything but getting out of here," Joey said, his voice a little hysterical. "That cop is still out in the street talking to the guy on traffic duty. He'll be back any minute and he won't be seeing the guard again."

"You damned fool!" Earl said. "Karl, get the girl," he ordered. "I'll nail up the opening."

He returned within a couple of minutes and Mario and Joey were already lifting the coffin. He helped them as they carried it out to the hearse.

**3.**

Billy Dale tucked the walkie-talkie into the large shoulder bag and opened the door of the convertible. Stepping to the street, she turned toward the bank. When she reached the corner, the cop at the intersection looked up and half nodded, smiling.

She smiled back and he lifted a hand, holding up traffic to let her cross.

Georgie was working on the hole, and he had dropped his air hammer to use a shovel. He looked up as Billy passed next to the saw horse with the warning sign, and she gave an almost imperceptible nod and continued down the block.

Georgie dropped the shovel and crossed to Shannahan and tapped him on the shoulder. Mike cut the air and laid down the hammer and the two of them stepped to the street. They moved to the truck and each took out large paper bags. Saying nothing, they started south on Amsterdam Avenue. No one paid them the slightest attention.

They walked two blocks south and then turned east halfway up the block, heading for the Cadillac limousine, sitting at the curb. Billy was already in the back seat. There was a parking ticket shoved under the windshield wiper.

Georgie got in front and Mike stood for a moment, next to the window. Georgie took off his jacket and opened the paper bag and took out the folded black whipcord coat and put it on. Billy handed him a face towel and he wiped his face and neck as well as he could.

He opened the window of the door and Mike handed in the other bag and Georgie removed the black fedora and pulled it over his forehead. He leaned down and removed the work pants which had concealed the black trousers underneath. By the time he had straightened up, Mike had already started up the street, heading for the nearest subway entrance.

No one had spoken a word.

Billy was putting on the conservative, small black hat with the half veil as Georgie started the car.

He made two lefts and a right turn and four minutes later had pulled alongside the curb, just east of the funeral parlor. A shiny black hearse, followed by a single limousine was just beginning to move out of the driveway. Georgie waited until the two vehicles had turned into the street and joined the procession.

Twelve minutes had elapsed since the nitro explosion had torn the steel door from the face of the vault.

Out of the corner of his eye, Earl saw that the patrol car was still standing in front of the bank. The driver had skirted around the hole in the sidewalk and was starting up the steps.

There was no sign of any workmen.

The traffic cop at the corner held up his hands, stopping crosstown traffic to let the small procession past. He gave a small salute which Earl answered.

Three blocks north Mario turned west and when he was halfway up the block looked in the rear vision mirror.

"All okay," he said.

"Good," Earl said. "Now let's get on that elevated highway as soon as we can. We want to be out of Manhattan before the alarm goes off."

His last words were drowned by the sudden scream of a police siren.

**4.**

Midtown traffic was murder and the driver of the cab which was taking Jake Epstein and Dr. Jordan uptown was stuck in the thick of it. Jake looked at his watch and saw that it was ten-thirty. He turned to his companion.

"Look," he said, "I want to make a phone call."

"Your phone call can wait," Dr. Jordan said, impatiently.

"I'll tell you what. I know how we can save about twenty minutes at least."

"Well how?"

"If I tell you can I make my phone call?"

"Listen, brother," Dr. Jordan said, swinging toward Jake, who instinctively cowered in the corner. "Listen—oh well—anything to save time. You can make your call. Now how do we ...”

"We get out and take a subway," Jake said.

Five minutes later, while Dr. Jordan paced impatiently outside the booth in the drugstore next to the subway kiosk, Jake dropped a dime into the slot and dialed the *Blade*. When the girl answered at the other end he asked for the city desk. He had to wait several minutes and insert an additional dime before a gruff voice answered.

"Yeah—city desk."

"Mr. Dewey?"

"This is Dewey. Whaddaya want?"

"This is Epstein," Jake said.

"Epstein? I don't know any Epstein."

"Epstein, Jake Epstein, your reporter," Jake said. "I ..."

"What do you want, Epstein?" Dewey sounded more harassed than usual.

"Well, Mr. Dewey, you remember about telling me to get a colorful story. To dig up ..."

"Look, Epstein," Dewey said, his voice raising from a growl to a roar. "Don't bother me now. I'm busy."

"But Mr. Dewey, I got it. I got a really great ..."

"Epstein, get off this line!"

"But I tell you I have a real scoop. I found a dead man ..."

"By God! Epstein!" Dewey said, and he was yelling now, "by God, get off this line and stop tying it up! You got a story, why then write it. In the meantime I have a brand new bank robbery on my hands and I want this line free."

"But Mr. Dewey ..."

"Epstein, I will ..."

There was a crash of a receiver slamming back on a hook.

Dr. Jordan looked at Jake when he came out of the phone booth and asked, "You get your party?"

"Yes," Jake said. "I got him."

"Well then let's get moving."


**5.**

The sergeant slammed the receiver down this time and spoke quickly.

"Captain," he said, "the man you sent to check at the bank. He just radioed in. He says he found the bank doors locked tight. He looked in through the glass and there wasn't a soul in the place. So he knocked and rang the night bell. He ..."

The captain was aware of his hand as it began to shake. He had an odd feeling around his heart.

"... he says he went around to the side and looked through a window and he could see something funny. There were mattresses on the floor and the place was smoky. He says it looks like something has happened. The guard wasn't in sight and he was there when he first arrived, standing by the door. He says ..."

Captain James Xavier Cooney whirled in his swivel chair. "Damn!" he said. "Damn!"

A second later he spat out his orders as he grabbed for his coat.

"Emergency squad!" he yelled. "Ambulance. Notify the detective division. Roadblocks. Come on, get on, get with it, man."

Two minutes later the siren of his car was wide open as the driver whirled out of the precinct house driveway.

"I knew it—by God I knew it," Captain Cooney muttered under his breath. "It would just have to happen to me."

He suddenly remembered the man he had sent over to direct traffic in front of the bank. He groaned. He could already hear the Commissioner's voice: "Nice work, Captain. We always like to keep traffic clear for the getaway car."

His head sank on his chest and the groan became a low moan.

The moment that they crashed the glass in the front door and entered the main lobby of the building, Captain Cooney knew that his worst fears were realized. He could smell the odor left by the nitro charge.

He walked to the rear and looked into the vault room and then he returned and just stood for a moment amidst the rising confusion. He looked down, almost idly, and saw the telephone receiver lying next to the instrument. He could hear an odd squawking coming from it. Like a man in a daze, he lifted it and put it to his ear.

"United States Weather Bureau forecast for New York City & vicinity...."

The captain threw the receiver halfway across the room. Turning to the uniformed lieutenant at his elbow, he spoke in a listless voice.

"Have them radio it in downtown," he said. "And let's start trying to find the bodies. They must be around somewhere."

It was the low point in the captain's life.

The deputy inspector arrived while the intern who'd accompanied the ambulance was still attempting to calm Miss Langley, who was suffering from advanced hysteria. Grace Clark sat at her side, saying soothing words and secretly feeling very proud of herself for not going to pieces. Mr. Fidman futilely attempted to interrupt Mr. Tilford, who was trying to explain what had happened and was giving completely erroneous descriptions of the men he had seen.

Clarence Chance stood off by himself, wiping the perspiration from his forehead.

He had already explained that he'd never had a chance.

The deputy inspector called Captain Cooney to one side. His voice was bitter when he spoke.

"The only one of my precincts with a clean record," he said. "And then you had to take it over, Captain."

"Acting Captain," Cooney said.

"Don't interrupt me. As I said, this is the only one of my precincts with a clean record. And then you take it over and mess it up. Well let me tell you something, Mister. This is your baby. All yours. And if it's the last thing I ever do on the force I'm going to see to it that you get full credit. By God—"

He threw up his hands in disgust "—By God, just to think of it! Sending a patrolman over to keep the coast clear while they operated!"

"But, Inspector," Captain Cooney said. "The gas company …"

"The hell with the gas company. I say …"

The inspector felt a hand on his shoulder and swung around. An excited little man with a beet-red face was glaring up at him. He was bursting with indignation.

"Who the hell put a hole in my sidewalk?" he demanded. "I want to know who …"

"And who the hell are you, sir?" the inspector asked, his own face beginning to match the other's in hue.

"I'm Department of Plants and Structures of the City of New York," the little man said. "And I asked you who the hell has been digging up my sidewalks?"

Captain Cooney took advantage of the interruption to slink off and he was halfway down the lobby when a slender youth with an eager, boyish face stopped him.

"Sir," he said, "I'm Epstein. Epstein of the *Blade*. I happened to be on my way next door and I understand that you have had a little trouble here. Now …"

"You are who?"

"Epstein, of the *Blade*. And this is Dr. Martin Jordan. We heard that ..."

"Get out of my way," Captain Cooney yelled. He turned to a patrolman who was looking vacantly into the wastebasket.

"Who let them in here anyway?" he asked. He was about to continue when a flashbulb went off a few feet away and he turned quickly and started in the direction of the photographer.

Dr. Jordan took Jake by the shoulder.

"Listen," he said, "I don't know why I let you drag me in here in the first place. Our job is next door and ..."

"But this is a big story," Jake said. "I ..."

"Your big story, boy, is to help me find out what has happened to Jane Mercer, my fiancée. And don't you forget it for a second! Now come on, let's go."


## 6.


Karl half turned to the girl at his side. She sat very erect, on the edge of her seat, between himself and the old man.

"Now you listen to me, sister," Karl said. "Listen close. If for any reason we get stopped and somebody asks you something, just keep your mouth shut."

"Her mouth is shut," Herman Wonder said. "It's taped shut."

"Well, what I mean is," Karl said, "you behave yourself. I have a knife here—" he pulled a switchblade knife from his pocket and the wicked gleaming steel blade shot out when he pressed the safety "— I have a knife here and you get it right in the ribs if you make one bad move. Understand?"

Jane nodded her head.

"Don't frighten the child," Herman said mildly. "There's no use frightening her. She'll behave all right, won't you, Miss?"

Again Jane nodded quickly.

Herman reached over and patted her knee.

"We have your daddy with us and we are just taking him up to where he can be buried," Herman said. "Now don't you worry about anything."

"Where they can both be buried," Karl muttered, half under his breath.

Herman Wonder leaned across the girl and his voice was harsh when he spoke.

"Listen, punk," he said, "I told you not to frighten this girl. I mean it. Nobody is going to hurt her, understand?"

"See here, old man," Karl began, but Herman quickly interrupted.

"One more word out of you and I'll take that toad sticker of yours and shove it down your throat," he said. "Now sit back and behave yourself."

He patted Jane on the knee again and his voice was soft and gentle when he spoke to her.

"He's a little rough, but he's a good boy really," he said. "You just do what we ask you to do and then everything will be all right. If we are stopped, remember you're in mourning. I'll do all the talking. Now, will you promise me you will do what we want you to?"

Jane nodded again. She turned so that she could see his face through the veil. Her eyes were utterly bewildered as she looked at him.

In the limousine in front of them, Earl spoke out of the side of his mouth.

"That siren," he said. "Probably means the alarm is out. I was worried about that cop who parked in front. An alarm must have gone off somewhere."

"They'd have sent more than one cop," Mario said.

"They knew they had a man on the corner," Earl said. "They couldn't figure a vault job—not at this time of day. They probably just made a routine check and I guess the cop looked in and noticed that something was wrong."

"Could be," Mario grunted.

"Well if the siren means what I think it does," Earl said, "we can expect a roadblock. The procedure is to close the island off. A radio patrol car at all the bridges and tunnels. You can't get off of Manhattan without hitting a bridge or tunnel."

"Well, we'll soon know. The George Washington Bridge is only a mile ahead. Traffic seems to be moving right along."

"Traffic is light here this time of day."

Earl looked ahead and frowned.

"Cars are beginning to slow down," he said. "I guess we will hit a block all right. You got your lights on? Maybe they won't stop us."

"Lights are on."

A couple of minutes later they were forced to come to a slow halt.

They were still a quarter of a mile from the bridge and Earl quickly opened the door and looked ahead.

It was the roadblock all right.

### 7.

Jake took his finger off the button and turned to Dr. Jordan.

"That's funny," he said. "I been ringing for five minutes and no answer. Who ever heard of a funeral parlor with no one around?"

Dr. Jordan said, "Maybe they are out planting someone."

"Still, I would think there should be somebody here," Jake said. "I suppose there must be some sort of reception room. Shall we see?"

Dr. Jordan reached for the door handle and turned it. A moment later and they were in a small room, obviously used as a reception chamber. There was a small table on which sat a lamp with a low-voltage bulb, three or four leather armchairs, and an umbrella rack. The floor was covered with a medium-priced oriental rug. Religious prints hung on the dun-colored walls. There were no windows, but opposite the entrance door was a second door.

A piece of paper was thumbtacked to the door and Dr. Jordan at once crossed over and read the message. It read:

WILL BE CLOSED
FOR TWO WEEKS
MARIO GALLUCCI

Jake, reading over his shoulder, sighed.

"That's that, I guess," he said. "But it sure is kind of funny." He reached down and tried the knob of the door and found it locked.

"Odd," Dr. Jordan said. "Funeral homes don't usually just close up shop."

He turned and again studied the note on the inside door.

"Looks like it was written in a hurry," he said. "Someone merely tore a leaf off of the desk calendar and scribbled on it."

He took the thumbtack out and examined the note again. "May tenth," he said.

"Say," Jake's eyes lighted up, "it's more than odd. The tenth was last Saturday. Didn't Dr. Frogg say that the hearse came from this place on Friday to pick up Jane's father?"

Dr. Jordan stared at him for a minute, perplexed.

"That's what he did say, all right. Now why, if they had a body here to bury, would they close up? And we know that Jane came here on Saturday. Or at least started for here. This whole thing seems awfully peculiar. In the first place, why should some strange woman have claimed the body to begin with? We can be reasonably sure that the dead man was Jane's father."

For several moments he scratched his head thoughtfully.

"I don't like it," he said. "Not at all. First a woman claims a body which doesn't belong to her. A funeral director picks up that body and closes up his shop the very next day."

"And then decides to disappear for two weeks," Jake said.

They stared at each other for several seconds and Dr. Jordan suddenly turned and knocked hard on the door with his fist.

There was no sound from inside. Jake looked at him curiously.

"I'm going in, fella," Dr. Jordan said. "Are you with me?"

Jake shrugged.

"Breaking and entering—five years. Why not?"

Dr. Jordan turned and crouched and then moved fast. His heavy shoulder smashed into the door and it sprang open.

"You'd make a great tackle," Jake said.

"I did—All-American."

Jake carefully closed the sprung door behind him when they stepped into the office just off the reception room. They touched nothing, just looked around. And then they went on into the chapel and again looked around.

It took them fifteen minutes to cover the first floor. The place was utterly deserted.

"Shall we try the basement?" Dr. Jordan asked.

"Isn't that where they, well, they keep the customers?" Jake asked.

"I would suppose so," Dr. Jordan said. "Keep the customers, drain the bodies, make with the plastic ..."

"Please," Jake said.

Dr. Jordan preceded Jake down the stairs and they entered a large bare room containing nothing but a number of clothes racks, filled with assorted garments.

"This joint looks more like a second-hand clothing store than a mortuary," Dr. Jordan said. "What do you suppose this guy Gallucci does—steal the garments off the dead?"

"Maybe all undertakers do," Jake said. He crossed to the nearest rack and pulled out the sleeve of a vicuna topcoat.

"Nice goods."

Dr. Jordan walked over and idly began to look at the collection. He was about to turn away when he suddenly stopped and a sharp gasp escaped from his throat.

Jake turned quickly.

Dr. Jordan's face had gone white and he was staring at the clothes rack. Slowly his hand reached out and he pulled a short-tailored jacket from the rack.

Wordlessly, his hand shaking, he opened it and his eye went to the label on the inside of the lining.

Jake, looking over his shoulder, read:

"Milady's Specialty Shop, Sandusky, Ohio."

# Chapter 8

The line of cars was slowly creeping forward when the motorcycle cop cut out from somewhere up ahead and started slowly south. He was making a traffic check and would report back if the jam was getting bad enough to make a detour necessary.

Cradle nudged Mario.

"Signal him," he said.

Mario opened the door and beckoned as the officer came even with the hearse. The cop touched his siren and wheeled his cycle around.

Mario looked from his wristwatch up into the goggled face.

"We're already late for the services," he said. "Couldn't we get through, officer?"

For a moment the policeman hesitated and then held out his hand.

"License and registration," he said.

Mario took out his wallet.

The policeman studied them carefully.

"Wait here."

Holding Mario's license and registration in one hand, he gunned his cycle and started back for the head of the line.

"Wait here!" Mario said. "Sure, we'll wait. What else?"

The man was back in three minutes and handed Mario his papers. "How many are you?" he asked.

"The two limousines behind us," Mario said.

"Follow me."

Mario cut the hearse out of the line of traffic as the officer lightly touched his siren. He was followed by the other two and as they passed the roadblock, the motorcycle cop slowed down and held up three fingers.

He escorted them for a half mile up the road and then pulled to the side to let them pass.

Cradle breathed a sigh of relief.

"How long do you figure to the barn?" he asked.

"One hour."

For the next twenty minutes neither spoke. Cradle was lighting a cigarette and Mario finally turned to him.

"What about the girl?" he said.

"She asked in on this," Cradle said. "She wasn't invited."

Mario was silent for several minutes and then again spoke.

"I didn't bargain for murder," he said.

Cradle looked at him sharply.

"Has anyone said anything about murder?"

Mario ignored the question.

"If anything should happen," he said, "it would be first offense for me. Robbery. Probably ten to twenty years and with time off, I'd be out in seven. With murder it's the electric chair."

Again Cradle studied him closely. He looked straight ahead when he spoke.

"You knew all along that the police would connect you up, didn't you Mario?"

Gallucci didn't answer.

"You knew it would have to happen," Cradle continued, "and you planned to blow when it was all over. You never did plan to return."

"I'm not stupid, Cradle," Mario said at last. "But my plans are my own. I am not asking you what you're going to do."

"Right," Cradle said. "You know if you ever get picked up, the girl can identify you?"

"I know. But I'm saying it again. I didn't bargain for murder. Maybe I get a hundred and fifty or two hundred thousand when we make the split. That's worth a chance on seven years. It isn't worth a chance on my life."

"There are the rest of us," Cradle said. "How about us? We have records. It wouldn't be seven years with us."

"You are faces—not names," Mario said. "The girl has seen you, sure. On the other hand, those people at the bank all saw you. They're still alive. The girl is no more dangerous to you than they are."

"You're smart, Mario," Cradle said. "As far as I'm concerned, and you can count Billy as going along with me, you don't have to worry. The girl is no more dangerous than anyone else who saw us."

"And about the others?"

"Old Herman is a bank robber—not a murderer. We don't have to worry about him. He's getting enough out of this to take his old lady down to Florida or Southern California and spend the rest of his life sitting in the sun. Herman lives modestly. He's a professional and would consider a needless killing stupid."

"There are still the other three," Mario said.

"Joey is your cousin—you know him better than I do."

Again Mario was silent for several minutes before he answered.

"Joey," he said, "is small time. A clown. This is the biggest thing he's ever been mixed up in. I think he'd listen to me, but I can't be sure. He might panic. But it isn't Joey I'm thinking about. I'm thinking about the other two."

"You know what they are," Cradle said. "Hoods. Karl would cut her to pieces for a laugh. I've already been having trouble keeping him away from the girl. She'd be a lot better off dead than in his hands. Georgie is the same type, but he isn't vicious. Those two don't use their heads, they use their muscle."

"You brought them in."

"Sure I brought them in. You always need muscle on this kind of caper. But I didn't bring the girl in."

"The thing to do," Mario said, "is pay them off and tell them we'll take care of the girl. As far as I am concerned, I want twenty-four hours. Just twenty-four hours and then she can yell her head off and it won't matter."

"I'll pay them off," Cradle said, "but I'm not sure about the rest of it. Karl wants that girl."

"You'll have to do something about it," Mario said. "I told you I didn't bargain for murder."

Cradle butted his cigarette and lighted another one.

"There will be no murder," he said. "And you'll get your twenty-four hours. Myself, I need a little more. I plan on about thirty-six. Thirty-six will get me where I want to go."

Mario said: "We understand each other then?"

"We understand each other."

"The trouble will come after we split up the money," Mario said.

"I know. I'm thinking about that."

**2.**

They stood there, for a full minute, staring at each other. Jake was the first to recover.

"Hers?" he asked.

"Hers," Dr. Jordan said. "Yes—hers. Jane has been here."

He swung around suddenly, with a soft cry, and then he was like a madman. Jake's eyes opened wide as he watched while Jordan began tearing at the clothes on the racks. Garments began flying in all directions. Within seconds Jordan had stripped the first rack and moved on to the second. He worked like a maniac, jerking suits and dresses and coats from their hooks, looking at them swiftly and discarding them.

It took him five minutes to complete his task and when at last he had finished, the sweat was pouring from his face. He threw the final garment on the floor and turning slowly, his eyes desperate, he fell into a chair.

"Nothing else?" Jake asked.

"Nothing. I thought—well, I thought if I found the rest of her things ..."

He didn't finish the sentence and he didn't have to. Jake understood what he thought.

"Get the police, Epstein," he said slowly. "Go next door and get the police. Jane has been here."

Jake shook his head.

"Listen, Doctor," he said, "let's look around a little more first. After all, we know she was here, but we don't ..."

"I said get them."

"But they're busy with a bank robbery and ..."

Dr. Jordan stood up, his mouth grim and his fists clenched.

"Please listen," Jake said. "Let me handle this ..."

"What are you trying to do, Epstein, get another scoop?"

Jake put his hands up in protest.

"No," he said quickly, "no. It's just that I know what would happen. You'd just get a runaround. Please listen to me. After all I did find about Miss Mercer's father when the police failed to come through.

Anyway, what could you really tell them? She came here and she came because her father's body was brought here."

Jake hesitated a second, thinking, and then spoke again.

"A few minutes ago, while we were over in the bank, I overheard that police captain asking the officer who had been outside about anything unusual he might have seen. The policeman told him that he had seen no one leaving the bank, but he did mention something about a funeral procession. Said a hearse and a couple of cars left from in front of here a few minutes before the robbery was discovered. Now isn't it just possible, assuming a funeral service was held here this morning, that it could have been for Miss Mercer's father?"

"If a funeral was held here, then how do you account for that note we found upstairs?"

"I can't account for it," Jake said. "Any more than I can account for a false identification of the dead man. On the other hand, mistakes are often made. The undertaker could have been embarrassed about the whole thing, although it certainly wasn't his fault. But we know the girl's father was brought here and now we know that she herself has been here. It is even possible that she left in that funeral procession—if it was for her father. Maybe she just felt so upset and all that she forgot to phone you. She could have been trying ever since you have been in New York, you know, and you wouldn't have known about it. Why don't we ..."

"Why don't we what?"

"Well, let's really go through this place. If I'm right and Miss Mercer was burying her father this morning, there is probably a record of it up in the office."

Dr. Jordan hesitated. What Jake said was true. It was just possible that Jane could have been upset and postponed her call until after he had left. It was possible that everything was all right. That the funeral procession which had left earlier was the one for her father.

"But her coat?" he said. "Why would she leave her coat?"

"She had a dress under it?"

"Of course."

"She was probably upset. Just didn't think about it. Look, do it my way. Let's look around first. Then if we don't find anything, we can go to the cops."

Again Dr. Jordan hesitated, but finally he nodded reluctantly.

"All right," he said. "You go on upstairs and check the office. I am going to take the basement. And don't miss anything, anything at all which might give us a clue …"

"I won't miss anything, Doctor."

"Marty," Dr. Jordan said. "You can skip the doctor."

Jake was halfway to the stairs when Dr. Jordan turned and started for the next room.

3.

If Mr. Gallucci's records were any indication, business was really lousy. Jake had found the card index on which the undertaker had kept a more or less complete file on his business transactions. On each card was a name and a date. The cards were cross-indexed, alphabetically and chronologically, and each contained the pertinent information concerning the deceased's address, his ultimate disposal, the type of casket, and the kind of funeral.

Jake looked for a card bearing the name Mercer and found none. He next checked the date on which Gallucci had picked up the body from the morgue and there was no listing for that day. The last corpse had passed through the establishment around the middle of the previous month.

Jake replaced the file and turned to the desk. The side drawers yielded nothing of value except a list of cemeteries and crematories, which he put in his pocket. He tried the top drawer and found it locked. For a moment he hesitated and then shrugged and reached for the letter opener on top of the desk. It took him only a minute to force the lock.

Almost at once Jake began to understand a great deal about Mr. Gallucci's private affairs. There were notices of called loans, threatening letters from creditors, dunning notes from suppliers. The picture was obvious.

Back in the corner of the drawer he found copies of recent correspondence.

Gallucci had been selling off his equipment and anything that would bring in a dollar. There was the receipt for the money he had gotten for the four Cadillac limousines. There were several letters from real estate brokers concerning a farm that the man apparently owned somewhere up in the Catskills. The last item Jake discovered was a tightly rolled tube of paper and Jake slipped the rubber band off and spread it out. It was a civil engineer's or surveyor's map of a property, showing boundary lines and giving geographical specifications in longitudes and latitudes.

Jake looked at it curiously and then shrugged. He was unfamiliar with plats and it meant little to him.

He had rolled it up and was about to replace it in the drawer when he heard the footsteps approaching.

Without thinking, he quickly pushed the rolled-up map into his jacket pocket and slammed the drawer shut. He was looking at a travel folder he had found on top of the desk when the door opened and Dr. Jordan entered.

Jordan spread out his hands.

"Nothing," he said. "Absolutely nothing. I went through the place with a fine-toothed comb. The only thing I can say is that our friend hasn't been doing any business lately."

"How could you tell?"

"I am not totally unfamiliar with morgues," Dr. Jordan said. "You have to have certain instruments to handle dead people. There were no instruments in the room where ..."

Jake held up his hand.

"I understand."

"They have to drain the blood and there was no sign of any fresh ..."

"Please," Jake said. "I have a queasy stomach."

"All right," Dr. Jordan said. "Now what have you found? Did you get a lead on where the funeral was to be held today? Which reminds me, that's another odd thing. Why a funeral if he had not been handling any ..."

"Miss Mercer's father had already been taken care of down at Bellevue," Jake said quickly. "It must have been him."

"Then there should be something here in the office."

"That's the strange thing," Jake said. "He has a cross-index file on every person he buried or who was delivered to him. There is no mention of Miss Mercer's father. It's indexed by date also and he has no card for last Friday or Saturday."

Dr. Jordan nodded his head, his eyes hard.

"There is something very wrong here," he said. "Thank God I didn't find what I was afraid I might find. But I've had enough of fooling around. We're going to the police ..."

The crash of the door as it was smashed open stopped him in midsentence and both he and Jake turned, their eyes popping. Acting Captain Cooney stood in the opening.

**4.**

"And just what the hell are you two doing here?"

The Captain's eyes were streaked with red and the vein in his forehead was throbbing. He spoke through gritted teeth and Dr. Jordan, looking at his flushed face, was unable to keep from reflecting that the man was probably subject to high blood pressure and a very good bet for a cardiac. He had to restrain himself from sounding a warning.

"I said, what are you doing here and how did you get here?"

"Well, we came in the front door," Jake said. "You remember—I'm Epstein, from the *Blade*."

"Damn it, I know who you are. Now just what are you doing in this place? What …"

"I'm looking for my girl," Dr. Jordan said.

The Captain swung toward him and for a second Jake thought he was going to start swinging. Dr. Jordan stepped back.

"I'm Dr. Martin Jordan from Sandusky, Ohio and I am …"

"You are looking for your girl. You just told me," the captain roared. "Well, by God, I want you two to get …"

"Now see here, Captain," Dr. Jordan interrupted, "I came here to find my fiancée and …"

"Your fiancée? And just who is your fiancée?"

"Her name is Jane Mercer and she's from Sandusky, too. She's a secretary …"

"That's enough," the Captain said.

"She's supposed to have come here …"

"Damn it, I said that's enough. Now you two listen to me. I have a bank robbery on my hands. A seven-hundred-and-fifty-thousand-dollar bank robbery. And you want to tell me about your girl! You want me to discuss Sandusky, Ohio! Get out! Get out of my sight and stay out of my sight. If you aren't out of this place within the next five seconds, I'll lock you up so tight …"

Jake leaned over and tapped Dr. Jordan on the shoulder. "You see," he said. "I told you …"

Captain Cooney took a step forward.

"What did you say, Epstein? What was that?"

"I said we are just leaving," Jake said. "Come on, Doctor, I think we should be going."

Dr. Jordan hesitated a moment and then shrugged. He followed Jake out of the office and through the reception room to the street.

"That's how far you get going to the police," Jake couldn't resist saying.

"All right, Epstein, all right. So what do we do now?"

"Have you got a hotel room?"

"Yes. I checked in at …"

"We go there. We get on the phone. We call every cemetery and crematory within the radius of fifty miles." Jake took a folded paper out of his pocket. "I have the list here," he said. "I got it out of the office."

Dr. Jordan looked at him with a trace of awe as they started for the bus stop.

**5.**

"Now let's go over it calmly and coolly," the Commissioner said. "Let's see just what we have."

He had taken Acting Captain Clooney's chair and the captain was standing next to the desk. Deputy Inspector Morgan was seated where the sergeant usually sat and the door of the office was closed.

The Commissioner spoke in a soft, pleasant tone of voice. Far too soft and far too pleasant.

"We can assume that the entrance was made through the Gallucci basement, is that right?"

Captain Cooney nodded, looking miserable.

"Right, sir."

"Fine. And so we can assume that the gang very likely worked out of the place. But we have not been able to locate Mr. Gallucci, is that correct?"

He didn't wait for an answer.

"But we don't know for sure if Mr. Gallucci was involved or not. He has no criminal record and is a reputable businessman. No known criminal associations. He could have been an unwilling participant, perhaps kidnaped and perhaps murdered. On the other hand, he could have been in on the entire scheme."

"He …" Captain Cooney began.

"Please don't interrupt me, Captain," the Commissioner said with exaggerated courtesy.

"But let's start a little earlier," he went on. "To begin with, you say, Captain, that you got a telephone call from the gas company?"

"That is right, sir."

"No it is not right. We know that the gas company did not call. We have found out …"

"But how was I to …"

"Please, Captain. There is such a thing as checking back. But let's get on with it. Two men with a truck from Consolidated Gas drive up in front of the bank and start digging a hole in the sidewalk. Is that right, Captain?"

"That's right, sir," Deputy Inspector Morgan said.

The Commissioner lifted his eyes and stared at him. "I'll get around to you in a couple of minutes, Inspector," he said.

"Anyway, these two men start digging up the sidewalk. So you, Captain, assign an officer to see that they are not disturbed by traffic. Am I correct?"

"Well, not exactly. You see …"

"I see very clearly, Captain. And please stop interrupting me. To continue. You learn a little later that the bank fails to answer its phone. You ultimately get around to sending a man over to see what has happened. The man stops to chat with the officer you have protecting those two chaps who are digging up the sidewalk and destroying public property."

"He was checking first …"

The Commissioner again raised his hand.

"Eventually this officer climbs the steps of the bank and looks in and sees no one. He suspects something is wrong. He calls in and you start for the scene. About this time, three cars leave from the establishment next door. Three cars that I have every reason to believe were carrying the gang that robbed the bank and some three quarters of a million dollars from the bank's vault."

"But we don't know …"

"We can make a very adequate guess," the Commissioner said. "We know that after the robbery, no one left by the front door of the bank. We know that they went through the basement and into the funeral parlor. We *know* that. We also know that when those three cars left, *after* the robbery had been discovered, one of your men, Captain, stopped traffic to wave them on. To hurry them to their destiny."

The Commissioner slowly stood up and his face was very pale. His voice was still soft, but there was little doubt about the effort he was making to keep it so.

"Yes," he said. "We know all that. There is no other possible deduction. Why we even know that when the funeral cars, which were being used by the gang for their getaway, reached the roadblock at the George Washington Bridge, one of our motorcycle cops was kind enough to escort them through and on their merry way."

The Commissioner sat down again.

"Which brings us back to you, Captain Cooney," he said. "Now we have our robbery and we have our getaway. Ultimately, you find the passageway in the basement which they used to make their entrance into and their exit out of the bank. You, you personally, Captain, go through that passageway and you enter the funeral parlor. You go upstairs to the office and what do you find there? I ask you Captain, what do you find?"

"Why, as I said, there were these two …"

"Exactly. Two men. Two men who very obviously had no right in the place at all. Two men who had, from the evidence of the broken door, forced an entry."

"This Epstein said he worked for a newspaper …"

"We have checked him Captain, and he does. Or rather, let me say he did. The *Blade* no longer considers Mr. Epstein as a member of its staff, I am happy to say. Well, you encounter two men, in the place where a bank robbery has been hatched—a place from which it has been exquisitely executed less than an hour previously. So what do you do, Captain? Do you hold them for questioning? Do you arrest them?"

Again the Commissioner stood up. He had reached the end of his control and this time when the words came out they came to a near scream.

"No, you do not arrest them! You tell them to leave! In fact, you threaten to arrest them if they *don't* leave!"

The Commissioner took out his handkerchief and wiped his forehead. There were several moments of deep silence and at last he looked up and again spoke. He had recovered his voice and it again came soft and slow.

"I am not taking you off this case, Captain," he said. "Oh no, you are going to stay right with it. When the newspapers want answers, somebody has to give those answers. And if that someone has to look like a damn fool, that, Captain, that someone is going to be you."

"I'd be glad to ..."

"One more thing, Captain. Do you happen to know anything about Staten Island?"

Captain Cooney lifted his chin and looked perplexed.

"Why no, sir," he said. "I live up in the Bronx ..."

"Excellent, Captain. I am really glad that you live in the Bronx. But about Staten Island. You are going to learn a great deal about it. A great deal. Because, Captain, as soon as this case is over and forgotten, if anyone ever can forget it, then you are going back into a uniform. And until the day that you retire from the police force you are going to be patrolling a beat at the far end of Staten Island. They never have bank robberies at the far end of Staten Island, Captain. They don't even have banks. They don't even have sidewalks—to be dug up!"

"If I may say so, sir," Inspector Morgan began, but the Commissioner turned and glared at him and his voice faded away.

"You may say nothing," the Commissioner said. "I only have this to tell you. You were in charge over Captain Cooney. He was and is your responsibility. I hope you are fond of him. Because when Captain Cooney goes out to Staten Island, you will be with him. You and the Captain will spend a lot of time together. You will be patrolling adjacent beats. It will give you a good chance to talk over the old days."

# Chapter 9

Jake Epstein dropped the receiver back on the hook and reached for his handkerchief to wipe his face.

"And that," he said, "is the last of them."

"The cemeteries you have in this town," Dr. Jordan said. "People must die off like flies. There must have been a hundred of them. I can't see how Gallucci managed to be in the financial trouble you say he was in."

Jake shook his head and looked at the clock.

"Three-thirty," he said, "and we're right back where we started. We've covered the cemeteries and we've covered the crematories. No Mercer and no Gallucci at any of them."

"But they must have gone somewhere," Dr. Jordan said. "They

couldn't have just disappeared."

"They went someplace all right. That's what the police are wondering about too. You've been listening to the radio bulletins. I guess we've been wasting our time. The police, without doubt, thought about the cemeteries as well as us."

Dr. Jordan got up and crossed the room to find the cigarette package he had left on the hotel room's writing table.

"It's time we saw the police," he said. "Past time. They should know about Jane."

"We tried to tell them," Jake reminded him. "You saw how far we got."

"I know. But they didn't understand. I think …"

"Listen," Jake said. "You've been hearing those broadcasts. Don't you realize that the police are looking for us also? Don't you realize they want us for questioning? That they also want us for breaking and entering?"

"We can explain …"

"We wouldn't have a chance to explain anything," Jake said. "I'm a newspaperman and I know how the police work. There's been a quarter-of-a-million-dollar robbery. We were at the scene. Right where the gang, who pulled the job, started and finished from. Sure, I know that in the long run we can clear ourselves. That is, clear ourselves of any connection with the robbery. But they still have that breaking and entering charge.

"Another thing. I know how the police work. Do you think they would be gentle or that some studious young assistant district attorney would question us? Not in a million years. It would take place in the back of a precinct house and what would happen wouldn't be pretty."

Dr. Jordan shook his head.

"What happens to us isn't the point. I am only thinking about Jane. If the police realized that she might have been kidnaped by the bank robbers …"

"We have no proof of that. And, besides they are doing everything humanly possible to catch up with them."

"But if it's a kidnaping, the federal people would come in on it. The FBI."

"The FBI is already in on it, Doctor," Jake said. "The bank carried federal insurance on its accounts. That brings them in automatically."

"All right, say I agree with you. We have nothing to gain by going to the police. Where does that leave us?"

"What we have to do," Jake said, "is to outthink them. We have to figure …"

Dr. Jordan tossed his cigarette in the ash tray and slumped in a chair.

"Epstein," he said, "you are suffering from delusions of grandeur."

"Maybe yes and maybe no. But let's try and figure a couple of things out. We have nothing to lose. To begin, we can assume that the gang did work out of the funeral parlor, as the police believe. We then assume that they made their getaway in that hearse and those other cars in the procession. Now the police know that and so the gang themselves will know that the police are trying desperately to find out what happened to the hearse and the other two cars.

"They would get rid of them as soon as possible. Probably within an hour or two of the time the job was pulled. It isn't easy to get rid of a hearse and a couple of long black limousines. That means, during the two hours or so of time they had, it was necessary to reach a hideout. It means the hideout must be somewhere within approximately a hundred-mile radius of New York."

"Sure," Dr. Jordan said. "But where is it getting us? You can hide a whole damned city within a hundred miles of New York."

Jake went into the bathroom and filled a glass with water.

"You know," he said, when he returned, "something keeps sticking in my mind and I can't think exactly what it is. Something about that funeral parlor."

"Something you saw there maybe?"

"Not that I saw. Something …"

He stopped in his tracks and his eyes widened.

"By gosh!" he said. "By gosh—now I remember!"

He ran to the chair where he'd thrown his coat and quickly reached into the inside breast pocket. When his hand came out he was holding the rolled-up surveyor's map.

"What …"

"From a locked drawer in Gallucci's desk," Jake said excitedly. "I just remembered it."

"What is it? Don't keep it a mystery," Dr. Jordan said. He refused to be excited.

"It's a map of a farm Gallucci owned up in the Catskills, if I'm not mistaken. Gallucci was trying to sell the place, according to letters I found in his desk."

Dr. Jordan leaned forward.

"You think—you think they could have gone there?"

"It's the right distance," Jake said. "And I know the general area. My folks used to go up there every summer. It's a particularly lonely neighborhood and almost nobody would be around this time of year. They could have gotten there without being observed by taking back roads once they had crossed the Hudson River. They probably went to the farm, divided the loot and then ..."

"And then ..."

"Well—disappeared. Dumped the funeral cars and just broke up."

"And if they had Jane with them?"

Jake shook his head.

"I don't know," he said. "We can only hope."

"We can go up and find out," Dr. Jordan said. "How long would it take ..."

"I'd say an hour to two hours. I can get my father's car—he keeps it in a garage off Riverside Drive in the Nineties—and we could drive up ..."

"This," Dr. Jordan said, "is where we bring the police in." His hand reached for the telephone.

Jake leaped across the room and grabbed him.

"Listen to me, Doc," he said. "Please—listen. Don't call the police. If you want to see Miss Mercer alive again, don't call them. You have to understand what could happen. In the first place, if they have her, the first thing they would do, in case of a raid on the hideout, would be to kill her. If they didn't, the chances are a cop's bullet would get her. Don't you understand?

"The police come in shooting. She'd be right in the middle. Either that or the gang would use her as a cover or a hostage. In either case, you would be putting her in terrible jeopardy."

"Well, what do you suggest? Do you think you and I, unarmed, can go up there and ..."

"So far," Jake said, "if we are right, we have outthought the police and out thought the mob. No, we don't storm the place or anything like that. We try and use our heads. The first step is to go up to the Catskills and find the farm. Find out if they are there. From that point on, we have to play it by ear. If we can find out that they are there, and there doesn't seem any way we can secure Miss Mercer's release, then we can always go to the police. We have nothing to lose playing it my way and everything to lose if we try anything else."

Jordan thought for several minutes and then again reached for the telephone.

"No, Jake," he said. "No, not again. I would have to be insane to listen to you. This is a matter that calls for professional handling. I won't risk Jane's ..."

"You're tossing her life away," Jake yelled, grabbing the telephone. "Can't you see it? Remember how that police captain acted when you tried to tell him about her? Remember? He wouldn't even listen to you. Sure, I admit, in time you might get through to them. But it would be after about twelve hours of sweating. Before they would even believe there was a Miss Mercer, they would check back in Sandusky. They would check the morgue. They would check up on the coat at the funeral home. It would take all night and then half of tomorrow. By that time your girl could be dead a dozen times over."

"I am a reputable doctor ..."

"You are, in Sandusky," Jake said. "Here you are just another guy wanted for breaking and entering. Wanted in connection with a bank robbery. They would figure you would have some cock-and-bull story and wouldn't even listen to you. Not until it was too late."

For a long time Marty Jordan was silent, staring at the floor. Finally he looked up, his face wracked with indecision.

"I may be making a mistake I'll regret the rest of my life," he said. "But what you say makes sense in a way. Either that or I have completely lost my mind. Come on. Let's get that car that belongs to your old man."

**2.**

At four-fifteen on Monday afternoon the information desk down at Central Headquarters reached Captain Cooney on the telephone.

"Captain Cooney?"

"This is Cooney."

"This is Lieutenant Means downtown. You still in charge on that Citizen's National stickup?"

"I am," Cooney said, defensively.

"Well I got a man on the wire says he may have some information for you. A Constable Bilins from up in Sullivan County. You want me to transfer it?"

"Yes."

Cooney drummed his fingers on the desk in irritation. It made about the hundredth call he had taken in the last couple of hours. Seemed like every crackpot in the country was getting in on the act. But he couldn't afford to miss any bets. Not any longer, he couldn't.

"Hello?"

"Captain Cooney speaking," Cooney said.

"You the one wants information on that bank robbery thing you been broadcasting about?"

"That's right. Who am I talking with?"

"Constable Bilins. And I think I have something for you. Old Mrs. Hawkins …"

"Who?"

"Mrs. Hawkins. That's Ed Hawkins' widow. Well, she found a body."

"She found what? This connection seems bad," the captain said.

"Found a body. Went out to the barn—it's about a quarter of a mile from the house, separated by woods—and she went out there around two or three o'clock this afternoon to pick up some eggs—she keeps some layers out there—and when she went into the barn, there was this dead man."

"Well, what about him, Constable?"

"He had a shirt and tie and coat on. No pants. No shoes, no underwear."

"I don't think I quite understand, Constable. Did you say …"

"I did. A dead man, no pants, no shoes, no underwear. Laying on the ground."

"Well what …"

"Next to him was an open casket."

Captain Cooney reached for his handkerchief to wipe his forehead.

"Listen," he said, "I can't seem to quite understand."

"Ed Hawkins' widow found a dead man, half undressed, and a casket in her barn when she went to get eggs."

"How does that tie in with …"

"There was a hearse in the barn next to the casket and the dead man."

Captain Cooney clutched the phone and said, "Say that again."

"A hearse. New York plates. I heard you people down there were looking for a hearse so I just thought so long as we found one up here I should call …"

"Have you got the license number?"

"Yep, just you hold the wire a minute now."

When the Captain hung up a few minutes later he had verified the license number and knew that Gallucci's hearse had been found abandoned upstate. As near as he could make it, from the slender information he had obtained from Constable Bilins, the vehicle had been abandoned sometime between ten o'clock in the morning and three in the afternoon. No one had the vaguest idea of how it had landed up in Mrs. Hawkins' barn.

The Captain relayed his information downtown, talking directly to the police commissioner.

"They switched cars without a doubt," he said. "But neither of the limousines have showed up yet. We still have a good chance …"

"They wouldn't necessarily have dumped them," the Commissioner said. "Once they lost the hearse, and the two limousines took separate routes, they would merely be a couple of black Caddies. Wouldn't even be noticed."

"Well, we have the license numbers …"

"Contact the federal people about the hearse," the Commissioner said. "Keep in touch if there are any fresh breaks."

The Captain hung up and breathed deeply. The old man had sounded a little gruffer. It was a good sign. Maybe, if things broke right, he might reconsider about that Staten Island thing.

3.

Three miles beyond the Thruway cutoff, Mario began to slow down and pull over to the side of the road. There were no cars or houses in sight. The two limousines stopped behind him and Earl opened the door and got out. He walked back to where Joey sat behind the wheel of the Cadillac. Joey lowered the window.

"Mario says we take the next turn on the right," he said. "The barn is only a mile beyond. You go on ahead. You remember how to get to the place all right, don't you?"

"I brought the cars up last week, didn't I?"

"All right, Joey. I'm going to have Georgie follow us in."

"Maybe it might be a good idea to take her with you," Joey said, twisting his neck to indicate the back seat of the car.

"She goes to the farmhouse with you," Earl said shortly. "I'm running this show."

"Sure." Karl spoke up from the back seat. "She stays with us. As a matter of fact, I'm beginning to get real fond …"

"Lay off, Karl," Earl said. "Leave her alone."

"Aw hell, what do you care," Karl said. "If I want a little fun before we …"

"I said shut up, Karl. You're going to do just what I tell you to do and when I'm not around, Herman here speaks for me. Is everything under control, Herman?"

The old man nodded, saying nothing.

"Listen Earl," Karl said, "I do what I want to do. See. Now if I want …"

Earl stared at him and he stopped talking, his mouth mean and nasty.

"You do what Herman tells you to do," Earl said. "Understand? What Herman tells you or, if I'm around, what I tell you. Until after we split up the money. Then you're on your own. But keep it in mind. The dough is with us. You get out of line and you might run into a little trouble, brother."

He turned to Herman.

"Take care, Herman," he said. "We'll be along about ten minutes after you get there."

"Right, Earl."

Earl walked back to the other car.

"Joey's going ahead," he said. "You follow us. We're turning into the next lane and going in about a mile. Then we take a right into the barn. You wait after we turn and Mario and I will get rid of the hearse and be back within five minutes."

Georgie nodded, saying nothing.

"Everything okay, Earl?" Billy asked.

Earl winked and held up his thumb and forefinger in a circle.

Several minutes later, as Mario turned off into the path leading to the barn, Earl said, "You sure no one can see from the house?"

"That's right. There's just the old woman and she's deaf as a doornail."

"How long do you suppose before someone finds …"

"Who knows?" Gallucci said. "It doesn't matter. All we really need is time to get out of here. Once we're at the farm we'll be safe. For several hours anyway. Long enough to divide it and split out."

"Don't be surprised if we have a little trouble," Earl said. "Karl is beginning to get ideas …"

"He's your problem," Mario said. "You brought him in on this, you know."

"He's my problem, but the girl is the problem of both of us—that is if you are still interested in keeping her alive," Earl said.

"I'm still interested."

"How far after we leave here?" Earl asked.

"Around twelve miles. All back roads. If anyone notices us, it would be a miracle. Not even the mail carrier hits the back roads we'll be using."

"Well, I'll be glad to get out of this hearse," Earl said. "You may be used to riding around with a stiff, but I'm not."

"I guess that's why I don't like murder," Mario said. "I get to see too many dead people anyway."

When Mario and Earl walked back to where the limousine was waiting at the turnoff, a few minutes later, Mario was carrying two heavy sacks containing the money. Earl had the guns, wrapped in a lap robe. Mario got in the front and Earl got in next to Billy.

Georgie turned the ignition key and then backed around.

"Better let me have the forty-five," he said.

"Wait until we get to the farm," Earl said. "The guns are all wrapped up."

Georgie shook his head.

"I feel better with a gun," he said. "We can always get stopped."

"Okay, Georgie," Earl said. He unrolled the lap robe and took out a forty-five automatic.

"This is yours?"

He handed it across the seat. George pushed it into his belt, between his shirt and his trousers.

Billy looked at Earl, but said nothing.

<br>

**4.**

<br>

Dr. Jordan left the phone booth and returned to the car. He said nothing until he was seated next to Jake.

"Well, that ties it. No Kastlebaum, at least not in Kingston, New York," he said.

"No Kastlebaum. Why, that's impossible."

"I'm telling you—no Kastlebaum. Neither under surveyors or anywhere else in the phone book."

"But the map was dated only ten years ago and …"

"Greene and Pinkus are listed under surveyors and someone named Tickelmann. That's all. Do we try either of them?"

Jake shook his head.

"I don't know. I sort of doubt that, unless they actually were familiar with the property. Say, I know what. Why not a real estate office? If that map is dated ten years ago, the property must have been on the market then. Let's find a real estate operator who has been in business since that time. There's a chance that the place was listed with them all and ..."

Dr. Jordan was already out of the car.

"Start with the yellow pages," Jake said, following him. "I'll get some change."

When Jake returned from the drugstore where he had changed a dollar bill into dimes, Dr. Jordan was already putting the receiver back.

"I got it on the second try. A man by the name of Peters," he said. "Peters and Ginger, Realtors. I got him at his home and he said he would meet us at his office in fifteen minutes. The office is three blocks down the street on the right."

"Did you tell him what we wanted?"

"No, I just said it was a matter of life and death."

Chad Peters looked across his desk at Jake and Dr. Jordan and shook his head.

"Kastlebaum," he said. "Sure, I knew him. Died seven years ago. Damned fine surveyor."

Jake took the rolled-up map out of his pocket and handed it across the table.

"This is the place, Mr. Peters," he said. "We are trying desperately to locate it. We felt that perhaps you, having been in business here for so many years, might be able to help us."

Peters took the plat and put on his glasses. He studied it for several minutes and then looked up.

"Does it ring a bell?" Jake asked expectantly.

Peters nodded his head.

"It does," he said. "I sold it only last week to Milt Swartz who owns Swartz's Hotel."

Jake and Dr. Jordan simultaneously released their breaths. "Thank the Lord," Jake said. "Just where is it, Mr. Peters?"

"You wanting to make an offer on it?"

"Well, not exactly, sir," Jake said. "We just want to find out where it is."

"Well," he said. "I don't rightly know as that might be ethical. Guess I'd sort of have to know …"

"Mr. Peters," Dr. Jordan said. "This is a serious matter. A matter of life and death—literally."

"You boys better get in touch with the sheriff if that's so," Peters said. "I'm a real estate man, not a …"

"Listen, Mr. Peters, you must try and understand. We just have to know where this place is. It's confidential." Jake was reaching for his wallet and he pulled out his newspaper identification card from the New York *Blade*.

"I'm a newspaperman," he said, "up here working on a big story. But it has to be kept secret until we are ready to break it. Now if you can tell me …"

"You going to run a story about this place?"

"The place enters into it indirectly."

Peters again shook his head.

"Can't say that Milt Swartz would be in favor of anything running in the papers unless he knew in advance exactly …"

"But Mr. Peters, Mr. Swartz really has nothing at all to do with it. This is the kind of story which would mean a lot and I can tell you this, if you give us the information we want, I'll see that Peters and Ginger, Realtors, gets mentioned and mentioned damned favorably."

"Well, that sounds as though it might be interesting. We sell a lot of stuff to New York people. You sure you'd mention us?"

"My word of honor," Jake said.

Peters thought for a moment and then slowly stood up. He crossed the room and pulled open the drawer of a long desk and when he turned around again he was unrolling a large map.

"County map," he said. "Now come over here and I'll show you exactly where that property is. You have to go out about eleven miles on the main highway leading to …"

It was exactly seven-thirty when Jake and Dr. Jordan left the outskirts of Kingston, driving due west.

The marked map, which Chad Peters had given them, lay on the front seat between them.

# Chapter 10

Earl Cradle pushed the final stack of bills across the table and leaned back in his chair.

"Well," he said, "that's it. Everyone satisfied?"

Karl, sitting directly opposite him, pulled his stack into his lap, saying nothing. Georgie, next to him, nodded. Herman muttered a "Sure," and Joey said "Yes." Billy, who sat next to Earl, just smiled.

Mario Gallucci, between Herman and Joey, stood up and gathered in his share.

"Fair enough," he said.

Earl looked at his watch.

"Seven-forty," he said. "Plenty dark out now. So, I guess that's it. Herman, Billy's driving you into Albany. She'll take the Chevy that's out in the garage. She'll drop you wherever you want to get off. Now I think you'd better be getting started. We want to break this up as soon as possible."

Herman stood up slowly and Billy reached down to the floor and handed him an overnight bag. He pushed the money in and pulled the zipper.

"I won't be seeing you boys again," he said. "It was a good caper." He moved over and shook hands with Earl.

"A nice one, Earl. You come see me and Mama someday, see."

"Right, Herman," Earl said.

Billy looked at Earl for a moment and then nodded her head toward the door leading into the next room.

"Don't worry, kid," Earl said under his breath.

She put her money in a second zipper bag and moved toward the door.

"I'll be waiting, Earl," she said.

Two minutes later they heard the sound of the Chevy engine as she gunned the motor.

Earl said, "Well, Joey, do you want to go along with Karl and Georgie or do you want to wait for us?"

Joey shrugged and started to open his mouth, but Karl spoke first.

"Why not leave together?"

"There are two Ford sedans in the garage," Earl said. "Both have registration papers in the glove compartments. You, Karl, and Georgie can take either one of them."

Karl stood up. He still had the forty-five in his belt. He started to edge back toward the sideboard and Earl spoke quickly.

"Stay away from that sawed-off shotgun, Karl," he said. His hand moved slightly, up toward the shoulder holster.

Karl stopped.

"What's the matter, Earl?" he asked. "Don't you trust us?"

"I don't trust anybody where there is this much loot laying around."

Mario fidgeted and looked studiously at the floor. Georgie began to move around nearer Karl.

"How about the girl in there?" Karl asked, looking toward the door.

"Don't worry about her, Karl," Earl said. "You and Georgie take off before it gets hot around here. Mario and I will worry about the girl."

"The trouble is, I do worry about her," Karl said.

"Look, what's everybody getting so unfriendly about?" Georgie asked. "What the hell, Earl, if Karl wants the girl, why shouldn't he …"

"I'm not arguing about it, I'm telling you. I'll worry about the girl. You guys be smart and move while it is still safe to get away from this spot."

"I'll move when I know about the girl," Karl said. "You think I want to walk into court someday and …"

"I've told you a dozen times not to be crazy," Earl said. "That girl is no more of a danger to you than any of the others who saw you in the bank. She …"

"The hell she isn't," Karl said. "The others didn't see Georgie here at all—but the girl did. The others maybe got one quick look at me if that. And then they were so frightened that they wouldn't remember. The others haven't heard my voice. She can identify it. What the hell do you think I am, nuts or something? I say the girl has to …"

"I didn't come in this thing for murder," Mario suddenly said. "So far it's nice and clean. Let's keep it that way."

Karl swung around and looked at him with hard, malicious eyes.

"You," he said, "sure, you want to keep it that way. You got a couple of hundred grand out of it. You'll be safe somewhere in Italy and they'll never get you. Anyway, you're the only one it wouldn't matter about. The cops know about your end already. You're the only one they do know about."

He turned back to Earl.

"And you, Earl," he said. "You got over two hundred grand and that blonde of yours has another fifty. You got enough to disappear forever. But how about us? How about Georgie and Joey and me? Fifty grand apiece. How long you think we can disappear on that?"

"What are you doing?" Earl asked, his voice icy. "Squawking about the split-up? You know what you agreed on when you came in."

"I'm not squawking about the split-up. But I didn't agree to kidnap some girl and then let her go so she could be a witness against me if we ever get tagged."

"Karl's got a point there," Joey said.

Earl swung around and glared at him.

"You stupid, two-bit punk," he said. "You got fifty grand there in front of you. Why you never had a five-hundred-dollar bill all at one time before in your life. I brought you in on this and the thanks I get is you turn against me."

He took the cigarette from the side of his mouth and threw it on the floor.

"Now listen to me," he said. "I planned this caper and I put up dough. I paid off the gas company guy and I did the brainwork. Mario shot his business, supplied the original idea, and contributed the cars and all the rest of it. We are entitled to our share and you all agreed on it. You also agreed that if you came in, it would be with the understanding that I was to run things."

"It's different now," Karl said. "The caper is all over."

"That's right, all over, Karl. Now you and Georgie go out and get in that car and blow."

"Can I say something?" Joey said.

"Yeah, say it."

"The argument seems to be what we do about the girl," he said. "Mario says that so far we've only pulled a bank job and that's prison and not the chair if they catch up with us. He's forgetting one thing. We drove that girl across a state line. That makes it a federal kidnaping. Penalty—the chair."

"He's right, Earl," Georgie said.

"You're damned right he's right," Karl said.

"Why don't we just sort of put it to a vote?" Georgie asked. "That's the fair way."

Mario pushed his chair away from the table.

"I said it before and I say it again. I want no part of no murder."

Earl's eyes went to him and he suddenly remembered that Mario was unarmed. Mario was on his side, but if it came to a showdown, he wouldn't be of much use.

Georgie had taken his forty-five from the pile of guns and had it on him; Joey could have a gun or not, Earl couldn't remember. In the meantime, Karl had again stepped back toward the table.

"You move any nearer that table, Karl," he said, "and the fireworks start. Now listen, all of you," he continued, speaking quickly before anyone had a chance to say anything. "We're acting like damned fools. What are we going to do, start shooting each other up for no reason at all? Hell, we got what we went after; it was a perfect caper. Now why the hell don't we act like human beings and work this out?" He hesitated, looking from one to the other.

"Look, Georgie," Earl said, "why don't you go in the other room and bring the girl in here? Then we can ..."

"Stay right where you are, Georgie," Karl said. "If you want the girl in here, Earl, let Mario or Joey get her."

"Leave the girl alone," Mario said.

"I'll get her," Joey said. He moved over to the door and turned the knob.

Earl suddenly looked over at the window at the other side of the room.

"Quiet," he said. "I thought I heard ..."

"Now Earl," Karl said, "you wouldn't really try to pull an old chestnut ..."

"Listen, you fool," Earl said in a harsh whisper. "I tell you ..."

"Take a look outside, Georgie," Karl said. "And Earl ..." Cradle's hand darted for his shoulder holster.

Karl didn't even try for his gun. He moved like lightning and smashed the heavy round table against Earl's body.

Earl had the gun out as he fell.

He shot as he was going over backward and the shot he had aimed at Karl, crashed into the back of Georgie's skull, throwing him hard against the wall before he slid down to his knees.

Mario had moved fast and he was trying to get out the front door when the bedroom door opened. Joey took deliberate aim and shot his cousin three times, each bullet striking his back and plowing through his chest.

Earl rolled as he fell and the table missed crashing down on him, but by the time he had turned, looking for Karl, he already knew that it was too late.

He felt the bullet plunge into his stomach even as he heard the sound of the shot.

He thought he heard the crash of breaking glass.

He also thought he heard, somewhere off in the distance, the thin wail of a police siren.

He couldn't be sure. He could never be sure because he was already dead before his arms had stretched out on the floor and the revolver had dropped from his hand.

## 2.

County Patrolman Flynn, driving a four-year-old souped-up Mercury, spotted the blue Buick sedan some five miles outside of town while he was parked in back of a large sign advertising a kosher restaurant. He smiled in satisfaction.

The Buick was tooling along at a good sixty and a good sixty was good enough for Officer Flynn. He gave them plenty of leeway, waiting until they were a couple of hundred yards past him, before he pulled out from behind the sign.

"Slick New Yorkers, eh?" he said, under his breath, and with satisfaction.

He played it cool, following behind with his lights off for another quarter of a mile before he pushed the button switching on the red flash on top of the car. Simultaneously he nudged the siren button.

It looked like a real nice one and he was smiling contentedly when it suddenly occurred to him that instead of slowing down, the Buick was speeding up.

Officer Flynn pushed hard on his throttle.

When the needle of his speedometer passed eighty, the officer was no longer smiling. His mouth had adopted a grim and determined line.

At eighty-five he swore and took his finger off the siren button. He wanted it on the steering wheel.

At ninety, he realized that he didn't have a lot left in the Mercury. And at ninety-five, he cursed a stingy county commission which kept the department on a budget that made it necessary to get that last damn mile out of its cars.

The Buick began to pull away.

Flynn would have liked to take his hands from the wheel and flip on the radio and contact the state police. The smart thing, of course, would be to slow down and try and set up a roadblock ahead somewhere. Flynn figured that anybody willing to risk his life driving at the speed the Buick driver was going, probably was trying to do a little more than avoid a speeding ticket.

But Officer Flynn was stubborn. He still had the twin tail lights in sight.

At the end of five miles, he knew that he was gradually losing ground. He was thinking seriously then about slowing down and putting in the alarm, when he suddenly realized the lights were no longer in front of him.

He pulled over to the side of the road and came to a full stop. A minute later he had contacted the state police. For a while he sat and smoked, cursing his own bad luck. It was damned funny, first the car was there, and then it wasn't.

Flynn spent quite a little time thinking about it.

Suddenly he opened his mouth and said, "Damn!"

He pushed the gear shift lever over and again started up the road.

He cursed himself again as he drove. He had sat there and wasted a good ten minutes, smoking and hating the county commissioners, instead of doing a very obvious thing.

3.

"Look, Doc," Jake said, "I don't think I should ever have let you drive."

"Don't worry."

"My old man would have kittens if he could see what you're doing with his car," Jake said.

"Is he still behind us?"

Jake looked back.

"Yeah. You know, my old man has had this buggy for a year and a half and he has never driven it over thirty-five miles an hour."

"He should have bought a Simca," Dr. Jordan said. "Are we gaining on him?"

"I think so," Jake said. "But honest to God, you're doing almost a hundred. Wouldn't it be easier just to stop and take the ticket?"

"They don't give you tickets at a hundred," Dr. Jordan said. "I'm not going to be stopped. I'm not going to be stopped by anything. I have a hunch …"

Jake took the flashlight out of the glove compartment and flashed it on the map.

"According to this," he said, "we got the turnoff on the next dirt road in just about half a mile."

Dr. Jordan nodded grimly and the throttle hit the floor.

"What the hell!"

"Putting a little air between us," Jordan said. "We'll corner fast."

"I'm not watching," Jake said. "My old man …"

Jordan leaned forward and cut the lights. There was a half-moon and he could make out the road as a vague white ribbon. He began to ease up on the throttle and touch the brake.

"Should be along here somewhere," he said.

Jake started to turn in his seat to look back, but as he did, there was the screech of burning rubber and the car lurched. Jake slid across the seat and banged his head on the window.

A moment later and he thought they were turning over. His body slid back and crashed against that of his companion and the car behaved like a demented meteor. By the time Jake had clutched the door handle, prepared to pull himself from flaming wreckage, Jordan had straightened out and pulled on the light switch and was again pressing the throttle toward the floor.

"Nice cornering if I do say so myself," he said. "Check the map. How far to the lane?"

"Doc, please," Jake said. "Don't think of my father—think of me."

"Check the map."

Jake retrieved the flashlight from the floor.

"Three miles exactly from the turnoff," he said after a minute. "And as I remember, according to that map, the lane is eight hundred and some-odd yards?"

"Right."

"When I turn in, I'll cut the lights again. If there is anyone there, we won't want to be seen."

"Well, if you do, drive a little slower," Jake said.

A couple of minutes later and the Buick turned into the lane leading to what had been, up until a few days ago, the summer farm owned by Mario Gallucci.

Jordan had switched the lights and was barely able to follow the road in the semidarkness and he had throttled down the engine until its sound was a bare whisper.

He drove for about five hundred yards and then pulled to the side and shut off the ignition.

"Up ahead," he said. "Lights."

Jake saw the outlines of a house in the distance. Dim yellow light came from a pair of downstairs windows.

Dr. Jordan reached into the back of the car and found the jack handle they had taken, out of the trunk.

"You take this," he said, handing it to Jake.

"You know, Doc," Jake said, "I've never been very good when it came to violence. Frankly, I am just a little chicken."

"Do you want to stay here?"

"Very much," Jake said. "But I'm coming with you. I guess, as a newspaperman, I have to take certain risks."

"Well, come on then, and be as quiet as you can. We're going to take a look in those windows."

They rounded the bend in the road a minute or two later and saw the large barn. Jordan took Jake by the arm and crept toward it. When he reached the building he saw that the wide doors were partly opened. Carefully shielding the flashlight, he turned the beam into the interior.

There were four cars sitting in the building. Two of them were black Cadillac limousines.

Dr. Jordan put his mouth close to Jake's ear and whispered. "You can stay here—I'm going to the house."

They could hear the sound of voices suddenly raised.

Jordan started creeping toward the nearest lighted window. For a moment Jake hesitated, and then he quickly followed. He was carrying the tire iron clutched in his right hand.

It was just as they reached the window that Karl spoke. He said: "Take a look outside, Georgie, and Earl ..."

And then came the crash of the exploding gun.

Jake never did quite understand exactly how it was he managed to get through that window and into the living room of the farmhouse. Later, he accused Dr. Martin Jordan of throwing him through.

Actually, Dr. Jordan himself never was quite sure of his own movements during those few first wild moments. He remembered hearing the words, quite clearly. He was already at the window then and lifting his head to see into the room. He remembered the words and he remembered his first quick glimpse into the room. From where he crouched he was facing the doorway of the bedroom and the first thing he saw was the fat man standing there in the doorway. But his eyes weren't on the fat man. They were on the tiny figure of the girl standing slightly to his left and behind him.

Dr. Martin Jordan was looking directly at Jane Mercer, his fiancée. And then the shot came.

Everything else was instinct. There was one thing and one thing only in his mind. To get into that room and to get to his girl.

It was probably some half-forgotten football tactic that he used in making his leap, but even as Earl Cradle was falling to the floor, he crashed through the window, taking glass and frame along with him. He cleared the falling table with one wild leap and Joey Gallucci probably never even saw him coming or knew what it was that hit him.

What hit him was Martin Jordan's closed right fist and it was a monstrous blow. It broke Joey's jaw so badly that he never fully recovered from the compound fracture. It knocked him completely unconscious for more than fifteen minutes.

Dr. Jordan's momentum carried him right on into the bedroom and he carried Jane with him, both of them ending up against the bedframe. He had his back to the door and it is probably as well that he did. He didn't see Karl as Karl swung around after sending the slug into Earl Cradle's stomach. If he had he would have seen that forty-five pointed directly at him.

Not seeing Karl, of course he didn't see Jake Epstein either. Jake Epstein, the boy who hated violence and frankly admitted to being a little chicken, brought the tire iron down across the back of Karl's skull. It was a beautifully aimed and timed blow.

Jake stood there temporarily paralyzed as he watched the body in front of him slowly sinking to the floor.

It wasn't until seconds later, when he heard the scream of the siren outside of the door, that he realized exactly what he had accomplished.

County Patrolman Flynn stepped into the room, his pad already in his hand.

"If anybody ever asked for a ticket …" he began.

And then he saw the shambles.

**4.**

Forty-five minutes later Jake sat at the sheriff's desk in the county seat and made his telephone call. He had his hat tipped on the back of his head and he was in his shirt sleeves. A cigarette dangled from the corner of his mouth and one foot was on the desk.

Jake looked like a newspaperman. At least, Jake was pretty sure that he looked like what a newspaperman was supposed to look like.

"Let me have the city desk, please," Jake said.

He waited a moment and there was a sound in the receiver and he looked surprised.

"Why, Mister Dewey," Jake said, "what are you doing there so late?" Suddenly he jerked the phone away from his ear.

"It's me, Epstein," he said. "I got the greatest story. Epstein, Jake Epstein, your reporter … Oh, I don't? … Well, Mr. Dewey please listen to me for just one second … The bank robbery … I have it all wrapped up … No, I'm not drunk."

Jake turned away for a moment and looked woefully at Jane Mercer and Dr. Martin Jordan.

"I tell you, I cracked the case … I am in Sullivan County with the Sheriff … Yes, I'll put him on."

He turned and held out the receiver.

"He wants to talk to you a minute, sir," he said.

The Sheriff moved over and took the instrument from his hand. He listened for a moment in silence and then spoke.

"Yeah, that's right, Jake Epstein. Yeah, it's the truth, we got it all wrapped up … That's right … No, you better let Epstein tell you about it … He is responsible for breaking it wide open … That's right … Here he is …"

Jake took the receiver again and shrugged his shoulders, smiling over at Jane and Jordan again.

"Right, boss," he said. "You'll take it yourself and write it … My byline—great—that's real great … Of course I know you're still a newspaperman … Sure … Sure—well, there was this dead man down at Bellevue—but this is the beginning of the story … That's right … This dead man down at Bellevue where I went to get some color as you suggested … Yes, I'll get on with it.

"What did you say boss? … Oh, I'm sorry … But some people here

… They were in it with me … They were distracting me for the moment … I know it's a long-distance call … What were they doing? … They were kissing each other, boss … Anyway, there was this dead man down at Bellevue, and he …"

THE END

# OBSESSION

## Lionel White

This book is for
Pat and John Kelley

# 1

It is very late, long after midnight. Although the windows are wide open, there is barely a breath of air. It is unbelievably hot. I am sitting in a straight-backed chair at the table in the kitchen, making a few random notes on a yellow lined pad.

Allie is in the adjacent room and I can see the silhouette of her slender, naked body as she lies sprawled out on the bed. Her eyes are wide open and she is staring at the ceiling. It is six months to the day since I first looked into those gray-flecked azure eyes and succumbed once and for all to their peculiar type of magic.

Joel is in the living room and he is slouched in one corner of the long Spanish leather couch, one lean brown hand holding the airline bag with the money and the other holding the loaded automatic.

I made the radio contact about fifteen minutes ago and it will take them at least two hours to drive out the lonely desert road which meanders for miles through the tumbleweeds and cactus and finally ends here at the long-deserted ranch house—the ranch house which is more than two thousand endless miles from the neat suburban split level where I first met Allie on that evening when Marta and I had our last bitter words.

Had Marta not been in a sense the catalyst, had my relationship with Marta been different, who is to say for sure that the resultant relationship with Allie would have been the same? Yes, the more I think of it, the surer I am that had it not been for the rather sordid and unhappy events of that day six months ago, when Marta and I for the last time joined in a duel of bitter recriminations, these things which have happened would never have taken place.

I want desperately to understand why they took place.

Six months ago. Noontime on March second. I, Conrad Madden, am in the bar of the Commodore Hotel, adjacent to Grand Central station, waiting for the train which goes north and east into Westchester County and Connecticut, following the commuter belt. I have a thirty-day ticket and the destination is Stamford, where I have left my four-year-old Ford station wagon. It will take me less than half an hour to drive from the parking lot to the middle-class suburb where I live with my wife, Marta, and our two children, Harold and Carol.

Marta and I were married fifteen years ago, soon after I graduated from New York University. She is a year older than I am, but looking at her slender, well-groomed figure, her small, heart-shaped face which she cares for with all the avid passion of an owner of a rare Stradivarius, her chestnut hair which she wears cut short like an Italian movie star, no one would guess it.

Marta looks much too young to be the mother of Harold and Carol. Harold is almost fourteen, a fat, awkward adolescent who suffers from acne, and Carol is a year and a half younger. I have often been baffled at the complete lack of any resemblance between them and either Marta or myself.

I have ordered my second Martini and, looking at my wrist watch, I see that I will have time to swallow it before making the telephone call to Marta to tell her what happened with my morning interview at the employment agency.

I drink the Martini and it fails to give me the necessary courage to make the phone call. The message I have to convey is one I have repeated to Marta too many times in the last few weeks. How does one go on continually reporting failure?

According to all recent surveys by those economic analysts who are supposed to know about such things, this is a temporary recession. Only a small fraction of the working population is supposedly out of work. Unfortunately, I am a member of this small minority.

"Things are rapidly improving, times are bound to get better." But when?

Certainly not this morning. This morning I heard only what I have been hearing for the last ten weeks.

There is a singular lack of openings for either an account executive or a copy writer. "But don't lose courage. Something will turn up. Keep in touch."

I wish the agencies which line Park and Madison avenues knew things are getting better. I wish …

I wish that I didn't have to return home with the same sad, unhappy story.

I have a third Martini and decide to postpone the trip back to Stamford. I will go to a movie and get a later train.

The four-forty has a bar car and I have a couple of straight whiskey and waters during the fifty-eight-minute ride. I no longer worry about breaking the news to Marta. She will have figured the answer long before I arrive at our mortgaged, seven-room split level. She will understand why I have not telephoned and why I have not returned earlier. She will also smell the liquor on my breath.

There will be no recriminations, no complaining, bitter words. Merely that look of sick defeat and disillusionment. The remainder of the insurance payment now long overdue. The tuition for the remaining quarter at Carol's school. The grocery bill. The need for …

Exactly what don't you owe and what don't you need after being out of work for more than two months?

I will tell her where I have spent the afternoon because I never lie to Marta. Again there will be no recriminations. Merely that same sad little smile and a shake of the head. A soft-voiced suggestion that perhaps tomorrow, if I return early, I can get to work on that television play I have been trying to do for so long. A reference to the play that I did do, and sold, some three years back.

Of course she will say nothing of my having quit my job when the check came in and my determination to write dozens of more successful half-hour shows. No mention of those twelve long months during which I wrote one show after another and failed to sell a single one.

Marta is very thoughtful, very discreet. She has infinite confidence in my ability as a provider. This confidence of course will not prohibit her from mentioning once more and for the hundredth time that perhaps after all it will be best if she goes back to her old job as a secretary in New York until things get better.

We both understand this gambit. She is being generous and loyal and thoughtful. She also knows, as well as I do, that the job would barely pay for her commutation, even assuming that she could still obtain the position. Certainly it would not cover the cost of a maid to stay at the house while she is working. The maid would be essential because Marta would never leave our children alone in the house, even for a few hours.

Marta understands that she will never take the job, just as she understands the ridiculousness of my spending time attempting to write and sell television shows. When a man is desperately worried about bills, demoralized by his failure to find work, unhappy and frustrated in his marital relationship, he doesn't exactly sit down and blithely turn out successful and salable freelance shows in a highly competitive market. Especially when he was unable to do so when he had a bank account and a degree of peace and happiness.

Oh, it will be the same old pattern. I will finally say that things will probably break any day and that the agency showed optimism. To forestall further discussion I will suggest making a drink for both of us before dinner and the answer of course will be the same. "Really, do you think we can afford to drink when the grocery bill is so long overdue? Is it morally right?" …

I will make the drink anyway and Marta will sip hers between hurt, disapproving lips. We will have supper and later Harold and Carol will take over the living room to wallow in the narcotics of television, Marta will retire to the bedroom to work at her sewing machine, and I will go into the study and stare at the blank sheet of foolscap in the typewriter.

But on that evening of March second, six months ago, it didn't turn out exactly that way.

Marta was on the couch, in a dressing gown, manicuring her nails, and she didn't look up when I entered the room. The television was going full blast and Harold was squatted on his haunches, less than two yards from it, staring through his thick-lensed, horn-rimmed glasses and with his mouth slack, his classic pose as he watched the endless drivel which poured forth from the screen.

Carol sat over at the other side of the room, buried in a comic book.

I tossed my hat on the table and crossed to the couch and leaned down to kiss my wife.

"Your breath," she said, without looking up. She turned her face away and my lips brushed the side of her cheek.

"I'm sorry I didn't call, darling, but …"

"Later," Marta said. "Not in front of the children."

Harold turned, annoyance on his face. He moved forward and snapped off the television. "How can I hear anything when everyone is yelling?" he said.

His mother looked at him and shook her head. "Why don't you go to your room and try out the new set?" she said. "After all dear, that's why you wanted one of your own."

It took a second or so for it to come through.

"One what of his own?" I asked.

Marta sighed. "Con," she said, "you can't seem to remember from one minute to the next. The portable television Harold has been wanting. We were in town this afternoon and I picked it up for him.”

For a moment I just stared at her. “You what?”

“I bought him the set. The one he wanted for his birthday.”

“His birthday isn’t until next month,” I said. “Anyway, I thought we agreed …”

“Please,” Marta said. “This is no time to discuss …”

“How much did it cost?” I asked, biting my lips and trying to keep the anger out of my voice.

Harold was halfway out of the room and he suddenly stopped and turned toward me. “I’m entitled to a birthday present, aren’t I?” he said.

I moved a step toward him and Marta spoke quickly, still using that reasonable tone of voice. “Darling,” she said, “of course you are. You go on and listen to your new set and dinner will be ready in a few minutes. Carol”—she turned to his sister—“Carol, perhaps you’d better get cleaned up and ready …”

Carol dropped the comic book on the floor and stood up. She didn’t look at either me or her mother but merely sighed and crossed the room and opened the door to the hallway.

I waited until they were out of hearing.

“For God’s sake, Marta,” I said, “this is hardly the time to be squandering money on nonessentials. I should think …”

Marta stood up, her face calm as she began to collect the various instruments which she had been using to improve her already flawless nails.

“How much money did you waste on liquor today, Conrad?” she asked.

Before I could say anything she gave me that odd half-smile which is so typical of her when she has coined an unanswerable remark. “Anyway, we don’t have time to discuss it now. I must feed the children and I suggest you shower and start getting dressed.”

“Dressed? Dressed for what?”

“Your memory, Con.” Marta shook her head. “The Halls’ dinner dance. You knew we were planning to go tonight and I do think you could have been home a little earlier. Anyway …”

“Marta,” I said, “I told you that I didn’t want to go to the Halls. I told you that I don’t feel much like celebrating these days. When I get home I just want to take it easy. My idea of taking it easy isn’t sitting around with a lot of suburban drunks and …”

“Some people *prefer* their drinking in the evenings,” Marta said.

"Anyway, we have no time to discuss it. Getting out will do you good and the babysitter will be here in less than an hour and a half and the Medows …"

"What babysitter?"

Marta sighed and turned toward me, shaking her head as though she were being confronted by a slightly backward child.

"The Medows are driving out from town and are going to pick us up. They know of this girl who babysits and they were kind enough to offer to bring her with them. And so now if you will just start to get ready …"

"Why in the name of God do we need a babysitter?" I asked, and in spite of an effort to control myself, I knew that I was raising my voice. "Why should we pay some adolescent to sit here when both Harold and Carol are old enough to be out sitting with someone else's children? Do you realize that your husband is out of work and looking for a job? Do you realize …?"

"I realize you are yelling," Marta said. "Anyway, you know how I feel about leaving the children alone. If anything should happen to them …"

"Nothing could happen to them which wouldn't be an improvement," I said bitterly.

Marta stared at me, unperturbed. "Take your shower, Conrad," she said. "You aren't really yourself, I'm afraid. I understand what you have been going through and …"

"You don't understand a goddamned thing," I said. "You seem to think …"

Marta interrupted speaking over her shoulder as she reached the doorway. "Black tie, Conrad," she said. "You'll find a freshly laundered shirt in the top lefthand drawer. Now hurry."

I went over to the corner cupboard and unlocked it and found the vodka bottle and there were about two inches in the bottom. I didn't bother with a chaser.

It was about when I was turning the hot water down and the cold up that I really began to feel a little like a son of a bitch. She had been reasonable and everything she had said had certainly been true. She hadn't bawled me out, hadn't even asked where I had spent the day.

If the children had more or less ignored me, well, I couldn't in all honesty blame them too much. There had never been any real bond of affection between us. We lived together in a sort of armed truce, competing for Marta's time and affection.

During the first years of our marriage, of course, it had been a lot easier. The children were younger and then, too, the relationship between Marta and me had been different. I am still not sure whether Marta and I ever loved each other, but at least we seemed to feel that we had a great deal in common and certainly there had been a real sexual attraction. If Marta had changed, perhaps the change was as much my fault as it was hers. In any case, this evening she had certainly behaved with a good deal more finesse and graciousness than I had.

By the time I was toweling myself down, I felt like a complete heel and I was determined to try to make things up. I took a clean Turkish towel from the rack and wrapped it around my waist, opened the door of the bathroom, and stepped into our bedroom.

Marta was standing in front of the long door mirror, holding an evening dress in front of herself, her head slightly cocked as she observed the effect.

I hesitated for a fraction of a second, watching her. Her slender beautifully molded body was as lovely as it was the day I had married her.

She didn't move as I crossed the room and stepped up behind her.

My hands slid around her waist and up and I pressed close. She didn't move, didn't freeze. Her head turned just slightly and she said, "Better get dressed. The Medows will be along pretty soon and …"

"Come over to the bed," I said.

"Now really, Conrad," Marta began, "this is hardly the time …"

"Damn it," I said, "we'll take the time. I want to talk to you for a few minutes. I want …"

She sighed and carefully folded the dress, slipping out from under my hands.

"All right, Conrad," she said. "As you wish."

She placed the dress over a chair and moved to the bed and sat down. I sat beside her and, turning, took her chin in my hand so that I could look into her face.

"I have been behaving like a damned fool," I said. "I'm sorry. But, damn it, don't you see, I need you. This is one time when I really need and want …"

"I'm always here."

"All right," I said. "Kiss me."

She leaned forward and kissed my mouth without opening her lips. My hands moved again and I started to put one arm around her as my body leaned back, but she moved quickly and stood up.

"I think that we had better start getting ready."

"Marta," I said, "don't you ever understand what I want?"

Marta sighed and looked at me, her eyes neutral, neither antagonistic nor warm.

"You should understand something of my emotions," she said. "You expect me to feel something that I just don't feel. The way you've been acting, the way things have been going, how can you expect me …?"

"I expect you to act like a wife should act," I said. "Is sex supposed to be something that only works in case I'm working? Is sex supposed …?"

"You're being foolish, Conrad," Marta said. "I either feel certain things toward you or I don't. Marriage is a great deal more than mere sex."

"Sure," I said. "It's love and affection and understanding and a hell of a lot of things. There are, however, certain demands of the body …"

"If you're asking me to give myself to you when I don't want to, you're asking me to be little better than a whore," Marta said.

I stood up and shook my head. "If happiness and money and security are the only coins which can buy you, then you are little better than a whore."

I started to turn away and then quickly turned back. "Damn it, honey," I said, "I didn't mean that and you know I didn't. It's just that I have been missing you a lot lately and what with one thing and another …"

"I understand, Conrad," Marta said. Her tone was insanely reasonable and polite. "I understand. Now hurry and get dressed. We haven't long until the Medows will be here."

I stared at her as she turned away, biting back the words which came to my lips. "Sure—sure," I said at last. "With the babysitter."

If I sounded bitter it was apparently lost on Marta. She was again standing in front of the mirror, this time holding up another dress to observe how it might look when and if it embraced her later that evening at the Hall's dinner party.

I wish I were able to say that when Allison O'Conner walked into the living room of our home that evening of March second, I had a sort of mystical realization of all that she was to mean to me.

The fact is, however, I was no more than dimly aware of her presence. This of course may well be because of the fact that she was preceded by Ned and Irma Medows, both of whom were already boisterously drunk.

I had answered the doorbell and they had crowded past me to enter the living room. I have never liked Irma Medows, who was one of Marta's schoolgirl chums, and I liked her husband even less. Ned Medows is a very successful real estate operator, one of those large, full-bodied men who have a talent for making money and an equal talent for telling the world about it. He also has a positive genius for saying the wrong thing at the wrong time.

Irma crossed the room to embrace Marta and Ned threw a heavy arm across my shoulder. "How's the old boy?" he said. "Got that new job lined up yet?"

He didn't wait for my answer, of course, but continued, apparently having some purely psychic source of knowledge. "Well, don't let it worry you. Just a mild recession. Hell, I didn't take in a dime more than three thou' all of last month. Anyway, a little struggle is good for an up-and-coming young fella."

He moved across the room to embrace and kiss Marta, who greeted him with a warm, moist mouth. I think that seeing Ned make his usual half-drunken, half-lecherous pass annoyed me as much as having him call me "young fella."

I am thirty-eight, but I am quite sure that despite his baldness and pot belly Ned is not more than three or four years my senior.

"The suckers must still be buying real estate in spite of the recession," I said, trying to think of something both clever and nasty and failing in each. In any case, the remark was lost on Ned.

"Brought the little lady here to sit with the young fry," he said, turning back toward the door. "Can't say," he continued with a smirk, "I wouldn't prefer to stay here with her than go on to the Halls, but you know the old war horse …"

The old war horse said, "Act your age, Romeo. And let's get moving. I need a little fuel."

"We have some vodka," Marta began, but I looked at her and shook my head.

"Vodka is for pigs and Russians," Ned said, exhibiting his usual social finesse. "Come on, we'll take my car."

Marta smiled at him and turned to me. "Take the sitter in and introduce her to the children, Conrad," she said. "You are—" She turned to the girl who still stood in the doorway.

"Allison—Allison O'Conner."

For the first time I really saw her then.

What I saw was an extraordinarily pretty child who seemed no older than my son, Harold, who at the moment was sitting in the dining room pushing pie into his overstuffed face. I saw a girl dressed in simple, nondescript clothes, a short plaid skirt, a rather tailored jacket, bare legs and loafers. Her hair was down to her shoulders, fine, honey-colored, and parted at the side of her head. She had very fair skin. The one feature which did strike me was her eyes. They were long and almond-shaped, unbelievably blue, and emphasized by the longest dark lashes I had ever seen.

At that moment Ned saw fit to slap his fat arm over my shoulder again. I slipped away from him and took the girl by the arm.

"I'll be right back," I said.

I steered her past Ned and through the door into the dining room.

Carol merely looked up glumly without nodding as I introduced her. Harold stared at her for a moment and said, "'lo." He turned back to the remainder of the pie.

"We should be home by midnight," I said.

"Don't rush," she said.

It wasn't until I was closing the front door, a minute or so later, that the thought struck me. Something had sounded odd and off-key when she had spoken those two short words. For a moment I thought perhaps it was the phrase itself and then it came to me.

She had looked like a little girl. It wasn't, of course, an analytical opinion, merely a general impression. But the tone of her voice, low and throaty, as she'd said, "Don't rush," utterly belied the impression. It was, in fact, the most completely sexy voice I had ever heard.

The Halls, like most of our friends, are really friends of Marta's. They differ from her other friends in only one respect. Instead of being merely middle-class prosperous or slightly wealthy, Lydia and Carl Hall are really rich. They live outside of Pound Ridge in a huge baronial castle with enough grounds to support a couple of dozen riding horses and half a dozen full-time gardeners. They are not actually germane to this story, and so there is no point in pursuing either them or their possessions; I may merely say that although the food and liquor at their brawls are of top quality, the guests are not.

The party, a so-called dinner dance, was as depressing and dismal as I expected it would be. I have often thought that the reason people like the Halls give parties is to offer their married friends a chance at adultery and drunkenness.

I managed, on that particular occasion, to avoid both, although I drank with a liberal hand. Ned Medows, however, after disappearing for more than an hour with the wife of a local high-school teacher, returned a little bit the worse for wear and became thoroughly and completely stoned. Had Ned Medows remained reasonably sober, or had he failed to disappear in the bushes with the wife of the schoolteacher, thereby antagonizing his own wife to the extent that she herself disappeared for the remainder of the evening with a sculptor from Bedford Village, I should not now, six months later, be jotting down these notes on a pad of yellow lined paper, more than two thousand miles away.

By eleven-thirty I had had enough. I was as drunk as I cared to get; anything more I drank I knew would merely further depress me. There was no one at the party I wanted to talk with, no one in fact who seemed to seek out my own company. I was tired; I was thinking of tomorrow. I was reaching the point where the money worries were all coming back, and the more I saw of these desperate fun-seeking, solvent citizens who had nothing to worry about but the next drink or the next bed, the more depressed I became and the more anxious to retire to my own bed.

I hadn't seen Marta for some time and I started looking for her.

She wasn't on the dance floor and she wasn't at either of the two bars. I finally discovered her in the library with a tall thin youth with a moth-eaten mustache, whom I vaguely remembered having met earlier in the evening. The youth held an opened book of verse and had obviously been reading aloud.

It seems utterly ridiculous, but the scene infuriated me. It was so typical.

I knew exactly what had happened. Marta was running true to form. She had found a sensitive soul. She had found someone to mother. I could have written the script. This tender, delicate boy had gone into the library with Marta because the two of them found the rest of those at the party vulgar and crude. In Marta he had found a fine, sympathetic person who had the larger understanding. And she had found someone who had need of her strength and her intelligence and her goodness. They had talked and he had told her all about himself. And then he had found the volume of poetry and read to her.

Nothing in this world could have been more innocent. And nothing could have given me a greater sense of nausea. I honestly believe that I would have preferred to have found her there on the couch with her clothes torn off.

Marta's purity and goodness, her desire to smother with mother love everyone she ever knew, merely pointed up the very frigidity and chaste sterility that she had substituted for the passion and emotion that a man wants in a wife.

It occurred to me that one reason Marta always liked to go to the sort of wild party which the Halls were giving was because her own behavior, by contrast with the behavior of the other guests, gave her a sense of righteousness and superiority. God knows, she certainly is superior to people like the Medows and most of the others, but I sometimes wonder if her particular form of bloodless superiority is really preferable. At least as a steady diet.

The boy stood up and bowed and left, still carrying the book of verse. He looked embarrassed. If he was, it was for the wrong reason.

"I'm tired, Marta," I said, "and I want to leave. Are you about ready?"

"I'm ready any time," Marta said. "The trouble is, Ned isn't. He passed out about an hour ago and the Halls had him put to bed upstairs."

"All right," I said. "Let's dig up Irma."

Marta smiled. "She's gone off with that sculptor fellow. I don't think she'll be back tonight."

It has always amazed me, the extent of Marta's knowledge concerning the sexual behavior of her friends.

"In that case," I said, "the hell with the Medows. We will take their car."

"But, Conrad, I hardly think ..."

I wasn't in a mood to argue. "I'm leaving. I'm taking the Medows' car. You may come or not."

For a moment she stared at me, and then shrugged. "We'll say good night to the Halls," she said.

"You say it," I said. "You have more to thank them for than I have."

We rode home in silence.

I parked in front of the house and started to turn off the ignition, but Marta suddenly spoke.

"You'll have to take the sitter home," she said.

I looked at her, bewildered. I had completely forgotten about the girl who was staying with the children.

"Remember? She came with the Medows and they were supposed to take her back. Wait here and I'll go in and get her. It will only take you a few minutes. She lives in town; I got her address from Ned in case we want to use her again sometime."

"Okay," I said. "Just hurry it up. I'm damned tired, I'm half drunk, and I want to get to bed."

"She'll be out in a minute," Marta said.

She stepped out of the car and closed the door and walked up to the porch. There was a light over the door, and for a second, as she stopped and turned the key in the lock, she looked back toward the car. And then the door closed behind her.

It was the last time I ever saw her.

# 2

"You turn at the next corner and go two and a half blocks. It's the apartment house on the lefthand side of the street. And may I have a cigarette, please?"

It was no longer a sexy voice; it was neutral and distant and she could have been talking to a cab driver.

It was a welcome interruption to the trend of my thoughts. I needed the interruption; my thoughts were not pleasant.

"Aren't you a little young to be smoking?" I asked, not really thinking or caring about what I was saying.

"I'm seventeen. I've been smoking for a long time."

I smiled. "Who am I to interfere with the habits of a lifetime?" I said. "Certainly you can have a cigarette."

I took one hand from the wheel and began a search of my pockets, and when I failed to find a pack in either my coat or trouser pocket, I switched hands and tried the other side.

"I'm sorry," I said. "I seem to be out."

There was a movement and she reached forward and opened the glove compartment. A moment later she said, "Your friend is thoughtful. May I light you one, too? And he keeps something besides cigarettes for an emergency."

A second later and she had flicked a match. I could catch her profile out of the corner of my eye as she lighted first one and then a second cigarette. I felt her hand brush the side of my face as she said, "Open your mouth."

I turned the corner, and by the time I had taken several puffs I saw the apartment house ahead and to the left. It was the only one in the block.

I drew up in front of the marquee which led from the door to the sidewalk and pushed on the brake. I didn't cut either the lights or the ignition.

"You don't talk very much," she said. She made no move to get out of the car.

"I haven't very much to talk about," I said. "I haven't had a particularly happy evening."

"I haven't either," she said and she laughed under her breath. Again I sensed her movement and again the glove compartment flipped open.

"Can you take it without a chaser?" she asked.

For some reason I wasn't startled. I wasn't even surprised.

"Another lifetime habit?" I asked.

"I have all sorts of interesting habits," she said. "And if you insist on a chaser, you may come up with me. I have some soda in the icebox. "

"Listen," I began. And then I too laughed. "You are a sort of odd babysitter," I said.

"I'm an odd baby," she said. "But let's not go into that. I asked you about chasers."

"You know," I said, "I must be a little bit out of my mind."

I reached for the ignition key and twisted it.

"I'll walk you to the door," I said. "I have a feeling your mother and father wouldn't quite approve of you pouring chasers for middle-aged men in the middle of the night."

"My mother and father couldn't care less. They're dead. And your son told me you are thirty-eight, which is hardly middle-aged," she said. "He doesn't like you."

"Who doesn't like me?"

"Your son. Neither does your daughter."

I laughed, not pleasantly. "No one likes me," I said.

"After an evening with your children, that sounds like a recommendation. Anyway, I don't want to sit here talking. You may come up or not, whatever you wish. I'm going inside."

The bottle she had taken from the glove compartment fell on the seat between us and the door opened and she moved to get out of the car.

I picked up the bottle and stepped to the street. Neither of us spoke as I followed her into the lobby of the building.

It was a run-down, rather shoddy apartment house with a small, dingy lobby, badly lighted. There was no elevator and we walked up three flights of stairs and she took a key and opened a door and flicked on a light and stepped aside, waving me in past her with a slight, enigmatic smile.

"Make yourself at home," she said, at the same time reaching out and taking the bottle from my hand. "I'll pour you a drink. I'm going to make myself a sandwich. Would you like one?"

I shook my head, not so much in answer to her question, but to sort of clear my mind. The situation was beginning to strike me as not only a little ridiculous but just a little unbelievable.

"You know," I said, "I'm beginning to feel like a character in a Françoise Sagan novel."

"I don't read much," she said. She turned and walked toward a closed door at the end of the small square room. "I'll only be a minute or two."

The door closed behind her.

For a moment I just stood there. I felt a bit dizzy and thought it was probably because I was very tired and had been drinking too much. And then again I shook my head to bring myself to and I turned and reached for the doorknob.

I had enough damned problems. The caprices of impetuous children who like to play parlor games were a little beyond my scope at the moment.

I started to open the door and the thought of returning home and crawling into my narrow twin bed for a restless, sleepless night suddenly seemed overwhelmingly depressing.

The door was half open when I changed my mind.

The hell with it. A drink was what I needed. A drink and a few minutes outside of myself and my own thoughts.

I closed the door softly. But at least, at that time anyway, I hadn't completely taken leave of my senses. My hand reached down and pushed in the button so that the door didn't relock on itself. I guess I am instinctively cautious. This child might like to play games to amuse herself, but sitting around a teenager's apartment drinking whiskey in the middle of the night behind a locked door didn't strike me as a very brilliant idea.

While she was gone I sat at one end of the couch, which faced the false fireplace, and I looked around the room. It was completely without character, one of those sterile, furnished apartments designed to be rented by the week. There were two upholstered chairs, a small low table in front of the couch, a faded rug on the parquet floor. Moth-eaten drapes covered the three windows and the venetian blinds behind them had been drawn. A couple of second-rate reproductions of bad oil paintings hung on the wall. A portable phonograph stood on top of a seventeen-inch, television set in one corner. There were no magazines or books, no personal possessions of any sort which might give an indication as to the type of person who lived in the place. The room was as bleak and burned out as I was feeling at that particular moment.

When she returned she was carrying a round plastic tray. She set it on the low table in front of the couch and then flopped down at the other end. I looked at the tray. It contained a bowl of mixed nuts, three white-bread sandwiches which I seemed to know were made of peanut butter, an eight-ounce glass containing a single ice cube and what from its deep amber tone must have been three quarters whiskey and a quarter soda, and an equal-sized glass of milk.

I guess it was the peanut butter sandwiches and that glass of milk which made me realize again how young she was.

She's a baby, I thought. Perhaps she's trying to be sophisticated, and perhaps she's playing games. But it doesn't really matter. She is just a little girl who is probably on her own for the first time in her life and she's lonely and unhappy and she wants somebody to be with her and talk to her and be nice to her.

I'm lonely myself. I want someone to be with and to talk to and be nice to me.

She reached for a sandwich with one hand and the milk with the other and said, "Grab."

I reached for the drink.

She ate two sandwiches and drank the milk and then, when I told her I wasn't really hungry, she devoured the last sandwich. She said, "I know all about you. Your children told me."

I turned toward her and smiled. "They must have been a lot more talkative with you than they are with me," I said. "But tell me, who are you? What do you do? How do you happen to be living here alone?"

Her forehead wrinkled and she pouted. "I don't like personal questions," she said. "I'll get you another drink if you like and you can find a couple of records and put them on the phonograph. Not voices. Dance music."

I looked toward the door, unconsciously. "Isn't it a little late?" I began, but she interrupted me, at the same time standing up and taking the empty glass from my hand.

"The only thing this grim little place has to offer is privacy," she said. "The kind of people who live here don't care if you shoot off fireworks."

She started for what I assumed must be the kitchen, but halfway across the room she stopped and turned.

"Take off your jacket and be comfortable," she said. "Is your friend's whiskey any good?"

"All whiskey is good," I said. "But am I keeping you up? Perhaps I should be going."

"You're not keeping me up. You can go of course if you want to. But you don't have to. I like to stay up myself. I don't like to be alone."

"I don't like to be alone either," I said. "Don't make the drink quite so strong. And you're a very nice girl."

"You're a very nice man," she said. She didn't close the door behind her this time and a moment later I heard the gurgle of liquid as she poured a drink from the bottle.

I crossed over to the phonograph. There were a half-dozen records already on the machine and I lifted them up on the automatic player device and turned it on, not bothering to look at what I was playing.

She carried the drink back and handed it to me and then, without saying anything, turned and left the room again. I heard a door open and close and I slumped back on the couch.

I was almost through with the drink when she returned.

She had changed her clothes and she was wearing a pair of orange slacks and had twisted something which looked like a bandana scarf over the upper part of her body so that it covered her breasts. Her stomach was bare and so were her feet and she had tied her hair back with a red ribbon.

She walked toward the couch and it suddenly occurred to me that

I must be drunk. I could have been given twenty years at hard labor for the thing I was thinking.

"You drink them fast," she said. "I'll get you another, but first, will you dance with me?"

I stood up, weaving a little. "I'm the world's worst dancer," I said.

"I'll teach you," she said.

She came over and held out her arms and looked up into my face. "Come on."

The record was almost over, and for about a minute and a half we danced in a small circle. I must have moved like a zombie. There was an unreal, dreamlike quality about the entire thing. My feet moved automatically and I didn't seem to understand what I was doing.

The music stopped and we stopped and stood there, her body close to mine, one small hand in my hand, the other on my shoulder. My right arm was around her waist and my right hand was pressed against the bare flesh of her body, just above the band of her orange slacks.

She was looking up into my face and her eyes were wide and her lips slightly parted.

I leaned down and kissed her.

Her mouth opened slightly and there was a sudden pressure and I felt the muscles of my body go tense. I dropped her hand and my other arm began to circle her and then suddenly she moved and in a second she was out of my arms and had stepped away. Her face had a gamin expression and she made a small noise, like a half-laugh.

"Your name is Conrad Madden, you're thirty-eight years old, you were in the Marines, you're looking for a job, your children don't like you, and your wife doesn't understand you," she said.

I stared at her.

"You're lonely and unhappy and the reason you don't go home isn't because of me but it is because you really have no home to go to. I'm going to get you another drink."

She turned and picked up my empty glass.

I said, "For God's sake."

"You've probably forgotten," she said, "but I'm Allison O'Connor. Call me Allie if you like."

I was on the couch again, wiping my face with a handkerchief, wondering if I was having some sort of dream, when she came back with the drink.

I started to say something, to mumble something about being sorry, thinking about having kissed her, and I guess she knew what I was trying to say.

"There's nothing wrong with your kissing me," she said. "I'm old enough to know what I'm doing. And you kiss nicely."

She handed me the drink and I carefully took it and laid it on the table and then I reached for her.

I know that I never did finish that third drink Allie poured for me because it was still sitting there in the glass on the table the next morning. I did, however, finish the rest of the whiskey in the bottle she had taken from the glove compartment of Ned Medow's car. The empty bottle was on the floor at the edge of the three-quarter-sized bed in the tiny bedroom off the living room when I woke up. There was a second empty pint bottle several feet away. I have no memory of the second bottle at all and only the vaguest sort of memory of having finished the first. I have no memory of how I got into the bedroom or of anything that took place after I did.

I do remember what happened after I placed the third glass, untouched, on the table in front of the couch. I remember every single ecstatic moment.

I know that sometime before daylight I left her and half staggered into the kitchen, drained and exhausted and no longer capable of feeling or thinking.

I know that I took a drink of straight whiskey from the bottle and I recall having turned and started back for the living room with some vague idea of gathering up my clothes and gathering up what fragments of sense I might have left. I must have fallen somewhere between the door of the room and the couch.

I didn't want to open my eyes. I wanted nothing but to escape the agony of my splitting head, of my aching limbs.

I could feel the sun on my cheek and I realized in a vague way that I was lying on a bed. Gradually it came to me that I must face whatever there was to face. Try as I might, I was no longer able to drift back into sleep and forgetfulness. But I still wouldn't open my eyes.

My hand, lying at my side, quivered, and I moved my fingers and then I felt the soft touch of flesh.

Lips gently brushed my lips and I opened my eyes and I looked into Allie's face as she leaned over me. I started to reach for her and the pain shot across my eyes and I dropped back on the bed and groaned. "Don't try to move," she said. "I'm bringing you coffee."

I waited until she returned before I again opened my eyes.

She put her hand under my shoulders and helped me sit up.

She held the mug of black coffee in one hand. She was fully dressed and she looked fresh and lovely and utterly beautiful. The blood began to pound in my head and I had to take my eyes away from her. She held the cup to my lips and I began to choke, but then made a supreme effort and swallowed several mouthfuls.

I pulled the sheet across me as I finally twisted my legs and sat on the side of the bed.

I said, "Oh, God."

"Don't try to get up," she said. "Can you handle a cigarette?"

I nodded and she moved away and I heard the scratch of a match. I lifted my head when she came back and she handed me the cigarette.

The sun was streaming through the venetian blinds.

"How are you feeling?"

I groaned.

"Are you able to understand me?"

I nodded.

"I have to talk to you," she said. "We haven't much time."

I tried to understand her.

"I'll get another cup of coffee," she said.

It must have been ten minutes later and after the second cup of coffee before I really began to come to.

She was sitting next to me on the bed now, lighting me another cigarette. I was far from a well man, but I was awake and could follow her.

"You must have hit your head when you fell," she said.

I nodded dumbly.

"I had a hard time getting you in here. But I managed. Anyway, all that doesn't matter now."

Nothing mattered now as far as I was concerned.

"Do you remember anything at all that happened—well, that happened after you went to the kitchen? I got you in here and you sort of half came to and you finished the bottle and then you finished the pint I gave you, but you were very tight and you didn't seem to know what you were doing. You finally passed out," she said.

"I drank the rest of the bottle?"

She looked down at the floor and I followed her eyes and that was when I noticed the empty fifth and the empty pint.

"You don't remember anything?"

I shook my head.

"I'm afraid I've some news for you."

I looked up at her.

"I have some for you," I said. "You're marvelous and I think I love you."

She smiled. "Tell me later. What I have won't keep."

"What you have," I began, but she quickly interrupted me.

"Try to come to," she said. "We don't have much time."

I suddenly became aware of the urgency in her voice.

I suddenly realized that she was being very serious, that …

"We've had visitors," she said.

This time I didn't have to pretend an interest. I looked up quickly.

"Your wife was here. You must have left the door unlocked. Anyway, about the time you passed out, while I was getting you under the covers, she came."

I sighed. I wish I could have felt what I was supposed to feel, but for some reason I didn't. All I felt was a sense of utter weariness.

"That was great," I said.

"She asked me to give you a message when you woke up." I nodded. There was no answer to that. "She said to tell you not to bother to come home. She would send your clothes when you wrote and told her your new address."

I didn't say anything.

"Do you care?" Allie asked.

"No," I said. "No, I don't think I care."

"That is that then," Allie said.

Again I looked at her. "You said visitors. Was someone with her? Who was it?"

"She was alone," Allie said. "The other visitor is in the next room. He came after your wife left, just after daybreak, and he let himself in with his own key. He's still here."

For a moment I just stared at her and then for the third time I said, "Oh, God."

I started to look around the room, I guess with some idea of finding my clothes. Perhaps I should have been frightened, I don't know. It still wasn't quite clear to me. I do know the thought crossed my mind that maybe it was her father, but then I remembered she had said her father was dead. A guardian? A …

I moved as though I had been bitten by a snake.

*"He had his own key."*

That's what she had said. Whatever color I had left must have drained from my face. I am no bigger a coward than the average man. I don't believe, but I do know that, in spite of myself, I was shaking as I started to my feet. His own key? I guess the bravest man is a coward if he finds himself sitting on the edge of a bed, stark naked, and is suddenly confronted with the thought of facing a man he has just finished cuckolding.

Quickly she reached up and took me by the arm and pulled me back.

"Sit down. Listen to me," she said.

I started to open my mouth but she put her hand over my lips.

"He's on the couch in the other room," she said in a soft voice. "But he won't bother us."

Apparently I was still having some sort of wild, impossible dream.

"Come on," she said. She started to pull at my arm and I came to my feet, automatically taking the sheet from the bed and wrapping it around me.

I looked down at her as though she were demented.

"I said he won't bother us," she repeated.

I was beyond thinking by this time. Beyond caring, I guess. I followed as she pulled me toward the door.

She opened the door and stepped back and sort of half pushed me. I stepped into the living room and slowly looked over at the couch. God only knew what I expected to see.

A second later I choked on the scream which began to form at the base of my throat. I forced myself to look again.

Somehow the sheet slipped, and I was stark naked as I stepped into the room and moved slowly toward the couch.

She was right. We had a second visitor and he was still there.

He was a medium-sized, dark-haired man and he wore a pin-striped blue suit, a white shirt, and a hand-painted necktie. He had patent leather shoes on tiny feet. He wore black silk socks with clocks. He was bareheaded and he needed a shave. He wore a large diamond ring on the third finger of his right hand.

I am very observant.

He wore the handle of a butcher knife just below the rib cage in the center of his body.

His brown eyes were wide open and he was looking directly at me but he was not seeing me. He was quite dead.

Allie passed me and she was carrying the sheet which I had dropped to the floor. She moved to the couch and draped the sheet over the man's body.

"His need is greater than yours," she said, and laughed.

I dropped into one of the upholstered chairs. I said, "Oh, God."

It was becoming a habit.

We were in the kitchen and the door was closed. I was fully dressed. She sat at the table drinking a glass of milk and munching a piece of toast while I leaned against the sink and consumed my fifth cup of coffee.

"His name is Patty Donovan, or at least that's what he called himself," she said. "I don't want to shock you, but I was his girlfriend. He paid the rent on this apartment."

"Nothing can shock me anymore," I said. It was a lie. The thought of anyone's having been her boyfriend, anyone's having paid rent on her apartment, shocked me. It upset me as much as thinking about the body lying under the sheet in the next room.

"We had split up. At least I had told him I was through with him and that I didn't want to see him again. I had forgotten that he still had the key."

I reached for the coffee and said nothing.

"It must have been a few minutes after your wife was here and left that he came. I didn't hear the door open. I was in the kitchen."

"You were in the kitchen," I said, meaninglessly.

"Yes. I heard the door when he opened it. He came in and looked around he called my name. I didn't answer. He went into the bedroom."

It still wasn't making sense but I tried to follow her. "He came into the bedroom."

"Yes. He turned on the light and then he saw you. He didn't move for several minutes, just stood there and looked at you. And then he reached into his pocket and took out his switchblade knife. He started to move toward the bed. I knew what he was going to do."

"You knew?"

"Yes, I knew. You see, I told you I had been his girlfriend. I had known him for less than a year, but had been going with a boy—a sailor—when Patty first met me. The sailor and I were engaged."

"What happened to the sailor?"

"Patty sliced him to ribbons. He's dead. Patty did it because he said that he was in love with me and wanted me to live with him. This boy, the sailor, objected and Patty cut him to pieces."

"And you think ..."

"I know. That's why I did what I did. The kitchen knife was lying on the table here and I had to move fast. He turned when he heard me enter the bedroom. He was very quick, but he wasn't quite quick enough."

"How did he get into the living room?" I asked.

"He tried to follow me as I backed out after I stabbed him. He got as far as the couch and then he dropped."

I still felt that I was having a nightmare. I felt that the whole thing was some weird alcoholic dream and that I would probably wake up any minute.

I stood up. I started for the living room. "Where are you going?"

"I'm going to call the police," I said.

She moved, standing in front of me. "If I hadn't done what I did," she said, "he would have killed you. Like he did the sailor."

I sat down again.

It took me a couple of minutes before I thought it out.

"Listen," I said, "we have to call the police. Where is the switchblade knife now?"

She shook her head. "It's in the dresser in the bedroom. But we can't tell the police."

"I know it will be tough," I said, "but we have to. We can't just ..."

"You don't understand," Allie said. "I have told you what happened. If I hadn't killed him he would have killed you. But do you think the police will believe it?"

"Why shouldn't they believe it?"

Allie laughed, but there was no mirth in the laughter.

"You didn't understand me. I told you that he was my boyfriend, that he paid the rent on this apartment. Call the police and you know what they will think? Not only think, but prove. He comes home and finds you here. In my bed, naked. And ..."

"Nobody can prove I was in your bed. No one ..."

"You are forgetting your wife," Allie said.

"But, dear God, do you think that Marta would ..."

"I think she would like to see you in hell and me along with you. But what she wants is not the answer. Patty is dead, stabbed to death. Killed in what, as far as the record is concerned, is his own apartment. The one he's been paying the rent on. You and I both will be as good as in the electric chair if the police come here and find him—and us."

"You better pour me another cup of coffee," I said.

She poured us each one.

"Tell me something more about him," I said. "Who was he? What did he do? How long …?"

"Patty was a bagman."

I looked at her blankly.

"A collector," she said. "You know, like a bookmaker. Only it was his job to go around to all the runners and poolrooms and places and pick up the money at the end of each day. He covered most of Connecticut and some of Westchester. I guess you could call him a racket guy."

"In that case, the police …"

"I've told you, we can't call the police."

I thought for several minutes. "Then just what …?"

"We've got to get out of here. Got to run."

I stood up and shook my head. "Listen," I said. "Listen to me. A few things you don't understand. If we run we have no chance. Sooner or later they are bound to get us. Running just establishes guilt. Anyway, let me explain something."

I reached down and pulled my trouser pocket out.

"I have, at the most, about three dollars and twenty-five cents. I haven't a dime in the bank, and although Marta may have as much as two or three hundred dollars, I don't quite believe she is in a mood to finance a getaway for us, if that is what you call it. If you were babysitting for a few bucks last night, I rather doubt that you have any money to speak of. So even if it were practical, just how do you think it would be possible to run?"

She looked at me and suddenly she smiled. I didn't see anything to smile about.

Without speaking she crossed the room, passing in front of me, and entered the living room. She went into the bedroom. When she came back she was carrying a briefcase. I said nothing and watched her.

She came to the kitchen table and laid the briefcase on its side and pulled open the zipper. The two halves fell apart.

"Don't bother to count it," Allie said. "I already have. It comes to something over sixteen thousand dollars."

It was an effort, but I avoided repeating my most recently acquired phrase.

Allie pushed the briefcase to one side and moved over and stood in front of me.

"We haven't very much time," she said. "I'm not too worried about the police—at least yet. But Patty's boss is going to be a little worried when he doesn't show up. We do have time, however, for you to kiss me before we leave."

**3**

I have long been aware that a bad hangover can act as an aphrodisiac. I know that, contrary to all sense and medical logic, a man may wake up exhausted by his night's labors, weak and shattered and with his nerve endings raw and jangling, and turn to a woman and want her with an almost unbearable desire. If you add fear and near panic, it merely increases the momentum of passion. I don't know what the chemical explanation of this may be. I only know that for long moments we were locked together and that my hands reached under the short sweater she was wearing and I was holding her small firm breasts and that I had pressed her back and across the table and …

There was no dead man in the next room, no sixteen thousand dollars in bills on the table, no police, nothing.

Just Allie.

I don't believe either of us heard the key turn in the lock of the apartment door; I am sure neither of us heard it open and close and the footsteps crossing the living room. It was only when the voice spoke, a couple of feet away from me, that I became aware of the intruder.

"Well, I'll be damned!"

My hands dropped and I stepped back, swinging around. Fear? Perhaps. I am inclined to think it was more a feeling of anger and frustration.

I swung around and there was Ned Medows, standing in the doorway of the kitchen, his blubbery mouth open and his chin wobbly. His hat was tipped back and his bloodshot eyes were wide with shock and surprise. For some reason or other, I noticed that he still held a brass door key in his hand.

We stared at each other for an endless time, neither one moving, neither one able to say a word.

It was Allie who broke the spell.

"Hello, Ned," she said.

*Hello, Ned*. No surprise. No shock. No embarrassment. Just *Hello, Ned*. You might have thought they were meeting unexpectedly at the supermarket or a PTA meeting.

I must hand it to Medows, whom I have never considered particularly bright and certainly not very fast on his feet. He was the first to recover.

He shook his fat head from side to side and he slyly smiled. An unpleasant, suggestive sort of smile.

"Well, well, well," he said. "I wouldn't have believed it." He hesitated and then stepped into the kitchen. "Conrad Madden, of all people."

I said, "What the hell are you doing here?"

Again he shook his head, an expression of fraudulent sorrow on his porcine face.

"Why, I came for the car," he said. "Stopped by your house and Marta"—he hesitated and actually winked at me—"Marta is burning up, by the way. Anyway, she said I would find the car here. She didn't tell me that you would be here, too. But the way she was acting, I might have guessed."

He looked past me, at Allie. "You work fast, baby," he said.

I started to take a step forward, my hands clenching.

"Now take it easy, Con," he said quickly, stepping back. "Take it easy. No hard feelings. Hell, we're both men of the world, aren't we? If anyone should be sore ..."

"How did you get that key?"

Allie spoke before he could answer. "He must have taken it when he came to pick me up last night. I had an extra one lying on the table and he must have ..."

He turned to her, a baffled look in his eyes. "Oh now, kitten," he said. "You know ..."

I suddenly remembered the dead man, sitting there in the next room, not ten feet away. A dead man with a sheet tossed over him.

My eyes instinctively went past Ned and I could see the outline of his figure. The sheet didn't completely cover him. A pair of ankles and two patent leather shoes protruded beneath that sheet.

I know that Ned must have come in, spotted us in the kitchen, and passed the couch without ever seeing it.

"You came for the car," I said harshly. "All right. It's down in front of the house. Take it and get the hell out of here."

"Now, Con," he began, in that phony salesman's voice of his, and then he suddenly stopped. I saw his oyster eyes widen and again his loose mouth dropped open.

I followed the direction of his eyes, turning.

He had seen the money scattered across the table. Instinctively he took a step forward.

"I said take your damned car and get out of here," I repeated.

He hesitated, looking at me with a sudden odd cunning. "You took the keys," he said. "They weren't in the car. That's why I came up."

But his eyes were still on the money.

I reached into my pockets and found his car keys. I held them out and when he made no move to take them, I spoke.

"For the last time," I said, "get out. Here are your keys. Now take them and get the hell away from here."

"Well, say," he began, backing away a step or two. "Say, maybe we can talk this over, chum. I come in here and find you with my girl and you start ordering me ..."

"You fat bastard," Allie said, "I am not your girl." She turned to me. "Throw him out," she said.

I moved fast, reaching out and grabbing him by the shoulders and swinging him around.

"You heard her. Out!"

I started to propel him to the door and I think I might have done it—gotten away with it—if I hadn't been careless, if I hadn't moved quite so swiftly. I had thought that I might get him through that living room and to the door and slam it behind him, tossing his keys out after him, and in the excitement of the moment he wouldn't see that sheet and what was under it. But I moved too fast.

As we passed in front of the couch, hands on his arms as I propelled him forward, I moved too close to the couch and his feet came into contact with those legs hanging out from under the sheet. Even then I don't think he would have noticed—if it hadn't been that he reached down to save himself from falling and his hand fell on the sheet and he clutched it.

He righted himself, the sheet still in his hand, and he turned just in time to see the sheet slide to the floor, exposing the body beneath it. He stood petrified for a split second, and then he pushed me violently away from him.

"The police will be interested in this," he said.

He began edging himself to the door, staring at me, white-faced. "You might think you can push me around, Madden, but I think the police will have something to say about this. I think it's time …"

I jerked his body around, pulling back my right arm, my fist doubled. I had to stop him.

But my fist never reached his jaw.

Even as I held him up with one hand, setting him up to knock him out, I caught the movement out of the corner of my eye. It's lucky I did. It saved his life.

Instinctively I pushed him, from me and the triangular flatiron, instead of crushing in the back of his skull, caught him a glancing blow on the side of his head. It made a sickening hollow sound and he began to slump.

"I'll kill him," she was saying and the small hand which had not released the iron was raising again and I knew that this time she wouldn't miss.

It took all of my strength to wrestle her across the room, to take the blood-smeared flatiron out of her hand. For a moment or so, after I had got it away from her and was holding her pinned to the wall by both arms, her blue eyes stared up into mine and there was a mad, unseeing quality to them.

And then, suddenly, the tension went out of her. "You're hurting my arms," she said. The words came out in a little girl's perplexed and slightly hurt voice.

I dropped my hands and stood back. "You could have killed him," I said.

She nodded. "I wanted to," she said. She looked up at me wide-eyed. "We have to get out of here now," she said.

She noticed the way I was looking at her. She pouted and her voice was defensive as she spoke. "He was going to call the police and I had to stop him. Don't you understand? It was for you, too. I had to stop him. It was him or us."

"I would have stopped him," I said.

I had crossed the room and was learning over him.

Blood was seeping out of his right ear. I felt his pulse and the beat was steady.

"He's alive," I said. "You may have fractured his skull."

She was still standing against the wall. "Let's get out of here," she said.

"And just leave him here like this?" I asked, turning to her.

"Leave them both," she said. "Get the money and take the keys. We won't have much more time."

For a moment I hesitated. My eyes went back to Ned Medows. He was unconscious but he was breathing regularly. It had been a nasty blow, but I didn't believe it would be fatal. On the other hand, if we stayed there and waited while I called a doctor, it could very well be fatal—for us.

Allie could have been telling the truth. Perhaps she had stabbed that man whose body slumped on the couch in an effort to save my life. Perhaps when she'd lifted the flatiron to strike Medows she had believed it was the only way to give us time to get away.

I wasn't thinking too clearly; too many things had happened too quickly. But one thing I did understand. If I were to cut and run now, I would be ruining any chance I might have of clearing myself.

I had killed no one. I had attacked no one. I had stolen no money. I had slept with a girl and I had probably destroyed the last bonds between me and my family. But I was not a criminal. Not wanted. I was broke and out of a job and had a hangover and that was about it. Nothing had changed from yesterday or any other day.

I had lost Marta, but hadn't I lost her a long time ago?

Why should I run? Because Allie wanted me to?

"We had better take his car," Allie said. "At least until we get away from here. I think New York would be best. A hotel somewhere until we have a chance to make plans."

She was watching me and her face held an expression of complete confidence. It was the first time in a long while that anyone had looked at me with confidence. Her expression seemed to be saying, "See, I have done what I had to do for you and now you will help me and take care of me."

I went into the kitchen and started to put the money into the briefcase.

When I returned Allie was packing an overnight bag, and I vaguely thought about fingerprints and things like that, but I quickly dismissed the idea of attempting to cover up any traces of my having been there. Marta had seen me; Medows had seen me and he would undoubtedly live and talk.

There was no covering up, no room for anything but running—

losing ourselves for once and for all.

We left the apartment ten minutes later, after I had found the keys to his car where they had fallen on the floor. We left the place just as it was, locking the door after us. She was dressed in a tailored suit and wore a pair of dark glasses. They made her look a little less like a child. She carried the briefcase with the money and I carried the overnight bag. I had washed up and combed my hair, but I needed a shave. My clothes were wrinkled and I felt like a tramp.

We climbed into Ned Medows' car and the engine started when I turned the ignition key. I was about to pull away from the curb when I heard a gasp at my side. I turned and as I did Allie slid low in the seat, putting one hand up to conceal her face.

"Hurry," she said.

I was aware of the white Cadillac pulling up at the curb on the other side of the street as I pushed the throttle down. There was a man wearing tinted glasses at the wheel, but he was not looking in our direction.

I started to say something, to ask her something, but she slumped lower and spoke urgently.

"Hurry."

We drove to New York, as Allie suggested, but from then on I took over, using every variety of cover-up technique I had ever read about. We didn't check into a hotel.

The first thing we did, after leaving the Merritt Parkway and entering the Bronx, was to get rid of Ned Medows' car. I took it to a garage and said I wanted to put it in dead storage for a month. I paid the rent in advance and left the keys. I gave a name and address picked at random.

We took the subway into Midtown and I had Allie go to a department store and buy a hat and a pair of high-heeled shoes. I didn't want her looking like a teenager. While she was doing this I found a barbershop and had a haircut and a shave. Later, in the bus station, I took the hair dye which Allie had purchased and went into a private toilet. When I came out I no longer had red hair; I had a jet-black crew cut.

We took the same bus, going south, but we bought our tickets separately. My destination was Washington and Allie's was Richmond, Virginia. We sat in separate seats but we both left the bus in Philadelphia.

We took the plane to Baltimore, again buying our seats separately and again not sitting together. The taxi driver who drove us into the city from the airport was a real smart cookie. An operator. I'd picked him by his appearance.

The minute I gave him the ten-dollar bill, over and above his fare, he understood. He knew exactly what we were doing, what I wanted. He smiled, very knowingly, when I told him the name was Smith.

"The kind of hotel," I said, "where the Missus and I can check in and well, you know ..."

Yes, he knew. Not exactly a fleabag, but certainly not a place where a Mr. and Mrs. John Smith on the blotter would look odd. I had hoped he would think she was just some young girl I had picked up on the plane, but I think he believed she was a professional hooker. With the orange makeup, the phony eyelashes, and the purple lipstick, she certainly looked like one.

The clerk at the desk had a mind which must have come out of the same mold. Fifteen a night for the room and bath and I was surprised that it was as clean as it was. Worth at least eight.

Allie and I went down the City Hall, to fill out the forms. We had to start somewhere. You can't have an identity unless you begin some place.

A marriage license is the best place to begin. For some reason or other, a marriage license is just about the only official document you can get without previously established identification. I guess it has never occurred to the officials who handle such things that anyone would go to the trouble of getting a phony marriage license. Certainly not anyone who looks like Allie.

We will have to wait twenty-four hours before the ceremony, of course. After that, the driver's license which will take two or three days. And then the car, and the registration.

Mr. and Mrs. Gerald Mahon will be leaving Baltimore on their honeymoon by the end of the week, if all goes well.


Thursday afternoon. March fifth. Six-thirty. Allie and I were married less than four hours ago, in a simple, utterly undignified ceremony at City Hall. A court clerk handled the thing. We are now legally Mr. and Mrs. Gerald Mahon. We have checked into a different hotel, in the heart of the city. A very respectable hotel. We have the bridal suite and it's costing thirty-eight dollars a day. The marriage certificate is lying on the long library table in the sitting room. It is a two-room-and-bath suite with a small closet-kitchenette. The luggage, good solid stuff even though secondhand and purchased from a hock shop, is stacked in the larger of the closets.

The dresser drawers are loaded with the clothes we have purchased.

Next to the marriage certificate are the papers from the Motor Vehicle Bureau, and Allie and I both—separately, of course—took our driving tests right after the marriage ceremony.

The New York and local newspapers are lying scattered on the floor at my feet. They all carry stories about what the police found in Stamford, Connecticut, the New York tabs giving a pretty comprehensive account and the local papers using condensed wire-service stories.

It makes very vivid reading.

Allie is in the bedroom, lying naked on the large double bed with a thin percale sheet over her. She is sleeping, or pretending to sleep. I will awaken her in another hour and we will call room service and have dinner sent up.

I am sitting in a pair of shorts and drinking a Scotch and soda and there is a tray with a bowl of cracked ice, a couple of unopened bottles of soda, and the remains of the Scotch at my elbow.

I have just left Allie and I am thinking about her.

I have come to a number of conclusions. The one which worries me the least is that I am, without doubt, out of my mind.

Allie, beyond question, is a congenital liar. She is, also, a murderess and a thief. She killed Donovan in cold blood. She would have murdered Ned Medows had I not stopped her. She would have murdered him for no reason at all, but she had a very good reason for killing Donovan.

She wanted his sixteen thousand dollars.

I completely discount her story that he was going to cut me up with a switchblade knife. I doubt if he even carried a switchblade knife. I don't believe he killed her ex-lover. I don't even think that there was a sailor or that there was a word of truth in her story.

Ned Medows had a key to her apartment and I don't think he picked it up when he arrived to bring her to our house to babysit. I think she gave it to him.

I don't think it was an accident that I spent the first night in her bed. I think she planned it at the very moment she climbed in Medows' car to have me drive her home.

I have no proof of any of this, but I know that I'm right.

The reason I say I'm probably insane is that I don't care. It doesn't mean one damned thing to me. The only thing which means anything is Allie herself, lying there naked under the sheet in the double bed in the next room.

I can see the outlines of her body, under the sheet, if I lean slightly forward in my chair. I know all about that body. She might just as well not have covered herself.

She is a child and she is also a woman. A full, ripe, and complete woman. She may be seventeen, as she says, or she may be younger or older. I don't know; I don't care. All I know is that she is completely lovely, intolerably desirable. And that she is mine.

She knows nothing and she knows everything. She knows things which it could take a lifetime to learn. They may be instinctive and they may be the results of God only knows what previous encounters with men and reality. About this I do not care. I am only aware of what she is, what she can do, how she can drive the blood coursing through my veins.

I know her lips and her mouth, her small shell ears, her slender soft throat, her firm breasts, and all of the secret places of her body. I know that as long as she is with me I am able to find something I have never found in anyone else and something I didn't believe really existed. Whatever it is, I want it and I will go on taking it for as long as I can.

Even the jealousy I have felt, when I have thought of what she has been and what she has done, when I have thought of that sleek gangster Donovan, the fat, sensuous, vulgar Medows, or any of those others who may or may not have known her—even the jealousy is meaningless when I have her.

If she lies, she lies like a child—without thought and almost without meaning. I believe that she is able to believe her own lies, at least while she is telling them. She has no guile, no sense of deceit. She merely does what is convenient to do at the time, tells the story which is suited to the occasion.

One thing she is unable to lie about. She cannot possibly lie in her reactions to our lovemaking. No one could be so superb an actress.

I pour a fresh drink and my eye automatically goes back to the newspapers at my feet.

And she did tell me tell me the truth about Donovan. He paid the rent on the apartment and he was a small-time racketeer. He was well known to the police. He was, as she had said, a collector for a bookmaking syndicate. He had been arrested on minor charges a number of times, had a disreputable background. It seemed, from the accounts in the press, that he had actually lived with his mother, somewhere in the Bronx, but he had rented the Stamford apartment under his own name and installed her. The police, if the newspaper accounts could be trusted, knew nothing of her or of her background. Just her name and the fact that she was quite young.

The stories in the tabloids hinted that Donovan had dealt in girls on the side and that she was probably one of his women whom he had set up in business as a sort of extracurricular occupation. But the trail ended there.

Ned Medows had been found in the apartment, still unconscious, after the police had received an anonymous telephone call. According to the press, police had grilled him. I could well believe it. For if the police knew little or nothing about Allison, they certainly knew everything there was to know about me.

Ned had not had to lie or exaggerate. He gave a straight story. He said he had met Allie when she had applied at his office for a job. He denied, of course, having a key to her apartment, but explained about arranging for her to babysit for us. He went on to tell about lending me his car (he didn't say why, of course) and arriving to pick it up after talking with Marta.

He told of entering the apartment, saying I had answered his knock on the door. He had seen a lot of money on the table, and when he had asked about it someone had struck him. He was not sure whether it was me or the girl.

Medows was still in the hospital and the stories read as though the police would like to keep him there for a while. He wasn't in the clear by a long shot.

Marta had been questioned. One other thing Allie hadn't lied about. Marta had been in the apartment and she had seen me lying on the bed. It must have been a very trying interview for her. Marta has a lot of pride, false or otherwise but still pride. She told of my driving the girl home and then failing to return, of her coming to the apartment, finding me, and leaving. She said that I had been out of work, worried, near a nervous breakdown. It was the only logical way she could explain my conduct.

A wife apparently always feels that when her husband finds some other woman attractive enough to sleep with, he must be suffering from some form of mental disorder.

In any case, everything from this point on was sheer speculation. The tabloids hinted strongly that I had killed Donovan for his money and then kidnaped the girl. It gave the thing a sort of fillip, I guess. The more conservative papers hesitated to make conjectures, but there were hints of internal gang warfare, feuding among bookmaking syndicates. They gave me the benefit of the doubt, some of them, suggesting possibly both the girl and I had been kidnaped after Donovan had been murdered by a rival faction.

But one thing they all agreed on, the reporters and the police alike. We must be found.

For a moment I could almost feel the cold angular arms of the electric chair embracing me.

Allie woke up within the hour and she was hungry.

She wanted milk and peanut-butter-and-jelly sandwiches. She wanted to know if I could call down and arrange to have a television set brought in.

She didn't ask what we were planning to do, where we were going to go. Nothing. Just the food and the television set.

Later, while we were eating (I had managed to talk her into a steak) I tried to question her. I mentioned the white Cadillac which had been pulling in across the street as we had left in Ned Medows' car. I mentioned the man in the tinted glasses. Someone, after all, had made that anonymous call to the police.

She denied remembering anything about the incident, denied having slumped out of sight in the seat of Ned's car as we pulled away from the curb.

She did say one thing, however.

She asked me, "How long do you think the money will last?"

I shrugged. "God only knows," I said. "Certainly not forever."

"Do you think we will be going out west anywhere?" she asked.

"Possibly. Why?"

"We can get in touch with my brother," she said. "My brother is out there and he can help us. He can see that we get a lot more money—when we need it."

# 4

I realized from the beginning that the longer we were able to avoid arrest, the better our chances were for continued freedom.

I knew also that we had much in our favor. The money we had taken was, in a sense, "safe money." It wasn't as though we had robbed a bank and thereby interested insurance companies or the federal people. It didn't seem logical that the owner of the money, a bookmaking syndicate which would have to admit its illegal source, would file any complaint. When money is not involved in a criminal case, the force and enthusiasm of the chase is lessened considerably.

Then, too, the man who had been killed was a petty racketeer and no one, at least officially, cared much about his death one way or another. Donovan was no great loss to society, at best, and society was not going to go out of its way to seek revenge for his death. In time the papers would drop the story, the whole thing would die down and be forgotten.

The only official police body interested was the local Stamford police force and it had a lot more important things to do than conduct an intensive investigation into a crime which meant very little to Stamford's citizens. When influential parties have no interest in a crime, and the public at large is neither indignant nor vengeful, police themselves soon tend to forget it and go on about their daily business.

All of this, of course, certainly did not mean we could sit back and relax. I knew I must do everything humanly possible to ensure our safety. I made one positive effort, during those two weeks we spent in Baltimore, to confuse our pursuers and throw them off our trail.

I wrote Marta a long letter and then I took a plane to Chicago and mailed it from there. I returned at once to Baltimore.

It took a long time to compose that letter and I knew I must be extremely subtle. The whole point of it was not only to lead the police into thinking I was somewhere in the Midwest, but also to indicate that, instead of looking for a man and a girl fleeing together, they must look for us separately.

I started the letter by begging Marta to keep it from the authorities. I told her that, in spite of everything I had done, I still loved her. I pleaded with her to withhold her own judgment until I could explain and clear myself, at least of the things which the papers were accusing me of having done. I said that, in view of our marriage and our years together, she owed me this much. I made it so strong that I honestly believe Marta would have withheld the letter from the police. But I was also smart enough to know that the authorities would be certain to intercept the letter before it ever reached its destination.

I wrote Marta just what had happened in the Stamford apartment that night when she had found me there. I admitted I had had an affair with the girl. I did not ask forgiveness, didn't attempt to gloss it over. I wrote that I had been unhappy (and certainly Marta knew this) and that I had got drunk. I accepted the full blame for what had happened. I explained that, once I was able to clear myself of other charges, I would grant Marta a separation and even a divorce if she demanded it, but that I was living in the hopes she would find it in her heart to understand and to forgive me.

This, of course, was the most difficult part of the letter. It was hard to make it sound convincing and I had to make it sound that way if the letter was to be successful. I wanted it to sound as though the basic problem I had was readjusting my life with Marta—at some future time and place.

And then I wrote about the dead man. I told Marta I was completely innocent; I had awakened from a drunken stupor to find him there, already murdered. I said that, after Medows had come and discovered us, I had completely panicked. I said that the girl and I had left together and gone to New York, and because of my temporary fear and hysteria, I had left her and hidden out for several days. I had been on the verge of giving myself up, after reading the stories in the newspapers, when I had suddenly realized that the truth would never be believed, that in leaving the girl I had lost the only possible witness who could clear me.

I told Marta I had a clue as to where the girl might have gone after we went our separate ways in New York. She had mentioned coming from Chicago and having friends there. And now I was hoping to find her. Or hoping that the police would turn her up. But until she was found I myself must stay hidden.

Back in Baltimore three days after mailing the letter, I had reason to believe that this carefully planted clue was at least partially effective. I purchased a Chicago newspaper and there, on the front page, was a photograph of me, taken some ten years before. The accompanying caption said I was wanted in the East for questioning in a murder and that it was believed I might be in the city. There was no mention at all of Allison.

We stayed on in our honeymoon suite at the Baltimore hotel for a full two weeks. By this time the newspapers no longer mentioned the case, and I knew that the time had come to move on and to start the second stage of building up our reborn identities.

I had not wasted our time. I realized we must establish backgrounds and unquestioned identifications in case we were ever suspected, and also as a guarantee that we wouldn't be suspected. And we must change our physical appearances as much as it was possible to do so. Fortunately the authorities had only fragmentary descriptions of Allie and no photographs. They had only that one photo of myself, taken when I was in my twenties.

There wasn't much I could do about changing my own appearance, but I did what I could. I purchased a pair of heavy, horn-rimmed glasses and the optometrist to whom I went prescribed them with no suspicion when I told him that reading gave me headaches. I had already changed my haircut and dyed it and I had started to grow a mustache.

Allie, in a way, was easier to disguise. The newspapers had described her as a teenager, saying she was extraordinarily pretty. Her long, honey-colored hair and large blue eyes were mentioned and the reports said that she stood about five feet two and weighed around a hundred and ten pounds. Well, there was nothing to be done about her weight, but I added a few inches to her height with high, spike-heeled shoes. She actually stood five four and the shoes added another three and a half inches. She didn't attempt to dye her hair, but did go to a beauty parlor and had it cut short and ragged in the Continental style.

Glasses seemed out of the question as her eyes proved to have perfect 20-20 vision, but she said the sun bothered her when she drove and the optometrist made her up a pair of clear glasses, with the lenses just slightly tinted with green.

The newspapers, in describing Allison, had always referred to her as "the babysitter" and I had a pretty good idea of the popular image of a babysitter—a kid in a short skirt and a sloppy sweater and bobby socks. To get away from this image, I was very careful in the selection of her clothes. I wanted her to look like a young woman who might have come down from Vassar and taken a job as an assistant editor or researcher, or perhaps one of those smart young girls who work in obscure capacities in the larger Madison Avenue advertising agencies. Smart, almost severely styled, and obviously expensively tailored suits. That sort of thing.

I think perhaps one of the most effective touches had nothing really to do with clothes at all.

I went to a very high-class pet shop and purchased a miniature blue-gray French poodle and insisted that Allie take the dog with her whenever she appeared in public. It didn't seem to me that anyone could possibly suspect a girl with a French poodle as someone being sought as a participant in a murder case.

My theory was that, rather than seek a facade of anonymity, the trick was to be just a little on the spectacular and flamboyant side. A couple who were obviously a little conspicuous could hardly be suspected of not wanting to call attention to themselves. I felt the police theory would be that anyone hiding out would attempt to melt into and blend with the crowd. And so we would do the exact reverse.

I believe that is why, when I decided to buy the car, I purchased a white Jaguar convertible instead of buying a nondescript Chevie or Ford.

We checked out of the hotel on a Thursday, at eleven o'clock in the morning, and I must say we made a rather impressive appearance as we pulled away in the Jaguar with the top folded back. Our luggage was strapped on the trunk rack and I was bareheaded, in a tweed sports coat, behind the wheel. Allie sat next to me, holding the poodle in her lap, and he was barking madly, straining at the ornate rhinestone collar, as she held him by the plaited red leather leash. She wore the tinted glasses and a long blue scarf was knotted around her throat. She looked like a million dollars.

In my inside jacket I had the car registration and my driving license as well as the insurance policy on the car, all made out in the name of Gerald Mahon. I also had a checkbook on the Maryland Savings Bank of Baltimore, showing that I had something under fifteen hundred dollars on deposit. I had a little more than seven thousand dollars in traveler's checks in my wallet, which I had purchased in odd lots in more than two dozen places. It was far from complete and perfect identification, but at least it would do in case of a minor emergency.

Heading south on Route 301, I looked over at Allie and I knew that I had done a good job on her. She looked exactly as I had wanted her to look. The facade was perfect.

Where I planned to go and what I planned to do next, however, involved a little more than mere physical appearance. I knew that I must play a sort of Pygmalion game with Allie and already I had started on the first stages. Certain things, of course, would be impossible, at least in the beginning. I couldn't give Allie the diction and the words and phrases to fit in with her new personality overnight. It would take time. But I did what I could.

"When we're in public," I explained to her, "you must let me do most of the talking. If we're eating in restaurants or hotels I'll do the ordering. And you must forget your passion for peanut-butter-and-jelly sandwiches. From now on you are smart and sophisticated and wealthy. You've come from a good family and a good school and you must talk and act and live like it. For instance, that dog in your lap is not 'Baby Doll.' From now on call him—well, call him 'Gigi.' When we leave a place, as we left the hotel this morning, and the doorman says, 'Goodbye, Mr. Mahon,' don't you say, 'Goodbye now.' Just give him that devastating smile of yours and nod your head slightly. Don't ask bellboys to bring a pack of butts. In fact, let me do the ordering. You stay aloof and dumb. When you do talk, avoid slang, pronounce your g's at the ends of words, and …"

She leaned across the dog and her lips kissed the corner of my mouth. "Can I do this, sweetie pie?" she asked. "I thought you liked me the way I am."

"You can do that any time, but not in public, honey," I said. "And don't call me 'sweetie pie.' I do like you the way you are; I just don't want to like you behind a set of iron bars."

She pouted but I knew that she understood what I meant.

That night we stopped at a motel down in Virginia and the next morning started south again. I had picked Aiken, South Carolina, as our destination and I knew exactly what I wanted to do when we got there.

We checked into what I assumed to be the best hotel in town when we arrived. We had dinner in our room. Allie was a little restless and wanted to go out to a movie but I talked her into watching television instead. In the morning I gave her a handful of bills and told her to go shopping and to meet me back at the hotel around lunchtime.

I stopped by the manager's office and introduced myself. I asked him for the name of a good real estate agent. In the course of the conversation I let him know that I was planning on settling in the neighborhood and would eventually buy an estate somewhere outside of the town. I explained that I hoped to raise Herefords and keep a few horses and said I had in mind something with around three or four hundred acres, a nice house, and, preferably, a swimming pool.

He hinted around, attempting to find out what business I was in and where I had come from, and I indicated that I really hadn't been in any particular business but that I was living on inherited money. I explained that I had only recently been married and was looking for a place to settle down.

The manager of the hotel, who had a habit of rubbing his thumbnail across his lower teeth as he talked, reached for the telephone and in a moment was speaking to someone named Randy who appeared to be a personal friend.

Randy turned out to be Randolph Cardle, of Cardle and Cardle, Realtors, and within a few minutes I was in his office. He took it for granted that I was an old friend of the hotel manager.

"Could you give me an idea of how much you would like to spend, Mr. Mahon?" he asked, after I had explained my wants. "I don't wish to pry, but it would perhaps save us time if …"

I told him that price wasn't a factor and went into details about just what I was looking for.

He wanted to take his car, but I insisted we use the Jaguar, and we spent the next two and a half hours looking at South Carolina real estate.

Around noon he suggested we have lunch together, but I told him I had to meet my wife and asked him to join us at the hotel. He accepted.

Allie was standing in front of the hotel and Gigi, the poodle, was performing a necessary rite at the curb as we drove up. Allie had several packages under her arm.

I introduced them and Allie smiled sweetly and started to speak, but I quickly reached for her arm and squeezed it, at the same time saying, "Mrs. Mahon is just getting over a bad case of strep throat, and you must forgive her if she doesn't use her voice. The doctor has warned her not to …"

I let it die out and Cardle said something sympathetic and Allie smiled at him again. The poodle spotted a man on a bicycle and began to bark and tug at his leash, and I quickly suggested Allie take him to our room and meet us in the cocktail lounge, which doubled as a lunchroom at noontime.

Everything went along smoothly during the lunch except for one rather bad moment when I ordered sweetbreads on toast for Allie, and she gave me a startled and slightly horrified look. The only other time she showed any sign of surprise was when Cardle mentioned something about the last place he had showed me, a very fine old thousand-acre estate on which the asking price was four hundred and fifty thousand dollars. Allie began to choke on a sweetbread but she recovered. As a reward I ordered her a chocolate sundae for her dessert. As soon as we were finished I outmaneuvered Cardle in picking up the check.

I excused myself to take Allie upstairs, explaining that she must rest after lunch, according to doctor's orders. She wanted to show me her purchases when we were alone in the room, but I told her to hold it for later.

"What was all that about a half-million-dollar estate?" Allie asked. "You haven't flipped, have you?"

I kissed her. "Part of the plan," I said. "Just part of the plan. Now you be a good girl and take it easy. I'll be back later and …"

"I don't like to stay alone."

"Then go to a movie, honey," I suggested.

That afternoon I looked at half a dozen more places and found nothing which quite suited me. By four o'clock Cardle had run out of possibilities and was getting a little desperate. He had asked a hundred questions during the day, trying to pin me down as to exactly what I wanted. Once, when I had shown a little more than lukewarm interest in a place, he had mentioned that it would stand a heavy mortgage, and I knew that he was attempting to learn just how much I was really planning to spend and how much cash I might be prepared to put down. I squared him away in a hurry. "For tax reasons," I said, "I will want a mortgage. However that is not a factor. Nor is the price, although I certainly don't plan to go over three or four hundred thousand. On the other hand, if I can find what I want for a hundred or a hundred and fifty, why so much the better."

It was along about then that Cardle really began to put on the pressure. He didn't want to miss out on that kind of sale.

But by four o'clock he was through and there wasn't a thing on his list that was quite right.

I let him stew for a while and then I spoke. "The country is right," I said. "I like the town and I like the general feeling of the neighborhood. A couple of the places would seem to fill the bill but ..."

"Just which ...?" he began, but I interrupted.

"None, exactly," I said. "Are you sure that you don't have something we may have overlooked?"

He pretended to think a moment and then spoke, his voice barely escaping a note of desperation. "I am positive, Mr. Mahon," he said, "that we can satisfy you. Cardle and Cardle, after all, handle the very finest estates to be found in this area. There are a couple of places I know of which the owners might very well wish to part with and if I can have a day or so ..."

"You know," I said, as though the idea had just struck me, "instead of rushing into something and perhaps not getting exactly what I want, it might be a better idea if I stayed around for a while and sort of got the feel of things. Perhaps it might be a lot smarter if I were to rent something for a while. After all, spending several hundred thousand dollars for a permanent home is no light matter and ..."

He nodded quickly. "You are so right," he said. "Of course, renting a place is a little difficult but ..."

"I would want something on a month-to-month basis, preferably furnished," I said. "I wouldn't quibble about the rent figure if a lease could be waived, and it wouldn't have to be anything elaborate. We would, of course, like a good neighborhood, preferably near the country club, with room for servants and ..."

I let him mull it over for a while and then we went back to his office and he got on the telephone. He set up two appointments for the following morning, and before I left him that night he came to me with the question I had wanted him to ask.

"You mentioned wanting to be near the country club," he said. "I presume you like golf. I would consider it a pleasure if you would accept a guest card to my club. Just happens I'm the chairman of the greens committee and used to be president. We have a sort of rule down here that a family has to be in residence for a year before a membership may be taken out, but I think I can arrange to have the rule voided in your case. Assuming of course ..."

Well, it worked out perfectly. Five days later I had signed a month-to-month lease on a furnished, nine-room colonial, a few miles out of town and near the country club of which Cardle was a member. The price was three hundred a month, expensive for Aiken, but cheap by comparison to other localities.

Cardle had lived up to his word and maneuvered things so that I was carrying a card certifying me as a member of the country club. He had also introduced me to the president of the Southern Trust Company and I had opened a checking account for a thousand dollars, giving a check on the Baltimore bank. I had endorsed several money orders and forwarded them to Baltimore and then deposited additional checks in the Southern Trust. I had signed transfer papers to obtain South Carolina license plates for the Jag and had obtained a driver's license.

Randy Cardle, still dreaming of how he was going to spend the twenty- or thirty-thousand-dollar commission he would receive when he ultimately sold me my estate, had introduced me to just about every socially prominent person he knew and also every important businessman in town, with the exception, of course, of competing real estate agents.

Allie had an account in the principal department store. I was made a member of a couple of luncheon clubs and a very exclusive businessman's club. I was being treated like royalty.

Along about the third day Cardle introduced me to the local manager of a New York brokerage house and spent a couple of hours watching the board. I took a small flyer for a couple of thousand dollars in an electronic stock, pretending to play it very cagey, and mentioned that I was seriously thinking of getting out of steels and oils and going into chemicals. I mentioned a reluctance to pay a large capital gains tax, hinting that I had held the steel and oil securities for several years, and let the broker attempt to persuade me to make an intelligent switch.

The broker, a slab-faced man named Gainsley, got me a membership in a very expensive private bottle club and within a couple of days was introducing me around as though he had known me for years. It was he who later on made the contact with a local politician and obtained for me an honorary police lieutenant's badge.

It is a peculiar thing, but once the assumption is made that a man is rich, people are very hesitant about asking personal questions. Of course there were certain incidental things which came up that I had to be very careful about. When a school was mentioned, I casually referred to having been educated in Switzerland (I did know the name of a prep school in Zurich). There was an embarrassing moment when someone asked about the Pendennis Club in Louisville, where I had indicated I had once lived. Wanted to recall the name of whosis, who had been the steward for years. I ducked that one by having a sudden coughing fit and quickly changing the subject when I came out of it.

But, all in all, everything went smoothly, and five days after we had arrived in Aiken, Allie and I were installed in our rented house in the suburbs, and I was able to walk down the main street of the town and say good morning to a dozen persons—as though I had been living in the place for years.

It wasn't completely foolproof, of course, but I had established an identity which, barring some freak accident, certainly would be as perfect a camouflage as it would be possible to obtain on short order.

We were to spend two months in Aiken, and in many ways it was the happiest two months of my entire life.

Yes, a perfect two months. By the end of that time there was no doubt about the solidity of my identity. I performed one touch of which I was really proud. The trophy committee of the golf club solicited me for a trophy and I surprised them by purchasing a silver cup for seven hundred and fifty dollars and offering it in perpetuity, to be awarded annually to the local top scorer as the Geoffrey Mahon, Sr. Trophy, in memory of my dead father.

It was very impressive and not only served to endear me to the club membership but also to establish the fact that I *did* have a father. There was even the usual joker—a hardware wholesaler named Kelvin Green one night while half-drunk told me in the club bar that he had once met my father in Cleveland and that he had known him well and that Geoffrey Mahon, Sr. was one of the finest gentlemen that it had ever been his privilege to be acquainted with.

It could have gone on forever—but for two things.

After two months had gone by I made a quick audit of the exchequer. Allie and I had less than eight thousand dollars left, and the only reason we had this much was because that little flyer I had taken in a completely unknown stock had, to my utter amazement, tripled in value and I was able to sell out at a four-thousand-dollar profit.

I knew that eight thousand couldn't last forever. But the money alone wasn't the only reason, or even the most important one.

The second reason was Allie herself. The life I was living as a fraudulent rich playboy was exciting and interesting to me, but it had no appeal for Allie. It wasn't that she hated it or found it uncomfortable. It was worse.

It bored her to tears.

And when Allie became bored, she did something about it.

From the day we took the furnished house, Allie hated it.

"All that grass," she said, looking out of the library window the morning we moved in. "It makes me lonely. Anyway, what do we want it for? I like to have houses nearby. I get frightened in houses that are lonely."

It was a little difficult for me to imagine Allie being frightened of anything, but I guess I understood. A lot of people brought up in city apartments feel that way in the country.

She objected to having live-in servants and only compromised on a cleaning woman every other day. She wouldn't tolerate the idea of a cook. Aside from the kitchen, where she loved to potter around, making sandwiches and stewing up batches of candy—she had a dozen recipes for fudge—the house meant nothing to her.

I gave her the Jag and I bought a Volkswagen for myself and I tried to get her to come to the country club and learn golf, but she gave up after one sorry session with the pro.

"Baseball is the only game I like and I only like to watch that," she said. We tried a couple of club dances, but Allie, who was mobbed by every man in the place, said they were all a bunch of creeps and squares and that the music was dead. She avoided the wives as though they had the plague.

Several times I invited people to the house, but it was the same thing all over again. The men were creeps and the women were ghastly bores. Halfway through the evening she would excuse herself and go up to the bedroom to read her movie fan magazines.

We would go to the movies about three or four times a week, and now and then she would talk me into driving into Raleigh where we would find a second-rate night club. Once we went to a circus and she had a great time, hitting every one of the sideshows and losing money hand over fist at the con-game booths. But mostly she was plain bored.

"Miami Beach, even in the summer," Allie would say. "Anything would be better than this dead backwater."

Finally she herself brought up the subject of money.

"We can't make it here and that's for sure," she said. "What we should do is leave and go out west. I have a brother out there. We can find him and he can tell us how to get some real money, and then we can go somewhere and have fun."

I didn't have much confidence in this alleged brother of Allie's and figured that she was just making him up so that we would move on. And I was becoming more and more conscious that sooner or later we would have to. But I was still trying not to look into the future. I guess I was afraid of what I might see.

It was the first time in my life I had lived from day to day, from sensation to sensation, and I didn't want it to change. It was Allie herself who brought things to a head.

We had been in the house for almost two months when the incident occurred.

It was a Monday morning and I had awakened around eight o'clock. I had an appointment down at the bank at ten, with Cardle, to talk over a deal that had me tremendously excited. I had met him late Saturday night at the club and we had gone into the deserted library for a couple of brandies. He had something to talk to me about.

He was a little tight, but he was plenty sober enough to make it clear. It seems that he had stumbled onto something and he was offering to let me in on it. There was a plan afoot to open an industrial development over on the south side of the town. His brother-in-law was a zoning commissioner and had tipped him off.

Anyway, the thing would be announced within the next thirty days.

The idea was that next to the development and part of it was a tract of some two hundred acres. It could be bought for a quarter of a million dollars. Cardle and his brother-in-law, acting through a dummy, along with the vice president of the bank and another man whose name he wanted to keep secret, were going to take a ninety-day option on the property. I could come in with them if I wanted. We would be able to get the option for twenty-five thousand dollars, each of us putting up five.

The minute that the zoning plans went through, the property would jump in value to a half million. In short, if I wanted a piece of it, I could invest five thousand dollars and within less than ninety days realize a profit of fifty thousand dollars.

It sounded a little screwy and a little too good to be true. But I knew that it was true and I knew why Cardle was offering to cut me in. He believed by this time that I was worth millions and he wanted to get in solidly with me. He still figured on selling me that fancy estate and he also figured that I would, being under a sort of obligation to him, come in on other real estate promotions he already had in the planning stage.

Well, as I say, I was excited about it. It just might work out. I have been around long enough to know that such deals do often work out and I also have been around long enough to know that it is usually some guy with half the dough in the world who is brought in on these things. Money attracts money.

So I was feeling pretty good when I woke up that Monday morning.

Allie was lying next to me in the bed and I turned to her and leaned over and kissed her lightly on the lips. Her eyes opened and she stared at me.

"Leave me alone," she said.

I reached to draw her to me.

It is a strange thing about my relationship with Allie, but although there was never a time I didn't want her, somehow or other the mornings always seemed best.

She turned quickly and pushed me away. "I said leave me alone."

"Now, baby," I began.

But it was no good. For the first time since we had been together, she refused me. She wouldn't even speak to me. I should have known something was coming, but I guess because of my excitement over the possibilities of that real estate deal, I wasn't thinking too clearly.

Anyway, I tried to kid her along and cheer her up. But she wasn't having any of it. She was still lying in bed, staring at the ceiling, when I left.

I had breakfast at the hotel and at ten I met Cardle at the bank. The other three men were present. Cardle's brother-in-law explained the thing in detail and we agreed to make the deal. We ended up shaking hands on it; Cardle, as the real estate broker, would handle the transaction. He said he expected it would take him two or three days to close the option. We should be prepared at that time to have the money ready. I offered to put up my share then and there, but they told me there was no hurry.

It's a good thing that they did.

I got back home a little after twelve o'clock and the cleaning woman told me that Allie had left a couple of hours before. By five o'clock the cleaning woman had gone, and Allie had not returned. I was beginning to get really worried, remembering how she had acted that morning.

At five-fifteen the telephone call came.

It was from a Captain Desiota of the police department and he was down at headquarters. He suggested I come down at once.

It didn't take long once I got there.

Captain Desiota was a youngish, well-dressed six-footer with soft understanding eyes and a quiet, subdued manner. I knew the minute he started talking that he was feeling sorry for me and trying to explain it as nicely as he could.

"She's over in the woman's ward, in a strait jacket and under sedatives," he said. "We would have called you before but we couldn't find out who she was—not until the matron went through her bag and we found an identification. She kept screaming that her name was Allie."

I guess I must have paled, but I maintained control. I still didn't know just what had happened.

"Must be some sort of sudden breakdown," the captain said. "She didn't appear to have been drinking. Nothing on her breath. Of course, it might be drugs. Does your wife take …?"

I shook my head, saying nothing. There was nothing I could say at this point.

"Well, anyway, it happened in some colored bar, over on the other side of town. A real tough place. They sell the stuff illegally. But it didn't start there as near as we can find out. One of the two men, a fellow named Mike Castor and he has a rep as a local pimp and worse, finally admitted he picked her up at the roller-skating rink. Then he and another man, a small-time hoodlum named Finkel, took her to a gin mill and they got drunk. Or at least the two men got drunk. Then the three of them went to this colored place and that's when the fight started. We don't know exactly what happened, but it seems it was a regular free-for-all. In any case, the woman who runs the place was cut up, the man Finkel was shot, and it was pretty bad. By the time the police arrived, the place was a shambles."

"Was Mrs. Mahon injured?"

"No. No, oddly enough, she seems to be about the only one who wasn't hurt in some way or another. But she was completely hysterical, according to the officers who arrived with the riot squad, and she tried to brain one of our men with a whiskey bottle. We broke it up and those who didn't have to go to the hospital were brought in. I hate to have to say this, Mr. Mahon, but the language your missus used and the way she fought …"

He shrugged.

"She hasn't been well," I began, but he stopped me.

"We understand that, sir," he said. "The doctor who gave her the shot said as much, or rather guessed as much. In any case, once we discovered who she was, we got in touch with you immediately."

"I suppose there will be charges?"

"No, I don't think so. Of course, the two men who were with her are going to have to face assault-and-battery counts. But in view of your wife's condition, so to speak, well, if you can get her where she might have the proper treatment …"

Allie was out like a light when the doctor and the private ambulance arrived and she stayed out for at least ten hours after we got her home.

The doctor gave her a second shot of morphine and suggested getting in a private nurse, but I told him I would stay with her that night and see him in the morning. We put Allie in bed and I sat up the rest of the night.

At eight in the morning the doctor telephoned to explain that he had been called out on an emergency and again suggested a private nurse. I told him that Mrs. Mahon was still sleeping and he said that she would be awake any moment and that he would be along in a couple of hours.

I asked him to hold off on the nurse until that time.

Allie came to while I was in the kitchen making a pot of coffee. She was lying on the bed, completely still, staring at the ceiling when I returned to the room. She looked at me and suddenly half smiled.

"How did I get here? I thought I was in jail."

"Allie, for God's sake," I began.

"Never mind," Allie said. "I guess you must have come down and picked me up."

"What in the name of God ever got into you? Why …?"

"I told you I hated this place, that I wanted to leave."

And that was every blessed thing I could get out of her.

I reasoned with her, argued with her, and pleaded. But it did absolutely no good at all. Nothing I said meant a thing. She was through. She was going to leave. She wanted what money there was left and she was taking off. I could come with her or not, just as I liked. But she was leaving.

I tried to explain about the deal, the money we could make, but it got me nowhere.

"We have about seven or eight thousand left—you told me so yourself a couple of days ago," she said. "I'm taking it and leaving. You can come or not."

And that's the way it was when the doctor came and that's the way it was after he left.

The next afternoon I sold the Volkswagen and we packed our bags. I had already paid the following month's rent on the house so I knew there would be no difficulty about that.

Aiken is a small town and things get around quickly. When I telephoned Cardle to give him some sort of story, he already knew what had happened. So I just said that I would be in touch with him but that I was taking my wife to a rest home and would be gone for a few days. Later on I would write, tell him I was too preoccupied to think of business, but assure him that once Mrs. Mahon was well, we would be returning, and he should keep on looking for that estate I wanted to buy.

I wanted my identification to hold up if I should ever need it.

At least I was leaving town without owing anyone money. I was leaving with a nice new identity and a good reputation—but with several thousand dollars less that when I had arrived.

The following morning Allie and I and Gigi the poodle were once more on the road in the white Jaguar. We were heading south for Miami Beach, where Allie wanted to go in spite of the heat.

# 5

It would be very convenient for me to believe that, during those months I spent with Allie, I was actually living in a state of moral and emotional suspension—a sort of period of amnesia in which I really didn't understand what I was doing or why I was doing it.

But this is not true.

I remembered everything and I knew full well exactly what I was doing. I even believe I understood why I was doing what I was doing.

Possibly the only thing really abnormal about both my behavior and my feelings was the fact that the future did not exist. There was only the present. And neither the possible future nor the very definite past had any effect on that present or upon how I felt and how I conducted myself.

I know that I often thought of Marta and of the children. I remembered all of the intimate details of our life together. I remembered the early years during which we may have been truly in love, or at least had lived a life together which I believed encompassed love. Had that love failed me, or had I failed love? Who is really to say?

I only understood one thing: I had changed.

For most of my thirty-eight years I had entertained a certain set of values and had followed the mores and conventions of a normal society. I don't believe that I had been either weaker or more indulgent than most of the men who lived in that society. But I had ended up by failing all along the line. I had failed as a husband and as a father; I had failed in my chosen career and I had failed as a member of the very society in which I had been born and raised. Everything I had done had turned out wrong; everything I had dreamed of and wanted had either turned out to be valueless or unattainable.

I knew, in thinking about it, that it would have been quite possible for me to have gone on living out the years and never changing, drifting from defeat to defeat, from one area of bitterness and unhappiness into other even more desperate areas. But then this thing occurred which changed everything, which was suddenly to bring a sharp and dramatic period to that stage of my life and catapult me into a world in which none of my old values or feelings and sentiments had any existence at all.

There would never be any going back, never any return. Whatever lay ahead was bound up with Allie and my life with her. This was so not only because I understood that, for realistic reasons, I should never be allowed to go back; it was because I knew in my heart I would never want to go back.

I have tried a thousand times to analyze my true feelings about Allie, tried a thousand times to understand exactly what peculiar enchantment she had for me. I was aware of the almost overpowering sexual gratification she gave me, but this alone was not enough to explain exactly what I felt toward her and why it was possible for me to identify her so thoroughly with this complete change in my life.

It may well be that Allie's very childishness, her lack of sophistication, appealed to me, made me want to protect her and take care of her. It had been completely different with Marta. Marta had been the dominating personality; Marta had been the one who'd insisted on mothering me. Marta had been confident and self-assured—utterly self-sufficient. In Allie I saw someone who needed me and someone to whom I had something to give.

Certainly when I would compare Allie with Marta, I was able to see that in a hundred different ways Marta had actually been far closer to me. We had many more things in common. Even though Marta and I had had our difficulties and disagreements, had grated on each other's nerves and often held violently opposite points of view, we still had a great deal to hold us together. I knew the limitations of Allie's mind; I realized that in many areas of human relationships we were totally unable to communicate with each other. I even understood that whereas she might want me sexually, she very likely didn't love me and was incapable of loving me. But none of this made any difference. I was obsessed with her and I was positive that our destinies lay together.

It is very possible that one reason I was able to ignore the future lay in the subconscious knowledge that it was impossible for me to visualize what the future might be. I only knew in my heart that we must share it.

Marta, in her own way, had given me many things, When she had failed me, I don't believe it was from a lack of trying. But Marta had an infinite capacity for hurting me and for doing small things which grated like a file on my sensitivities and rubbed my nerves raw.

What Allie gave me was not given because she tried or even cared. It was there for the taking.

The story of Marta and myself is an old and tired story, a story which has been lived by millions of men. The story of Allie and myself is something quite different.

Until the last week, the three months that Allie and I spent in Miami Beach went by so fast it seemed almost like one long afternoon in the sun.

We arrived around the first of June. With the season already over, we had no difficulty in finding a small efficiency apartment a couple of blocks from the beach itself. The rent was extremely reasonable, and although the weather was becoming very warm, there was an air conditioner and the place was quite comfortable.

Almost at once our lives began to assume a regular pattern. Rarely did we get up before noon and we would have breakfast in. If the day were pleasant—and the days were, almost without exception—we would drive down to the beach around two or three o'clock and spend the next few hours there. Allie very rarely went into the surf, but she liked to lie on her back in the sun, her eyes shaded by dark glasses.

She always carried a portable transistor radio and seemed thoroughly content to listen to the music, rarely speaking. I would alternate swimming with reading.

Returning to the apartment, we would dress and then go to a cocktail lounge or tavern and I would have two or three drinks. Allie herself never drank, but she would order cokes and play the jukebox, if there was one, or listen to the music in places where they had a pianist or entertainers. On those evenings when there was something she particularly liked on television, we would return home after having dinner; on other evenings we would go to the movies. About once a week we went to places where we could dance.

Around midnight we would have a late supper. Often we drove over to Miami and sometimes went as far north as West Palm Beach to find new places.

We were usually back home by two o'clock and we would go to bed. The light never bothered Allie and I would often stay up and read for hours after she had fallen asleep. We rarely talked aside from trivial comments on the picture we may have seen or subjects equally unimportant.

It was a peculiar characteristic of Allie's that she hated to be asked questions and she never had the slightest curiosity about my own past life.

By the time we had been in Miami Beach for several weeks, I had almost completely forgotten that we were actually hiding out. The days and weeks and months of idleness had given me a sense of security and I almost never thought about the fact that we were both wanted on murder charges.

The one time that it came vividly to my attention was on an evening when I was reading a newspaper and Allie was sitting next to me on the couch fondling Gigi, the poodle, and yawning. I was reading an article about a certain well-known racketeer who had been indicted on income tax evasion charges. He was a man named Blackmer who was said to have cheated the government out of some three quarters of a million dollars during the last three years.

I whistled, half under my breath, and spoke unconsciously aloud. "Three quarters of a million," I said. "Boy, he was no piker."

It wasn't until Allie answered that I realized she had been reading the same article over my shoulder.

"That's what I always told Patty," she said. "I knew that he could afford to pay him more than the peanuts he was getting."

I didn't look up from the paper.

"Patty who?" I asked.

"Why, you know. Patty. Back there in Stamford. Patty Donovan."

And then I did look over at her.

"You mean this guy, this Blackmer, was the one he worked for?"

"Sure."

I started to ask her more about it, but she got up and stretched, dropping Gigi to the floor.

"Tired," she said. "I think I'll go to bed. You coming?"

It was all I was able to get out of her, but it told me several things. It told me that Blackmer was the head of the bookmaking syndicate for which Donovan had worked. It told me that he was without doubt the man whose money Patty was carrying when he was killed. It told me that this Blackmer was a man who probably wanted me and Allie even more than the police wanted us. And it reminded me that I was living in a fool's paradise, that we would never really be safe, never really stop running.

Only on one other occasion did Allie slip up and mention anything even vaguely connected with her past. It was on a night when I suggested we run down to a gambling joint on the Keys which we had visited several times in the past. Allie shook her head and said in a bored voice, "No, Con, I don't think I want to go. That joint is dead; not at all like Vegas where you can really get some action. I like Las Vegas. When we get tired staying here, let's go out there. Maybe I can find ..."

And then she stopped and, making an excuse, left the room. When she returned she carefully changed the subject. We ended up going down to the place on the Keys after all and she won a hundred and sixty dollars at the crap table and I dropped fifty playing twenty-one.

The incident which ended our stay in Florida was, I suppose, inevitable. Our luck couldn't hold out forever.

It had been an inordinately hot day, around the end of August, and Allie had been behaving very strangely. For hours on end she had sprawled out on the rug which covered the floor of the living room, lying on her back and staring at the ceiling. She wore a bikini and lay with her legs crossed and her hands under her head.

I had tried talking with her a number of times but she refused to answer. I had asked her if she wanted anything, a cold drink or a magazine or something to eat, and each time she had shook her head and pouted.

Around eight o'clock I told her I was going out to eat and asked if she wanted to come along. Without a word she got up and went into the bedroom. When she rejoined me, still without speaking, I could see that she had put on one of her prettiest dresses. When I asked if there was any place in particular she would like to eat, she merely shrugged and said nothing. Believing that a change of scene might do her good, I carefully avoided our usual spots and instead drove to what was, at that time of the year, the finest and most expensive hotel on the beach.

Allie seemed to cheer up visibly as we entered the lobby and made our way to the main dining room. The place was less than a quarter filled, and as we waited for the headwaiter to guide us to a table, I noticed that a small five-piece combo was over on a dais directly opposite the door. They were playing a rumba, and when the headwaiter returned, I slipped him a couple of singles and suggested a table as near the music as possible.

Allie surprised me by suggesting that we have a wine before ordering dinner and I ordered sherry. From where we sat we had a perfect view of the small orchestra, and although the music was a little too loud for my taste, it seemed to please Allie.

There was another rumba while we sipped the sherry and it ended as we waited for the waiter to take our order. I was studying the menu, about to make a suggestion, when I became conscious of the fact that someone had approached and was standing next to the table. It wasn't until I heard Allie's gasp that I quickly looked up.

He was a tall, slender man in his mid-thirties and he wore evening clothes which fitted him loosely. He had a slender, lantern-jawed face and eyes shaded by heavy black lashes. His mouth was wide and twisted upward at the corners. The second I looked up and saw him standing there, I knew that I had seen him before.

I had seen him on the dais with the five-piece combo; he had been playing the piano.

"Hello, Allie," he said.

My eyes darted quickly from his face to Allie's. She had gone dead white. For a moment I thought she was going to bluff it through, but then I guess she figured she would never be able to get away with it.

"Freddie," she said. "Why, Freddie—it's been a long time."

"A long time," he said, his eyes noncommittal. "A very long time, Allie."

I started to get up.

"Please don't bother," he said quickly, putting his hand on my shoulder. "We're just taking a couple of minutes off and I've got to get back on the stand right away. Enjoy your dinner."

Allie opened her mouth to say something, but before she could speak he had swung around and was walking away from the table. It wasn't until I had given our order and the band was again playing that Allie spoke.

"Fred Pension," she said. "Used to play in a band up in New York. He was a friend of Donovan's." Her face had regained its color and her voice was calm, but I could sense the tension in her.

"We better get out of here," I said.

"No—no, he won't do anything. I'll send him a note and ask to see him as soon as he gets off. I can handle him all right. We were friends once."

"It would be safer if we just got up and ..."

"No. We'll finish our dinner and then you leave. Let me handle him. I can stall him off long enough to be sure nothing will happen until we have a chance to get out of town."

"What do you think he might do?" I asked. "Go to the police?"

Allie shook her head. "Not the police."

"Then ..."

"Do what I tell you," Allie said. "I know him. I can handle him. But you will have to leave. Go back to the apartment and start packing up. Wait. Just don't worry. Get ready to leave and wait. I'll be along."

"But suppose ..."

She again shook her head. "I said I can handle him. You must do it my way. He won't do anything until I can talk with him and I can handle him."

We were just starting with the dessert when once more the music stopped. Allie leaned forward and quickly whispered to me. "They'll be taking a few minutes' break again," she said. "Go to the men's room or make a phone call or something. It will give him a chance to stop by."

I quickly pushed my chair back and mumbled something, dropping my napkin on the table. I walked toward the door leading to the lobby and didn't turn until I was through it. I saw that the pianist had stopped at the table and was leaning over speaking to Allie.

It wasn't until I again heard the music coming from the dining room that I returned.

Allie spoke at once. "He gets off at ten when a dance band comes on," she said. "He's going to meet me in the lobby."

I looked at my wrist watch. It was nine-thirty.

"What did he say?" I asked. "Do you think …?"

"I think he has some idea of shaking me down," Allie said. "But he won't do anything until we have a chance to talk."

"Wouldn't it be better if I stayed with you? Perhaps …"

"No. You do what I say. Pay the check now and go back to the apartment. Get things packed. I'll be along. Just stay and wait and don't worry. I know I can handle him. If it's a shakedown I can stall him off long enough to give us time to get away."

I didn't like it, but there was nothing I could do about it. And so I called the waiter and got a check and paid it and then I left. I did as Allie suggested and returned at once to the apartment.

Something had gone wrong with the air conditioner and the heat in the place was almost unbearable. I opened several windows and stripped down to the waist and began packing. By eleven-thirty I had things pretty well organized, and I was dripping wet. I took off my trousers and shoes and went into the bathroom for a quick shower. When I was finished I found a pair of slacks and a thin sports shirt and slipped into them.

There wasn't a breath of air and the perspiration was dripping from my face. I turned the radio on low and sat down to wait. The station I had selected was located somewhere in Central America and it was broadcasting a rumba band.

I got up and turned the radio off.

For a while I tried to read, but I was unable to concentrate and finally tossed the magazine away.

I was sweating it out—literally and figuratively.

Imagination can be a terrible thing. Where was Allie and what was she doing? She had said she could handle him. How? How was she handling him? Knowing Allie, the possibilities were not pleasant to contemplate.

She had said she suspected he would attempt to blackmail her. And how would she handle that? What would he want? What coin would he wish to be paid off in?

By twelve o'clock I was pacing the floor. I cursed myself for taking her advice and returning to the apartment. I should have stayed with her and we should have faced him together. At least I should have stood by, seeing that nothing happened to her.

I thought vaguely of calling back the hotel where this Fred Pension played and trying to find his address. I went so far as to look up the hotel's number in the book, but then changed my mind. I must give her time, must trust her to do what she said she could do. Handle the situation.

By one o'clock I think I was beginning to go a little out of my mind. Could he have called the police after all and turned her in? Or could Allie have gone somewhere with him and were they even now ...?

It was a thought I didn't want to pursue.

Jealousy is a strange and inconsistent thing. Until now I had never experienced it with Allie. Oh, I knew that she'd had other men, perhaps dozens of them. But that was part of the past and I had accepted it as such.

But this was something different. This was something which could be happening now.

I decided to give Allie until two o'clock to call, and if I failed to hear from her by then, I would do something. Just what I wasn't sure. Certainly I could hardly call in the police to find out what may have happened to her. But I could follow my original idea and try to find where this man Pension lived.

Quickly I leafed through the phone book, but I failed to find any Fred Pension. Once more I checked the clock. It was five minutes to two.

I reached for the telephone to call the hotel and as I did the instrument rang.

It was Allie and I don't believe I would have recognized her voice if I hadn't been expecting her call. She spoke in a whisper, and the moment I attempted to interrupt and ask where she was and what happened, she shut me up.

"Don't say a word," she said. "Just listen and do as I say. Do exactly as I say. Everything depends on it. You must get a cab and come to the address I give you. Memorize the address—don't write it down. And don't bring the car. Take a cab."

And then she gave me the address of a house out past Hialeah on the other side of Miami. She said there was no number on the house, but she described it. She said that I must leave the cab a couple of blocks away and described the filling station on the corner where I should get out of the cab. She told me how to get from the filling station to the house.

"You can't miss it," she said. "The only one on the street, a small bungalow a hundred yards off the road. All by itself. When you get there, come in. The door will be open. I'll be waiting."

Again I started to interrupt, to ask her what had happened, to ask if she was all right, to ask … But she cut me short.

"For God's sake hurry," she said. And then the sound of the receiver being replaced interrupted my own words.

I wasted only enough time to call a cab company and ask to be picked up. I didn't turn off the lights as I started for the street in front of our apartment. I stopped at the dresser just long enough to grab up a handful of bills which were lying next to my wallet. I was careful to be sure the door was locked behind me. There was a little more than two thousand dollars packed in one of the suitcases waiting on the floor for Allie's return.

The taxi I'd phoned for probably took not more than ten minutes to arrive, but it seemed like an hour.

The trip over the Causeway, through Miami proper, and out to Hialeah seemed endless. The cab driver had a little trouble finding the street on which Allie had said I would find the gas station, but he finally obtained directions from a cruising patrol car.

"Sort of a lonely neighborhood," he muttered when at last he found the right street and swung west.

He was right. It was a run-down section with houses far apart and without street lights.

The gas station was where Allie said it would be, and when we drew up and stopped, the driver used a flashlight as he made change. I could see that he was highly suspicious and I muttered something about a friend who was supposed to be there waiting for me. I tipped him with a ten-dollar bill and then spoke.

"It's damn lonely and I guess my friend is going to be a little late. You couldn't spare that light, could you, Buddy?"

He thought for a moment and then handed me the flashlight. "For the ten-spot I guess I can," he said. "I can get another for seventy-eight cents."

He pulled away and I started walking west to the first corner. I turned and went two blocks and passed but a single house. And then off to one side of the street I saw the dark shape of another house. There were no lights. There was no car in the driveway and no car in front of the place. I thought I must have the directions wrong.

I went beyond the darkened house for another block and then I retraced my steps. I went an extra block the other way and found nothing.

I returned to the darkened house.

It had to be the place where Allie had said she would be waiting.

I walked up the path leading to the front door. Something was wrong, something had to be wrong. There was a small open porch and I stumbled over the two steps leading onto it.

I took out the flashlight and, shielding it, looked for a bell. There was a bell and under it was a name plate. I had found the right place. The name was Fred Pension.

For a moment I hesitated, wondering what to do. And then I remembered. She had said the door would be open.

I reached for the knob and twisted it and a moment later I was inside. I closed the door quietly behind me and I stood there listening.

There was no sound at all.

I took the chance, flicked on the flashlight again.

I was in a rectangular living room and the heavy curtains had been drawn tight over the windows.

I used the flash only long enough to find the light switch.

The room was completely deserted and looked as though no one had been in it for a long time. I stood there for several moments, waiting to see what would happen. And then I moved toward a closed door.

The next room was a small kitchen.

The sink was filled with dirty dishes and there was a coffeepot on the stove. It didn't look as though it had been used for a long time.

But the bottle of partially filled Scotch on the side table had been used recently. The ice bucket next to it was half filled with melting ice. There was an empty club soda bottle standing next to the ice bucket and two highball glasses.

There was still no sign of life in the house. Returning to the living room, I saw that there was another door leading into a hallway. At the end of the hallway was a bath, and between the living room and the bath was another closed door.

I held the flashlight on as I opened it. But I didn't need the flashlight. Someone had left a small night light on over the large double bed. I hadn't seen it from outside because of the heavy drapes covering the windows.

The bed had been used.

It was still being used.

Fred Pension was lying on top of the covers, stark naked. He looking up at the ceiling and he paid me no attention to me as I slowly entered the room. He didn't say a word.

He couldn't. His throat was cut from ear to ear.

Why I bothered to search the place I'll never know. I knew in my heart that she was gone. Nevertheless, I went through the bungalow with a fine-tooth comb, searching closets, looking behind furniture, and going into the attached one-car garage. There was a Ford sedan in the garage and the keys were in the ignition. But there was no sign of Allie.

I don't even know why I bothered going back to the bedroom, but I did. Perhaps I had some idea of covering up any clues that Allie had been there. And certainly there was no doubt but what she had.

A lace brassiere, which I had myself bought for Allie only a week before, was caught under a pillow on which the murdered pianist lay. There were pale orange lipstick stains on his chest and smeared across his own dead-white lips. There were other things.

Fred Pension had collected and he had also paid in full for whatever he had taken.

The knife which she had used was still there beside the body. I picked it up and, using the edge of the sheet, wiped it clean. I returned to the kitchen and wiped the glasses which stood beside the partly filled bottle of Scotch. And again I returned to the bedroom.

His clothes were neatly hung over the back of a chair. He hadn't been in any hurry.

I am not sure what I expected to find, but I began to go through his pockets. The wallet yielded the usual identification cards and a few bills. There was a collection of keys on a ring, a soiled handkerchief, and a silver dollar. There was a checkbook on a Miami bank and there was a crumpled bit of paper. I spread it open. It was a blank check. There was writing on the back of it.

He had apparently sent a telegram and he must have written it out first on the back of the check. The penmanship was bad, but I was able to make it out.

"Art Blackmer—Addison Hotel—Palm Beach—Allie will be at my place this evening—believe boyfriend with her—you had better come as don't know how long I can hold her."

There was no signature. I guess he'd had no difficulty in remembering his own name.

I didn't need a design. I understood. Allie had said Fred Pension was a friend of Donovan's. And Donovan had worked for Blackmer. It was no wonder she had gone pale when he had spotted her and recognized her while we were having dinner.

Yes, I needed no blueprint. Sometime during the evening he had reached a telephone and he had sent the wire.

And somewhere, right at this moment, a heavyset man wearing tinted glasses was on his way to this lonely bungalow on the outskirts of Hialeah.

I suddenly understood why Allie had not waited. She too must have seen this copy of the telegram. She too must have gone through his pockets. And she too must have known that a heavyset man with tinted glasses ...

The sharp command, coming from the doorway, sliced through my thoughts and froze me as I stood there holding the crumpled sheet of paper.

"Don't move."

I didn't move.

This time I heard the steps and someone crossed the room and I felt a breath on the back of my neck. Hands moved swiftly up and down my body, patting my pockets and under my left armpit. The steps receded and again the voice spoke.

"Turn around."

There were three of them. A short, curly-headed man in his twenties with large brown eyes and freckled face. A nondescript middle-aged man with a felt hat partly concealing a face which showed only a broken, twisted nose and a chin that jutted out like a spade.

The one who stood in the middle was the only one who was not holding a gun and who seemed completely relaxed. I don't know what color his eyes were because he was wearing a pair of tinted glasses. He was smiling and he had very white teeth which were too true to be anything but false. He needed a shave and he had a very dark beard. His hair was tombstone white and parted in the middle. His clothes were expensive, immaculate, and on the sporty side. He was smoking a cigar which he didn't take out of his mouth when he spoke. He did shake his head a little, from side to side, rather sadly.

"Poor Freddie," he said. "Seems we got here a bit too late. But I guess he's with friends. Who are you, chum?"

"I'm—I'm a neighbor. Heard a noise from next door and I ..."

"Hit him."

I didn't have a chance to duck. The one with the curly hair and the freckles moved like lightning and the barrel of the revolver he held in his left hand slashed across my forehead. I staggered back, but I kept on my feet.

"Let's try it again. Who are you?"

"I'm a friend of Freddie's and I ..."

Apparently it wasn't necessary to give instructions again because Freckles once more waved that gun. This time he opened the flesh not more than a half inch over my eyes. They gave me a couple of minutes to come to.

"All right, chum," the big man with the glasses said, "I guess you are too shook up to know who you are. We'll try something else. Where's Allie? I suppose you must know Allie. Freddie's friends all knew Allie. So just tell Art Blackmer where Allie is and then we may get back to you."

I started to shake my head. I wanted to get a chance to collect myself. To try and think.

But Blackmer and his boys were not going to give me any chance to think. No chance at all.

"All right, Al," Blackmer said. "Into the bathroom with him. You and Red put him through some exercises. Clear his mind. Just keep him sane enough so that when you bring him back he can tell us his little story. I want to look around for a few minutes."

They walked me out of the room, each one holding an arm. They walked me down the hall and into the bathroom and they closed the door and then someone turned on the shower.

The room was pretty small, but it didn't bother them at all. Not at all.

**6**

It is fantastic the amount of punishment the human body is able to absorb—especially when the punishment is being administered by experts—without collapsing and dying. I know. I was the recipient of it.

The details make gory reading. Even the memory is macabre. It should be enough to say that Al and Red were thoroughly expert in their field.

They carried me out of the bathroom after about twenty minutes and I had to be carried. I couldn't have walked if I had wanted to.

A half glass of whiskey forced down my throat and a few slaps with a wet towel were enough to bring me around so that I was able to understand Blackmer when he spoke to me.

"I'll make it easy for you, chum," he said. "I'll tell you what I know, just to let you understand I am leveling with you. And then I am going to ask a question and I want a very straight answer. To begin with, I know who you are. Your name is Conrad Madden. You were with Allie O'Conner that night she stabbed my boy Donovan and walked off with sixteen grand that belonged to me. You have been hanging around with her ever since. Now I have nothing against you personally, although I can't say I like you. But you don't really interest me. I am pretty sure it was Allie who handled Donovan, just as I am pretty sure she did this little job on Freddie. So I don't hold that against you."

He stopped for a second and then said, "A little more of the wet towel. He's beginning to fade."

They used the wet towel again.

"You hear all right? Good. So, as I say, you aren't of prime interest. But the girl is. And I want that girl. Now you are going to tell me exactly where to find her. It's your last chance. You either tell me now or you are going to get beaten to death. Think about it for a minute while you get your breath and then talk."

Well, I thought about it. I had been thinking about it all the time I had been taking the beating in the bathroom and all the time he was talking. And I had already made my decision.

I wasn't going to tell them a damned thing.

They could beat me to death but they couldn't make me talk. You see, there were a couple of things I knew. I knew that I wasn't going to take much more pain. I wasn't able to. A love tap would probably throw me into another faint. A man reaches a certain threshold of pain and then there is no more pain. There is nothing but unconsciousness.

Given time, of course, and they could eventually get their information. This I also understood. The Russians had proved that and so had the Japs and the North Koreans. But if a man doesn't want to talk within a short period of time, there is no way in this world of making him, short of using the truth serum. And I didn't want to talk. I knew just what would happen if I did.

They would catch up with Allie and that would be the end of her. It would also be the end of me. I knew very well they had no intention of letting me off with a mere beating.

There was something else I knew that they didn't know. Without Allie I wouldn't even care.

It was hard speaking through the broken teeth but I made it.

"Go to hell."

It wasn't what they wanted to hear.

This time they didn't take me into the bathroom. They just went to work where I was. And I was right about one thing. The real pain was over. It was just a matter of bringing me to long enough to knock me out again. It probably went on for quite a long while.

In a way, it wasn't actually as bad as it may sound. I knew that the only way in the world they could catch up with her, at least for the time being, was if I did talk. They had, of course, searched me and they had found no wallet, no identification. I had left everything back at the apartment when I had received Allie's telephone call and run out with a handful of bills to catch the cab. So whatever they learned would have to come from me.

In a perverse sort of way, this knowledge gave me strength, made me superior to them.

It was during one of the more lucid moments, when I was more or less conscious, that I made a sudden change of plans. Why not just give them a phony address? It wouldn't work, of course, but it might put a temporary end to what I was going through.

And that is what I did. I managed to mumble the few words necessary, telling them that we were living in a bungalow up in Hallandale. I gave them a street and a number.

I must have passed out then for a second or so because, when I next came to, they were discussing it among themselves.

"One of us could stay here while we check," a voice was saying.

"Take too long. We have to be sure. God, he must be telling the truth. He knows we would be back."

"Bring him to again," said a voice which I recognized as Blackmer's.

They brought me to.

"Listen," he said. "Listen for the last time. We don't want you. We don't want anything from you, not even this."

He took a handful of bills and threw them at me. "All we want is the right address. You are buying your life with it. It's the only thing which will buy your life. Now for the last time ..."

I again mumbled the address in Hallandale.

It seemed an hour later when I was again conscious of a voice. I assumed it was Blackmer, but I am not sure.

"So it's either the truth or it isn't. If he's lying, then believe me, he never will tell us. The only thing to do is check up before she gets suspicious and blows. Red, take care of him. We're leaving."

A second later and something hit me on the side of the head. I don't know what it was, but it disproved a theory I had formed. I could still feel pain. That is if something which makes you feel your skull has suddenly exploded can be interpreted as pain.

It was the bar car on the five-forty out of Grand Central to Stamford and I kept trying to catch the bartender's attention so I could get a double Martini. They were crowding me, all of those who also wanted a double Martini, and they kept stamping on my feet and shoving their elbows in my ribs.

I kept hearing the sound of the flat wheel as it rode over the rails and it bothered me. I'd write a letter. And the damned bartender never did get to see my glass and so I started looking out the window, giving up, and that's when I saw the tracks running parallel to those we were riding on and suddenly my mouth opened and I tried to scream a warning. The other train, the one coming down those parallel tracks, was moving over and heading directly for my train. I screamed again; I wanted to warn the engineer, to tell him what was going to happen. But no one heard me, so I turned and tried to run back through the train. But all those double Martinis were in front of me blocking my progress and I was frozen in a world of highball glasses and shot glasses and wineglasses and still I could see that other train rushing toward me.

I made one last effort and this time when I yelled not a sound came and I knew that it was the end. No one could hear me because I couldn't scream out loud.

The impact was unbelievable and there was that terrible shattering and grinding and the next thing I knew I was lying there dead beside the tracks and I knew that Marta would never believe it and think I had made the whole thing up. Another one of my excuses when I didn't get home when I should.

I opened my eyes because Marta was there beside me, gently accusing me of dying on purpose. In a minute she was also going to accuse me of causing the train crash, so I opened my eyes again so that I could explain to her. Only she wasn't there. And the shattered wreckage of the train was now nothing but a sheet hanging from the side of a bed.

But the crash was right because there was a naked bloody body half falling off the bed.

I didn't want to see that body because it seemed he was an old friend of mine and so I closed my eyes again. I wanted to shut everything out and just sleep.

But the pain didn't let me sleep.

If I could get away, maybe I could leave the pain behind. So I began to crawl.

I guess it was when I ran into the wall at the side of the room that I first really became conscious.

It was probably a full hour before I was able to get to the bathroom. When I was finally able to pull myself up by the sink and stand wobbling as I held on, I looked into the mirror through the one eye which was not swollen all of the way shut.

I knew I was alive all right, but I couldn't for the life of me understand why. They wouldn't have left me there alive. And the things they had done to me wouldn't have left me alive. But alive I was; if nothing else told me so, the agonizing pain verified the fact.

Three fingers on my left hand were crushed and the wrist may or may not have been fractured. I wasn't able to use it or move it. At least one rib on my right side was broken, and the others on both sides felt as though they were. My body was bruised from my knees to my head and the pain in my groin made me wonder if I would ever be good in a bed again, although at the moment I couldn't have cared less.

One eye was closed and my forehead was sliced in three parallel ridges. My left ear was badly torn. Several front teeth were broken and my lips badly cut, but I could move my jaw.

And I had shooting pains in my kidneys. But I was alive and I could walk, so long as I found something to hang onto when the dizzy spells came.

I didn't ever want to go back to that bedroom again, but I forced myself to. I wanted the money which I remembered seeing lying on the floor.

There was a clock on the night table beside the bed and the hands pointed to nine-thirty. I could see traces of sun coming through the heavy curtains and so I knew it was daytime.

Picking up the money on the floor, I turned to leave and it was then I became aware of my blood-soaked clothes. I hated to take anything from that dead man on the bed, but I went to his clothes closet nevertheless and I found slacks and a shirt and a sports jacket. His shoes were too small so I kept my own in spite of the blood on them. I wouldn't touch his underwear or socks to keep from going out of that house naked.

I had a hard time with the overhead door in the garage, but I managed it at last. And then I crawled into the front seat of the Ford. There was a pair of dark glasses on the top of the dashboard and I put them on. It made it hard to see but I wanted to conceal my beaten-up face as much as possible. I couldn't have worn a hat had I found one, because I already had covered most of my head and face with bandages from the bathroom.

I must have resembled a recently excavated mummy as I slowly drove out of the garage.

For the first couple of blocks it was fine and then I felt one of the dizzy spells coming on again. I knew then that I would never make it through Miami. I had to find some place where I could get sleep and rest.

I was not sure where I was going, but I saw the glassed-in phone booth on the corner. Now I would stop and I would call Marta …

It wasn't Marta I had to call, but Allie. What was Allie's number? I couldn't remember. I knew that the number was unlisted and I should remember my own number, but I simply couldn't.

I started the car again and I must have gone half a mile down the empty road when I came to a sign pointing to the left. It said, "House for Rent."

I turned.

My good eye was bleeding again, but I made out the house. It seemed to be a new house in what would someday be a development. I turned in the driveway and the garage door was open and I drove the car in. I got out and I managed to pull the garage door closed.

And then I climbed into the back seat of the Ford. Whether I fainted or fell asleep I will never know. But when I next came to, it was completely dark outside.

I have always known that ten or twelve hours of solid unbroken sleep is about the only and the best cure for a severe hangover. I know now that it is also probably the best therapy for broken bones, fractures, contusions, bruises, and general injuries to the physical body.

When I finally woke up I was far from a whole man, but at least my head was clear. Every bone in my body still ached and I felt as though I had been through exactly what I had been through, but at least I was able to move and I felt the will to move.

I had no idea where I was when I left that garage, but I headed back in the direction of what I assumed must be Miami. The light reflected in the sky gave me a general sense of direction.

Somewhere on the outskirts of the city I found a telephone booth. The only coin I had was a quarter and I dropped it in the slot and dialed the number I had failed to remember before. The phone rang for a long time and there was no answer.

I knew that every minute I spent in Fred Pension's car I was courting disaster, but I was afraid to leave the car. I headed on into Miami.

It was when I passed the hospital that the idea came to me. I pulled up half a block away and got out of the Ford.

It took a long time because walking was hard, but at last I made my way back to the hospital. There was a long circular drive and I moved halfway up it and stopped.

In less than three minutes the taxi left the entrance of the hospital and came toward me.

I waved feebly and it pulled up.

The driver helped me in. "Boy," he said, "they must be pressed for beds to let you out in this condition."

I managed to give him the address of our apartment over in Miami Beach.

I remember crossing the Causeway and I must have passed out soon after. The next thing I remember was the cab driver leaning in the door and looking up and seeing Mrs. Taylor's face over his shoulder. The driver was speaking.

"This is the address he gave me, Ma'am," he was saying.

"Why, it's our Mr. Mahon. Goodness, he looks as though he's been in some sort of accident. Do you suppose …?"

"Please call my wife," I said.

The driver stepped aside and my landlady looked in at me.

"Mrs. Mahon isn't home," she said. "Can I …?"

"Would you please help me?" I muttered. I fumbled in my pocket and pulled out a handful of bills.

The driver and Mrs. Taylor together got me into the apartment.

"I think he should be taken to a hospital," Mrs. Taylor said.

"That's where I picked him up—at the hospital."

Mrs. Taylor said "tish tish" and the driver looked at me curiously and then turned and left.

"Is there anything I can do for you until Mrs. Mahon ...?"

"If you have a family doctor," I said, "you might call and ask him to come by. And a glass of water, please."

It was agony getting the words out so that she understood me.

The little man with the gold-rimmed glasses was standing at the side of the bed and we were alone in the room. I remembered him only vaguely from the other two times he had been there. He had removed the glasses and was caressing the side of his nose with them as he talked.

"I would have put you into the hospital at once," he was saying, "but you absolutely refused to go. Your wife wasn't here to commit you and Mrs. Taylor, your landlady, hesitated to accept the responsibility. I will tell you something else. If I had found a stab wound or a bullet wound, I would have made a report to the police. I might have in any case, but for the fact that Mrs. Taylor vouches for you."

"How long have I been lying here, Doctor?"

"A little more than two and a half days. Most of the time you have been under heavy sedation and unconscious. You talked a good deal but none of it made sense."

"I've been alone?"

"Mrs. Taylor took turns with the nurse. The nurse is in the other room and I suggest you keep her for another few days or at least until your wife returns."

"And just how bad ...?"

"As I say, I don't know what happened to you, although I might guess. But whatever it was, you are lucky. There will be no permanent damage. You'll have to see a dentist, of course, and you should have your eyes checked by a specialist. The hand will heal in time and so will the ribs. I have you all nicely strapped up. You need rest and a lot of it. I would certainly suggest you get in touch with your wife as she should be here with you. Mrs. Taylor says ..."

"Is there any reason I can't get up?"

"None except common sense. You've been through a bad time. I've done what I can, but from now on only nature will make you well.

I'm leaving now and Miss Smyth—that's your trained nurse—will take over."

I asked about a bill, but he said he would mail it. He brought in Miss Smyth and introduced her before he left. I vaguely remembered having seen her around during the last day or two.

When he was gone, I told Miss Smyth that I thought I would be fine and I gave her an extra day's pay and dismissed her. And then I called Mrs. Taylor in and asked her several carefully phrased questions.

She had not seen Allie since the night we had left the apartment together. Sometime the following day she believed that my wife had returned because she had heard someone moving around the place. And that was all she knew. When she left me, I knew that she believed Allie had packed up and deserted me. She was very sympathetic.

The minute I was on my feet, I started a careful search of the apartment. Allie's bags were gone and so was Gigi. The money I had packed was gone. Everything was gone except my own personal possessions. A little later I went out to the garage and I was surprised to see the Jaguar still there. Again I searched the apartment. There must have been some message. But there was nothing.

The possibility that Blackmer had found Allie was too remote to consider. Certainly if he had, he wouldn't have taken the poodle nor would he have taken her clothes. I was left with but one conclusion. Allie had left me of her own volition. Could she have panicked? I doubted it. Allie never panicked.

Why had she telephoned me to come out to Pension's place and then left before I arrived? And how had she left? His car was still there in the garage and there was every reason to believe they had arrived at the place together in it.

How had she returned to the apartment? And why, after returning, had she left, leaving no message?

Was it because she figured Blackmer had found me there and killed me? Certainly this could be a logical answer, especially when I myself had not returned immediately after finding her gone.

I wanted to believe this. I wanted to believe it very much.

I waited in the apartment for a solid week, hoping each moment the phone would ring and I would hear her voice. I sent out for food and never left the place.

And nothing happened.

At this point had I been a normal person, I would have hated her. I had been willing to die to protect her and she had deserted me at the first indication of danger.

I didn't hate her. I had never expected loyalty of Allie.

During this week, as I waited vainly for a message, I sent out for the newspapers. They were full of the murder of Fred Pension. Police had received an anonymous tip and had gone to the house near Hialeah to find the body. They had learned that the musician had left the hotel with a woman. They had a theory that he had taken her to his place and that a jealous lover or husband had shown up and killed him. There were the signs of a fight and an examination had shown two types of blood splattered over the apartment. The thing which baffled them was the fact that although there must have been a tremendous battle, Pension's body showed no bruises and no wounds except for his slit throat.

Sooner or later the cab driver who had left me off near the house would show up to tell his story. Every minute I spent in Miami I was in jeopardy. I knew that I must leave. I knew I must find Allie.

On the eighth day after my return, I told Mrs. Taylor that I had heard from my wife and that I was going north to meet her and would be away for a couple of weeks. I paid a month's rent in advance and packed a single suitcase, leaving everything else in the apartment. I asked her to hold any mail and told her I would send for it later.

Throwing the suitcase into the Jaguar, I left the Beach and checked into a motel just north of Miami. I began to canvass the railway stations and the airlines. I had a little under four hundred dollars in cash.

Ticket agents are amazingly cooperative people. This is especially so when they believe they are helping a man who is looking for a wife who has been under a doctor's care for a mental ailment. I had a story—a pretty blonde girl with a poodle and she was probably buying a ticket to Las Vegas to see her brother.

I hit pay dirt on the third try. The clerk at Western Airlines recalled a girl with a small French poodle coming in very late at night or early in the morning. She had wanted a flight west and the reason he remembered her was because they didn't have a plane stopping at Las Vegas. He'd gone to a lot of trouble explaining that she could go directly through to Los Angeles and that the airline would arrange transportation from International Airport to Burbank, where she would be routed back to the Nevada city. She had wanted to take the dog in the cabin with her and had offered to pay for an extra seat, but he had explained it would be impossible and that the dog would have to fly in the baggage compartment in a special crate.

I didn't bother to return to the motel. My bag was already in the trunk of the Jag and I left the airport and started north to Tallahassee, where I would pick up Route 90 going west.

I pulled into Las Vegas exactly three days and seven hours after leaving Miami. Four times I had stopped at motels long enough to get a hot meal, a shower, and several hours' sleep. Aside from those brief intervals, and stops for gas and oils, coffee, hamburgers, and cigarettes, I had driven steadily. My left hand still bothered me a great deal and I'd found night driving very tiring on my eyes. I was exhausted when I finally reached the outskirts of the town.

There was a bungalow courtyard at the edge of the city and the vacancy sign was out. I pulled in and rented a room and bath and within minutes I was dead to the world. I slept around the clock.

In starting my search for Allie, I knew full well that I had no guarantee that she had ever come to Las Vegas in the first place. I had no reason to believe that if she had, she might still be there. I had no reason to believe that if she was, I might be fortunate enough to encounter her in a town where she might already have found sanctuary with someone else and be buried away in some obscure apartment or hotel suite.

But I was positive I would find her.

Las Vegas is divided into two principal areas. There is the downtown section, filled with cheap gambling dives, shoddy hotels, and broken, desperate-eyed strangers who carry their defeat in their pale, drawn faces.

And there is the Strip—that gaudy, glittering, neon-lighted stretch of luxurious hotels and gambling casinos which are inhabited by the rich and the famous, those children of fortune whose destiny it is to receive only the pleasures and enchantments of existence.

Allie could have been found in either area. A roller-skating rink with its blaring tin-pan music or a cocktail lounge where the sound came from a string quartet were equally appealing to her. She received the same thrill playing roulette with ten-dollar chips as she did playing a nickel pinball game where the stakes were merely another free game.

I started in the downtown area because that is where the movie theaters were and I knew her passion for pictures.

Three days of wandering around the sad confines of Las Vegas' cluttered downtown and I was ready for a change of climate. The heat was terrific. Where the poor play their games of chance, the management doesn't believe in pampering its clients with air conditioning.

The first four places I hit on the Strip used up a full four days. I spent one in each. On the fifth day I entered the Egyptian, newest, most expensive, and by far and away the most luxurious of Las Vegas showplaces.

There was a continuous, twenty-four-hour round of imported Broadway shows, three fabulous restaurants and a half-dozen oyster bars and smaller dining areas, two Olympic-size swimming pools, nurseries for those who couldn't stand to be away from their children even while drinking and gambling, and God only knows what other adjuncts to the modern gambling casino. There were, of course, the usual game rooms. Roulette, twenty-one, chuck-a-luck, the slots, poker chemin-de-fer, bridge, dice—you name it. The Egyptian has it.

The atmosphere falls somewhere between a cathedral, a bordello, and an opium eater's dream of heaven. I think they must have a rule that only beautiful women and handsome men be admitted as guests. Or perhaps it is the general tone of the place which makes everyone seem beautiful and careless and rich.

The hired hands, from bartenders to croupiers, from cigarette girls to hostesses, all seem to have been hired from Central Casting. The place has a branch brokerage office and a board on which ticker prices are chalked, for those conservative gamblers who like to take major risks between sessions at the dice tables.

In spite of its elegant decor, the lobby is lined with slot machines, and as I passed through, I stopped in front of a dollar machine and plunked a coin in the slot.

I thought for a minute it was an air raid or at least a three-alarm fire. Three camels showed in the glass, a sort of innovation. There was no click of coins but lights began flashing on and off.

I was still wondering what had happened when a slick-looking character in evening clothes came up and informed me I had hit the jackpot. Six hundred dollars and he paid me off in twenty-dollar chips.

It was a great beginning. I had been down to less than a hundred and fifty dollars when I entered the place. I moved on to the next room and I couldn't help thinking how my attitude toward money had changed. I don't believe that at any time during my marriage to Marta I had been worth less then several thousand dollars. It may have been tied up in a house or furniture or cars or something, but everything added and subtracted, I was never down to a hundred and fifty bucks. I had never failed to have a more or less permanent roof over my head and at least a day-to-day security. And I certainly had not been on the lam. And yet I had lived then in a constant state of fear and frustration.

Now I had entered the Egyptian with a hundred and fifty dollars and enough problems to drive a man to insanity, and I felt fine. I hadn't found Allie, but I wasn't worried and I was sure things would work out all right.

It didn't make any sort of sense, but then again, nothing I had done in the last five and a half months made sense.

I didn't want to push my luck, so I went into one of the less auspicious dining rooms. The Blue Horizon Room, as I remember. It was probably designed for people who were a little ahead of the game and wanted quiet relaxation and a good meal while they made up their minds about returning to the tables and giving their money back to the house.

There was no orchestra, merely a bald-headed fat man playing a soft baby grand over in one corner. He was playing "As Time Goes By," which sounded just as good as it always had. It reminded me of one night Marta and I had gone to a place down in the Village and heard the boy play it who had done the original job on the song in the movie *Casablanca*. Marta couldn't understand why I gave him a five-dollar bill so that he would play it a couple of extra times.

The room was almost empty and I took a table near the door. I was feeling fine.

I looked over at the pianist. I was thinking of giving *him* a five-dollar bill and asking *him* to play it over.

A man and woman were sitting at a table just to the right of the piano. They were leaning toward each other talking.

The girl's back was toward me and I noticed that she was dressed in a very tight-fitting silk sheath sort of thing with a very low back. She had honey-colored hair, cut short.

The man was thin-faced, dark, with long, beautifully combed hair. He had dark, intense eyes, a thin nose, and delicate, almost effeminate lips. He suddenly stood up, shaking his head and saying something that I thought from his expression must be unpleasant. He shook his head again and then left the table and started for the door.

He looked straight ahead as he passed me. The girl turned slightly to watch him.

I had found Allie.

She hadn't seen me and turned back to face the pianist.

I waited a moment or so for the man to get out of the room and then I stood up and walked over to the table. I circled and sat in the seat the dark man had just vacated.

She looked up at me.

"Con," she said. "Hello, Con."

"Hello, Allie," I said.

The pianist started all over on "As Time Goes By," without my giving him a five-dollar bill.


# 7


"You don't seem very surprised to see me, Allie."

"I'm happy to see you, Con."

The thing is she did look happy. She reached across the table and took my hand and squeezed it. "Maybe you'd like to tell me …"

"Not here, Con. I don't want to talk here."

"Then where?"

"We'll leave. Have you a place to stay?"

"I have a place."

I wanted to ask her if she had a place to stay. And where it was. And whose place it was. But I didn't. I wanted her to do the talking. I knew that asking Allie questions would get me nowhere.

"Well, wait a minute and I'll be right back."

She moved to get up and I said, "What do you have to do, explain to the guy you were with?"

"He's not a guy," Allie said. "He's my brother. His name is Joel. He works here. You wait. I'll be right back."

So she got up and I stood up too and pulled her chair back and she left. I sat there, for ten minutes, wondering if she was going to return. There wasn't anything else to do. She either would or she wouldn't.

When she returned, he was with her. He was smiling as they

approached. He had his hand out and spoke before she had a chance to introduce us.

"Allie has told me a lot about you," he said. "I'm glad to know you. The name is Joel. Joel Ricco."

I nodded, saying nothing. The name Ricco sort of threw me. But I wasn't too surprised. In Allie's circle, names didn't mean a great deal. I tried for a second to find some family resemblance, but I could see none. The only thing they had in common was that they were both good-looking.

"You call me later, eh, kid," he said to Allie. "And I'll be seeing you around," he said to me.

He walked us to the door.

We climbed into the Jaguar and I drove out to the place I had taken at the edge of town. Neither of us said a word until we were inside.

I turned to lock the door after us.

"Get yourself a drink, Con," she said. "Bring me a coke if you have one."

I turned to her. "Allie," I began, but she put her fingers to my lips and shook her head.

"A drink first, Con."

Well, I needed a drink. I was feeling a little dizzy. So I went into the kitchen and struggled with an ice tray. I poured a double shot of Scotch into a glass and filled it up from an already opened bottle of soda. I got a second glass and found a bottle of coke. Then I downed the Scotch and poured myself a second double. I went back into the other room.

The black sheath dress was lying in a heap on the floor along with a pair of silver slippers. I guess she hadn't been wearing anything under the dress.

She was already in the bed with the sheet pulled up to her chin. She was looking at me and smiling.

"The coke, Con," she said.

I gave her the glass. I didn't bother to drink the Scotch, but put it on the table beside the bed. I went over and checked the venetian blind to see that it was securely closed. And it didn't take me any longer to strip off my clothes than it took her to drink the coke.

It was just like it always was, only better if possible. I hadn't been with her in more than two weeks and you would have thought she'd been saving up for as many years. Three minutes after I climbed in beside her I didn't give a damn if she had set me up for murder, I didn't care if she had walked out on me, I wasn't even interested in knowing whether Ricco was actually her brother. I only cared about one thing and that was the thing I was having.

There are no possible words to describe it.

Sometime during the early hours of the morning we talked. Allie talked. She came as close to really telling me something as she ever had. I didn't even have to ask questions.

"… and I telephoned you to come when he said it was money he wanted," she said. "I thought maybe the two of us might take care of him, some way or another. He didn't know that I called you.

"But then, long before you were due to arrive, I found out it was something else he wanted. Well, I gave him that. I had to. I thought it might be enough. But later on, in bed, I knew. It was something about the way he was talking and acting. He was too smug, too sure of himself. And then he told me he'd sent word to Blackmer, Patty's old boss, just in case I didn't cooperate. So I did what I had to do. I went into the kitchen and I got the knife …"

She stopped talking and I didn't say a word. I knew if I interrupted her, she might not say another thing. "Well, anyway, after I did what I had to do, I went through his pockets. I found his message to Blackmer. It was then I guess I lost my head. I thought Blackmer would be in New York, but he wasn't. He was in Palm Beach. I guess maybe I really did panic. Because I knew he could arrive any second.

"So I dressed and I got out. I wanted to go down to that gas station and warn you before you got to the house. I was so frightened, I didn't even think to take his car. And somehow or other I got lost. You remember, there were no street lights. I wandered around for a long time. I never did find the gas station."

"I know," I said. I couldn't keep a trace of bitterness out of my voice.

She went on talking, ignoring the remark. "I must have wandered around for an hour or more. I did what they say you do in books. I made a sort of circle and I ended up and back at Fred's place. There was the car in front and I could see that it had New York plates. I sneaked up and lighted a match. Then I went to the house and I couldn't see inside, but I could hear. They were going to kill you. I heard them say so."

"They damned near did."

"I just turned and ran. I don't really know where I went or how far. But sometime later, a car drove by and it was a milkman and he stopped and picked me up. He took me to where I could get a taxi and I went back to the apartment. I thought that you'd be dead. I took my bags and Gigi and I got out. I came out here."

"How come you didn't take the Jag?" I asked.

Allie leaned over and kissed me. "I didn't want to leave it at the airport, in case you came back," she said. "I called a cab."

"But you could have left me a note—in case I came back."

"I was afraid to do even that. There was the chance they could have gotten the address from you."

She kissed me again. I didn't say anything for a time. I was busy with other things.

Later, I asked the question. "You made no effort to get in touch with the apartment?" I said.

"I thought you were dead, Con. And if by chance you weren't, I figured you would be in the hospital for a long time. I heard what they were doing to you. That's the way it happened, just like I've told you."

I could believe her story or not. It could all be just as she explained it. Or the entire thing could be a tissue of lies. Yes, I could believe it or not. But what I did was neither believe nor disbelieve. I accepted it. There was really nothing else to do.

"And where are you staying now, Allie?"

"I'm staying with you, dope," she said. "I'll get my things in the morning. I'm staying with you."

And that was every last thing I could get out of her.

We hardly moved from the room for the next three days. Allie took the Jag the following morning and disappeared for a couple of hours. When she returned, she had her luggage and Gigi, who seemed glad to see me. I noticed that she also had a lot of clothes I had never seen before.

The three days were like all of the times I had spent with Allie when she was happy and contented and wanted nothing but to be with me. We lost track of time, of days and nights, and there was no world except ourselves locked within the geography of our own passions.

On the fourth day Allie said she wanted to go into town and do some shopping. She wanted to go alone and I didn't argue with her.

She returned in less than an hour and I knew at once that something had happened. She was nervous and intense.

"I talked with Joel," she said.

"Joel?"

For a moment I had completely forgotten the slender dark boy who had been sitting with her at the Egyptian when I had found her.

"My brother," she said. "He wants to see you."

I looked at her curiously. "See me?"

"Yes. He has something to talk to you about."

"Well, tell him to come on over and talk."

"We're going to meet him out at the airport."

I shrugged. I didn't ask any questions. Maybe he was going away and wanted to say goodbye. I couldn't have cared less.

An hour later we drove out to the airport, leaving Gigi behind, locked in the room.

He was waiting at a private hangar and he didn't smile when he pulled up and climbed out of the Jag.

"Come on," he said, and turned and started for a four-place Cessna which was warming up on the air strip. No one spoke as we climbed aboard. Joel took the controls, and by the time we were airborne, talk was out of the question.

We headed northwest, over the desert, and we must have been flying for about two hours when he began to circle and lose altitude. Looking down, I saw nothing but miles of wasteland, sand, and windswept emptiness below. And then, almost before I realized it, the wheels touched the ground and he gunned the engine and swung in a half circle and we traveled over the floor of the desert for ten or fifteen minutes.

It wasn't until he opened the door and we stepped down out of the plane that I noticed the ranch house. It was a long, low adobe building without a tree or a bush to shield it from the merciless sun. Faint twin tire tracks showed where a road may have been at some time in the past. There was no water tower, no outbuildings, nothing. Just the house.

Still not speaking, we followed Joel Ricco to the front door which he opened with a key.

I saw at once upon entering that someone must have recently furnished and partially restored the place. There was a large stone fireplace in a huge, semi-furnished living room with very small windows to keep out the sun. Indian rugs had been thrown carelessly on the floor and the walls were bare of decoration.

"Sit down," Ricco said. "Scotch or rye?"

I said Scotch.

He went into the back somewhere and a moment later I heard the sound of an electric generator. When he returned he had a couple of straight drinks. There was no glass of milk so I guess he didn't have it on hand or didn't know his sister's tastes.

I was sitting on the couch but Allie had walked over to the side of the room and opened the doors of an old Spanish highboy which turned out to be the storage place for some sort of complicated hi-fi set. Allie was busy pushing and pulling switches and turning knobs. "How do you work this jukebox anyway?" she asked.

"Damn it, take your hands off that," he said, his voice suddenly tense with anger. He put the glasses on the table and, moving quickly, crossed to her, knocking her hands away and closing the cabinet doors.

"I was only trying to get a little music," Allie said.

"You don't get music on that piece of equipment," Joel said. "That's a shortwave radio set. I've got several bucks in that equipment and I don't want anyone fooling around with it."

"Are you interested in ham radio?" I asked. "I used to fool around a little with it myself."

"Yeah?" He turned toward me and for the first time his expression showed animation. Almost friendly animation. "I made this outfit up myself," he added with pride. "One of my few hobbies. You wanta take a look at it?"

He reopened the cabinet doors and I crossed over as he swung the cabinet around on casters and dropped the back so that the various components were exposed.

"I have picked up stations from all over the world," he said. "And they have heard me in Hong Kong, in London, in Berlin, and everywhere."

For several minutes he talked and I looked over his equipment. It was really good and especially so when I realized he was generating his own power.

Before he closed it up I noticed his call letters: WG-1556.

We went back to where he had put the drinks down and he handed me one and lifted his own. We drank.

Allie and I seated ourselves on a long leather couch and he pulled a chair up and faced us.

"Like the place?" he asked.

"I guess so," I said.

"Bought it a couple of years ago," he said. "Nobody knows I have it. Fixed it up myself. Flew everything in by plane except the stones for the fireplace and I brought them in by truck. Did the work myself. "Makes a nice hideout."

"I should imagine."

He nodded, a sort of self-satisfied smile on his lips. "Allie tells me that you and she might be interested in getting hold of some money."

I didn't know what it was all about or where he was going, so I just nodded and let him talk.

"I don't know you, Bud," he said, "but if you're okay with Allie, you're okay with me."

"Thanks."

"You're sort of an amateur, I understand."

I shrugged. "I guess I am," I said. "In most things."

"From what Allie says, you learn fast."

I shrugged again. I still didn't know what he was leading up to.

"Well, here's the pitch. I can use you. You and Allie. There will just be the three of us. Three of us and about two hundred and fifty to three hundred thousand dollars. You interested?"

I was very interested. I said so. Allie said nothing. "We cut it two ways, half for me and half for you and Allie. I get half because I set it up."

"Seems fair," I said. I still didn't know what he was getting at. I had sort of an idea he might be junked up. He sounded like something out of one of those grade B pictures Allie was always going to.

"Allie tell you what I do?"

"She told me you worked at the Egyptian."

He nodded. "Right," he said. "I have sort of a sensitive job."

"Is that so?"

"That's so. I won't go into everything I do, but I'll tell you the part that's sensitive. The Egyptian operates like most of the places on the Strip. They got a steel-and-concrete-lined office and in that office is a Diebold safe. There's a guy with a machine pistol guarding that safe twenty-four hours a day. Even if he wasn't there, nobody in this world could break in and get away with it. Electric alarms—that sort of thing. It's foolproof. Take my word for it—foolproof."

I took his word for it.

"About four times a day money is picked up around the place and put in that safe. It stays there until the third Monday of each month."

I was beginning to get the drift of his conversation. I still didn't know where it was leading, but I wanted to sound like an intelligent audience. "Didn't you say something about just the three of us?"

"Don't interrupt. As I was saying, the third Monday of each month the money no longer stays there. It is packed up into money bags after being counted and audited. It is then taken out and carried to the bank downtown. It's always on the third Monday, but never quite at the same time of day. And that's where my sensitive job comes in. I drive the money to the bank."

It was getting a little clearer. "You—alone—drive the money to the bank?"

"Me—alone. Except I am not completely alone. Two of the boys walk out back with me and place the money in a sedan I usually use. There are plenty of other boys around. I get in behind the wheel, still alone, and take off. But I am still not altogether alone. There is a car right behind me and there are two guys in that car. They are experts in their field. They each carry submachine guns. They follow me right up to the bank, and when I get out, there are a couple of guards from the bank waiting. The money goes into the bank, from which point it is insured and from which point the management of the Egyptian ceases to worry about it."

"That part sounds pretty foolproof also," I said.

"It is. After all, the people who own the spots on the Strip aren't exactly babies. They've had a lot of experience, some of them on both sides of the fence. They have another thing going for them, also. The kind of mob which might be able to knock off the dough on the way to the bank never gets to land in Las Vegas. You may not know it, but people who arrive in Vegas are screened. Of course now and then a racket guy gets in. A lot of them get in. But I can tell you one thing. For a big-time mob to filter into this town, even one by one, would be impossible. And nothing less than a big-time mob could handle that sort of stickup.

"Besides, Las Vegas is situated smack in the center of the desert. There are three ways out of town—by road, by train, and by airliner. Even assuming that a mob big enough to pull the job was imported, and assuming they got away with the money, they would have no place to go. No place at all."

"I am willing to believe that," I said.

"It's true. It's also true that the three of us, you, Allie, and myself, can take that money and get away with it."

He sounded very convincing, but I was pretty sure by now that he was either doped-up or crazy. Hopheads and psychos are always convincing.

"Maybe you would like to tell me how."

He stood up and went in for another drink and this time there were thin flakes of ice in it. I figured he had a darned good generating plant.

"So assuming I explain, how do you feel about the deal?"

"How does anyone feel about that kind of money?" I asked in return, trying to play it as cool as possible. After all, the entire conversation had a sort of unreal quality about it. It wasn't as though someone were asking me if I wanted a long drink or a short one. I didn't have to give a serious answer.

He shrugged. "I have to assume you will be interested," he said. "From what Allie tells me you are both on the lam and if the lam isn't successful, then you burn. You don't lam successfully without dough and I happen to know that you haven't got a lot of that."

This time I nodded and I was a lot more serious. What he said was only too true.

"All right. Here's the pitch. You are going to stick me up. When I …"

I shook my head a little sadly. It had sounded as though he might really have something for a moment there.

"And those two boys with the submachine guns are just going to stand around and watch, I suppose?"

"I said let me do the explaining and listen," he said. "Those two guys are not going to be standing around and watching and for a very good reason. Because about six minutes after we leave the Egyptian, something is going to happen to their car. Something which will keep them from following me. And I will be going on alone. And three and a half minutes after they have ceased to follow me, you are going to run me into the curb in another car, stick me up, and take those money bags—the ones with the bills. It is going to be a daylight robbery and there will be witnesses. There will have to be witnesses."

Again I shook my head. "You don't have to go into the rest of it," I said. "You can stop right where you are. Are you trying to make me believe that if that car behind you stops, you are not supposed to stop also? Are you trying to tell me that your bosses are so stupid that in case of engine failure or a flat, you haven't been instructed to pull up and wait for those two boys with machine guns to get out and climb in with you?"

"Damn it, will you let me tell it?" he said. "Who said anything about a puncture or an engine failure? Of course if anything happens to them, I am supposed to stop. I have to keep them in my rear-vision mirror and I am never supposed to be more than four car lengths in front of them.

"But there is one circumstance under which I don't stop and wait for them to climb in beside me. That's in case they aren't there."

"You want to make it a little clearer?" I asked.

"Yeah, I'll make it very clear. They'll be flying off in several directions. That's what usually happens when a blast of nitroglycerine goes off under a hood."

I'm afraid I went a little pale then. Up until this point I had thought he was either crazy or just kidding himself. I was even vaguely willing to consider the possibility of a simple robbery, assuming I thought we had even a remote chance of getting away with it. But nitro—

I stood up. "Count me out," I said. "I don't buy murder."

He looked at me queerly for a moment. "You are wanted for murder," he said.

"That may be. I still don't buy it."

"All right, keep your pants on. I haven't said anything about murder. I said a shot of nitro goes off under that hood. It doesn't have to be a very big shot. It doesn't actually have to much more than stop that car. It just has to be good and loud enough so that I can reasonably say I didn't know what had happened and I was afraid to wait and find out. That the safest thing seemed to be for me to race on to the bank."

"You mean to tell me …"

"I am telling you. I can plant it so that it will blow hell out of the motor, and sound as though an atomic bomb were going off. But that's an armored car, the same as the one I will be driving. They look like plain sedans, but the bodies are made of armor plate. The two guys in that car will be shook up and shook up bad. But they won't be killed and they probably will suffer nothing but a few bruises."

I looked over at Allie. She shrugged.

I knew that it wouldn't make much difference to her either way.

"There is one reason you can believe me," he said. "I know that there is always a slender chance I could be picked up. You think I want to face a murder rap when it could be a robbery charge just as easily?"

Well, he had a convincing argument there. "Let's hear the rest of it," I said.

"All right. So, you stick me up. I have it planned so I'll have witnesses but you'll be safe. You grab the dough. You drive a certain route, end up at a certain spot—a secluded, quiet spot where you will have about a minute of complete privacy. Allie is going to be there in a second car. You transfer the money. You leave your car and you start out on foot. You won't have the dough, you will have gotten rid of your gun—which won't be loaded in any case. You are clean. So far so good?"

I said so good.

"Allie drives back to your joint. Except it's a different joint than where you are now. A small house at the south side of town which I am renting for you. It has a garage. She drives into the garage."

"Still with the dough?"

"Still with the dough. You get back to the house. A couple of days later, you both leave town, a nice conventional couple with the identifications Allie says you have. And you got the money with you."

"And I suppose every car that leaves town will not be searched. Hell, you can't hide a fig leaf in the Jag without …"

"You can the way I've planned it. Because when you get back to the house, the one with the private garage, you have a little job to do. You take off your shirt and go to work. Jacking up the wheels and pulling off the tires. They are tubeless tires. And into each one of them goes the dough. Then you get those tires back on the rims and back on the wheels. You fill them from a few portable compressed air cans I'm going to supply you with. From that point on they are going to be very special tires. Tires riding on somewhere around a quarter of a million dollars."

I thought about it for quite a while and he let me think. He went out and got a couple of more drinks. When he came back he said, "Any flaws?"

"One. We'll be stopped and we'll be searched. You can bet on that."

"You will. But you have the right identifications, you look legit. They'll search, but they won't do a thorough job of it. And, besides, they won't have any idea of who they are looking for. You see, after the stickup, I'm going to be taken down to headquarters and run through the mill. And you can bet the description I give of the stickup guys—there will be at least two of them according to my version—

won't resemble you in any possible way."

It was beginning to look as though he really did have something.

"What happens to you?" I asked. "They'll be damned suspicious …"

"They sure as hell will. They'll really take me over the coals. But they won't be able to prove a thing and they'll know it. Sooner or later the pressure will let up. When it cools down enough, then one day I get in the plane and I come out here. You and Allie will be waiting. Next stop—Mexico."

Allie spoke up for the first time. "Joel's pretty bright isn't he, Con?"

"Yes," I said. "Yes, he's pretty bright. Let's go over it again."

He went over it again, this time in detail. I stopped him a half a hundred times to ask questions, and he didn't object. He wanted questions. He was trying to find flaws himself.

Finally he was through and I was through and even I couldn't see any flaws in it. Except one.

I was the flaw.

I had done a lot of things during these last months. I had condoned things I never believed it possible for me to condone. I had violated about every rule in the book. But all along, I had considered myself sort of a bystander. A free rider. My crimes had been crimes of omission rather than commission.

At no time had I considered myself in any way a criminal.

I still couldn't quite picture myself deliberately setting out to commit a violent felony. I had changed, in every possible way, but not in that way.

I stood up and yawned, forcing the gesture. "I'd like to think it over," I said.

"There's nothing to think about."

I didn't like the way he said it. "No? Suppose I tell you I don't want any part of it."

"Now, Con," Allie began, but Joel turned quickly and said, "Shut up."

"Let her …"

"I'll do the talking," he said. "It isn't quite a case of whether you want in or not. You are in."

"And supposing I say I am not in?"

"You are in. If you won't do it for Allie here, then you'll do it for yourself. You see, I know all about you, friend. Everything. You don't come in, then you know too much. And I know too much about you. If you don't play along, I can make a little telephone call to the cops …"

"And Allie?"

"I'll protect Allie, friend. But between you and me, I wouldn't make the call to the cops. It wouldn't be enough. I'd go a little bit further. I'd get in touch with your old friend, Art Blackmer. Yeah, I know all about him. And this time, he wouldn't miss. He'd fly a boy out here or, quicker yet, call a certain party in L.A., and you'd be dead before you could get to the city limits. Believe me, I know. So give up any thoughts about not coming in. And don't bother to think it over. You are in. You and Allie both. Both in."

He smiled suddenly and held out his hand. "Shake," he said. "We're partners."

We shook.

We landed back at the Las Vegas airport just before dusk and he walked over to the car with us. He took a piece of paper from his pocket and scribbled an address on it.

"This is the place I want you to rent. Belongs to a man named Creary and he rents it out furnished by the week to parties coming here to gamble. I happen to know that it's vacant, so get over and tie it up. Be damned sure not to mention my name."

He seemed to take it for granted that everything was set, that I would be going along with him. As a matter of fact, at the moment I wasn't ready to disagree with him.

"Right," I said.

"You and Allie go out on the town and have yourself a time tonight," he said. "I'd invite you down to the Egyptian, but I think it might be a good idea to stay away from the place from now on."

Allie said "Right" this time.

"Have fun, kids."

He swung around on one heel, going back to the hangar to check up on the Cessna.

Allie and I got in the Jag and started back to town. "This brother of yours," I said, "he's something, isn't he?"

Allie didn't answer.

"He is your brother, isn't he, Allie?"

She turned and stared at me. "I said he was, didn't I, Con?"

"You said so, Allie," I said. I wasn't going to argue with her. I couldn't argue with her.

It was, I suppose, a pretty brotherly thing he was doing—cutting his sister and her boyfriend in on a quarter-of-a-million-dollar heist.

# 8

This thing was insane.

I had been right all along. It was preposterous; it was totally and completely impossible. I should have listened to my sense of reason, if not my conscience.

Why, less than a half minute ago a cruising patrol car passed and the two officers looked over at me curiously. I was thankful for one thing at least. I was in the U-Rent-It Ford, which itself was stolen. But at least the arrangements had been made, or I prayed that they had been made. It wasn't to be reported stolen until after the robbery had taken place.

The officers looked at me. The driver slowed down slightly and I felt a shiver go down my spine. But they were no longer looking at me. They were looking at the two drunks sitting on the stoop across the street, nursing the half-filled sherry bottle.

I thought for a moment they would stop, but they didn't.

The drunks were the only thing right about the scene. I knew they were supposed to be there. I knew Joel had arranged for them.

But how about the patrol car? How about the dozen or so other persons who were walking around and constantly passing to and fro?

He had sworn to me that there would be no one at all, no one but those two drunks. And he had figured it wrong.

My eye went to my wristwatch and I saw there were still three and a half minutes to go. It was going to take him exactly three minutes from the time the nitro exploded in that car which was following him, until he turned the corner up ahead and swung into the street on which I was parked.

But his calculations had gone sour. This street was not going to be deserted. It wasn't going to be a simple case of two stooges verifying his false identification of the stickup men. It was going to be a case of any number of people making that identification. And those people were going to identify me. One or more of them was going to remember the license number of the car in which I sat. Not only would I be caught; it was doubtful if I would get as far as my rendezvous with Allie.

Joel Ricco was smart, but he had missed on this one.

I reached forward and turned the key in the ignition. The motor caught and my hand tightened on the wheel and I started to press down on the gas pedal.

This whole thing was insane and I would be insane to let it go any farther.

The car began to move.

And then it came.

I don't know for sure whether it was the concussion or the sound which reached me first. But it doesn't really matter. I was totally unprepared for either.

It was to take place more than a half mile away and it hadn't even occurred to me that I would actually hear anything.

But it came and it came with all of the fury and crashing might of an atom bomb. The car in which I sat appeared to be nudged sidewise by the concussion. And the sound—well, there is no real way to describe it.

It took me a full ten seconds to identify it, to realize what had happened. The nitro had gone off under the hood of that armored sedan which had been following Joel and carrying his two armed guards.

Joel must have planted enough to blow up half a city block.

I think it was the sudden shock that made me put my foot on the brake and bring the car to a halt.

The full implication of what had happened came to me slowly. I didn't have to be on the scene to guess what havoc that explosion had wrought. The guards would be dead and God only knows how many others might have died in that fantastic blast. Innocent pedestrians, passersby in other cars, residents of nearby houses. But then I remembered we had driven by the spot where he had planned it and it was in the middle of a block without buildings. It was a small comforting thought.

I shook my head, trying to gather my senses. I looked around me. The street was deserted. There was only myself and the two drunks on the stoop. A man came out of the building opposite and started running up the street toward the sound of the blast. I knew then that the others had gone off in the same direction.

There would be no police in a patrol car to witness the fraudulent stickup which was about to take place. There would be no casual witnesses. Everyone within hearing of that blast would be converging on the scene of what must be a major disaster. Joel had not lied about what was to happen. His lie had been about the two armed guards in that car following him. No two humans could have survived that tremendous explosion.

I was suddenly no longer a collaborator in a robbery. I was an accessory before the fact in a double murder.

A car was turning into the street at the next corner and I recognized it at once as the one Joel would be driving. There was time. All I had to do was stay, right where I was—not make the move we had planned on and rehearsed so many times—just sit still and let him pass and there was nothing he could do but continue on to reach his destination at the doors of the bank.

I couldn't save the lives of those two men who must have died in that explosion, but I could keep the thing from going any farther. I could withdraw. It would take no overt act. It would merely mean my doing nothing at all.

It is amazing the rapidity and clarity with which a dozen random thoughts can pass through the human brain within a small fraction of a minute.

If I did nothing the plan would fail. There would be no robbery. But if Joel would be unable to complete the robbery it didn't mean that he would be unable to take care of me—and of Allie. There was not the slightest hope either of us would be able to leave Las Vegas alive.

Even assuming we might manage to escape his vengeance, the police would be bound to pick us up. In either case, we had no out.

Perhaps, had I time to really think it through, to consider every possibility, to formulate a plan … But time had to run out.

He was no more than fifty yards up the street, moving fast.

I jerked and swung the wheel, pressed hard on the gas, and the tires cried out on the hot pavement. My foot jammed on the brakes and I pushed my spine into the back of the seat.

There was the squeal of his tortured tires as he rammed down hard on his brake pedal and then the sudden harsh jar as the hood of the sedan smashed into the side of the car I was driving.

There was the crash of shattering glass and I was out of my car, the unloaded gun in my hand, as I reached the side of his car.

He only had time for the five quick words before the barrel of my gun crashed down on his head.

"The five top bags only," he said.

I departed from the script when I smashed that gun across his forehead. It was supposed to be a light, gashing stroke, the kind which would open the flesh and draw fast blood, but would cause no serious damage. The blow drew blood all right because it struck hard and true and I twisted the gun in my hand as it hit him. Whether it caused serious damage I didn't know at the time and I didn't care. I was remembering the sound of that explosion.

The bags were where he had said they would be and I pulled the door of the sedan open and reached for them. They were small, leatherbound canvas sacks of the sort banks use for transporting money. I tossed them, two at a time, into the back of the Ford. The last one I carried with me as I climbed back into the front seat.

The engine was still running and I shoved the car in reverse. For a second or so it failed to move and I could hear the tires slip. Somehow or other, when he had struck me, his bumper must have gotten caught. There was no time to find out. I threw the gearshift lever in forward and then threw it in reverse. On the second try I was clear.

A blind man with silver hair was standing in the very center of the street, a few yards from the corner, and he was turned facing me, motionless. He held a seeing eye dog on a harness. The Ford rolled up on two tires as I jerked the wheel to circle around him.

The next turn right, according to the way we planned. And then another right, the alley a half block ahead, a left, and now I was driving at a normal speed again.

The stop light was against me as I pulled to a halt.

There was a policeman walking fast, halfway down the block. I waited for the light to change. I felt completely calm.

Seven minutes later I pulled into a parking lot at the side of the supermarket. It was a large lot with room for two hundred cars or more, but there were less than a dozen spaces occupied.

The Pontiac which Joel had obtained for Allie was exactly where it was supposed to be. There was a Mercury station wagon next to it and the tail gate was down. A boy in a white apron was standing next to the gate, one hand on the aluminum handle of a wire basket cart which was filled with groceries. He was smiling and talking with a pretty dark-haired girl who was smoking a cigarette. She held a small boy by the hand.

I pulled in on the other side of the Pontiac. There was no one in it; no one was supposed to be in it. Allie would be in the store, casually shopping, watching—waiting until she saw me make the transfer.

Five minutes went by and the grocery clerk continued to talk to the pretty, dark-haired girl. He was in no hurry at all to unload the cart.

I began to worry. Allie should realize that every extra minute I spent in the Ford increased my risk. I was about to get out of the car and go in and get her when the boy began to unload the cart. But it was another five minutes before he finished and opened the door for the girl and leaned on it to light her a final cigarette. Maybe it was a part of his job, being sociable with the carriage trade.

I could have cheerfully killed him.

Once the coast was clear, it took me less than two minutes to put the canvas money bags into the two airplane zipper bags and to transfer them to the tonneau of the Pontiac. I forced myself not to look over toward the supermarket as I climbed back behind the wheel and started the engine. I could have left the Ford in the lot and just walked away and I was tempted to do so. But it would add a possible element of risk. If the car were to be found there, someone might remember the Pontiac.

Had anyone else but Allie been coming out of the store to get in that car and drive it out to the small house we had rented ten days previously, I would have taken the risk. But I didn't! I put the Ford in gear and drove off.

Looking into the rear-vision mirror as I left the parking lot, I saw Allie leaving the supermarket, several bundles in her arms. It would take her less than twenty minutes to get home. She would drive the Pontiac into the double garage and close the overhead doors. The Jaguar was waiting there, the tires already removed, all four wheels up on jacks.

It would take me twelve minutes to dump the Ford at the place which we had prearranged. It would take me another forty minutes to walk back to the bungalow. I didn't worry about the forty minutes. I worried about those twelve minutes. I was behind schedule, thrown off by that grocery clerk who liked to talk to pretty, dark-eyed customers. By now that Ford would have been reported stolen. The license number would have been radioed to every cop in the city. That call had to go in as close to the time of the robbery as possible in order to protect the man who had rented the car.

Two blocks from the supermarket I made the left turn and I had gone less than fifty yards when I heard the siren. My hands froze on the wheel and for a fraction of a second I found the impulse to jam my foot on the throttle irresistible.

I no longer had the money and there was some question if the Ford could be identified as the robbery car. Certainly Joel and the two drinkers of sherry he had hired to witness the stickup would fail to identify me.

But the Ford was stolen. I would be taken in and questioned and fingerprinted. Within a matter of thirty-six hours, at the very outside, Stamford, Connecticut, police would have been alerted and extradition proceedings would be under way.

Joel had been brilliant. The money would still be safe. Well, didn't I want it that way? Didn't I want Allie taken care of, irrespective of what might happen to me?

I never had time to figure out the answers.

The siren had been coming from behind me and its wail had increased in crescendo and suddenly it was upon me. From sheer instinct, I pulled to the curb.

It wasn't until the fire engine passed and was almost out of sight far ahead that I came to and realized what had happened. The sweat was dripping from my face and my clothes were glued to me.

My hand was shaking so badly that I had to try twice before I could turn off the ignition. I looked around as I started to reach for the door handle. Two women were standing on a porch across the street and looking over in my direction.

Again Joel had been right. Take the car to a safe place where you can leave it with no one seeing you and tying you in with it, he had said. It was the lesser risk. So once again I started the engine. Once again I put the car into gear.

It was a vacant lot beside a warehouse, utterly deserted. There was no other building within several blocks on each side. No one in sight.

I took time to wipe the steering wheel, the gearshift lever, and any other part of the vehicle I might have touched, before I finally left. I looked at my wristwatch. I was fourteen minutes behind schedule.

But it wouldn't matter now. I had done it. I was safe.

Until that moment when I started walking back to the outskirts of the town, I don't believe I had ever really believed we could get away with it. But we had. And I had carried through my own part successfully. I felt a peculiar sense of exhilaration, a sense of what might be considered perverse pride. I wasn't proud of what we had done or what I had done, only proud that I had been able to do it. All I could do was keep repeating, half under my breath, "We did it. By

God, we really did it."

I was still mumbling the words when the car pulled up alongside of me and slowed down and stopped. I don't believe I would have even noticed it at all if the driver hadn't poked his head out of the window and spoken.

"Want a ride, Mac?"

He had to ask me twice before I really understood him.

I started to say no, and then I figured it would be the wrong thing to say. The natural thing would be to take his kindness as it was offered. I wanted to do the natural thing.

"Where you headed?" he asked, after I was seated next to him and he had the car under way again.

I was supposed to walk some twenty blocks and then turn off and cross over and aim for the bungalow. That had been the plan. But it was a plan which called for no witnesses. And he would be a witness.

"Oh, anywhere downtown," I said, casually.

"Right," he said.

I took out a package of cigarettes and offered them to him and he took one. He said thanks. He didn't say anything after that but concentrated on his driving. He was a goodhearted guy. He'd picked up a hiker to do him a favor, not to find a captive audience.

I smoked quietly, buried in my own thoughts. My own plans.

Allie would already be back at the place. She would have locked the garage doors, leaving the airplane bags in the car where I had tossed them. She would be in the house, probably in the kitchen, making herself a sandwich and pouring a glass of milk.

Joel—well Joel would be down at headquarters. He would be having a hard time. He expected to have a hard time. The two drunks would be there also, telling their stories, and it would be the same story Joel would be telling.

State police would have been alerted and the road blocks would be up. Solemn, hard-faced men in plainclothes would be at the airport, the depot, and the bus stations. Top police brass would be closeted with executives from the bank and from the Egyptian. Detectives and uniformed police, on foot and in squad cars, would be combing the city, picking up men with known records, picking up suspicious persons. The dragnet would be out.

And somewhere in the city, down at the morgue …

"As far as I go, Mac," the man beside me said.

I turned to him and he smiled as I said, "Thank you. This will be fine."

He leaned across me to open the door. "We're here," he said.

It was an odd remark and I hesitated, turning and looking at him again. He was staring past me, sort of looking up so that the whites showed on the underpart of his eyes. I turned instinctively to follow his gaze.

I had never seen the building before but I knew what it was.

He had parked in front of police headquarters.

I knew what the building was, but I still don't quite believe it came through to me. I turned to him, honestly curious. I started to lift my hand to take the cigarette out of my mouth before speaking.

My hand didn't come up. It couldn't. Because his hand was next to it and the stainless-steel bracelet which had somehow become attached to my wrist was connected by a slender chain to the one on his wrist and he wasn't ready to move his hand.

"Yes," he said. "We're here. It was nice of you to come."

The first two sessions had lasted less than fifteen minutes apiece. This one was longer. I guess, during those first few hours, they were busy, asking so many questions of so many people, they just didn't have time to do a thorough job on anyone.

I sensed, this third time they brought me back from the cell block to the oak-paneled office on the first floor, that they were through playing around. They had found time to be a little more thorough, or perhaps they had found something else that made them want to be.

The one who looked like a greyhound and wore shell-rimmed glasses still sat behind the desk. He had introduced himself on the first time around as Lieutenant Stacy. Now there were three others in the room, one in uniform, the others in plainclothes. One of the two in plainclothes was the man who had picked me up and given me a lift. It was another reason that I sensed this third time would be the main act. But they were still polite, still courteous. At least in the beginning.

"All right, Madison," Lieutenant Stacy said. "Please sit down again. A couple of things we would like to go over. Cigarette?"

I took the cigarette he offered me and the uniformed patrolman crossed over and lighted it.

"We checked," he said. "Everything you said, or at least what we have been able to check, is right. You are registered at the Midtown Hotel. You came in three days ago. You gave the name of Harry

Madison and San Francisco as your home. No street address. We have your wallet and we have looked into it. Two hundred and sixty dollars in assorted bills. No driver's license, no credit cards, no business cards, no social security number, no identification. Not even a photograph of the wife and kids.

"You had a handkerchief in your trouser pocket, a key to your hotel room, forty cents in change, two toothpicks, and a half a pack of Marlboros. You had two empty envelopes, addressed to Harry Madison, General Delivery, San Francisco, in your jacket pocket.

"You tell us you came down here to try your luck at the tables. You say you don't want to tell us where you work in Frisco, because you might lose your job. You tell us you don't want to tell us where you live in Frisco because your wife would leave you if she knew you came down here to gamble. You tell us you don't know a soul in this town who can identify you. You don't even want to give us the name of someone in San Francisco who can identify you. You say you are a salesman. In short, you give us your name and your occupation, but not even a serial number. Maybe you think you are observing the Geneva Convention Rules or something.

"Well, I got news for you. This is a police station and this is a police investigation. I haven't had lunch, I've only had a cup of coffee for breakfast, and I doubt if I'll find time to have dinner. My stomach aches and my nerves are getting a little frayed. And, brother, in just about one minute you are going to improve my nervous condition. You are going to cease being the great stone face and you are going to start babbling like a moonstruck monologist."

He stood up as he finished speaking and leaned forward and his hand swept across my face knocking the cigarette out of my mouth. He sighed, shook his head, and sat back.

I still needed more time; I still had to think. I still had to stall.

"I'm not trying to be evasive, Lieutenant," I said. "I'm not trying to be a wise guy. But you have picked me up and brought me in here. You haven't told me why I'm here, you haven't placed a charge against me. This is not Russia; this is the United States of America. I think I am entitled to know why I'm being held here and questioned."

He went a little pale and he started to get up again, but then he once more sighed and sat back.

"You tell him, Jonesy," he said.

The one who had driven the car moved over and sat on the edge of the desk and faced me. He still seemed to have a pleasant, kind face.

"Around nine o'clock this morning," he said, "a couple of men were killed. They were blown to death in a dynamite blast. They were murdered." He paused and he was no longer smiling. "A few minutes later a car was rammed by a second car and the driver of the first car was robbed. Of approximately a quarter of a million dollars. Want to hear any more?"

"What has this to do with me? Why have I been placed under arrest?"

"Well, you know when this sort of thing goes on in our town, we like to know why and we like to know who is responsible. We have to start somewhere."

He spoke as though he were explaining that two and two make four to a slightly backward child. The Lieutenant sighed again and Jonesy imitated him.

"We start by picking up suspicious people and asking them all sorts of intimate and personal questions."

I nodded. "All right. And just what makes me suspicious?"

He hunched off the desk. "Because you have been so completely uncooperative," he said sarcastically, "I shall answer that question. But it will be your last question for quite a while. We will start the questions next and this time you are going to answer.

"I picked you up this morning because I happened to be driving down a very lonely stretch of road. I passed a deserted warehouse. No one was in sight and there were no cars around. I drove on for maybe five minutes and then I turned around and started back. The next time I passed the warehouse there was a car beside it—a Ford sedan with a side partly caved in. No one was in the car, no one in the warehouse. I drove on. I came upon a man walking in the direction of town. He had to come from somewhere. It seemed logical to me he had come from that smashed car. I happened, at the time, to have a particular interest in cars with their sides partially caved in. Because, you see, whoever got away with that quarter-million dollars was driving a car with its side smashed in."

He stopped talking and this time the Lieutenant did stand up. "All right," he said, "the story time is over. We will now …"

He stopped talking as someone knocked on the door. The uniformed officer looked at him and then moved over and opened it a crack. He shut the door and crossed over, whispered something to Lieutenant Stacy, who nodded his head. He returned and opened the door. A patrolman stepped into the room followed by four men in civilian clothes.

Immediately behind the patrolman was Joel Ricco. He was followed by the two drunks who had been drinking sherry on the stoop. The fourth man had detective written all over him.

They stood just inside the door and no one said a word. We had all turned and faced them. Slowly, carefully, they looked at first one man and then the next until they had very carefully observed everyone who had originally been in the room. It took almost four or five minutes. They were very thorough.

Joel was the first to turn. He looked at the one whom I had taken to be a detective. He shrugged, almost imperceptibly, and shook his head. The other two did the same. They turned and filed out. As they did the telephone rang and the Lieutenant picked up the receiver. He listened for a minute or so and then swore. He jammed the receiver back on the hook.

"Come on, Jonesy," he said. He started for the door, and then stopped and turned back to face me.

"Madison," he said, "I want to say something to you. We have had you printed. Within twenty-four hours we are going to know if you have a record. Personally, I would be willing to bet my right arm that you have. In this town we use three methods in seeking information. If the man being questioned is a reputable, decent taxpaying citizen, we are reasonably considerate although we still get the truth. If he is unknown but doesn't have a record, we might be just a little more crude. If he has a record, we simply skip the amenities.

"We never hurry things. We don't have to. We have time. In your case all we need is twenty-four hours, and during these twenty-four hours you are being held on a charge of vagrancy. I have to go out for a while, but the boys here are going to have a little talk with you. If you have any sort of story to tell, any sort of tale which makes sense, do yourself and us a favor and tell it. Save yourself grief."

He turned and left.

It was a simple statement, said without heat. There was no doubt at all of what he meant. I could feel the sweat beginning to come out of the back of my neck. Twenty-four hours.

It wasn't Lieutenant Stacy I worried about at the end of those twenty-four hours.

It was what was going to happen when the reports on my fingerprints came back over the teletype.

# 9

I don't know what I was waiting for. Perhaps there is something to that old bromide that "while there is life there is hope." I had twenty-four hours—or less—and then there would be no hope. None at all. In the meantime there were the realities of the moment to face and they were not pleasant realities.

Those men who were questioning me knew full well I was concealing something. Hell, I am concealing everything. It is usually, and rightly so, an assumption on the part of a cop that when a prisoner refuses to talk he has something to conceal, that in refusing to talk he is confessing guilt by omission. This evasive characteristic on the part of the questionee brings out the very worst in the questioner. Detectives Zany and Carter were no exceptions.

Carter was the one who played the sympathetic part and Zany was the heavy. It should have been the other way around. Carter was a big fat, wide-shouldered man with the face of a dissipated chimpanzee. Zany was short, slight, pale, and had the face of a Latin scholar. He had an acquaintance with Judo and a superb technique with a leather belt.

They didn't beat me in the classic sense of police procedure. Zany merely used his techniques to keep me awake and snap me to when I seemed to be dozing. Carter brought me coffee, lighted my cigarettes, and sympathized with me.

And neither of them got to first base. But they weren't trying too hard. It was just a sort of finger exercise before the real concert began and that would begin when the fingerprint report came in.

When they finally tossed me back in the cell, sometime shortly before dawn, I thought I might find sleep. I didn't. I lay awake and began to think of Allie.

I was in jail. Allie was not in jail. Allie was sitting on a quarter of a million dollars, a good part of which she would eventually own.

This man Joel, who had masterminded the entire venture, was being questioned, but he was bound to be freed. Could the entire thing have been a very subtle plot to use me? To have it end as it so obviously had ended?

There was only one flaw to this theory. All I had to do was to talk.

They—Allie and Joel—would have known this. It was impossible that I could have been framed. Should I talk, it wouldn't matter what I could prove and couldn't prove. Allie and Joel would be picked up and there was no remote chance they could have withstood the most cursory investigation.

They couldn't have double-crossed me. Whether or not their particular type of amorality would have permitted them to, they never could have afforded to have done so.

Whatever sense of logic I still retained convinced me that my own predicament had nothing to do with either of them. It was a matter of sheer bad luck.

A man reaches a point of physical exhaustion when it no longer becomes possible to stay conscious. He also reaches a point of emotional and mental exhaustion when it is no longer possible to think or to understand. I probably arrived at each barricade simultaneously.

I fell into a dreamless sleep.

The guard apparently had difficulty in awakening me. When I finally opened my eyes and stared up at him, became conscious of his activity, I realized that he was slapping my face with a water-saturated towel.

"Get up, fella," he said. "There's someone here to see you."

I knew at once where I was, why I was there. Someone to see me? At once the thought crossed my mind that the fingerprint reports had arrived. My old companion Lieutenant Stacy was without doubt waiting.

I pulled myself up, went to the triangular sink in the corner of the cell, and washed my face. I was far from bright and alert some five minutes later when I faced the well-groomed man with the briefcase, in the visitor's room.

He wasted no time.

"Name," he said, "Finney. Bail bondsman. You Harry Madison?"

For a second the name didn't ring a bell, but I came to in time. I said I was.

He took a paper out of a briefcase. It was all routine to him.

"Held on a vag charge," he said. "Also suspicion of armed robbery and murder. Bail, twenty grand. It's been paid. We'll stop at the desk and you can pick up your stuff."

He turned and started to walk away.

He was short and took small, delicate steps. I reached him and grabbed his arm.

"Listen," I said. "Listen. Who …"

"You want out?"

He turned and stared at me.

I drew a deep breath.

Yes, I wanted out.

"Yes."

"Come on then."

So I followed him down the hallway and we went into a room and he signed some papers and then gave me something to sign, lending me his gold pen. It only took three or four minutes and then we were again in the hallway. I was stuffing my wallet in my pocket. Again I reached for his arm.

He turned, swinging around as though he were on a swivel. He stopped me before I could open my mouth.

"Take your hand off of me," he said. "You wanted out and you are out. Maybe you got friends—I wouldn't know. But take your hand off of me."

I stepped back and he turned and walked through the double glass doors and started down the steps leading to the street.

I don't know why, but I didn't follow him, at least not for a moment or so. I guess I was too stunned. I just stood there.

They had returned my half-empty pack of cigarettes.

It was in my side coat pocket and I found it and took out a slightly bent cigarette. I put it in my mouth and started for the door, searching my pockets for a match. I didn't have a match. I hesitated at the door and for some reason my eyes went down to the street.

That is when I saw him. He was sitting in a cab and he had leaned forward to say something to the driver. Even without the tinted glasses I would have known him. I would have recognized him from the silver hair.

I took a couple of backward steps, turned, and walked swiftly down the hallway until I opened the door and went down a flight of steps into the basement.

I have no memory of the intricate passages. I only know that sometime later I lifted the latch on a door and pushed it open and climbed several steps and I was in an alley and the sun was cutting down across the asphalt in front of me.

At the end of the alley was a street and I started for it. I walked blindly, mindless of my direction.

I no longer needed a sense of direction. I needed no map, no compass. I didn't even have to think or to figure. I understood. At last, I understood.

The alley I had left led into the street running beside the police station and I walked up to the corner and started to turn when I realized my course would take me past the entrance of the building. I stepped back into a doorway and looked ahead and saw that the taxi with Art Blackmer was still standing in front of the entrance. There was a flight of granite steps leading up to the opened front door and on each side of these steps, with their backs turned to the entrance so that I could see their faces, were Blackmer's two boys, Al and Red.

It was perfectly clear. They were waiting for me to come out, waiting to escort me into the cab.

There was only one way in the world Blackmer could have known I was being held. He would have had to have been informed long before I was even picked up. He would have had to have known the name I would be using, because there was no doubt at all in my mind that it was he who had arranged for my bail.

There were but two persons who could have given him this information—Joel and Allie. They must have figured it almost to the split second. In another half dozen hours the police would have made the check on my fingerprints and then there would have been no chance of my getting free on bail. But whoever tipped off Blackmer wasn't interested in having the police hold me. I had not been set up for the electric chair or a long term in prison. I had been set up for a murder.

I had served my purpose. It wasn't a case now of my merely being expendable. So long as I was alive, I represented a positive danger.

Standing there in the doorway, I knew I had reached the end of my rope. There was no longer anywhere to go. I believe at that moment I was ready to turn around and retrace my steps, find the nearest policeman, and give myself up for once and all.

I started to move away and then again I hesitated.

Was there one remote possibility Joel had been alone in arranging the double-cross? Could it be possible that Allie was not involved? Could he have double-crossed her as well as myself?

I wanted to believe this. I had to believe it.

Slipping out of the doorway, I turned and started back down the street, away from the police station. There was a cab sitting by the curb as I neared the intersection and I quickly climbed into the back seat. I gave the driver directions and fifteen minutes later he pulled up a half a block from the bungalow Allie and I had rented.

Paying the driver off, I started for the house. I knew there was no point in attempting to approach without being seen if anyone was there.

It was broad daylight and the street was deserted.

I walked boldly up to the front door and tried the knob. The door was locked. I rang the bell. Nothing happened. I rang again and waited for several minutes. A car turned in at the next corner and passed the house and I waited until it was out of sight. Putting my shoulder against the door, I leaned back about a foot and then quickly hunched forward. The door flew open.

As I turned to close the door I heard a soft rustling behind me and I swung around. Gigi stood halfway across the room, straining at the thin chain which held him to the leg of the couch where Allie had tied him some twenty-four hours before, when we had left the place together, me to keep my rendezvous with Ricco and she to wait at the supermarket. The poodle was whining softly and watching me with pleading eyes.

The bowl of milk we had left for him was empty. I released him from the lead before I started to go through the house.

The place was exactly as we had left it. Allie's clothes were still scattered haphazardly around the bedroom. The unopened toothpaste tube still lay on the edge of the bathroom sink where she had left it. Nothing had been disturbed, nothing moved.

I took time out to go to the icebox and refill Gigi's bowl with milk and then I opened the connecting door to the garage. The Jaguar was there, on blocks. It had not been touched since I had jacked it up and removed the tires. The tires themselves lay on the floor, still waiting for their cargo of stolen money.

Going back to the bedroom, I made a second search. It was obvious that Allie had never returned to the bungalow. I wanted to find some clue to tell me whether she had ever really intended to return when she had left the previous morning.

There was nothing, nothing to give me a hint. The money which we had kept in the top dresser drawer was no longer there, but she might well have put that in her bag when she left. Some of her jewelry was gone, but none of it was really worth a great deal and Allie never had any particular feeling about possessions. My wallet, which contained a few bills and my identification as Gerald Mahon, lay on the dresser next to my cigarette lighter. By the time I ended my search only one thing was still clear to me.

She had never returned to the bungalow.

I went into the kitchen and put on a pot of coffee. I needed time to think. While I was waiting for the water to come to a boil, I turned on the small portable radio and I was in time to get the tail end of a news broadcast. I learned that the police had only just released a statement admitting they had no definite clues as to who had dynamited the car carrying the two guards. They were hard at work on the case and believed there was a strong possibility that the robbery and dynamiting were an inside job, but were forced to confess they had no positive leads. A number of suspects were being questioned, but as of the moment the authorities were unable to offer any solution to the crime.

The news merely verified my belief that Allie had not been picked up. But if she hadn't, then where was she and why had she failed to return to the bungalow? Could there be any possibility that Blackmer had found her?

I doubted it. Joel Ricco may have tipped him off as to my whereabouts, but he would have had to protect Allie if he wanted to protect the stolen money I had turned over to her. There was but one conclusion I could draw. Allie had never intended to return.

Could she have double-crossed Joel as well as myself? I couldn't see how; she would have needed him in any plan to get away, once she had the money.

I began to remember Joel's deserted ranch house out on the desert—a lonely isolated ranch house somewhere within two hundred miles or so of Las Vegas.

Even assuming I might be able to avoid being picked up again by the police, and avoid being found by Art Blackmer, and make my escape from Las Vegas, how was I ever to locate the place? Certainly when Joel had purchased it he had not used his own name. I might, by some wild stretch of luck, be able to search into records and look for property transfers which had taken place within the last couple of years or so.

I had one or two clues of course. When he had left Las Vegas we had gone in a general northerly direction. We had been in the air for a couple of hours.

I was pouring a cup of coffee when I became conscious that the program coming over the radio had changed and that a morning soap opera was starting. I leaned over to cut the switch and it was then I remembered.

There had been a radio in the ranch house. A shortwave radio. With private call letters. Yes, I remembered them well. Ricco had been very proud of that ham radio and he had made no effort to conceal his call letters. I could still see the printed plaque screwed to the cabinet. WG-1556.

Ten minutes later and I was talking with a clerk in the district office of the Federal Communications Commission in Los Angeles. He didn't even bother to ask me to identify myself when I asked for the information. It took him several minutes to look it up and he suggested I call him back, but I told him I would wait.

The exact location was a little vague but the postal address was a box number in Duckwater, Lincoln County, Nevada. He believed the station itself was on a ranch somewhere on a line between Duckwater and Warm Springs. The name of the owner and operator was George Richards. If I had any complaints, if WG-1556's signal was interfering …

But I quickly reassured him I had no complaints. I hung up as he was still talking.

The next telephone call was a lot more complicated. It was to the county clerk in Tonopah, the county seat. I wanted the location of a ranch owned by a George Richards, somewhere in Lincoln County, and I believed the property had been purchased some two years previously.

It wasn't the sort of information that they gave out over the telephone and anyway it would take considerable time to look up. He suggested if I were to come by personally … I explained that I was in Las Vegas and told him that I was calling from the offices of Murphy and Dexter, Attorneys. I was Allan Dexter, Judge Allan Dexter, and I would appreciate any effort he might make to help me. It was a matter of some importance.

I think it was the "Judge" which did it. He would try to get me the information. He would call me back.

I wouldn't let him go to the expense and trouble of returning my call; I would hold the wire.

But it might take an hour or more to get the information. I gave him the telephone number from which I was calling and asked him to return the call collect.

While I waited I looked up a local number in the telephone book. I was playing a straight hunch this time.

The phone rang at the other end several times, and when a woman's voice answered, I asked for the control tower. A man who identified himself as Rathbone picked up the receiver.

"I wondered if it would be possible for me to get a message to a Mr. Joel Ricco," I said. "I was supposed to meet him at his hangar this morning at nine and I have been delayed. It is quite important or I wouldn't bother …"

"Mr. Ricco's plane left the airport less than half an hour ago," Rathbone said. "I'm sorry but you're a little late. He was cleared for Los Angeles and perhaps if you were to put in a call to International …"

I thanked him. I was tempted to ask if Mr. Ricco was alone when he took off but I was afraid to continue the conversation. I didn't understand how Joel had managed to get away, but I knew that there was a strong possibility someone would be around checking on his plane. I didn't want to create any suspicion, give them any opportunity to trace my own call in case someone might be there even now checking on Joel.

Hanging up the receiver, I began to understand what could have happened. How they had managed it.

Allie would not have been on that plane when it left the airport. And neither would the money. The police would have known about Ricco's plane and it would have been the first thing they would have checked after the robbery. They might not keep him grounded, but they certainly would never have let him leave the airport without making a thorough check of both the plane and any luggage he might be carrying when he had taken off.

He must in fact have had an excellent story to have been allowed to leave at all.

Allie would never have gone near the airport. There was never any real necessity for it. Somehow or other she must have managed to get past the city limits between the time I placed the money bags in her car and the time the road blocks had been established. They must have arranged a temporary hideout at some spot not too far out from town, so that she would have been off the roads by the time the police began their patrols.

Then, probably early this morning, she had driven out into the desert to a prearranged rendezvous where Joel would have been able to make a landing and pick her up.

At this very moment they could be circling in to land at the ranch house. It would be a safe hideout for an indefinite length of time. The radio would keep them informed of any progress in the police investigation. There was no doubt that sooner or later the police as well as Joel's bosses at the Egyptian would realize his own part in the robbery scheme; no doubt they would figure he was the inside man who had masterminded the job. But the knowledge would do them little good. No one knew about the ranch, and when they decided to leave, he would still have the plane in which to make his final escape.

The basic plan would proceed as he had outlined it to me. With one exception. I would not be along.

I knew that waiting around the bungalow presented a serious risk. On the other hand, anything else which I might do would place me in even greater jeopardy. I was safe so far as Blackmer was concerned as long as I stayed where I was. He couldn't have known about the bungalow. Joel would have concealed this information from him in order to protect Allie.

There was another reason I must stay where I was, at least for the time being. I wanted to get that return telephone call from the county clerk at Tonopah.

The call came at ten minutes before noon.

A George Richards had purchased the old Amon Forthing ranch in Lincoln County, two years and eight months ago. The property consisted of some six hundred and eighty acres. The clerk began to read off a description of the place and its boundaries, giving me latitudes and longitudes. I interrupted to ask how I might find the place by car.

"It would be extremely difficult," he answered. "Are you at all familiar with the general locality?"

I said that I wasn't but that I had a road map of the state in front of me.

"Won't do you too much good, but I can give you sort of general directions and if you are lucky you may find the place. Drive north on Route 95 until you intersect Route 6 at Tonopah. Cut east on 6. When you come to Warm Springs you continue on perhaps another forty miles where you come to a branch road going north. It isn't much of a road. You follow this until you come to the Hot Creek ranch and again you branch off driving east and north. You go another seventy miles, more or less, and you come to an intersecting road on the right. It's little more than a cow path and there may or may not be a sign.

"The Forthing ranch was known as the Bar Q, but Richards may have changed the name after he purchased the place. If you follow this road long enough, and assuming you can find a road to even follow, you will probably come onto the ranch house. I would guess it would be a matter of thirty miles or more."

We talked for a few minutes more and he warned me that the country was extremely desolate and suggested that I make an effort to contact the place by mail and have someone meet me.

"A very deserted section," he said. "Seems to me I heard somewhere or other that the new owner merely uses the place as a sort of hunting retreat and doesn't actually live on the property. Keeps his taxes paid up, however. I know this country fairly well myself, but I would certainly hesitate to try to find it by car, alone."

I thanked him and told him to look me up the next time he was in Las Vegas. He promised that he would.

I had written down his instructions and I spent a half hour studying the old road map of Nevada that I had found in the glove compartment of the Jaguar. I had picked it up on my way west when I had driven from Florida.

Later, I found food in the icebox and fed Gigi and made myself something to eat. I wanted a drink, but there was nothing in the place and I was afraid to go out and buy liquor or send for some.

There was nothing at all I could do until after dark. I knew that by now probably every cop in town would be looking for me. The fingerprint report must surely have come in.

I thought of going out to the garage and getting the tires back on the Jag. It would be transportation. But how far could I expect to get? Without a doubt the road blocks would still be up and no car would be able to leave town without being stopped.

It was almost dark and I was in the unlighted living room, sitting in a chair staring out the window, wondering what possible move I could make, wondering how I could possibly escape from the bungalow and the town, when I noticed the large moving van across the street and down several doors. The driver had backed up across the lawn so that the van's opened side door faced the front porch of the house. Men were moving furniture from the house into the van.

In the dusk I was able to read the legend on the side of the vehicle. It said: THREE BROTHERS VAN COMPANY and under this was printed *Los Angeles*.

At first all I could think of was how much I would like to be in Los Angeles at this very moment. And then gradually the idea came to me. I pulled the shade a little to one side and watched as three men went in and out of the house, carrying out chairs and tables and beds and odds and ends of bric-a-brac. After a number of minutes had passed, one of the men took a heavy dolly out of the van and his two companions followed him, carrying quilted blankets.

Suddenly I understood what they were about to do. They were preparing to move a piano.

It was almost dark.

Within less than a minute I was out of the house. I crossed the street swiftly and, praying no one was watching, quickly climbed into the side of the truck. It was pitch black and I felt my way cautiously. The van's body was packed almost solid, but I managed to squeeze myself past a large piece of furniture which seemed to be an old-fashioned wardrobe.

I shifted it slightly, straining every muscle, and managed to create a narrow space between it and whatever had been stored behind it. My hand came into contact with a chair and I wedged it into the space. I pulled a rolled-up rug from above and drew it over me, cowering under it.

There were sounds outside and someone cursed and I felt something heavy hit the floor of the van. A moment later and a flashlight went on. The wardrobe moved and shifted and pressed hard against me and for a moment I thought I would be crushed. There was the sound of grunting and again something banged on the floor of the van. Again the wardrobe shifted slightly, pressing even harder against me.

They had moved the piano aboard and were lashing it down. Someone said, "Well, that does it. Let's hit town and get something to eat. We got a long night ahead."

It was less than fifteen minutes later when I heard the van's engine roar and the vehicle began to move. I was in complete darkness. I knew that the side door of the truck had been closed and locked.

Some fifteen or twenty minutes later the van came to a halt and the sound of the engine died. I heard the van door slam.

It was almost impossible to estimate the rate of passing time but I assumed they must have found the diner and gone in to eat because I had dozed off and when I came to it was to the sound of the engine starting again and I heard the grinding sound of gears shifting. It was difficult to move in my cramped position but I managed to push the wardrobe forward an inch or so and reach into my pocket for cigarettes. I knew that the three men in the cab were probably intent on the road ahead.

I found my cigarette lighter and was about to flip it when I sensed the truck slowing down. I hesitated and it was as well that I did.

Once more the vehicle came to a halt and once more the engine died out. I could hear voices and again a door slammed.

A moment later and I knew someone was at the side door of the van. I heard a chain rattle and the sound of a heavy iron latch being lifted and then a light hit the top of the van over my head. This time the voice was very distinct.

"No, buddy," the voice said, "it isn't that we think you are bootlegging or running contraband or anything like that. We just have our orders to check every car and truck leaving Vegas tonight and that's what we're doing. Any objections?"

"No objections at all officer," a second voice said. "But we would sure as hell hate to have to unload this stuff. We just got through piling it in less than an hour ago and that piano is damned heavy. Maybe if you were to tell us what you are looking for …"

"We're looking for a man," the first voice said. "A man and maybe something else."

"There ain't a damned thing in this van but house furniture," the first voice said. "You can check all you want but you won't find nothing but furniture."

The reflection from the light moved and came through a small space between the piano and the wardrobe behind which I crouched and I could feel the sweat beginning to come out of my forehead. There was nowhere to go, nothing to do but stay where I was.

A new voice spoke up. "You want to move this stuff, why, go right ahead. But me and the boys are dead tired and we got a long haul. I can save us all time and trouble by telling you there isn't a thing on here that can interest anyone but the guy we are moving from Vegas to Barstow. So suit yourselves. You wanta check the contents, then go right ahead and start moving this junk out. But if you do, I want you to put it back the way you found it."

The voices moved off, still talking. Several minutes passed and then someone returned and I could hear the doors again closing.

Five minutes later and we were under way. I breathed a long sigh of relief and took a chance on lighting the cigarette. We had passed the road block.

While the match still flickered I took bearings. I saw that there was room between the piano, which stood on its side, and the top of the van. Quickly I pulled myself up and climbed on top of the piano and again flicked my lighter. There was some clear space between it and the back end of the van, occupied by a number of heavy blankets.

I dropped down on them and made myself comfortable. I knew that I was in for a long ride. As I figured it, Barstow was across the California line, some hundred and eighty miles away. It was now around eight-thirty and we should be arriving sometime after midnight.

I was still wondering how I would manage to get out of the van when I fell asleep.

It must have been the sudden silence that awakened me. The van had come to a stop, very likely at its destination in Barstow. I pulled myself up on one elbow and started to reach for my lighter. But once again I heard a sound just outside and someone was rattling the wide door of the van.

I ducked back and pulled one of the heavy quilted blankets over me. It was fortunate I did.

The voices reached me at once and apparently two of the three men who had been up in the cab were standing just outside of the opened doors.

"Ed's a damned fool, spending six bucks on a motel room when we got to be up and unloading this bus in less than four hours," a man said. "I got a jug back here and I'm going to take a couple of snorts and hit the deck. Hell, I can sleep here for nothing."

"I'll join you in a couple of those slugs, Charlie," a second man said. "But if you don't mind, I'll go back and stretch out in the cab. You better be careful and not let Ed know you got a bottle. You know how he feels about drinking on the job."

I could hear someone climbing into the back of the van and moving around and I lay dead quiet, not daring to move, waiting any second to be stepped on.

"I put the damned thing in a drawer in this bureau, Horace,"

Charlie said. "Lemme have that flashlight a second."

A moment later and I heard a drawer being pulled open. A light went on and then off and I heard the pop of a cork being pulled. There was no sound then for several seconds.

"Another one?"

"No, that's fine, Charlie. I'm going on back to the cab. You sure you'd just as soon hit the deck back here?"

"Yeah. I'm sure. Just pull the door shut but not all the way. I want a little air."

Something heavy fell beside me and I could feel the blanket which covered me being pulled away. There was the sound of the door being partly closed and then a second gurgling sound, followed by a long sigh. It seemed to come from less than a foot from my head.

I lay there like a dead man, almost afraid to breathe. For a matter of some five or ten minutes there was no sound but soft breathing and then I heard a gurgle again. It seemed less than five minutes later that the sounds of deep snoring supplanted the heavy breathing.

I waited for a long time, or what seemed to me a long time. Once he turned and the snores were interrupted by a deep cough and then were resumed.

Slowly I began to move. I didn't dare show a light, hardly dared to stir more than a fraction of an inch at a time. I had to play it by memory. It must have taken me at least fifteen minutes to slowly crawl out from under the blanket and reach the side of the van. The snoring continued without interruption.

I felt along the wall until I found the edge of the door and then I slowly moved along until I reached the opening. There was a dim gray light outside and I knew it was the sky.

The opening was little more than a foot wide, but I squeezed through without difficulty and a moment later dropped to the ground. The van had driven up in front of a motel which had a neon vacancy sign over its entrance. There was a dim light in the office but no sign of life about the place.

Down the road, to the right, were the lights of a town which I assumed must be Barstow. Quickly I started in that direction.

The motel must have been at least a mile out from the town limits and twice cars passed me. Each time, seeing the headlights approaching in the distance, I moved into the shadows at the side of the highway.

The bare dark fields gradually gave way to dwellings and within a few minutes I was approaching the center of the town. I passed an all-night gas station and garage and then came to the bus depot. The lobby was open and two uniformed sailors were stretched out on wooden benches sleeping. No one was behind the ticket counter, but to one side was an all-night restaurant.

I went in and ordered coffee and a hamburger from a sleepy-eyed woman who apparently doubled as waitress and cook. When I had eaten I returned to the main room of the bus depot and found the telephone book. Looking into the yellow pages I saw the ad for a car rental agency.

It took a long time before a sleepy voice answered. My watch showed twenty minutes after three and I knew the place must be closed for the night.

I explained that my car had broken down at the outskirts of town and that I was on my way from Los Angeles to Las Vegas. I wanted to rent a car, any kind of car. I had to argue for some time before the man at the other end of the wire finally agreed to see what he could do. He told me how to reach his home, out of which he operated his rental service. It was some three and a half blocks down the street.

Ten minutes later and I had showed him my identification, the credit cards, and other necessary documents I had taken out six months previously in Aiken, South Carolina.

He made me leave a deposit of fifty dollars and I tipped him an extra ten before climbing into the front seat of the three-year-old Ford sedan which he rented out at fifteen dollars a day plus mileage.

By four o'clock I had left Barstow behind, heading west on Route 66, which in turn would put me on Route 395. At Bishop I would turn off on Route 6 and, a few miles farther north, cross the Nevada state line.

Sometime before noon, if all went well, I would have passed through Tonopah and Warm Springs and have reached the intersection where I must turn north on that obscure desert road which would eventually lead me into the tracks which led to Joel Ricco's ranch.

# 10

Somewhere beyond the Hot Creek Ranch, while I had been searching for the final right-hand turn, I must have found the wrong set of tire tracks wandering off south into the rolling sand hills of the desert. It was long after noon and I had been driving for hours. Three times I had stopped to refill the radiator from the several water bags I carried.

I had passed no human habitation for miles and now the tracks had finally faded out and there was nothing but sand and wasteland.

The heat was overpowering and long ago I had stripped to the waist. My gas needle showed less than half a tank, but this alone didn't worry me too much. I had the three five-gallon tins of gas I had picked up early in the day when I had turned off of Route 6 after passing through Warm Springs.

I knew that if the instructions I had received had been correct, I had made a wrong turn, and so I stopped and swung the car around and headed back.

By four-thirty I was again on what passed for a secondary county road and again I swung north and east. I had gone less than five miles when I saw an ancient pickup truck parked at the side of the road. An Indian was standing in front of the steaming radiator. I stopped alongside of him.

He was out of water and I gave him one of the bags I had supplied myself with. He grunted and didn't thank me. After he had filled his radiator, I offered him a cigarette which he took without a word. I held out my lighter.

"The old Bar Q ranch," I said. "I understand there is a turn-off somewhere around here."

He looked at me quizzically for a moment and grunted. I mentioned the name George Richards and then Forthing and a semi-intelligent look came into his face.

He pointed up ahead and grunted.

"How far?" I asked.

He shrugged. "Follow," he said.

He climbed into the pickup truck and slowly pulled out. He kept his speed well under twenty miles an hour, and after some forty or forty-five minutes I pulled ahead of him and stopped and he stopped. I got out and went to the side of his car and again questioned him. He merely shrugged and repeated what he had mumbled before.

"Follow."

Again the slow procession began. For more than an hour I kept behind him until at last he slowed down and stopped. There was a stake at the side of the road and next to it a barely discernible pair of tracks leading off to the right. I should never have noticed them had he not stopped.

This time he got out and came up to where I had parked. He pointed at the tracks and nodded.

"Bar Q," he said. Or at least that is what it sounded like.

"How far?" I asked.

He shrugged. "Two hour—three hour maybe."

I didn't know whether he meant at his speed or what might have been my speed. But I thanked him and gave him another cigarette. I waited until he had pulled ahead and then climbed in the Ford and turned into the tracks.

The sun was rapidly fading in the west, and for the first half hour or so I didn't have too much difficulty following the tracks. But by the time it was dark I knew that if I were to continue much farther, sooner or later I would lose them. I began to feel a sense of desperation creep over me. Something told me that unless I came across Joel Ricco's ranch soon, I would never find it.

By eight o'clock it seemed I had been driving for hours. It was not completely dark and I had lost the road a half-dozen times. It was only after getting out and walking in circles that I had been able to find the faint tracks again and resume my journey. I had, fortunately, purchased a flashlight the last time I had stopped. Without it I would have been hopelessly lost.

It was shortly after nine-thirty that I lost the road for the last time. The only way I knew it was because the rear wheels suddenly sank in soft sand and the Ford came to a stop. I had thought of water and extra gas, the flashlight and cigarettes, but not a shovel.

It took me more than an hour to free the car from where it had stuck and it was only by jacking it up and using the seat cushions under the wheels, going a few feet forward and repeating the process, time after time, that I eventually again reached hard ground.

I was so exhausted by my labors that I lay down on the ground beside the car, too bone weary to move. I must have stayed there, spent, for at least another hour.

At last I got to my feet and I again took the flashlight and started walking in widening circles, seeking for the tracks I had been following.

I never found them.

There was a slender sliver of moon and periodically I would look back to locate the silhouette of the car as my ever-widening circles took me farther and farther away from it.

It wasn't until more than a half hour had gone by that I turned back, realizing that finding the tracks was hopeless.

I could feel the chill of desperation come over me and instinctively I began to run in what I thought was the direction of the car. I stumbled, fell, and pulled myself to my feet. I moved again, and realized I was climbing a small hillock. It was then, as I was about to turn, that I saw the lights. They were off to the left and came from the windows of a long low ranch house, silhouetted against the skyline.

I had seen that ranch house once before, in the daylight. I recognized it at once. Joel Ricco's rebuilt Bar Q lay some five hundred yards away.

I approached slowly and by the time I was two hundred yards off I saw the outlines of Joel's Cessna where he had parked it next to the house.

Someone had turned on the radio and music was coming from the opened window behind which the light showed. It was, I knew, the living room.

I circled wide and came on the house from the rear. There was a light at the side and I knew this was one of the bedrooms. Cautiously, making no noise, I moved in and approached the window, crouching low. The steel casement was wide open; venetian blinds had been drawn and partly closed. I lifted my head as I crawled under the window and risked a look.

Allie was standing in the center of the room, stark naked. She turned slowly as I watched her and started for the bathroom. A moment later and I heard the sound of a shower.

I moved past the window and rounded the corner of the house. This time the window was wide open but there was no light in the room. The venetian blinds had not been drawn. It was a smaller window than the one in the bedroom and I thought that it must be the kitchen.

I took off my shoes and then carefully hoisted myself up and stepped into the room. It was dark but I knew at once that I had been right. I was in the kitchen and the door leading into the living room was opened a bare crack. The sound of music came through as I crept up and put my eye to the crack.

He was sitting on the couch and I could see the back of his head. There was a bag at the side of the couch and I recognized it at once. It was one of the two airline bags in which I had stuffed two of the canvas bank sacks.

I gently pushed the door and it began to swing in noiselessly.

It wasn't until I was actually in the room, standing not three feet behind him where he sat on the couch, that I realized what he was doing. He had the second airline bag on his lap and he was mumbling under his breath.

He was counting money.

I took another step forward.

He couldn't have heard me; I had made no sound.

But suddenly he knew. I could see his hand shoot forward to where the gun lay on the table in front of him. At the same moment his head turned and he saw me.

His hand was on the gun and he was raising it, turning and coming to his feet.

He saw me. There was no mistake about that. He saw me and he recognized me.

The side of my hand cracked across the back of his neck before he had fully turned and before the gun had swung around.

He didn't drop the gun and he didn't drop the airline bag which he still held in his other hand. But he slumped and started to fall back on the couch.

I struck him two more blows in quick succession and then my arm was around his neck and I was pulling his head back.

He had sunk into the couch and he never made a sound.

My arm moved and I had both hands on his throat and my hands had reversed so that I held his head bent forward. My thumbs were deep in his jugular.

His body jerked and for a moment he struggled and then he became still. But I continued to press my thumbs into his throat. I must have maintained the position for at least three or four minutes.

When I finally released him, he still retained an upright position. He still held the gun in his right hand and the airline bag in his left.

The money had partly fallen out and lay scattered on the floor.

It was not necessary for me to walk around the couch and look at him. I knew that he would never move from where he sat until someone moved him.

I crossed the room and I could still hear the sound of the shower coming from the bedroom, although the door was closed.

She had left the bathroom door ajar but she was in the shower and the curtain was drawn and she didn't hear me as I quietly entered the bedroom and closed the door behind me. I moved over to the bed and I slowly let myself down on it.

My feet were bare, and I had stripped to the waist hours before. I loosened my belt and sat there in my shorts as I waited.

The water in the shower went silent and a moment later she stepped into the room. She was humming under her breath, in tune with the radio music coming from the living room.

She had a towel to her head and was rubbing her neck. She didn't see me until she had almost reached the bed.

The towel dropped and she was suddenly still, staring at me with those great almond-shaped azure eyes.

She looked like she had looked that first night I had met her and known her and loved her.

She looked like a little girl.

I said, "Hello, Allie."

For a split second her eyes darted around the room and lingered for a moment on the dressing table. There was a pair of manicure scissors lying on its surface.

"No, Allie," I said.

She turned back and again stared at me. Her face was completely without expression.

"Joel?" she asked.

"We don't need Joel, Allie," I said. "Joel won't bother us. Come here, Allie."

I stood up.

She took a step forward, walking like a woman in her sleep.

She took another step forward and staggered a little. I reached out and caught her.

We fell to the bed together.

I waited until she cried out, her body writhing under me, her nails deep in the flesh of my back, her limbs tense and straining.

I waited until her throat was blocked with the sob and her sharp white teeth had closed on my lower lip.

I waited until the moment of consummation.

And then my own two hands closed on the slender column of her throat.

It took me some time to figure out the radio set, to get through to an amateur station in Los Angeles. The man I eventually reached thought at first that I was either insane or pulling some sort of grim practical joke. But at last I made him understand. I made him realize what he must do, that he must call the police in Las Vegas and relay the message I had to give them.

He radioed back after some fifteen minutes and he said he had gotten through to them.

They were already on their way.

It would take them a couple of hours or more. Well, the time is almost up and they will be here any minute now.

Every light in the place is turned on and they will have no trouble finding me.

I will be here, waiting.

Allie will be where I left her, naked on the bed in the next room.

But I am no longer thinking of Allie. I am thinking once again of my wife Marta and of my two children. I hope they will understand this last thing and know that it was the only thing I could do, that it was the only way I could cure myself of an obsession which I can't hope to explain.

For some reason I have no fear and no regrets.

For the first time in more years than I can remember I am at peace with myself.


THE END

From the master of the big caper....

# LIONEL WHITE

### Marilyn K. / The House Next Door $19.95
A lone driver picks up a beautiful woman and gets more than he bargained for, and the perfect heist is made complicated when a drunken neighbor climbs in the wrong window. "Pure noir."
—James Reasoner, *Rough Edges*.

### The Snatchers / Clean Break $19.95
Two classic heist novels, the first one a kidnapping gone wrong, the second a perfectly orchestrated race track robbery, filmed in 1956 by Stanley Kubrick as *The Killing*.

### Hostage for a Hood / The Merriweather File $19.95
A failed caper involving a bankroll heist and a missing wife; and a clever mystery in which many secrets are revealed when a body is discovered in the trunk of a husband's car. "Insidiously potent."—*Kirkus Review*

### Coffin for a Hood / Operation—Murder $19.95
"These two caper novels are gripping and tense, reading them is like watching a lit slow burn fuse, you can hear it sizzle, see it spark and you know where it's headed - an explosion, or in this case a blood letting... noir to their core."—Paul Burke, *NB*.

### "Lionel White wrote some of the finest caper novels in the genre..."—George Kelley

### Steal Big / The Big Caper $19.95
"*The Big Caper* is the story of how a criminal mastermind plots a crime by bringing together a team of individuals ... told in a matter-of-fact manner, this style of writing is top-notch."—Dave Wilde, *Amazon.com*.

### The Money Trap / Love Trap $19.95
"... two cops figure that if they rip off a drug dealer, who cannot call the police, they can get off Scott-free... a taut, nasty little thriller, a model of its kind."—Ronald Koltnow.

### Invitation to Violence / A Party to Murder $19.95
"Classic and solid noir. I felt I was transported back to the forties and in a black and white film..."—Steve Scott.

### The Mexico Run / Jailbreak $19.95
"From seedy motels to abandoned coastal villas, White takes advantage of atmosphere and environment to create his riveting portrait of betrayal and intrigue."
—*Paperback Warrior*

### Rafferty / To Find a Killer $19.95
"Many a character in a Lionel White novel thinks his detailed plan is perfect only to have the whole thing unravel."
—Elgin Bleecker, *The Dark Time*

### Too Young to Die / The Time of Terror $19.95
"Terse and exciting melodrama."
—Anthony Boucher, *New York Times*

**Stark House Press, 1315 H Street, Eureka, CA 95501**
**griffinskye3@sbcglobal.net / www.StarkHousePress.com**
Available from your local bookstore, or order direct or via our website.